BERLIN
WILD

Also by Elly Welt

JOANNA REDDINGHOOD

BERLIN WILD

A Novel by

ELLY WELT

VIKING

VIKING
Viking Penguin Inc., 40 West 23rd Street,
New York, New York 10010, U.S.A.
Penguin Books Ltd, Harmondsworth,
Middlesex, England
Penguin Books Australia Ltd, Ringwood,
Victoria, Australia
Penguin Books Canada Limited, 2801 John Street,
Markham, Ontario, Canada L3R 1B4
Penguin Books (N.Z.) Ltd, 182–190 Wairau Road,
Auckland 10, New Zealand

First published in 1986 by Viking Penguin Inc.
Published simultaneously in Canada

LIBRARY OF CONGRESS CATALOGING IN PUBLICATION DATA
Welt, Elly, 1932–
Berlin wild.
1. Holocaust, Jewish (1939–1945)—Fiction.
2. Berlin (Germany)—History—1918–1945—Fiction.
I. Title.
PS3573.E496B4   1986   813'.54   85-40779
ISBN 0-670-80925-X

Grateful acknowledgment is made for permission to re-
print the following material:

Excerpt from "Bells for John Whiteside's Daughter" from
Selected Poems, Third Edition, Revised and Enlarged, by
John Crowe Ransom. Copyright 1924 by Alfred A. Knopf,
Inc., and renewed 1952 by John Crowe Ransom. Reprinted
by permission of Alfred A. Knopf, Inc.

Printed in the United States of America by
R. R. Donnelley & Sons, Harrisonburg, Virginia
Set in Granjon

It would not have been possible without the help of my friends:

John Ciardi, who praised and scolded me through the last two years of writing;

the late John Cheever, who urged me to begin and encouraged me through the first draft when I was his student at the Iowa Writers Workshop;

Eleanora Walker Tevis and her late husband, Walter Tevis, who directed me to an outstanding agent;

Molly Friedrich, my marvelous agent, who sent *Berlin Wild* to a dynamic editor;

Nan Graham, my wonderful editor;

and all the other superlative Vikings;

and at Northern Kentucky University, Professors Doris Brett and Margery Rouse; President Leon E. Boothe; Provost Lyle Gray; my assistant Becky Williams.

and the
National Endowment for the Arts

E.W.

For Peter my love

I am thy father's spirit;
Doom'd for a certain term to walk the night,
And for the day confined to fast in fires,
Till the foul crimes done in my days of nature
Are burnt and purged away.

—*Hamlet* (I, 5)

If I were to tell you the truth I would have to lie.

—The Chief

CONTENTS

PART I

OCTOBER 10, 1967
IOWA CITY

CHAPTER · ONE

Winemakers

On Tuesday, October 10, 1967, the day the surgical resident advertised him as the German who just came down from McGill, Dr. Josef Bernhardt realized he had been in a depression since the end of the war. Not a clinical depression—he was functional—but in an emptiness lasting twenty-two years.

"Who is he?" the circulating nurse had whispered to the surgical resident.

"He's the German who just came down from McGill."

His patient was asleep and already paralyzed, and Dr. Bernhardt was preparing to insert the endotracheal tube before turning him over for surgery, when he noticed that the resident was folding down the sheet.

"He's not intubated yet. Cover him, please."

But the resident, preoccupied with the pretty circulating nurse, continued to fold down the sheet, exposing the naked body of the patient, an elderly black man. Dr. Bernhardt kicked at the tripod stand holding the unwrapped sterile water basin. The empty stainless steel container clattered on the tile floor. All looked at him: the surgical resident and the circulating nurse, the intern, the orderly, the scrub nurse, and the surgeon.

"Cover him!" Dr. Bernhardt shouted, voice shaking, body trembling with rage. His large, dark eyes above the white mask were half closed with pain. He could see his pulse, rhythmic, making waves, distorting his vision, and feel his diffuse headache throbbing in tune.

The reflexes of the resident and the circulating nurse were a jump and a rush to pull up the sheet. Hands met. Heads bumped. They covered him.

"This is Mr. LaRivière," said Dr. Bernhardt, extending his arm. "If he were awake and in control, would he wish to expose his genitals to you in such a way?"

The resident and the nurse shook their heads, faces drained of color.

"Then while he sleeps, you will treat him with the same consideration as you would if he were awake. And if I hear again of such indignity to a patient in this hospital, the wrath of the Lord will descend upon you, and it will come through me." He bowed slightly to the surgeon. "I beg your pardon, doctor."

"Thank you, doctor, very much," said the surgeon.

"Who is he?" hissed the nurse.

"He's the German who just came down from McGill."

The operating room was small; Dr. Bernhardt could not help but hear. He, at the head of the table, hemmed in by the anesthesia machine with its gas cylinders, valves, and meters, could not escape, for LaRivière was asleep and already paralyzed.

· · ·

The anesthesiologist must interview his patients while they are fully conscious. Josef Bernhardt visited LaRivière on his rounds the afternoon before surgery, having no idea that this would be his final case. At the station on Four North, a nurse handed him his chart.

"Thank you," he said mechanically, without seeing her. He leaned heavily against the counter and opened his second pack of cigarettes for the day, feeling so tired that any movement was extraordinary effort.

"Dr. Bernhardt? May I get you a cup of coffee?"

"I beg your pardon?" He glanced at her face—young, late twenties or so. The name tag on her left breast read *Susan Ingram, R.N.*

"Coffee? May I get you a cup?"

"No, thank you, Miss Ingram. But if you have an ashtray?"

She turned away and was back in an instant.

"Thank you very much." He extended the pack of Camels. "Would you like a cigarette?"

She shook her head. "I think you smoke too much."

Her face was even-featured and pleasant, her dark hair pulled back neatly behind the stiff white cap.

"You are right." He leafed through the chart, several pages on a clipboard. "Are there any old charts?"

"No. He hasn't been in a hospital for thirty years, and that was in France and was some kind of fracture."

Dr. Bernhardt lit his cigarette.

"I'll see if I can get the lab reports up before you leave the floor."

"If you would be so kind. I would really appreciate that."

She addressed a student nurse who sat at a desk at the rear of the station. "Telephone the lab, please, and see if you can get the results on Mr. LaRivière before Dr. Bernhardt leaves the floor."

"That's the pilonidal cyst in four-oh-nine North," said the student.

"His name is Auguste LaRivière."

"He's the cranky old colored guy in four-oh-nine North."

"His name," repeated Miss Ingram, "is Auguste LaRivière."

Auguste LaRivière, 72, Professor of Chemistry, retired. R.C. No Last Rites. The nurses' notes listed many complaints: that the nurses would not let him sleep; that they awakened him to give him a sleeping pill he did not want; that they would not tell him the name of the sleeping pill; that they restricted him to his room and would not let him go down to the cafeteria; that they took away his bottle of wine. All in all, the patient seemed crotchety but fit.

Dr. Bernhardt extinguished his cigarette and was about to walk down the hallway.

"Wait a minute, Dr. Bernhardt." The student nurse was waving a piece of paper and moving toward him. "I've got the lab tests." She came out from behind the counter to hand it to him. "How do you like it so far in Iowa City?"

"Fine, thank you." He looked at the paper: routine preoperative lab work was well within normal limits. No obvious problems.

"Do you mind if I ask you a personal question?"

Reluctantly, he looked up. "I can't promise to answer."

"Are all the anesthesiologists up at McGill like you and Dr. Borbon? He came from up there too, didn't he?"

"Yes."

"Do you want to know what the girls are saying about the two of you?" She giggled and leaned provocatively close. "They say you're good-looking enough to be obstetricians." She was a blandly pretty blonde, typical of the region, corn-fed and bursting with health. "Dr. Borbon says that obstetrics is the only specialty chosen while standing in front of a mirror."

"I've known it to happen, Miss . . ."

"Burke. Debby Burke: 555-4765. And I'm partial to older men."

The station nurse, Susan Ingram, was still at the counter. Dr. Bernhardt looked at her; they exchanged smiles. She was a small woman, full-bosomed. Her crisp white uniform was buttoned to the throat, and she wore a thin gold chain under the collar with a small peace symbol resting between her breasts.

"And I like your accent."

"You'll have to excuse me, Miss Burke."

He clipped the lab report onto the chart, walked down the hallway to 409 North and knocked on the door.

"*C'est ouvert.*" The voice informed, curtly, in French, that the door was open.

Dr. Bernhardt entered and scrutinized the patient: LaRivière sat up in bed reading, a red plaid robe over his pajamas. Magazines and newspapers were stacked neatly on his bedside table. His slippers were so placed on the stool beside the bed that one could assume he walked freely about. He was in no obvious distress; if anything, he was at ease and fully in control of himself. He was a Negro, so dark that Dr. Bernhardt could not tell whether or not his color was good, but there was no obvious breathing difficulty and no evidence that he smoked. Although his hair was gray, he looked younger than seventy-two.

"Good afternoon, sir. Are you Mr. Auguste LaRivière?"

"It is I." The patient spoke English with a pronounced French accent.

"Excusez-moi, Monsieur LaRivière. Je m'appelle Josef Bernhardt. Je suis votre docteur, votre anesthésiste." Their conversations, thereafter, were in French. "I will be putting you to sleep before your surgery tomorrow."

"You'll be administering anesthesia, you mean. Contrary to your opinion, *monsieur le docteur,* not all of us with dark skin are in want of education. I have a doctorate from the Sorbonne. But I should not correct you. At least your French is perfect. Nevertheless, you will forgive my hopefully incorrect assumption that you are like the rest of them and won't tell me what you are going to give me."

"What kind of anesthetics have you had before, monsieur?"

"Ether! Once!"

"Have you any allergies?"

"They asked that before. It should be written."

Dr. Bernhardt looked at him without speaking.

LaRivière glared fiercely, but the doctor remained silent.

"All right, doctor, there's not a thing in the State of Iowa I'm allergic to but the racial bigots and being wakened in the middle of the night to be given a sleeping pill they won't tell me the name of."

"How much alcohol do you drink?"

"Do you mean here in this prison, or when I'm a man?"

The doctor waited.

"You're not a talker, are you?"

Dr. Bernhardt shook his head.

"Hmpff! Every night at home—with my dinner—I drink a small bit of my own homemade wine. One glass or two. I brought some with me, but the nurses made my wife take it away. Then at night, when I get into bed, I sip a little Scotch whisky with the ten o'clock news before I go to sleep."

"How do you take your whisky?"

"I used to take it pure, but my stomach can't stand that now, so I mix it with a little water. Are you going to tell me what you are giving me in the morning?"

"Laughing gas." Dr. Bernhardt smiled.

"Nitrous oxide? That won't even touch me, much less put me to sleep."

"It will be combined with other drugs."

"What other drugs? *Sacré coeur,* doctor, if you would look at my chart as you are supposed to, you would see I'm a chemist!"

"Sodium thiopental to put you to sleep. Succinylcholine to paralyze you and small doses of meperidine, nitrous oxide plus oxygen for sleep and analgesia."

LaRivière was startled. "Succinylcholine. That's a muscle relaxant."

Dr. Bernhardt nodded. "It blocks the nerve impulse to the muscle by keeping the neuromuscular junction in a state of depolarization."

"But why would you want to paralyze me? I won't be able to breathe!"

"I do so that the level of sleep need not be very deep. One needs less of the drugs. And I am there to breathe for you."

"Artificial respiration," he said quietly.

"Yes. In the morning before they take you up to surgery, you will be given shots of meperidine and Nembutal, and also some Bellafoline to reduce secretions. I see from your chart you prefer not to have a sleeping pill at night."

LaRivière nodded.

"I'll leave an order for a glass of wine with your dinner and at eight o'clock or so a shot of Scotch whisky and water. After that, please, nothing by mouth until after your surgery."

"I thank you, doctor."

"You're welcome." LaRivière seemed shaken, chastened. Dr. Bernhardt had not intended that. "I would like to apologize in advance for the wine they will bring you. It will not be like your own."

"You're damned right it won't," LaRivière exploded in English; and then, in French, "It's those nurses. And my wife—she took mine away. Did you ever make your own wine, doctor?"

"No. But I remember that my uncle did." For an instant the image surfaced in Dr. Bernhardt's mind of the bulging cheese-cloth, stained wine-red, dripping over the bucket in the cellar of his uncle's apartment house in Berlin. Passover wine. "It was for sacramental purposes. Very, very sweet. As a child I loved it."

"He must have used sugar. I add no sugar! Only the grape. I add no yeast! My hands and the grape, which I grow myself."

"And what of the happy little winemakers, the first wine-makers, the *Drosophila,* who are kind enough to walk about on your grapes with yeast on their tiny feet and start the process of fermentation?"

"Ah, yes, the little fruit flies; we couldn't do it without them, could we? They wrote the book." He smiled. "You're different, doctor. Where are you from? You're not like the rest of them."

This classical cliché of bigotry brought Dr. Bernhardt back to his usual feeling of extreme fatigue. "Berlin. I was born in Berlin. I will see you in the morning, Monsieur LaRivière. I will put you to sleep and stay with you until your own protective reflexes are present again."

. . .

The trolley or the train, he couldn't remember which, rammed into a brick wall. His propulsion was cushioned by the bodies of the other passengers, whom he was on the verge of knowing but

could not identify. He smashed them to bits. The trolley or the train was cut open with a carpenter's ax, and he was lifted out. Saved. But the unremembered others, mashed and broken by the impact of his body, lay in pools of their own gore—crushed, dismembered, beheaded.

Dizzy, nauseated, Dr. Bernhardt swung his feet over the side of the bed and reached for a cigarette. This horror had not surfaced since near the end of the war, and he could not understand why after so many years the dream returned that morning. He lit up and inhaled deeply. He was exhausted—more exhausted than when he'd gone to bed—and he had to get up; he was due in surgery at seven.

. . .

Auguste LaRivière was wheeled into surgery at seven-thirty, groggy from the meperidine and Nembutal. The intern and the orderly helped him move from the cart to the operating table, then covered him with a sheet, removed his hospital gown, and secured him with a strap about his hips.

Dr. Bernhardt was wedged in at the head of the table checking his equipment. "Good morning, Monsieur LaRivière. Do you remember me?" They spoke in French.

"Morning, doctor. The wine was terrible."

They both smiled.

Dr. Bernhardt asked the orderly, "Would you be so kind as to stay until we have turned Mr. LaRivière?"

The orderly nodded and continued talking with the intern. The surgical resident was talking to the pretty circulating nurse.

"Is the surgeon here?" Dr. Bernhardt asked the scrub nurse.

"He's already scrubbing up."

Dr. Bernhardt pushed the operating table forward and came out from behind it on the right side of the patient. "Monsieur La-

Rivière, I'm going to put a blood pressure cuff on your arm. Will you give me your right arm, please?" He put the cuff on the right arm, then lifted the left from beneath the sheet and laid it in an arc above LaRivière's head, straightened the sheet, moved back to the head of the table, and pulled it into place, locking himself into the small space. His chest felt constricted; he was having difficulty breathing and experienced a momentary vertigo. He had felt particularly unwell since awakening that morning and now was experiencing the disquieting sensation that his arms and legs were asleep and that any movement was an effort of supreme will. He sat on his high stool to rest for a moment. Dr. Bernhardt couldn't remember; it was either a trolley or a train. The image came to the edge and receded. He rose and said, "I have to start an intravenous drip, Monsieur LaRivière, so you'll feel a needle prick." His hand trembled as he inserted the needle in the patient's arm. "Monsieur LaRivière, you will be getting sleepy."

"This stuff tastes . . ." and Auguste LaRivière was asleep.

The surgeon came in and said, "Good morning, doctor, is he ready for turning?"

"No. You still have a few minutes."

"Fine. No hurry." He turned to the scrub nurse, standing across the table from him, and asked if she had the 3-0 silk and his own needle holder.

Dr. Bernhardt put the mask in place, watched LaRivière breathe the oxygen—his airway was fine—and injected the paralyzing agent, succinylcholine. Within seconds LaRivière's muscles began twitching; then he lay still, paralyzed. Dr. Bernhardt gave him a few breaths of oxygen, his hand squeezing the breathing bag, and then, in order to see the expansion of his chest in breathing, he pushed down the sheet enough to bare the chest. The resident, talking with the circulating nurse, must have noticed that movement out of the corner of his eye and without thinking loosened the strap around the hips and folded down the sheet. Ignoring Dr. Bernhardt's first admonition to cover LaRivière, he exposed the naked body.

In an astonishing rage, Dr. Bernhardt kicked over the tripod stand and shouted, "Cover him!"

The empty sterile water basin clattered to the floor; Dr. Bernhardt squeezed the breathing bag; they covered him; Dr. Bernhardt, all the while watching LaRivière's chest, loudly offered the wrath of God, apologized to the surgeon, then, headache pounding and vision wavy, began inserting the endotracheal tube through which he would give the nitrous oxide and oxygen. It was then that he heard the surgical resident bruit it about the operating room that he was a German.

All the while ventilating the patient, Dr. Bernhardt secured the endotracheal tube and bite block with tape, checked the blood pressure, and began the nitrous oxide and oxygen. After checking the dials on the machine, he announced the blood pressure and pulse. The patient began to show movement: a feeble attempt to cough. The muscle relaxant was wearing off. Dr. Bernhardt started the intravenous drip containing succinylcholine and injected a dose of meperidine before reporting, "One hundred fifty over ninety and pulse eighty. Ready to turn." He was saved, but the others were smashed by the propulsion of his own body. Their identity was on the edge of his memory, but he could not bring it forward—like a name on the tip of the tongue: one knows it but cannot remember. Dr. Bernhardt's lips were numb; he felt faint and nauseated. He knew that his blood pressure was quite high, but he could not succumb to it. He must continue to breathe for LaRivière until he was turned and attached to the ventilator. He detached the anesthesia machine and assisted those who were not scrubbed—the orderly and the circulating nurse—with the turning: a fast and gentle flip onto his stomach. With shaking hands, he reattached the anesthesia machine, ventilated the patient, checked the vital signs, then looked to be certain that LaRivière rested so that there were no pressure points. He asked the orderly to place a pillow to lift the legs, and he rearranged the donut under the face.

They were almost ready. The circulating nurse handed Dr. Bernhardt the metal arc for the screen, and he put it in place. The scrub nurse threw the first drapes over the screen, separating the surgical field from that of the anesthesiologist, and he was finally secure in his tiny space at the head of the patient. He asked the surgeon, "Is the position all right?"

"I want the patient a little higher and the table flexed. I don't think I need a kidney bar."

The orderly pumped up the table with a foot pedal.

"Wait," said the surgeon, "too high."

All was adjusted and flexed. The unscrubbed tightened the straps so that LaRivière would not slip down. The surgeon asked Dr. Bernhardt, "How is the patient?"

"Pulse is ninety, blood pressure one sixty over one hundred. He reacted a little to the change in position; I'm going to deepen anesthesia slightly, and the patient will be ready for you by the time he is prepped and draped."

The intern began the prepping. Dr. Bernhardt put LaRivière on the ventilator, then in a cold sweat, palsied, he perched on the high stool. The unremembered others buffered his propulsion so that he was saved. But they, crushed by the impact of his body, lay smashed in pools of their own blood. The incision had begun. Dr. Bernhardt forced his mind away from the nightmare that had come back to haunt him after twenty-two years, forced his mind away from his own symptoms, for he, Josef Bernhardt, was his patient's pulse, his heartbeat, the guarantor of his homeostasis. That is what he would tell his residents during their training, and he would say that being an anesthesiologist is a secret wish fulfill-ment. One becomes a guardian angel watching over the sleep of a being who has given up his will, is totally defenseless, for not only is his monitoring system anesthetized, but also his motor system is paralyzed. The technical skill makes one omnipotent, with the power to gas another human being into a deep and dreamless sleep. And what could be more pleasant than that? But after the cutting is done, one must see that the being awakens again. Mother. One becomes in his tenderness and love as a mother to her unborn child—its very life and breath.

The surgeon removed the pilonidal cyst from LaRivière's back, and since there were no complications, it was only ten minutes before the intern leaned over the screen and said to Dr. Bernhardt, "Ready to close." Then, blinking at him in his tiny isolation behind the arc, he added, "Don't you have claustrophobia?" And he disappeared from view.

The implication that one should feel claustrophobic in such a confined space acted on Dr. Bernhardt like a posthypnotic suggestion. He broke out in a cold sweat and began to wheeze. Bronchospasms. When he glanced at the blood pressure gauge to see how LaRivière was doing, he could not read it: double vision, two gauges instead of one. He was drenched, suffocating, and his impulse was to flee. But he was unable to escape without shoving the table forward, or crouching and crawling underneath it, or without pushing past the surgeon. The complicated defense system that had allowed him to function since the war, already weakened, blew apart. It was as though an electrically indifferent neutron was introduced into a mass of fissionable material. Nuclear fission is a process of structural simplification. Dr. Bernhardt became simple. He could no longer force unwelcome thoughts from his mind, nor could he control his physical symptoms. He was ajangle. Through the din, a memory imposed itself counterpoint to the mangled and bloody dismembered bodies, and his will was unable to silence the invasion: Berlin. He, sixteen and a half, locked into the tiny control booth in the corner of the Radiation Laboratory monitoring the linear accelerator, a small atom smasher, used in genetic experiments on *Drosophila*—fruit flies. He irradiated them with fast neutrons to produce mutations. The little booth was supposed to have been protected from the radiation by the half meter of paraffin blocks, twenty-five centimeters of concrete, sheet of lead, and windows only fifteen centimeters in which the contractor had put one pane of lead glass, a vacuum, then another pane of lead glass.

Years later, of course, he realized that even after the Chief and the physicist, Dr. Maximilian Kreutzer, filled the vacuum with water, one was not protected. But at that time, he looked through the aquarium of glass and water into the Radiation Laboratory and felt safe. Even when the in-house Gestapo—the Security Officer for the Institute—was brought in each day for his x-ray treatment, he had felt protected, never considering that one should feel claustrophobic in such a confined space.

He did not know how long he had been abstracted when he heard the surgeon tell the intern to do the dressing. The operation was over, and during the moments of the depth of his anxiety, he had left LaRivière unguarded. This is inexcusable. He heard the surgeon asking if the patient was all right.

Dr. Bernhardt was shocked by the sound of his own voice. "Just fine. No problems." He looked again at the gauge. His vision was still distorted, wavy, but there was only one gauge and he could read it. LaRivière was all right. But he had left him unprotected. This could not be forgiven.

"Then I'll grab a cup of coffee and see you in the lounge." The surgeon left with his resident.

The intern and the scrub nurse dressed the incision; the circulating nurse left to find the orderly and a stretcher; Dr. Bernhardt lightened anesthesia but did not bring LaRivière out of it yet, because he still must be turned.

It was not that he had ever forgotten the Institute, but that he tried not to think about it and had steadfastly refused to discuss his two years there with anyone, even with his wife, Tatiana, who had been there, too. But then they never had discussed anything.

The orderly came with the stretcher. Dr. Bernhardt, in a trance, on the verge of his own reality, was able to care for LaRivière automatically. The years of medical training and practice taught one to seem controlled under almost any circumstance.

"Will you straighten the table please," he heard himself say to the orderly, his voice hollow and distant. And then, to all, "Let's push these instrument trays and stands away." The intern, the orderly, and the scrub nurse helped him. "I prefer to turn the patient on the table and move him onto the stretcher only when he is extubated and has his own protective reflexes."

The period of awakening is a critical one. Feeling returns, muscle power is restored, and protective reflexes: coughing, sneezing, vomiting. This is where the art comes in—removing the endotracheal tube one second before the patient coughs or before he awakens enough to try to pull it out with his own hand but not before he can take care of his own airway—breathe on his own and protect himself against the aspiration of vomitus. One had to make certain that the return again to life was not so great a shock that it induced a violent reaction.

Dr. Bernhardt stopped all medication but continued to give LaRivière pure oxygen. They turned him and strapped him down again, which was very important now, for he might try to jump when he first awakened. Dr. Bernhardt checked the vital signs and watched the patient for eye movements, twitching, slight movement of head, and the slight elevation in pulse rate which should come as he awakened. One of LaRivière's fingers moved. A small shaking of his head. Dr. Bernhardt removed all secretions from the airway with suction, turned off the respirator, and had to wait five long seconds before LaRivière took a breath on his own; then, with the next exhalation, he swiftly, smoothly removed the endotracheal tube. LaRivière reacted with a slight gagging but kept on breathing regularly. Dr. Bernhardt checked the vital signs: pulse 90, blood pressure 160 over 95. LaRivière opened his eyes.

"Monsieur LaRivière, the operation is over. You are fine. We are going to move you onto the stretcher, and you will remain in the Recovery Room until you feel ready to go back to your own room."

LaRivière looked bewildered and made a grunting noise.

A loving circle for the moving: the intern on one side, the scrub nurse at his feet, and the orderly on the side by the stretcher. The orderly bore most of the weight, leaning over the stretcher and pulling LaRivière onto it. Dr. Bernhardt held LaRivière's head and kept talking quietly as he was moved so that the continuity of his life would not be broken. Then he and the intern wheeled him to Recovery, where Dr. Bernhardt completed the anesthesia record and attached it to the chart before leaning over and touching LaRivière's arm. "Is there anything I can do for you?"

LaRivière opened his eyes.

He repeated, "Is there anything I can do for you? The operation is over, Monsieur LaRivière. You are fine. I will tell the surgeon you are awake, and he will come to see you."

"*Monsieur le docteur,* by now you know me so intimately, can we not use the familiar *tu* instead of the formal *vous*?"

Dr. Bernhardt was so touched by this, he felt tears rising. He had not felt like crying since the war. "I am honored." Then, using the familiar *tu,* "Are you comfortable? Can I do anything for you before I leave?"

"No, thank you, Josef." Auguste LaRivière closed his eyes.

· · ·

In the dressing room, the surgeon was sprawled on a chair smoking a cigarette. He offered one to Josef Bernhardt.

"Thank you, no. Mr. LaRivière is awake. I told him you'd be in to see him."

"How is he?"

"Fine. He's in remarkable health for his age."

"Thank you, doctor. It's a pleasure to work with you."

"Thank you." A slight bow to him. "And good-bye."

In the scrub room, Josef found the resident in charge of scheduling.

"You'll have to cancel my other cases for this morning," he said. "I am unwell."

"Oh, Christ," said the resident. "What's wrong? Are you sure you can't get through the morning?"

"I'm sure."

"Oi vey," said the resident, picking up his scheduling list and tearing from the room.

Josef showered, put on his charcoal gray suit and black tie, and headed down the corridor to his office in the Anesthesiology Suite.

It was in chaos, unpacked cartons randomly stacked, papers and journals covering every surface. The Department of Anesthesiology was so understaffed that he had begun working the day after his arrival in Iowa City, leaving no time to make order of his office or house. Carlos's housekeeper, Camila, and her two daughters had been kind enough to unpack the kitchen and arrange the furniture, but his clothes and his papers and books were still in suitcases and boxes.

He dropped into the swivel chair behind his desk. If one resigns, one must, he supposed, write a letter about it. He rummaged through the desk drawers for stationery. He found it and also a sphygmomanometer and decided to take his blood pressure. Leaving it untended was a stupid form of suicide. He didn't want to have a stroke or a heart attack unless it would kill him. In any case, he would need time to get to his safety box at the First National.

Josef stood, removed his jacket, rolled up his left sleeve, and attached the cuff: 200 over 110. Higher than he'd estimated. Actually, he was feeling better, although, curiously, since the intimate scene with LaRivière, he was on the verge of shedding tears. The severe physical symptoms had abated, but his head still throbbed, he was nauseated, and there was that fatigue he'd had for months—an almost irresistible urge to sleep; yet when he would lie down, he was unable to sleep. He was tired. Josef had allowed himself no holidays, had worked steadily since he entered the Institute in April 1943, when he was sixteen. He was forty-one, now, and too tired.

Jacket on again, Josef sat behind his desk and telephoned the office of Dr. Elizabeth Duncan in Student Health. Her nurse said she was over at Mercy. He dialed Mercy and had her paged. While waiting, he removed the opened pack of Camels from his pocket and dropped it into the wastebasket. Over two packs a day now. He had begun smoking in earnest when he went to the Institute. But then he began all his vices in earnest there. Everyone smoked. It was a wonder they didn't blow themselves up, with all the fumes from the ether and the alcohol. There were signs all over, warning of the danger: DO NOT SMOKE. CAUTION: DANGER OF FIRE AND EXPLOSION.

He could picture the signs—and himself, so young, so thin—emaciated, really—in the Biology Lab, leaning into his microscope and puffing away on those dreadful cigarettes they rolled from tobacco grown in the greenhouse and cured in the basement of the Institute, each scientist with his own nauseating recipe. One could not buy tobacco in Berlin during those last years of the war. The Chief, who was director of the entire operation, cured his leaf with prune juice and extract of dried figs. All Josef's co-workers in the lab were able to do the tedious sorting of the fruit flies and smoke simultaneously because of his famous little invention, a metal cigarette holder attached at mouth level to the body of the binocular lenses. He could not breathe. A recrudescence of his phobic symptoms. Josef's noisy lungs had lost all compliance. He began to sweat profusely, and the incipient tears let go and rolled freely down his face.

"Dr. Duncan here." Elizabeth's warm voice brought him to, but he could not answer her immediately. He mopped his face with a handkerchief, took a shallow breath, and exhaled.

"Hello?" she said.

"Elizabeth." His voice was hoarse and shaking. "How are you?"

"Josef? Is that you? I can hardly hear you. Can you talk a little louder?"

"Yes." He was calmer. "Can you hear me now?"

"Yes, yes, that's better. How good to hear your voice. Just last night John and I were lamenting that we haven't seen you since you came down. We saw more of you when you were in Montreal. How have you been?"

"Just fine, thank you. And how is your family? John? The boys?"

"We're plugging along. What can I do for you?"

"I wonder if you might have time to see me today?"

"Of course. What's the problem?"

"My blood pressure has been a little high."

She hesitated before answering. "You know I'm always happy to see you, but you should go to a good internist. I hardly think you need a doctor who takes care of all the young ones around here."

"Elizabeth, I . . . I want to talk to you."

"Of course, my dear. Your blood pressure. How high is it?"

"Fairly high."

"How high?"

"Right now it's about two hundred over one hundred and ten."

"How long has that been going on?"

"Three quarters of a year or so."

"That high?"

"It's usually around one seventy over just below a hundred."

"Did it go up all at once?"

"I think so. I checked it one day last spring—in Montréal. It was up, and it hasn't come down since."

"What are you taking?"

"Nothing."

"Not even a diuretic?"

"No."

"Good God, Seff, there are more efficient ways to commit suicide."

Josef was silent.

"Can you come over to Student Health in about an hour? Around ten?"

"Ten. Yes, that would be fine. And thank you."

He hung up and, feeling calmer, began to compose the letter of resignation. The facts were simple. He was not competent; therefore, he could not work. But how much detail must he convey? They would be displeased no matter what he said, so he might as well keep it brief. He pivoted his chair to face the typewriter on the small table beside his desk, inserted the University of Iowa letterhead, and glanced up at the wall calendar: Tuesday, October tenth.

UNIVERSITY OF IOWA
COLLEGE OF MEDICINE
IOWA CITY, IOWA 52242

Department of Anesthesiology

October 10, 1967

George M. Jenkins, M.D., Head
Department of Anesthesiology

Dear Dr. Jenkins:
I resign, for reasons of health, effective immediately.

Yours truly,
Josef L. Bernhardt, M.D.

It was thin. Joseph did not want Jenkins to think he meant to be rude, for he did not. But what more should one say? Some "deeply regrets", or "sincerely sorrys"? That had never been his style. His high school composition teacher had always complained that although Josef's essays were mechanically correct and to the point, they lacked embellishment. His papers were forever decorated in red ink with "embellish" or "invent." The Nazis were quite good at that kind of thing, at taking a so-called fact, usually an invalid premise, and building it to a conclusion with loaded language.

Biological science has shown that only the pure race will survive and that mixed-bloods inherit only the worst characteristics of their ancestors. Therefore, the bastardizing of pure

*German Aryan blood with degenerate Jew-infested blood has
to be outlawed.*

In math he could invent—elegant proofs. Out of the depths of his
memory emerged the image of his high school math professor, a
very old man, retired from the University of Berlin, called back to
teach at the Collège Français de Berlin because of the shortage of
teachers in Germany during the war.

With this recollection, Josef's symptoms once again returned:
shallow, fast inhalations through his mouth; he was unable to exhale. He tried to think of anything else: the mechanics of the remainder of the day; the walk to the bank so he could empty his
safety box, destroy some memorabilia of no concern to Tatiana,
and send the rest of the money to her in Berlin. The bank would
seal the box and their joint accounts as soon as they read his obitu-
ary. He had a little tuft of white hair above each ear. He was the
most marvelous and exciting teacher. He saved Josef's life. The
other classes were so boring. Josef jumped to his feet, put his hands
firmly on his desk, and bent over, hunching his back, mouth open,
straining his neck and abdominal muscles, trying to pull the air out
of his noisy lungs until, finally, the chest constrictions eased and his
breathing became easier. Drenched with sweat, exhausted, Josef
dropped in his chair and, elbows on desk, rested his face in his
hands. Bronchodilators would raise his blood pressure, and he
didn't want to have a stroke or a heart attack unless he could be
assured it would kill him. He could breathe now and felt calm
enough to sign his letter and type the envelope.

He knew Jenkins would be outraged by his resignation. Josef
had been on the job a little over two weeks after over a year of
intensive manipulation on the part of Jenkins and Carlos Borbon
to get the Bernhardts residents' visas and to secure a position for
Tatiana in Biochemistry, which, after all their effort, she refused.
He'd wanted to stop the damn thing after the first delays, begged
Carlos to stop pushing it. And Tatiana never had wanted to go to

Iowa. Her family was alive in Berlin. All she ever wanted, she said over and over, was to return to Berlin.

He inserted the envelope into the typewriter. There was a knock on his office door. Carlos. Josef grimaced as he removed the envelope and shoved it and the letter into the center drawer of his desk. A second knock; the door opened and Carlos Borbon, in wrinkled surgical greens, unshaven, his mask dangling, entered the office, stood by the door, and stared critically at Josef.

"You can come in, Charley, if you'll stop examining me."

"I've just got a minute." Carlos crossed the room and dropped heavily into a chair. "Do you have a cigarette?"

Josef recovered the pack of Camels from the wastebasket.

Carlos raised an eyebrow. "You file them in the trash can?"

"I stopped smoking." Josef handed him the pack and an ashtray. "Keep them."

"I heard you're sick." Carlos leaned over and retrieved the lighter he kept tucked in his left sock. "What's wrong?"

"I suppose it's just an advanced case of *la grippe*. I'll be all right." Annoyed by his friend's scrutiny, Josef swiveled his chair to face the window, and, looking out, was shocked to discover that it was one of those rare and brilliant October days, the yellow oak, the red maple against emerald lawn and deep sky.

Carlos lit up and inhaled deeply. "Surgeon said you blew up at his resident this morning."

"That has nothing to do with it." The day reminded him of an image in a poem by some American author: white geese against green lawn—and apples. Elizabeth had sent him the anthology when he was interning in Montréal: *When you can understand the metaphors, then you'll know you know English,* she had written. It was "Requiem for . . ." No, that didn't ring a bell. It was a little elegy, a condolence letter for the death of a child, and he was annoyed he couldn't remember it. He had always prided himself on his memory. He would have to ask Elizabeth.

"In the five years I worked with you at McGill, I never knew you to miss a day. You're the only person I know who's more obsessive and compulsive about work than I am."

Josef sighed and turned to face his friend. "Did it ever occur to you to mind your own business?"

"This is my businesss. If it weren't for me you wouldn't be here."

"Look, Charley, I was going to write you a note. I . . . I can't make it to dinner tonight. Tell Matsumoto I'm sorry to miss him."

"He'll be sorry too. He's just had a break-through on that pituitary hormone. I wouldn't be surprised if he's nominated for the Nobel prize." Carlos snuffed out his cigarette, took the pack of Camels and his lighter from Josef's desk, shoved them into his left sock, and stood. "I've got to go," he said. "You're one of the few people Matsumoto enjoys talking to."

"I've enjoyed talking with him, and always with you. Those Tuesday night dinners—in Montréal and now here—were the one thing I did look forward to." He choked on the words. The tears were rising again, and Josef, mortified by his loss of control, jumped to his feet and walked to the window. His lips were quivering; he leaned his forehead against the cool glass to recover himself.

Carlos strode to the window and tried to put an arm around him, but Josef shrugged him away.

"Why don't you let me find a bed for you, and we'll give you a thorough going over."

Josef shook his head. "I'm going to see Elizabeth. I'll be all right."

"Elizabeth! You need an internist, not somebody who takes care of the healthy young kids around here."

"She's a good physician."

"That's not the point, Seff. She sees nothing but students who've caught a dose of the clap or—" He stopped mid-sentence. "What time are you seeing her?"

"Ten."

"Over in Student Health?"

Josef turned from the window to say, "Never mind where. Don't call her. I mean that."

"This move has been too much for you," Carlos said. "First the hassle over the visa, and then we didn't give you time to unpack and settle before digging in." Carlos looked around the cluttered office at the cardboard cartons. "Maybe I shouldn't have hounded you so to come down here—especially after that damned visa came a year late. I suppose you worked in Montreal right up to the last minute?"

"Yes."

"You need a rest. Do you have the time?"

Josef looked at his wristwatch. "Nine thirty."

"I've got to go." Carlos strode to the door, stopped, and faced Josef. "Isn't there anything I can do for you?"

Josef turned again to the window. "You've done quite enough already."

"I'll drop by after surgery."

"I won't be here."

"Then I'll call you later this afternoon." Carlos left, closing the office door behind him.

Forehead pressed against the cool glass, eyes closed against the beauty of the October day, Josef, on the verge of tears, laboring for each breath, felt that he was drowning. Why had he told that intrusive bastard he was going to see Elizabeth? And the visa, it was not one year late. It was twenty-two years too late. He pushed himself away from the window. There was just enough time to hand in his resignation and pick up the succinylcholine before meeting Elizabeth at ten. It was a punishing death, a suffocating death, but the insurance companies would not be able to prove suicide. The heart continues to pump the blood, but all voluntary functions stop—he would have to take enough for five minutes or so—one cannot breathe or even blink, so if the eyes are open, they remain open, or if they are closed, they remain so. He would lie down, and he must remember to close his eyes. The corpse looks as though it suffered a heart attack or a stroke. The autopsy, of course, would disprove this. It was not a bad idea to take a little tranquillizer or barbiturate to control vomiting and to throw them off the track. But the succinylcholine they would never find. It gets broken down by metabolism into normal constituents of the blood or serum, even after death. He would put it into enteric-coated capsules that don't get dissolved in the stomach but in the guts.

PART II

1943–1944
BERLIN

CHAPTER · TWO

First Day

There was a modest brass plaque on the stone gatepost:

KAISER WILHELM INSTITUTE
FOR
NEUROPHYSIOLOGICAL RESEARCH
BERLIN-HAGEN
MCMXXVIII

Beneath it was a wooden placard, white with black stenciling:

FORBIDDEN: TO ENTER
Authorized Personnel Only

There were no guards. I walked through the open gates, stepped onto the lawn, and, shielded from the road by the stone wall, shrugged the rucksack off my shoulders onto the grass, unbuttoned my ski jacket, and searched through my pockets for the necktie. I promised Mother I would wear it—and a suit and clean white shirt—if she would promise not to get up with me. I had to beg her not to get up with me that morning of my first day. My commute, on two trains and a bus, to the northeasternmost border of Berlin would take two hours. Hers was only one, and she needed the extra hour of rest. Mother peeled potatoes each day for the glory of the Third Reich in a factory midtown. Her chosen profession, medicine, was taken from her in 1938, but in September 1942 it was replaced with the new one. Adolf Hitler was so kind as to provide her with a first-rate potato peeler.

The tie was stuffed somewhere in the pockets of my knicker-bocker suit along with all the other junk I carried: screwdriver, pliers, one ocular from Mother's microscope, a stub of pencil, a fountain pen, or so. I found it, a narrow striped thing, in the pocket of my knickers, wadded together with the paper my father had given me with the names of the Director of the Institute and of his secretary. I held the names between my teeth, slid the neck-tie under the collar of my white shirt, and tied a small tight knot.

As I swung the canvas rucksack onto my back, I was hit by the fumes of the salami Mother had put there the night before. I was to deliver it to my uncle and aunt—her brother and his wife—on the way home that evening. They both had to wear the yellow star and, therefore, had difficulty shopping. The salami was from Italy and stank of garlic.

I walked around the circular drive, past a flagpole that, curiously, flew no Nazi flag, to the main building, which was in the shape of a Y. The central rectangle was six stories but the two wings, which made the prongs of the Y, were only two stories. This main building was not far from the gate at the northeastern end of the Institute's huge and beautiful grounds, acres of grass and trees and April flowers: tulips, daffodils, violets, and the like.

There were no guards at the double-door entrance, either. The only sentries were a swarm of troublesome fruit flies who seemed determined to enter with me. I shooed them away with wild wavings of my arms, but despite my precaution, some of the little fellows sneaked in anyway.

It was twenty to eight in the morning, and except for the fruit flies, I was alone in the lobby. My father had told me that work began at eight and that I was to report to the Director's secretary, Sonja Press, before that time. There was an unattended Information Desk to one side. Directly behind it was a sign forbidding smoking: NO SMOKING.

And there were other signs around the lobby walls:

CAUTION: DANGER OF FIRE AND EXPLOSION:
DO NOT SMOKE

FORBIDDEN: TO SMOKE

DANGER: SHHHH: THE ENEMY IS LISTENING

NO SMOKING

·   I thought it strange that there was no picture of Adolf Hitler, nor was there a directory with the location, for example, of the Director or his secretary—only the signs warning one not to smoke and not to talk. And it made no sense that there was music. From a room opening off the lobby, I could hear a pianist, superb, practicing a Bach toccata, the same phrases over and over and over.

I sat on the edge of a leather chair near the Information Desk to wait for someone I could ask. It was quite warm; the lobby was actually heated. I unbuttoned my ski jacket partway and sat there involuntarily inhaling the Italian garlic salami in my rucksack, its smell permeating my clothes, my skin. Shortly before eight, people began to walk through the lobby, some from the main entrance and others from interior hallways. There were many young women—girls, really. The men, mostly middle-aged and older, wore either white lab coats, everyday clothes, or the uniform of the Luftwaffe. I could not tell the scientists from the workers. At times the lobby was full. Altogether two hundred or so people passed through, almost all smoking cigarettes or pipes. They smoked and chattered to each other.

No one paid any attention to me. I looked younger than my sixteen and a half years because I was so thin, and I looked down at the floor most of the time. The chronic disease—mixed-blood—I had suffered for ten years, since 1933, had made me abnormally shy.

By nine, the flow of people stopped, the pianist had moved on in the toccata to other phrases, and I was already more than an hour late. I knew I must ask the next person passing where to find the

Director's office. I did not like to talk much, so to avoid actually speaking to anyone, I took a school tablet from my rucksack and wrote the secretary's name in large printed letters: SONJA PRESS.

The next person passing was a tall, thin officer, an *Obersturmbannführer,* in the black uniform of the S.S. He walked with an awkward, shuffling gait, his arms held away from his body like a primate; he was pale and seemed ill. I looked at the floor. He looked down also. Then a man in a white lab coat, most likely a scientist, came into the lobby from a hallway. He was smoking a cigarette. I stood and held up the tablet. He read the large print: SONJA PRESS. He asked me in a very loud voice, "Young man, are you deaf?"

I put my finger to my lips and pointed to the sign DANGER: SHHHH: THE ENEMY IS LISTENING, under which was another sign prohibiting smoking. He read the signs, grinned at me, and pointed his cigarette toward the right wing.

"Follow me." He had a pleasant face and looked somewhat younger than my mother, who was forty-five.

I bowed slightly, said, "Thank you," and followed him to the right prong of the Y and up one flight. The Bach toccata and the garlic trailed us, Bach growing fainter as we walked down the long, warm hallway, which was generous and dark, with storage cabinets on one side, laboratories on the other. The smells emanating from those laboratories were strong but not necessarily unpleasant.

The man in the white lab coat stopped halfway down the corridor at a laboratory marked RARE EARTHS. "Stairs at the end of the hall to the penthouse. Chief's office." He pointed with his cigarette.

A penthouse off the second floor? I bowed again. "I thank you, Herr Doktor."

"You are quite welcome," and he disappeared through the door of Rare Earths.

The lobby on first and the corridor on second were spartan. By comparison, the penthouse up the spiral staircase from the right wing was rich, with oriental carpets, leather couch and chairs, and oil paintings of landscapes. There was no portrait of Adolf Hitler there, either, only the landscapes and charts of insects and an atomic table.

I thought it must be Sonja Press at the desk taking dictation from the Director, Professor Avilov, who was pacing back and forth. She was an attractive brunette of twenty or so, with a tiny figure, not at all boyish, but quite round. He was as I remembered him when he visited high school to lecture to my biology class: stocky, not too tall, with thick light-brown hair and powerful arms and chest. His son, Mitzka Avilov, who had been my schoolmate and friend, told me that his father had been a swimming champion in his youth. Professor Avilov was a world-famous geneticist, and that is why he was invited, two or three times each year, to speak to the students at my high school.

When he lectured to us, the first thing he did was push aside the desk with the lectern. He began in French. *"Excusez-moi, messieurs . . . dames."* Although my high school was in midtown Berlin, every course except German language and literature was taught in French, even Latin and Greek. He paced, as he did now, hands behind his back, bent forward slightly, but always looking at us, as he now looked at his secretary. He talked to us without notes, partly in German so we would be sure to understand, about his genetic research at the Institute with the fruit fly, *Drosophila,* and about the little atom smasher—a linear accelerator—they had built themselves. It produced fast neutrons and artificial radioactive substances, producing a wide spectrum of ionizing radiation which induced a great number of gene and chromosome mutations in the irradiated *Drosophila.* They could then analyze this information and form hypotheses about the mechanism of actions of genes. His lectures were always marvelous, and even though he was one hundred percent Russian, his French and German were faultless, except for a deep Russian voicing of the sibilants. He said "voize" instead of "voice"; his was low and soft. Russian.

When he finished dictating, Professor Avilov turned to me and

said, "You are one hour and seven minutes late! Come along!"
And to his secretary, "I will be gone less than fifteen minutes."
Then he ran down the spiral staircase to the second floor, I trip-
ping after him, rucksack and all, with the stench of the salami for
Uncle and Aunt wafting after us. He talked to me as we moved.
"This whole wing is devoted to genetics. We work *only* with insects and other animals, mostly *Drosophila*." He stopped for an
instant and turned to me. "Do you understand?" Running along
once more, he continued, "The teacher of mathematics tells me
you are the only one in the class who understands. Is that true?
Eh?"

What can one say to such a question? My face grew warm with
embarrassment.

"Come! We'll see if they can take you in Physics." We stopped
in the laboratory at the farthest end of the Genetics wing.

It was a junkyard, the Physics Laboratory, the center table a
junk shop, the floor a scrap heap. Total disorder. A man of middle
age—older than my mother, fifty or so—impeccably dressed in a
suit with vest, sat on a high stool at the table, peering through his
glasses at two pieces of rusty metal which he seemed to be trying to
fit together. The lab was huge, and one could see other, smaller
laboratories opening from the central scrapyard.

"Herr Professor Kreutzer, could you use a helper?"

Herr Professor did not even look up but waved us away with
the rusty iron.

"Come along. We'll try Chemistry." And Professor Avilov was
off, racing down the hallway.

The Chemistry Laboratory was a busy place, but orderly, a long
room with a center table running its length, on which flasks bubbled and tubes carried liquid here and there. The smells were
overwhelming, and some were new to me. An older man with
totally gray hair and two young women tended the operations.

"My dear Grand Duke," said Professor Avilov, "do you need a
helper?"

The Grand Duke spoke with a strong Russian accent. "Tell me,

Nikolai Alexandrovich, has he ever taken a course in qualitative analysis?"

Everyone looked at me: the Grand Duke Chemist, the two girls, Professor Avilov. I shook my head. My face burned.

"Well, then, has he ever worked in a chemistry laboratory?"

I shook my head again, and they all laughed at me. One girl sat on a stool with her legs spread apart; her skirt was quite short. The Grand Duke shrugged and said, "Such help we are not in need of at present."

Professor Avilov walked quickly; I followed. At this point I could again hear the Bach floating up the stairwell. Quite obviously, Herr Director Professor Dr. Nikolai Alexandrovich Avilov had failed to tell anyone of my coming; most probably, he himself forgot. It was not surprising. My situation was hopeless. And even Goebbels's School Proclamation, which I had seen the previous morning on the way to high school on the S-Bahn, was no great shock to me. After all, I was born in 1926, and most of my life had been lived in the lunatic asylum of the Third Reich.

. . .

As always on school mornings, I caught the 7:09 originating in Zehlendorf, so I could get a seat. A man across from me was reading *Der Angriff,* a Nazi Party daily for the workingman. I scanned the front page and saw the Proclamation in the lower right-hand corner. I changed seats to get a look at another daily, *Die Morgenpost,* and found it there too:

> We have received innumerable protests from teachers and the Hitler Youth who will no longer attend classes where the contamination of Jewish presence is being tolerated. In response to this overwhelming protest, and in order to ensure the superior education of the German youth
>
> IT IS HEREBY ORDERED AND DECREED THAT, as of

April 15, 1943, no one with Jew's blood in his blood vessels
is allowed to set foot in a German school.

> Dr. Josef Goebbels
> Minister for People's
> Enlightenment and
> Propaganda
> Gauleiter Berlin

My first reaction was to look around at the other passengers and
wonder if they could tell by my curly dark hair, my dark eyes—
and my nose—that I would no longer be able to go to school. My
second reaction was relief: I hated it! Two years before, the math
professor had taken me as far as he could in mathematics. All my
friends were gone—Sheereen, Petter, Mitzka Avilov. And I had
always a bad conscience about school because I never did the
homework.

The train was racing into the station. The acceleration and de-
celeration was very fast and smooth—electric. The seats would fill
up here and by the next stop, Steglitz, the aisles would be jammed.
I opened a schoolbook and pretended to study so some adult would
not force me to stand. There was no sense even showing up at
school, and I did not want to go home until I was certain Father
had left for his office. He caught Trolley No. 177 at 9:45. Mother
had taken the 6:49 train to her potatoes. So! I had over two hours
to kill.

The 7:09 pulled into Potsdamer Platz at 7:25. Most of the south-
east and southwest suburban trains converged there and were underground; I had to climb up the stairs to get to the regular
railroad station, Potsdamer Bahnhof. It was a busy place with
waiting rooms, kiosks, restaurants, ticket and information booths,
and racks and racks of timetables for all the German railroads. I
liked timetables and, when I was a young boy of six or so, had the
fantasy that I would be like my grandfather—my father's father—
who had been the schedulemaker for all the German international
trains.

One of the few times he came to Berlin to visit, he had been very kind and taught me all the intricacies of reading the complicated tables: the different printing, regular and italicized; the numbers, in bold and light, and other symbols. Everything had some kind of meaning.

I studied the racks for quite some time to figure out a difficult problem to pose to the Potsdamer Bahnhof information clerk, one with a line change to a local line and then to a narrow gauge and then to a bus. To make it more interesting and complicated, that time of year—April—both the winter and the summer schedules were hung. The information clerk had memorized every train of the German Railroad network: the stops, the times, the connections. He was famous for this and was written up, now and then, in the newspapers. Mitzka, Petter, and I used to visit him every month or two, and not once did we catch him out. He got tired of our game and, sometimes, would not cooperate, so I was hoping that he would not remember me.

He sat behind the information window at a desk loaded with timetables, a normal-looking man, wearing a railroad uniform, dark, with gold buttons. I was third in line. While waiting for my turn, I rehearsed what I would say to him.

"Good morning. I beg your pardon. I have to go from Berlin-Gartenfeld to Stäffelstein."

"What day and what time do you have to be in Stäffelstein?"

"The second Tuesday in June, in the afternoon, or very early Wednesday."

"The second Tuesday is June eighth," he said without consulting a calendar. "May I see your ticket?"

"My father hasn't bought it yet."

He hesitated. Perhaps he recognized me. "All right," he said, finally. "You have to leave Gartenfeld on Tuesday, June eighth, at six fourteen A.M., then catch the six fifty-one train at Potsdamer Bahnhof to Nuremberg; this is an accelerated train so you have to have a surcharge ticket. It will arrive at three thirteen P.M. at Naila, and at three forty-five P.M. you have to leave on the narrow-gauge side with a train going to Kronach-Süd, which arrives at four thirty P.M. It is the third stop. There will be a bus waiting, departing at four fifty P.M. to take passengers along the Main. Fifth stop, Stäffelstein, at six thirty-seven P.M." All this, of course, was without consulting a timetable. "Do you want me to write that down?"

"No, thank you. I looked it up myself already. I just wanted to make sure. You are very correct."

"Why not?"

After that I spent some time at the kiosks looking at the erotica in the magazines and trying not to see the repulsive pornography in the lower-class Nazi newspapers. One could not help but notice the *Stürmer* posters on the station walls: *Schmul Salomon Jew Bloodsucker caught in the act.* Pictured was an old man, watery-eyed, hook-nosed, demonically grinning, bloody knife in hand, in the act of raping a beautiful blond child. His supposedly huge and distorted sex organ was masked by a blob of blood. Or there was the poster that showed a caricature of an old Jew committing incest with his own children. The caption read: *And he blames the S.S.*

In my heart, I thought my curly hair and my face the essence of the caricature, and that everyone around me could see it in an instant.

I hopped on a train to the next main station, Friedrichstrasse, where I went through a similar timetable routine, except that the man behind the information booth at that station had to look everything up, and it took him a very long time. The most frightening poster of all was hung in the Bahnhof Friedrichstrasse. It was an actual photograph of a United States embassy with an endless line of Jews standing before the closed iron gate. The caption read: *No one wants them.* It was true, of course.

I timed it to arrive back at our house at exactly ten, and had a rare day to myself at home.

*

Our shelty, Dritt, met me at the door, tail-wagging and smiling. "Well, Dritt, my little friend, are you hungry, eh? If you'll be a good boy and help me pick up some twigs for the fire, I'll go and get some delicious, semi-rotten, stinking meat for you and your friend Mies." Mies was our cat.

I went into the basement, picked up a large canvas, and Dritt and I went out into the garden—which was relatively large with many trees—and filled the canvas with twigs and branches. Mies jumped out of the bushes and followed us around, and the pigeons came, too. I let them all back into the house with me. The pigeon coop was in the basement, but they liked to fly around the house when Mother wasn't there. Then we all went into the music room.

In the music room were a Bechstein grand piano, my father's two cellos, my violin—which I refused to play after I was dropped from our high school rowing team when I was twelve—a record player, a radio, a couch, and some chairs. It was forbidden by law to listen to shortwave, and I was not permitted to play records at full volume when my parents were at home. I searched through the collection and decided on the Brandenburgs—good music to work by—and put the volume as loud as it would go. Then we all went into the kitchen and deposited some of the wood in the bin and down to the basement to prepare the old woodstove in the laundry room to cook Dritt's meat, which I would have to get in Steglitz.

Then I began to change all the tubs of water in the entire house. Every available vessel was filled with water or sand against incendiaries—washbasins, bathtubs, pots. Also, in case of a break in the service, we needed a secure supply of water for drinking, washing, and cooking. The water had to be emptied every so often and then refilled. Bach, Dritt, Mies, and the pigeons followed me about the house. It took quite some time, and I had to race into the music room rather often to change the record.

After that, we went into my room, which was on the third floor, and got the antenna wire I kept hidden behind my books. I climbed through the trap to the attic, fastened an end as high as I could to the eaves, unrolled and trailed it down to the music room, which was on the first floor, and attached it to the radio. I searched the 16- and 19-meter bands and, finally, got something which sounded like news originating from a radio station not controlled by Goebbels. And, indeed, after a few minutes, there came the announcement, "This is London calling." It was a BBC German-language broadcast:

Allies hold their own in the Pacific but with heavy losses. Heavy Allied losses to German submarines in the Atlantic. The German Army reorganizes in the mud in Russia after a huge winter defeat. Mass graves of more than four thousand Polish officers found in Katyn; there is some discussion as to whether or not this massacre occurred before the German invasion, and the Soviet Union breaks off diplomatic relations with the exiled government of Poland in London. The British Eighth Army in Africa continues successful offensive.

I detached the antenna from the radio, rolled it up as I ran up the stairs, detached it from the eaves in the attic, and hid it, once again, in my room.

After that, I went into my father's study and, with a hairpin, unlocked his bookcase. I could open any lock in the house. He kept law and sexology books in there—marriage manuals or so—but the most interesting was Fuchs's *Moral and Custom History of Imperial Germany Before and During World War I.* It was all about sexual misbehavior. There were also old textbooks, collector's items, such as a nineteenth-century gynecology.

When I was through reading, I put Mies out, set the pigeons in their coop in the basement, said good-bye to Dritt, and took the trolley, No. 177, rather than the S-Bahn, to Steglitz, an adjacent suburb, because the trolley stop was only two blocks from the pet shop, where I would stand in line for two or three hours to get the rotten, smelly meat. I timed it so that I would arrive home after my parents did. And, of course, the first thing was for Mother and me to put the meat to cook in the laundry room in the basement— with all the windows open against the smell. Mother was always quite grateful for whatever I did around the house. It had been several years since our maids left—Jews were not permitted to hire Aryans—and my father, although he tried now and then to help, just didn't know how. Once the meat was simmering in the laundry room, Mother told me that my father was waiting to see me in his study.

He sat, as usual, on his thronelike tapestry chair, wrapped in blankets, a green corduroy dressing gown over his suit. Berlin is cold, and there was no heat in our house by April 1943, except in the kitchen from the stove. His spectacles dangled, as always, by one loop from an ear, and he held a sheaf of legal papers. On his lap lay Dritt, who was actually my father's dog, a gift of gratitude from the Crown Prince of Imperial Germany, whom my father's criminal law firm had extricated from some kind of trouble with a woman. Along with the shelty came an autographed photo portrait of the Prince sitting on the lawn, looking thoughtful. The photograph was subscripted *Wilhelm der Dritte*. Of course, he never actually became Wilhelm the Third, and my father had to keep the picture hidden in a drawer. Mother stood beside Father in her gray shawl and black suit, her hand resting on the back of his chair, a classic pose, ready for the photographer, and I knew there was to be a pronouncement.

"You are aware, Josef, that because of your background the authorities will not permit you to complete high school."

My background! My father, like all lawyers, had learned to obfuscate. He always spoke of it euphemistically as my "background." Our eyes met, but I said nothing. It would do no good. I was never permitted any choice about my life.

"Well? Answer me."

"Yes, Papa."

"Other arrangements have been made." He pressed his forehead between thumb and fourth finger. Dritt waggled his tail and blinked at me. I think he appreciated that I was willing to stand in line for hours at the pet store in Steglitz to get that foul-smelling meat for him and Mies. Even with all the basement windows open, one could smell the stink of the cooking meat.

"Because of the recommendation of your mathematics teacher at the Collège Français—to whom you must be grateful—the scientists at the Kaiser Wilhelm Institute at Hagen have offered to complete your education."

"But Papa," I blurted out, "I would be of great help to Mutti if I could remain at home."

"You don't know what you are talking about. You are too young to understand these things."

"But—"

"You are to be there before eight and report to Professor Avilov's secretary." He handed me the paper with their names. "You know, of course, who Professor Avilov is." It was not a question, but a statement requiring no answer. He knew that Mitzka Avilov had been my good friend. Then came his stock admonition: "At all costs, avoid drawing attention to yourself. Remember what happened to your Uncle Philip." He was through with me. Without another word he began to read from the legal briefs he held in his hand.

Mother and I retired to the kitchen. She, hugging her gray wool shawl about her, leaned for warmth against the huge coal- and wood-burning stove. I, at the table, in my ski jacket, was eating my supper of cabbage and potato soup and trying to persuade her not to get up with me the next morning.

"Please, please, Mutti. I must leave the house by five thirty if I want to get there before eight. There is no need for you to get up that early."

"You must promise to dress properly. A suit and a tie."

"I will." It was ridiculous. I would wear a clean white shirt, a suit and tie, but my underwear was all in shreds, my socks mend on mend, and I had no proper shoes and would have to choose between gym shoes or work boots. My warm Loden coat I had outgrown the year before and Mother wore it now to the factory. She dare not wear a fur. So I would wear my knickerbocker suit with work boots and my ski jacket, which was shorter than the suit coat.

"Your dark blue Eton suit—*not* the knickerbocker. And a clean white shirt."

The knickerbocker was my favorite. It was pale blue wool gabardine, soft and roomy, with a long jacket belted in the back, and big patch pockets. "Mutti, it's a science institute, not a fancy-dress ball."

"Josef, I needn't tell you how important . . ." Her voice trailed off.

"There is no need for you to get up with me. I promise I will wear a suit and a tie."

"And a clean white shirt?"

"Of course."

"Perhaps you should try the Loden coat?"

"Mutti, you know it doesn't fit."

She sighed. "I'll make your breakfast for tomorrow, then."

"I can do that. Please."

But she turned to the stove and prepared my breakfast for the next morning: a thin slice of bread sparsely spread with a paste of margarine and yeast, which she placed on white china with a gold border, Limoges. I would make myself a cup of ersatz coffee in the morning. Then she packed my rucksack with two one-kilo loaves of bread, a small jar of the paste, and one half kilo of the Italian salami that smelled so strongly of garlic, which I was to drop off for Uncle Otto and Aunt Greta on my way home from the Institute the next evening.

At least once a week I took them food from our house and from the Central Market across the street from their apartment. My father was "German" and, therefore, Mother and I were considered "privileged," did not have to wear the yellow star, and could shop at regular markets. Uncle and Aunt were both one hundred percent Jewish.

Mother tucked money—from my father—and some of our ration stamps for Uncle and Aunt into my rucksack along with the food, then turned to me. "Your father said that you would be given lunch at the Institute."

I nodded.

Poor Mother. Her eyes were pleading. She left the warmth of the stove, crossed the kitchen, and rested her hand on my arm. Her arm was thin and white, her wrist transparent. I knew that she sacrificed herself to give me extra rations. As a physician she knew only too well that growing bodies need food. And then she delivered her usual speech which had nothing at all to do with any reality we were living. "My dear Josef," she said, "I know you will behave at the Institute as a responsible and honorable boy and that you will do nothing unclean."

Responsible meant not deflowering a virgin and not impregnating anybody. *Honorable* meant no sex, and polite manners. *Unclean* meant venereal disease. There was a history of maternal propaganda behind each term, the most impressive on venereal disease, which she reinforced with select pages from her medical books. Gonorrhea with its painful strictures and possibility of blindness was bad enough, but the big scare was the late stages of syphilis. One did not want to have a horribly painful or crippling disease of the spinal cord or to go completely insane. On a lighter note were the gumma, the hideous, pussy, running sores chronic to late syphilis. One could see people running about Berlin with gumma, and Mother never failed to point them out. Anyone with a lesion was suspect.

"Please don't worry yourself, Mutti. I promise to wear a suit and a tie and to behave myself properly."

It was still night at five thirty the next morning. I put my dish and cup in the sink, turned out the light, and felt my way down the dark hallway—past the dining room, the two parlors, and the music room—and let myself out our front door, locking it behind me, then out the iron gate to the sidewalk. It promised to be a sunny day. The moon and stars cast light enough for me to see clearly. There were some tulips and hyacinths blooming in our neighborhood, but mostly one saw muddy ground with the remains of last summer's vegetable gardens. Only a few bothered with grass now, the next-door neighbor, Von Chiemsee, for one. Our suburb had not suffered extensive damage from the bombing—a crater here and there in the yards and broken window glass replaced with cardboard, but only two burned-out houses, so far, on the way to the station in the village, Gartenfeld, where the only noticeable changes were a few boarded-up shops, the button lady's, for example.

Our next-door neighbor was quite upset when he'd gone into Gartenfeld one morning the summer before and found her and little Hans gone and the button shop boarded up. He rushed home and out into his back yard, saw my mother and me, and shouted, as was his habit, over the back fence.

"Frau Doktor, Frau Doktor!"

Mother and I walked over to the fence.

He carried a suit jacket in his hand. "Frau Doktor, I took this into the village to match the button." He shook the jacket in her face. "I have lost one button and might as well throw it away if I cannot find a match."

The button lady—Frau Levy—kept, in her little shop in the village, jars and bottles and boxes of old buttons and shelves and drawers of needles and pins and every conceivable color of thread. Little Hans was her grandson. His parents had been taken the year before.

"They have taken her away." He was quite agitated. "Surely, she has done no harm to anyone."

Von Chiemsee was a Baron from Bavaria. He was wealthy, kept many servants, and yet, for reasons which I could never understand, liked to mow his own vast grounds. This gave rise to the weekly summer conversation he would have with my mother over the back fence, until September 1942, when she was gone all day because of her new career, peeling potatoes seven days a week in a factory midtown.

"Frau Doktor! Good day!" he would holler.

She, neighborly, would march to the fence.

"If you would be so kind as to tell me which day you think would be best for the laundry this week?"

"I think that tomorrow it might rain and that perhaps later in the week would be better—perhaps Thursday."

"Even with the rain, one could wash, but I know that you would agree—I know my laundress does—that drying the sheets outside is of utmost importance."

"I couldn't agree with you more, Herr Baron. They smell so fresh."

"Then if it won't interfere with your drying, I will mow my lawn today before the rain." He was too much of a gentleman to mow his lawn when either his wet laundry or ours would be soiled, and, of course, he expected the same courtesy from us.

The Baron was a charter member of the Nazi Party and a total idiot. He ended each over-the-fence conversation by clicking his heels, throwing up his arm, and shouting, "Heil Hitler!" even though he knew my mother was a Jew. She never failed to start when he did this.

The station was one kilometer from our house—exactly twelve minutes. I timed it to catch the train originating at Zehlendorf, two stops before ours, so I could get a seat. That early the passengers were mostly working people dressed like clowns in ragged remnants, stinking and unclean. There was no deodorant, no dry cleaning, and little soap in the Third Reich. Locked into the small compartment with them and with the garlic perfume I carried on my back, I could hardly breathe, so I threw open a window. The wretched man sitting across from me shouted, "Shut it! Better warm stink than cold ozone." So I closed the window and avoided taking deep breaths. Breathing through the mouth was no better, for then one could taste the stink as well as smell it.

. . .

"What is that pungent bouquet you carry?" Professor Avilov asked me as we continued down the corridor.

"Salami. Italian."

"Hmmm. It's not offensive, just strong. We'll try Rare Earths." We entered the lab of the man who had, earlier, directed me to the penthouse. The Rare Earths Laboratory was mostly storage closets with some worktables, and the man in the white lab coat seemed to be the chemist in charge.

"No, thank you, Chief." He smiled at me. "Can't use him." He was smoking a cigarette.

There were two more laboratories in this second-floor wing. Both were biology. Both rejected me, but there was a wonderfully kind woman in charge of the first. She was plain, very much like my mother, but much younger—thirty or so.

The work in her small laboratory was highly specialized, the microscope unlike any I'd ever seen. She and her assistant sat across from each other at a narrow table, each able to look at the same time straight ahead through binocular eyepieces and perform some sort of surgery with a syringe under the objective.

Professor Avilov addressed her as Frau Doktor and asked if she needed help. She stood, looked at me, and said, "What is your name?"

A little bow. "Josef Bernhardt, Frau Doktor."

"How do you do, Josef Bernhardt. I would like you to meet my assistant, George Treponesco."

"How do you do." I nodded at him.

"We are not planning to run a kindergarten here," he said to me.

I found out later that he was Roumanian and a biologist.

"Ah, Josef," said Frau Doktor, "disregard George. He is quite jealous of your strong and beautiful eyes and afraid you'll be competition for the hearts of the pretty young girls." She laughed and patted my rucksack. "Why don't you take this off—and your coat. It's quite warm in here."

It was warm. The building was surprisingly well heated! I slid the rucksack off my back, and that damned Roumanian sniffed audibly at my Uncle Otto's salami. I unbuttoned my ski jacket all the way but didn't take it off, and Frau Doktor explained to me the work she was doing. Using a hypodermic syringe under the microscope, she would suck up a piece of larval tissue that would later be the eye of an adult fruit fly and transplant it into a genetically different larva. Then, by observing the developmental interactions between the host and the transplant, she might study genic effects on hormonelike materials. The larval tissue was called an imaginal eye disk, the mature fly an imago. She seemed a wonderfully kind woman.

Frau Doktor made the Roumanian Biologist stand up and let me sit in his place to look at the larvae through his microscope.

"Kindergarten," he said again.

She ignored him and asked me, "Tell me, have you used a microscope before?"

"Yes, Frau Doktor."

"Was it in school that you used one?"

"No, Frau Doktor."

"Where then, Josef? Tell me."

All this while Professor Avilov was pacing in his usual way, silent, and not missing a thing.

"I used my mother's microscope. She is a physician."

"Is it similar to this?"

"No, Frau Doktor, it is much different."

"In what way, Josef, is it different?"

"It has a single eyepiece."

"And in what other ways?" She forced words from me.

"The magnification is much higher. Also, it has an oil-immersion objective, allowing for a higher resolution."

Then we discussed how a physician like my mother needed to have the higher magnification in order to count blood cells, to look at smears for V.D., and so on. And she demonstrated to me how these microscopes with the binocular eyepieces, although of lower magnification, gave a stereoscopic view of the object, right side up.

She and I looked together through the microscope at the two larvae. She showed me how one takes them out of a slimy solution, puts them on a slide under the lens, and performs the little operation. I thought it mechanically clumsy, with much wasted effort, but, of course, I was much too shy to say this.

"When you know all about the *Drosophila,*" she said when I was about to leave the lab, "I would very much enjoy working with you. I think you would do well because you have steady eyes and a steady hand."

I thanked her, bowed slightly, and shook her hand. Professor Avilov thanked her, bowed deeply, and kissed her hand. The Roumanian Biologist George Treponesco said, "Don't forget your sausage, Kindergarten."

All Roumanians are named George.

The next and last laboratory on the floor was huge, the rejection so humiliating that if there had been one spark of self-esteem left in me, I would have walked out.

Professor Avilov addressed the man in charge as "Dr. Krupinsky" and asked him if he could use me.

"Tell me, fellow," said Dr. Krupinsky, "do you know a virgin from an ordinary female?"

The question embarrassed me, and I blushed.

Professor Avilov laughed. "He talks of virgin *Drosophila.*"

I shrugged.

Krupinsky said, "Or tell me, do you know what is a *cubitus interruptus?*"

I had read certain books.

"Wrong!" yelled this Krupinsky. "It's not what you are thinking at all. Look it up in the dictionary."

Nothing was worth this embarrassment. Were we to go through the entire Institute with an insult at each stop?

No, we were not. Professor Avilov headed back to the penthouse, I at his heels like a puppy. If he could not place me in Genetics, it looked as though he would not place me at all. So! He had given up.

"Fetch Max," he said to Sonja Press, then strode into his private office and slammed the door shut.

"Why don't you take off your jacket?" she said to me. "We have plenty of heat. And here"—she tugged at the shoulder strap of my rucksack—"give this to me. You don't have to carry it around all day." She put the rucksack and jacket in the corner behind her desk and then, before she ran down the stairs, she patted my hand. Her hand was warm. She was more than just attractive—quite pretty, really.

In the waiting room were books and journals. On her desk I found a dictionary of scientific terms and looked up *cubitus interruptus*. It meant "deficient venation in the wings." Veins! Ha! The bending of Latin was as stupid as ever. *Cubitus* in Latin means "elbow." So the elbow on a fruit fly is a certain vein on a wing. Why can't they say *vena interrupta,* "interrupted vein," instead of "interrupted elbow"? Latin. I detested it. Imagine a boy of nine forced to translate from Latin to French and back again, knowing neither language. Seven years of it—just because of religious persecution. The Catholics threw the Huguenot Protestants out of France in 1685, and they fled to Prussia, where some tolerant archduke or other opened a gymnasium—a high school—for them in Berlin and put in the charter that French was to be its primary language.

I despised the languages, but not half as much as history, which was just distorted Nazi facts—propaganda—to memorize one day and forget the next:

> *The German Army was not defeated. The German Army was winning the First World War, but the Jewish-Bolshevistic Imperialists corroded the will to win of the home front and through such Jewish-Bolshevist agitators as Rosa Luxemburg and Karl Liebknecht inflamed the home front to knife the glorious German Army in the back. This will not be permitted to happen again!*

Of course, it was out-and-out lies. The truth is that the German Supreme Command begged the Emperor on bended knee to sue for peace, to seek an *immediate* armistice in order to avoid a military catastrophe.

Had it not been for some of the Calvinist ministers who ran the school, my life would have been even more intolerable. They were Old Testament Christians who taught that grace is predetermined and who encouraged me to believe I might have it, perhaps confusing grace with survival, which, I found out later, is not at all the same. I turned to them briefly after Sheereen left and my father refused, absolutely, to take Mother and me away to Switzerland. I began to attend chapel and even confessed to the school chaplain, Herr Wäsemann, that if I were not so young—fourteen—and if only I could speak to people more easily, I might think about becoming a minister myself.

He was a gentle man who took this most seriously and talked to me about the prophet Jeremiah, who had insecurities similar to mine. "Oh, Lord, Lord," Jeremiah was supposed to have said, "I am not fit to preach because I am too young." And the Lord was supposed to have answered him, saying, "Do not say 'I am too young.' But you should go where I do send you and preach where I tell you." Then the Lord stretched out his hand and touched Jeremiah's mouth and said to him, "Hark! I will put *my* words into *your* mouth."

That sounded pretty good to me, and I allowed myself some comfort from Calvinism, the religion of my father, until within two months, during chapel, I suspected what a swindle it was, too, and that there was no one of my parents' generation who had any sense whatsoever. A visiting minister preaching the sermon that day insisted that one did not question Paul, who said that the governing authorities, without exception, are ordained by God and are God's servants. To support his argument, he read from Romans 13: *Let every person be subject to the governing authorities. For there is no authority except from God, and those that exist have been instituted by God.*

Immediately following the service, I sought out our school chaplain, who was standing at the front of the chapel. "Surely, Herr Wäsemann, he cannot mean that Adolf Hitler is God's servant?"

I could see our chaplain was upset by my question. "It is ambiguous, Josef, and there is much argument among the clergy."

A fellow student, Dieter Schmidt, who had also approached Herr Wäsemann, overheard our conversation. "My God," he blurted out, "Saint Paul could never have meant that a government of criminals was ordained by God." Dieter Schmidt was as much an outsider as I, not because he was a cross-breed but because he was from a working-class family. There were even rumors that he was a Communist, and behind his back the other students called him "Commie." At the time, I didn't believe it, for he was quite religious. However, I found out later that I was wrong.

Dieter Schmidt talked so loudly he drew attention to us, and the visiting minister walked over to join the discussion. "Luther himself," he said in a condescending tone, "wrestled with these verses, and in his famous footnote to Romans Thirteen he teaches that in contrast to the Jewish idea, one should be obedient even to evil and unbelieving rulers—"

"But wait a minute!" said Dieter Schmidt.

The visiting minister held up a finger to silence Dieter and raised his own voice about ten decibels. "And he quotes from Peter, who says that everyone must be subject to every human institution, whether it be to the Emperor as supreme or to the governors as sent by him, for, as Luther explains, it is God's will!" The visiting minister was thundering now. "Even though the powers are evil or unbelieving, yet their order and power are good and of God."

"I don't believe it!" shrieked Dieter, losing his head completely and drawing a group about us. "Luther was a revolutionary who broke the rules of those religious authorities governing him when he knew they were wrong and when they went against his conscience. We know our present government is wrong and goes against our conscience—and compared to the malignancy of the Nazis, the Catholic Church in Luther's time was benign."

Herr Wäsemann, crimson, gasped, "Schmidt! This impertinence will be recorded in the Daily Diary of your class!"

Now we were surrounded by faculty and many students. One of the older students, who wore the brown uniform of the Nazi Youth, with much gold braid about the shoulder, stepped forward and addressed the school chaplain directly. "How do *you* interpret it, Herr Wäsemann?" It was a dangerous situation.

Voice shaking, Herr Wäsemann answered, "Romans Thirteen, Verse Two, merely reinforces One: *Therefore he who resists the authorities resists what God has appointed, and those who resist will incur judgment.* That is"—he paused—"they will receive damnation."

At this, Dieter Schmidt wheeled about, strode out of the chapel, and disappeared. I did not hear of him again for years.

Another teacher, also a minister, ashen-faced, stood now beside the chaplain in a protective way. "Say what you will," he said, "we are servants of the State. We have all signed a loyalty oath"—he raised his voice so all could hear—"and I, for one, and Herr Wäsemann here, for another, will not go back on our word."

"Heil Hitler!" Up shot the right arm of the boy in uniform, who then looked at the chaplain for affirmation.

Herr Wäsemann, stony-faced, nodded, as though in agreement, and walked woodenly down the center aisle of the chapel and out the door.

. . .

There was no door to the penthouse. One came up the spiral stairs and stepped into the reception room. I heard steps: Max?

Max! Herr Doktor Professor Maximilian Kreutzer, the physicist of the junkyard, appeared. His hair was graying, his face stern, his clothes impeccable. He stood straight, a bit of a belly. He looked very important and authoritative. He wore eyeglasses. He strode past me and knocked twice—two quick, hard raps—on the door of the private office.

"Enter."

He entered, slamming the door behind him.

They emerged together. Professor Avilov began to pace. Professor Kreutzer, across the room from me, took from his pocket a glasses case, removed a pair of small round spectacles with a narrow black shell rim, and returned the case to his pocket. He extracted from another pocket a small patch of cloth and began to clean the spectacles, looking at them through the gold-rims he was wearing, holding them to the light of the window and then to the light of the electric fixture in the center of the room. When he seemed certain they were clean, he removed those he was wearing, slipped them into the case, returned them to his pocket, and put on the black-rims.

Then he looked at me, a direct stare, but over the black-rims, or so it seemed, and not through them. Then, my good Lord, he pulled another case from his pocket, removed from it a pair of small round rimless spectacles, and, using the same cloth, cleaned them, holding them this way and that, and, when he thought they were clean, removed the black-rims and put on the rimless. He placed the black-rims in the case and put them in his pocket.

He looked at me. Directly, through the glasses, he stared.

I could not meet his eyes. I, little dog, looked at the floor. Professor Avilov still paced, hands locked behind his back, humming a quiet tune. When Professor Kreutzer was through staring at me, without a question to me or a word, he took from his pocket the original gold-rimmed glasses and repeated his cleaning and changing routine once again before he was able to say to Professor Avilov, "Why don't you call Krupinsky and tell him he has a new lab assistant?" That was all. He strode off. Professor Avilov ran after him, down the spiral staircase, returning shortly with that Krupinsky person from Biology who had rejected and humiliated me already.

Professor Avilov pointed to me. "This boy has to work here."

Krupinsky said nothing.

"He's in the same boat as you."

Krupinsky made some kind of motion with his hands and shoulders, a complicated shrug which one could read as *You win* or *All right, I know when I've lost*. "O.K., Chief," he said, "what do you want me to do with him?"

"I'll tell you, Krup: he doesn't smoke, he doesn't drink, and I assume he doesn't . . . Teach him. He's all yours."

"Sure. What school does he come from?"

"Collège Français de Berlin, the same as Mitzka."

"Come along," said Krupinsky.

I picked up my jacket and rucksack from behind Sonja Press's desk and followed him. On the way to his lab he asked me questions.

"Do you listen to BBC?"

"No," I lied.

"Do you know English?"

"No." Actually, I could read it, but I felt no need to tell him.

"Do you want to study medicine?"

"No! Never!"

Although he was in charge of the largest Biology Laboratory in the Genetics and Evolution Department, he was not even a real scientist—just a medical doctor.

There were two other men in the lab and two girls. He said to one of the girls, "He will be your assistant. Show him how to use the microscope, how to handle the flies, and what kind of labeling system we have here." And he left.

It was ten in the morning.

The girl pointed to one of the binocular microscopes on the worktable in front of the window. "This one is yours. Come along." Then she led me out of the lab and down two flights to a basement storage room. There, in two large suitcases, were the extra parts to my microscope. I carried both suitcases up to Krupinsky's lab. The girl told me to fix it so I could sit and look through "that thing" for hours at a time.

It was a beauty, a Greenough binocular with paired objectives and paired eyepieces, with Porro prisms for erecting the image. It had a large dissecting table attached, and a place to put my arms so I could lean comfortably into it as I worked. As with the microscope of the kind woman biologist, Frau Doktor, this, too, permitted one to look straight ahead, rather than down, to see the objects below. I opened the two suitcases and prepared to see what the possibilities were, but the girl was back with two trays filled with small bottles which she had taken from the incubators lining the entire wall behind me. Each bottle contained ten to fifty fruit flies.

"Look at these *Drosophila*. See how they are labeled. Become thoroughly familiar with them by tomorrow." She left and came back with two more trays and two more.

My good Lord, they all looked alike to me. What was I looking for? Virgins and *cubitus interruptus*? Krupinsky returned; he had been gone an hour or so. "You're supposed to go over to Physics," he said to me. "Kreutzer wants to see you."

I left the trays of *Drosophila* on my worktable and walked down the hall to the Physics Lab, where I found Professor Kreutzer behind the desk in his office. There were journals and books scattered everywhere and a table beside him heaped with scrap metal and other junk.

"Sit down!" He changed from the rimless to the black-rims

before he addressed me again. "What do you know about ionizing radiation?"

I did not know what to say. I had read about it in the science periodical *Die Naturwissenschaften* and had heard several lectures on nuclear physics at the Technical University by a physicist named Heisenberg.

"Well! Speak!"

"I know there is something like it."

"You will have to know quite a lot more than that by next week."

I shrugged.

"What is your background in physics, chemistry, biology?"

Again, I shrugged. I did not mean to be rude. It was difficult for me to speak about myself.

"Listen! Professor Avilov knows you, and he is not an idiot. So don't try to lead me to believe that he does not know what he is doing when he recommends you. He would not send an idiot to waste my time."

I said, "I have not studied—"

"I am not interested in what you do not know. I am interested in what you know."

"I have some elementary knowledge in basic sciences but it is all hypothetical, not even theoretical, and there was no practice involved. In the sciences, for the most part, I have read books and passed tests; for example, although I never have had a course in qualitative analysis, I read books and journals and passed the tests." I paused. "With high marks!"

"Yes! Yes! What else?"

"I have a solid background in mathematics."

He turned from me, changed to the rimless, and began to look through the scientific journals stacked on his desk.

· · ·

Mathematics: It was that solid background which kept me in the school. Collège Français de Berlin was difficult academically, and many students were failed the first few years. Only those with the best marks were retained. After I was dropped from the rowing team, I almost flunked out.

I was pacesetter, and we were winning. Nevertheless, in 1939, when I was twelve years old, I was ordered one morning to the office of the Director of the school. I had no idea why he wanted to see me; as far as I knew, I had not committed any infraction serious enough for such a summons. When such a crime did occur, the teacher making a charge would send a note to the Director with the complaint: tardiness; leaving the building during school hours to go to the candy shop around the corner; being on report in the Daily Diary of the class more than two times in one week. Diary offenses were, for instance, laughing or talking or any other disruptive behavior in class, inattention, disrespect to the teacher or to other students, and so on.

The malefactor would be sent first thing in the morning to the office of the Director, where a great part of the punishment would be anticipatory, for he was made to wait in the anteroom for what seemed a long time before the secretary would say, "You may go in now."

Once in the Director's office, proper form was to bow, click one's heels, and say, "Heil Hitler." Also acceptable was, "Good morning, Herr Direktor."

Herr Direktor would look quite stern. "Bernhardt, it says here that you have been displaying disruptive behavior. What is it you have been doing?"

"I laughed during Latin grammar."

"I do not want to hear of it again. It is not suitable behavior for a German citizen. Do you understand?"

"Yes, Herr Direktor."

But that morning in 1939 was different. I was not made to wait, and the Director himself came into the anteroom and beckoned to me. When I followed him into his office, I saw the rowing coach sitting in a chair in the corner.

As I said, I was the team pacesetter, and we were winning.

The Director seated himself.

I bowed, clicked my heels, and said, "Good morning, Herr Direktor."

He shuffled papers on his desk while he spoke. "Bernhardt, you will no longer be permitted to be on the rowing team. You are not strong enough." He could not look me in the eye.

Rowing was important to me when I was twelve, and track and field, and winning. But rowing was the most important, and I spent many hours working out. Twice each week I practiced on the rowing machines at the University of Berlin.

The Director's office was on the second floor and had large, arched windows. I looked out at the River Spree across the way— just a stream, really—and listened to the rowing coach make a weak attempt on my behalf. "He doesn't look strong, but he is very wiry."

"He is not strong enough!"

And that was that. At the time, I felt that it was the end of my life.

Word got around school. My friends, Sheereen and Petter, were sympathetic, and Mitzka Avilov, who had never even conde-scended to speak to me before, stopped me in the hall and said, "You have more stamina than all the rest." And he began to be my friend, even coming to my house, now and then, to help Petter and me with the secret cave we were digging in my back yard.

It was just a hole in the ground, really, and I started it because I was fascinated by the possibility of finding ground water. Father said the ground water was quite high in our back yard, but I had doubts about it. There was a steady slope downhill to a channel half a kilometer from our house. The channel was deep and navi-gable, with boats and ships going through. So I thought that since we were uphill from the channel, and that since our very deep laundry cellar was absolutely dry, there couldn't possibly be water anywhere near the surface. I was certain my father was wrong!

Petter was with me the day I started digging, and I was so sure there would be no water that we planned to dig a secret cave and play Trappers and Indians. I had the mistaken idea they mostly lived in dugouts. Digging wasn't at all difficult since Berlin was in a glacial stream valley, and the top soil was moist sand and clay. We were very careful to hide all the earth we dug up, and we obscured the entrance so cleverly that I thought my parents would never discover what we were up to.

But two weeks after we'd begun, I was shoveling away, and there, at my eye level, were Father's black shoes and gray spats. I expected he would put an end to the whole thing, but he didn't. It was several weeks after I had been removed from the rowing team, and my parents had been making an effort to divert my mind—to keep me busy with white mice and pigeons, books and radios.

"Josef!" said my father. "Because it is so easily dug and so hard to maintain, you will need to support the walls with lumber."

I was quite astonished that he even knew anything like that. At that time I still thought Father was an impressive person, but I didn't think he knew how anything worked. Later, Mother told me that he had been an officer in the Pioneers—the corps of engineers—during the First World War. "If it had not been for me," she said, "he would now be a high officer in the army."

"I have no lumber, Father."

"Yes. I have opened a charge account for you at the hardware store. You may buy what you need."

I had another open charge at the bookstore and could buy there whatever I liked. My room, consequently, was stuffed with books.

Father stopped each day and gave exact advice, using technical terms, on how to place the rough wood to keep the sides from caving in. He even helped me design a roof and showed me how to turn old stovepipes into air ducts. When the bombing began, Father and the Baron von Chiemsee seriously considered using my dugout as a bomb shelter. But they decided our laundry cellar would be best for that.

My hidden cave so intrigued Mitzka that he hunted about his own yard until he found a secret place for himself. He invited me to see it. "It leads right into the apple orchard next door," he told me, "and when the apples are ripe in late August, we can sneak through and get some."

So I took my first train ride to Hagen with Mitzka when I was twelve and discovered that his "yard" was a huge and beautiful park of more than thirty acres, surrounding a Kaiser Wilhelm Institute, with many willow and birch trees and winding and curving drives lined with lindens, beeches, oaks, and cedars.

We played freely about, and when we tired of our games— Trappers and Indians, an elaborate hide-and-seek with intermediate wrestling, or *gorodky,* a Russian version of cricket—we would crawl into Mitzka's secret place, which was absolutely concealed, first by a group of willow trees, then by a tunnel of hedge one had to crawl through head first. Mitzka had snipped the wire fence on the other side and bent it back so one would emerge not too badly bruised into the smaller hedge in the orchard. The cut fence was hidden in the shrubbery in such a way that no one would know if he was not shown.

We tried to dig a cave, but at that location the ground water was only three feet beneath the surface. So we contented ourselves by clearing out enough space so that we could lie side by side, our bodies touching, on a bed of soft branches and leaves beneath the boughs that arched above us like swords raised, and we plotted revenge against Adolf Hitler and the Thousand Year Reich.

Mitzka Avilov's friendship was the greatest of honors, for he was the school leader and hero, adored by students and teachers alike, because he was handsome and clever. That's how he got his nickname, Mitzka, from *amitzka,* which in Russian means "pass-key" or "false key," implying someone who could get in and out of any door. He was the one at school, for example, who was able to unlock the door to the bell tower, climb to the top, and wrap his necktie around the clapper so the bell would not ring to announce the end of recess, and all this without even being put on report. He was the ideal Aryan youth—except that he was one hundred percent Russian. He looked just like his mother, Madame Avilov, tall, blond, with purplish-blue eyes, but he had the vitality of his father.

Although he was a year and a half older than I, we were in the same grade. I had been moved ahead a year, and he had remained behind. He was not stupid, to the contrary, but he was not at all interested in schoolwork, only in athletics and girls, and later in politics.

I, on the other hand, had been quite a good student until I was dropped from the rowing team. Mother told me that I was dropped for my own health and that from that moment on I must never again go out for track and field, that I must never again be the class Optimus—even if my grades were at the top—and that I must not stand out or draw attention to myself in any way, I was to become invisible.

So I began to sit in the farthest corner in the back, away from the teacher. I would not speak unless called upon. I took all tests, for not to do so would draw attention to myself, but whenever possible I avoided doing assignments. Sheereen and I became closer than ever.

The school was in the habit of mailing the failure notices to parents immediately before Christmas. That thirteenth year of my life I found only one thing under the tree: an envelope containing a failure notice. I was saved from being suspended by the math teacher who came to our school shortly after Christmas. He was an old man, a retired mathematics professor from the University of Berlin.

He dictated problems, which we were to copy into our note-books and work out at home, then discuss in class the next day. I always took down the problems but never again looked at them. The second week he was there, he walked about the room picking up notebooks and looking at them. I prayed he would not look at mine. He did. Of course, it was empty but for the questions.

He asked, so the whole class could hear, "Would Bernhardt like to go to the board and copy for the class, from his notebook, the solution and the means to that solution of problem number six of the day's assignment?"

I looked at my notebook: the questions were concerned with the role of dimensions in physics. Number six was on the derivation of laws governing the oscillation of a pendulum.

I took my notebook to the board and pretended to study it carefully before I began to write. I pretended to copy each step, and in several minutes half of one section of the blackboard was filled. I put a large dot after the solution and underlined it twice, so heavily that the chalk broke.

The Professor said, "Do number seven."

I repeated my performance.

"Now," he said, "do number eight, putting only the solution on the board."

I looked at the question, closed my eyes, pressed my forehead against the blackboard. The figures began to arrange themselves in my mind. When they were through, I opened my eyes and put the solution on the board, crumbling the chalk with the dot and the underlining.

He gave me more chalk and asked me to do numbers nine and ten in the same way. I did.

Then he said, "Now we will do a simple one." He asked that the class compute in their workbooks and that I do so on the board. "Add together all the whole numbers from one to twenty as quickly as you can."

Most of the other students bent over their copybooks and began to write down the numbers in a column. I closed my eyes. The numbers danced brightly through my mind: 1 to 20. They arranged themselves in convenient pairs: 1 and 20, 2 and 19, 3 and 18, 4 and 17, and so on. Within five seconds I wrote on the board: 210.

"Josef will now tell us how he arrived at the figure of two hundred and ten."

I wrote on the board: $21 \times 10 = 210$.

The old professor came to the front of the room, shook my hand, and said to the class, "You have before you a mathematician."

I was not suspended from school, and my father bought me a

complicated electric train. I refused to play with it.

The math professor began to work with me four times a week until, two years later, when I was fourteen, he told me that he had taken me as far as he could. "All that we can hope for is an early end to the war so that you will be able to study as you should. You have a future in mathematics."

The day he said that, I thought about it on the ride home on the S-Bahn. It was all that I wanted in the world. If I could study mathematics, I would ask for nothing else. It was during my brief religious phase, and I actually made it into a prayer. But by the time the train pulled into the station at Gartenfeld, "hope" and "future" were blue-bleak embers, and in order not to call Providence down upon my head for such selfishness in those times of horror, I made a deal with God and exchanged my life as a mathematician for the life of my mother. I felt noble about this, never dreaming I might end up with neither.

. . .

Professor Kreutzer had finished looking through the journals on his desk; he changed from the rimless to the black-rims and handed me ten or so journals he had selected.

"Look at these."

"When?"

"Why not now?"

The first one went into the application of some dosimetry, had very little text, and was mostly math. To me it seemed but ten seconds later that he asked me what the article was about. I told him that I hadn't read the introduction yet.

"Read!"

It seemed but ten seconds more when he asked, "What is the important factor in the discharge of the condenser?"

"The replacement of the fixed value in the exponent of e by a differential equation."

He told me to come back the next day to get more articles and books. There was no dismissal, no good-bye. He turned to a small scrap heap on the table beside his desk and began to change his glasses.

I went back to Krupinsky's lab carrying the journals.

My good Lord, while I was gone, my work space had been filled with bottles of flies. Sonja Press came in with even more.

"These are most of the common mutations we have in stock. The Chief wants you to be familiar with them by tomorrow."

She left and I sat at my worktable and stared at the thousands of little fruit flies in the cotton-stoppered flasks. I picked up a flask and looked. All the same to me. I took out the stopper. Three flies clinging upside down to the cotton flew free. In trying to catch them, I squashed one and lost the others. Meanwhile, four or five more escaped from the bottle. I put the cotton back and captured one escapee, put him on my open palm, slowly, slowly moving him closer to my eye. He flew away.

Sonja Press returned with books and journals on *Drosophila,* realized my dilemma, and explained. "You must anesthetize the little fellows before you can examine them, Josef." She took the time to demonstrate. "First you put a few drops of this ether, here, on the cotton. Like so. Not too much.

"Now you tap the flask to shake the flies on the cotton stopper back down, like so. Then you remove the stopper and—very fast—turn the flask upside down, putting the opening into this smaller bottle. You see?" She looked at me.

I nodded.

"Now you tap gently to dislodge the flies but not hard enough to loosen the polenta pudding in the bottom." She handed the two joined flasks to me. "Here, you try it."

I did it correctly.

"That's it. Now stopper the bottle with that etherized cotton. Right! See? You can do it easily."

When the fruit flies were safely asleep, Sonja had me turn them out on a creased white card, spread them with a tweezer, and then insert the card under the microscope.

"Now you can take a look." She touched my arm. "Before long you will do it with ease. Now," she explained, "we begin the actual sorting. The useful flies—the virgins and some of the males—we put to one side, like so."

"What do you do with the unuseful ones?"

"Here. Dump them here." She pointed to a mass grave—an alcohol jar—heaped with dead *Drosophila*.

Sonja sat close to me, actually touching, while I practiced transferring the flies from one bottle to another. Before she left, she pressed my arm gently. "Don't worry, Josef, you are doing just fine."

She was more than just pretty, and she smelled like roses.

I looked again at the flies. I knew in theory the anatomy of an insect, but to see if there is one vein in the wing missing or if the eye color is yellow instead of red—I just didn't know. I opened the books Sonja Press had brought in, found the charts with the makeup of each chromosome, and began to read. Her face and body were in my mind, and my arm, where she pressed it, was warm. She was an attractive woman, and I was quite in love with her. Her manner, her warmth and sweetness, reminded me of Sheereen, although Sonja was nowhere near as beautiful.

I was alone in the lab for what seemed a long time, and I was desperately hungry. The others must have been at lunch. I looked at my wristwatch: almost one o'clock. My time with Professor Kreutzer had not been fifteen minutes or so, but more like two hours. It is always that way when I do mathematics. But it seemed more than the eight hours since I'd eaten breakfast at five that morning.

When they finally returned from eating, they were all different toward me. Krupinsky showed me around the laboratory and explained the work they were doing. The girl whose assistant I was told me her name was Marlene. She was unattractive and had suspicious-looking sore pimples on her face. The Rare Earths

Chemist, who was in our lab using some of the measuring equipment, said, "If Krup doesn't have any work for you here, come into Rare Earths any time." And they all teased me: "We hear you don't drink, Josef. Is it for religious reasons?" or "We hear you know something about math, so maybe you can help us with a problem. How much is five times six?"

A marked change. Just like that. No longer "you" but "Josef." Apparently I had been discussed over lunch. I was relieved. Krupinsky showed me where the bathroom was on our floor, and when I was done at the urinal he explained to me about the shower.

"There's plenty of hot water here, and you can shower whenever you like." Then he threw open a huge cupboard filled with clean, starched, white lab coats. "We don't have any towels, so just use a lab coat to dry yourself. Here. Take off your suit jacket and put this on. Take a clean one whenever you need it."

I hung my jacket on a hook on the wall, and when I was properly attired, Krupinsky took me down to the first floor, to the cafeteria that served the entire Institute.

"Is this where I eat?"

"Sure, if you've got money and ration stamps."

"I don't."

"You mean you don't have either?"

I hesitated. "Not exactly."

"Look, Bernhardt, either you do or you don't."

"There are other possibilities." I was quite sarcastic. "I do have both, but they are for my uncle and aunt. I'm going there after work today."

"What about that pile of garlic you've been carrying around? Didn't you bring a lunch?"

"No. That's for them, too."

Krupinsky led me back to the second floor and took me into a small greenhouse off the Genetics wing which had a tiny kitchen where, I soon realized, there was always a pot of polenta for the personnel. He turned on the gas, and while the polenta was warming, lectured to me. "We use this stuff to feed the yeast which feeds the fruit flies," he said. "For us we cook only cornmeal, water, and a little salt. For the yeast we add molasses, agar-agar, which is a dried algae to make it stiffer, and nipagin, which is a benzoic acid derivative—a good preservative that prevents mold but allows the yeast to grow."

He ladled a bowlful of the warm yellow porridge, then drowned it in thick brown molasses. My impulse was to rip it from his hands and drink it in a gulp, but I restrained myself and waited while he dug around in a drawer for a spoon. Then, slowly, I spooned in the first mouthful. My hand shook so, I was embarrassed. Hunger is dehumanizing and humiliating. I did not like to eat in front of others when I was so famished.

"Would you like a glass of vodka?" Krupinsky nodded toward a huge vat filled with clear liquid, which I had assumed to be water. There must have been seven or eight gallons of vodka in that vat.

"No, thank you."

"We can eat and drink as much as we want here, but it is against the rules to take any home with us." He very kindly left me alone for ten minutes or so while I wolfed down four more bowlfuls. It had been eight hours since I'd eaten my meager breakfast, and I had gone to bed hungry the night before. Perhaps that was why it wasn't sitting too well. I felt queasy.

Krupinsky breezed in waving several pages of newspaper. "You're taking money and ration stamps to an uncle, you say?"

"And some food. Uncle and Aunt."

"What is their name?"

"Jacoby."

"The Chief said you can take them some cornmeal." He rolled the newspaper into a cone and filled it with the dried meal, then filled a small flask with molasses. "Be sure and bring the flask back," he said as he corked it. Then he looked quizzically at me. "You O.K.?"

I nodded yes.

"You look kind of pukey."

The polenta was sitting uneasily in my chest; I was going to regurgitate the whole mess. "I'm just fine, thank you," I said weakly. Beads of perspiration on my forehead, weak-kneed, I felt faint. "I think I'm going to vomit."

"You're white as chalk. Here, sit down in this chair and put your head between your knees."

I dropped into the little wooden chair in a corner and put my head down. I could hear Krupinsky fiddling around in the refrigerator. "Give me your wrists," he said.

I extended both arms and he rubbed ice cubes on my wrists and then on my temples, and the nausea abated somewhat. He put the ice cubes in my hand. "Keep rubbing."

"Shall I keep my head down?"

"Doesn't hurt. How're you feeling?"

"Better. Thank you." I tried to take a deep breath but had trouble expelling it, which made me sweat even more. "I'm having trouble breathing."

"Just relax. You'll be O.K." He grabbed a tumbler from the cupboard, tilted the vat of vodka, and poured me a stiff drink. "Drink this."

It must have been three or four ounces. I hesitated, but he shoved it at me. "Drink!"

I took a sip.

"Chug-a-lug. All of it."

I drank about half in the first gulp and the rest in two or three shorter sips.

"Now take a deep breath and push the air out of your lungs. Push in your gut."

I did, and the exhale was a powerful belch emanating way deep down inside. "Whew. That's better," I said, pounding lightly on my chest. I could breathe, wheezily.

"You have asthma?"

"I used to when I was younger. Thank you, I think I'm quite drunk."

"You'll be O.K. What we usually do around here is space the polenta out through the day—a bowl or two when we get here, and now and then during the day; then, before we leave, we often come in and have one more and a snort of schnapps to get us through the trip home."

He gathered up the cornmeal and molasses for my uncle and aunt, and we returned to the Biology Lab, where I fell into the chair at my worktable and put my reeling head into my hands.

I was drunk for the second time in my life. The first time, my father had settled a huge case and his client invited him to a restaurant in the village for dinner. For some reason, he took me along—I was six years old—and they ordered a bottle of champagne. No one paid any attention to me, and I gulped down several glasses of the pleasant-tasting stuff before they realized it. I felt quite contented, but my lips were numb, and the singing seemed to come from a great distance. I turned to locate it, a reedy tenor voice singing a corny Italian art song, *"Caro mio ben,"* and as though through the wrong end of the ocular on my microscope, smaller and far away, at the lab entrance, stood Professor Avilov— the Chief—in a white lab coat and, behind him, side by side, two clowns, a tall, thin one, also in a lab coat, and a short, fat one, a dumpling with a bay window, in a dark suit with vest. He was the one singing, the dumpling, and he had a vibrato so terrible that he never seemed to hit a note directly.

The Chief's arms were outstretched, and he held a glass bowl, like an offering. "Sunflower seeds, anyone?"

Then the tall, thin one in the white lab coat leaped forward like a dancer and said, dramatically, "My dear Krup, how many flasks do you need for the new cultures?" He wore shiny black pumps.

Krupinsky assumed a mock ballet position and said, "My dear Yugoslav, why don't you tell us about Belgrade?"

The Chief, stepping forward into the lab, repeated, "Sunflower seeds, anyone?" and the dumpling, still singing, swooped over to pimply-faced Marlene. *"Credi m'al men,"* he vibrated in her ear.

"Belgrade!" The Yugoslav twirled about. "One cannot speak of

Yugoslavia without music," and he catapulted into the center of the room and began to dance in earnest—rather fine dancing. I found out later that, in Belgrade, he had been a professional ballet dancer, and that now he was a zoologist doing neurophysiological research with primates and other animals. The singer was a Russian named Bolotnikov. He did genetic research with *Epilachna,* a kind of ladybug, and he grew sunflowers in the greenhouse off the first floor to feed his ladybugs; consequently, there were always plenty of seeds to eat.

I was not sure all this was happening. I turned away from the commotion and stared for a while at all the bottles of *Drosophila* on my worktable and at the newspaper filled with cornmeal and the flask of molasses, which I knew I should put away in my rucksack.

I heard Krupinsky's voice in my ear. "How are you?"

"I'm quite drunk."

"Careful you don't knock those flies on the floor."

"What's wrong with him?" I heard the Chief's voice.

"I gave him vodka."

"He's not used to it. Come along. I want to take you up to Personnel."

At first I didn't realize the Chief was speaking to me, but then he clapped my shoulder. "Come along, Josef."

I stood and was dizzy. Bolotnikov still sang to Marlene; she ignored him completely and went about her work. The Yugoslav Zoologist had moved to the corner where the Geiger counters were stored and was talking to the Rare Earths Chemist.

I was no longer nauseated and my breathing, although slightly musical, was all right. But my gut was distended, and I used all my concentration to keep my flatulence from being too obvious; that is, I tightened my rear sphincter to keep the gas in—which was a loud mistake—then attempted a loosening to let it out in little farts: *blip, blip, blip.*

The Chief ignored my problem. "You must come to the fifth floor and speak with the Director of Personnel. Tell him the truth and trust him. In order to protect you, he has to know your background. He's an Alsatian and hates the Nazis. So far, he has been able to keep them out—that is, all but one, and that one is useful." And that was the first time I heard him say, "A Gestapo in the house saves one from a Caesarean section." It was a parody on a famous line from Schiller's *William Tell*, "An ax in the house saves one from the carpenter." Even in my drunken condition, I was able to understand that, somehow, it was the covert duty of the black-coated S.S. officer I had seen limping through the lobby that morning to see that one was not untimely ripped from the Institute.

I reeled after the Chief, blipping and burping, concentrating now on not sliding down the three flights of stairs we had to ascend to the fifth floor, where, for a moment, I was the warm and glowing center of a magic circle and everything outside it was another world—remote and strange—all the way down the long, dark hallway, lined on both sides with shelves and shelves of jars and jars of human brains. Mother had one pickled brain in her office at home, and, of course, I had studied biology. I knew what they were. The vodka loosened my tongue. "Whosh brainsh are those?" I asked the Chief.

He stopped abruptly, and I rammed into his back.

"Excush me."

"How much vodka did Krup give you?"

I held up three fingers.

"Three vodkas?" He grinned broadly at me.

"Ounces." *Burp. Blip.*

"These"—he waved his hand at the shelves—"are the brains of young men just like you." He looked at me intently—ominously—no longer smiling. "They like to get the cream of the crop."

My good Lord.

He raced to the end of the hall and popped into a doorway, leaving me frozen in my tracks in the warm, dark corridor, surrounded by the brains of young men just like myself. I turned my head fearfully to my right and to my left, but my feet would not walk.

The Chief stuck his head out the door and motioned firmly for me to join him. "Come!" he shouted.

Reluctantly, I moved toward him. Above the door was a sign: PERSONNEL.

As I stepped in, the Chief ran out, leaving me alone with the man behind the yellow oak desk. The nameplate read R. WAGENFÜHRER. He was, I hoped, the Director of Personnel. I could hear the Chief's steps echoing away from me.

"How do you do, Josef Bernhardt. Before I ask you about your background," said Herr Wagenführer, "you must fill in the forms. Sit down!"

I melted into the chair and looked at the three sets of forms wavering before me on the desk. He told me exactly what to write, and with most intense concentration, I was able to do so. The questions were mostly the same: NAME, ADDRESS, TELEPHONE NUMBER. For RACE he said to put *German* and for RELIGION, *None*. But there was no way, he told me, that I could avoid MOTHER'S MAIDEN NAME: *Jacoby*.

Then he asked me in great detail about my background. I answered truthfully; he listened intently but wrote nothing down. By the time the questioning was over, I was almost sober and feeling extremely tired.

"I think that will do," he said to me.

I stood.

"No, wait. I want to give you some information now."

I sat down again.

"You are to be employed as an apprentice laboratory assistant. You will receive a small monthly stipend plus commuting money, or, if you elect not to commute from Gartenfeld, you will be given extra money for room and board away from home. We do have some rooms and apartments here on the grounds, or there are places available in the village of Hagen.

"What I will tell you now is of utmost importance for your survival, so listen carefully. The name of this place, as you know, is the Kaiser Wilhelm Institute for Neurophysiological Research, and it is actually composed of three different and separate units. According to the records I will set up, you are now employed by the Kaiser Wilhelm Foundation, a private foundation especially endowed for scientific research. We have here also at the Institute private research by Mantle, which is a corporation, and also by the Luftwaffe. The brain research is almost all Luftwaffe. I have had you fill out three forms for these three different operations. It may be necessary from time to time—say, when the comptrollers are checking the books, or when there is an inspection of a certain section—to switch your forms from one file to another.

"Understand, each section is distinct from the others, so there is never an inspection of all at the same time. We might at any given moment—and with no warning—ask you to say you work 'here' instead of 'there,' if you are asked, which, most likely, you will not be. For example, when the Foundation is being checked, we will switch your file to Mantle or to Luftwaffe. The inspectors, one can hope, will not see it at all. If they do—if, say, the Ministry for the Study of Working Conditions should come across your file—any questions about your background would be out of their jurisdiction. We have been lucky and have known in advance about most inspections. Do you have any questions?" He stood.

I stood. Yes, I had questions. The brains. I wanted to ask him whose brains were lining the hallway, but I did not. "No, Herr Wagenführer," I said, "and thank you."

We shook hands. "You just do as I say, and we will do our best for you."

I was quite sober by now and the brains didn't bother me quite as much. But, just the same, I ran the long, dark corridor and raced down the stairs to the second floor. In the lab, I found Krupinsky,

Marlene, and the other girl—her name was Monika—putting away the equipment and the flies.

"How'd it go?" Krupinsky asked, scrutinizing me the way Mother did when she thought I had a fever.

"Fine."

"You're feeling better?"

"Yes."

"He's a nice man, that Alsatian."

I nodded. "Could I ask you a question?"

Krupinsky shrugged. "How could I stop you?"

"Is the neurophysiological research the main work done here?"

"I'd say so. The brain research by the Luftwaffe takes up the third, fourth, and fifth floors. It's important."

"Then why is it that the Chief is Director of the whole Institute? His specialty is genetics, and he isn't even German."

"It's complicated." Krupinsky slouched against my worktable. "The Chief is a really famous geneticist—world-famous?"

"Yes, I know that."

"Well, you know how those Nazis are obsessed with the study of genetics."

I nodded.

"And as for his not being German, he's from an upper-class Russian family that escaped to Germany during the revolution. You know Hitler hates the Communists almost as much as he hates the Jews."

"He calls them Jewish Bolshevists."

"Right." Krupinsky was silent for a moment before continuing. "But maybe the center of it all is the linear accelerator he uses for his research. You know about that?"

"I've heard him lecture."

"An atom smasher has to be of big interest to the military. So for all those reasons, and also because he is an incredibly capable administrator, he was appointed Director of the entire Institute. Of course, it was before we were actually at war with Russia." Krupinsky, still leaning tiredly against my worktable, unfolded his tall, thin frame until he stood in his usual round-shouldered stance. "Does that make any sense at all to you?"

"I think so."

"Well, it doesn't to me. Any other questions?"

"Yes. Whose brains are those up on the fifth floor?"

"Actually," he said, "they are all over the third, fourth, and fifth floors."

"Well, whose are they?"

He leered menacingly at me. "You'll find out soon enough. Now why don't you get to work like the rest of us and help put this stuff away so we can get out of here?"

I helped Marlene and Monika file away the rest of the flies into the incubators. Then we went into the little kitchen, where the polenta was already warming on the flame. Krupinsky insisted that I down another jolt of vodka before eating a bowl of polenta and molasses.

I did.

We didn't take the bus. A large group of us walked together the three kilometers to the train station in Hagen. I know I had my stinking rucksack with me, and I must have had an armful of journals and books. I don't remember for sure, for I was extremely tired and not sober. I cannot picture the scene or the weather. There must have been weather. It was April. The apple trees in the orchard beyond the Institute were blossoming in the evening of that first day.

CHAPTER · THREE

Sheereen

Here is the recipe for heavy water:

Take 5700 teacups of ordinary tap water. Put in bowl. Put enough electric current through to electrolyze down to 1 teacup.

"It looks just like regular water," I said to Krupinsky.

"It isn't, though."

I knew that. It was now enriched deuterium oxide. "What would happen if I drank it?"

"You could try a small amount, I suppose, but if you drank a large amount, mostly you'd die." Krupinsky poured it into a flask, corked it, and put it into a cupboard.

One then had to electrolyze the heavy water again in order to separate the heavy hydrogen from the oxygen, then feed the deuterium gas into a near vacuum in which there is a high-powered electrical field. This will make ions out of the deuterium, and then one feeds the ions into the linear accelerator, D ions, deuterons. I had to learn this and much more before Professor Kreutzer, six weeks later, would take me into that central room which housed the linear accelerator: the Radiation Laboratory.

I have lost track of the chronology of my education at the Institute. They crammed my brain with information: the anatomy of the fruit fly—how to tell the males from the females, the virgins from the egg-layers, one species or subspecies from another. I learned dosimetry, the accurate measuring of doses. I learned to handle radioactive material, to work with high-tension equipment, to make and use Geiger counters, to cook polenta in the kitchen in the little greenhouse off our second-floor wing, and so much more.

My education was broad, deep, concentrated, and thoroughly disorganized. For example, one afternoon the first week, after we were finished with the sorting of the fruit flies, the Chief ran into our lab, pulled a dead frog from his pocket, and placed it on the dissecting table of my microscope. Beside it he placed a scalpel, scissors, and tweezers.

"See what's inside," he said. And he began to pace.

I took the scalpel, and very generously I slit the frog open as one does a fish he wishes to fry. All the guts spilled out, and I had an excellent view of the interior. I was pleased. The Chief walked back and forth behind me as I poked about in the frog's insides.

"Notice," he said, as he paced. "Notice how carefully he uses the scissors and the knife to open the skin of the frog to expose air sacs. Notice how carefully he dissects several layers of muscle to enable him to identify the nerves and blood vessels, and then notice how he discovers another membrane, the peritoneum, and opens that up."

Everyone in the laboratory came over to my table to notice: Krupinsky, Marlene, Monika, several scientists from Mantle who were using the counting equipment.

The Chief pulled another frog from his pocket, dropped it onto the table of my microscope, and left. Everyone wandered back to what he was doing before, except Marlene. She stayed and tried to comfort me by patting my arm. I wanted her to go away so I could concentrate on the dissection. But she was still there when Sonja Press returned with a zoology book written in English. Sonja pulled up another chair to my table and leafed through the book, showing me the various pictures and charts.

"You see, Josef? It has much information about frogs and other animals. And the English language should not be at all difficult for someone of your intelligence—it is so similar to German. I could help you, if you wish."

"Thank you very much. I would appreciate that." Having studied English in high school, I could read it passably, especially in science where the words were almost the same. Of course, I didn't tell her.

"Study this tonight, and then tomorrow I can go over any questions you have."

"That would be quite helpful."

She smiled at me. "Shall we meet for lunch at noon in the cafeteria?"

Marlene had stood there the whole time, and when Sonja left, she asked me if I would like to go with her to the darkroom to take a photocopy of a page in a book. Actually, what I wanted to do was read as much of the zoology book as I could before I met Sonja the next day so I could amaze her with my brilliance. But I was curious about the darkroom and went along with Marlene, thinking it wouldn't take long.

It was a large room on the third floor, a photographic studio as well as a darkroom. There were no windows, the door was extra-heavy, and one could pull a thick black drape over it to ensure darkness. Consequently, the room was also soundproof. Marlene locked the door so we would not be disturbed.

I was beginning to get the picture, and I was uncomfortable.

This first visit to the darkroom occurred my second or third day at the Institute, and I was unable at that time to see the irony in my fear of the secondary stage of syphilis while still feeling my own death inevitably imminent. Marlene had suspicious sore pimples on her face; most likely, they were not syphilitic rashes but only adolescent acne. However, one couldn't be sure.

There were several cameras. Marlene used one mounted on a table that was aimed at a frame. She opened the book, placed it on the frame, adjusted some lighting, put a plate into the camera, and took the picture. She forgot to turn the red light on before switching off the others, and she said, "Oh, excuse me, Josef," when she gave me a full frontal bump in the dark. I jumped away from her, and all the while she was developing I stood in a far corner, feeling wretched and cowardly.

Aside from my concern with the "unclean," I thought her most unattractive. Furthermore, I am sensitive to odors and hers was not pleasant to me.

I was in a no-win situation. If to be "honorable" is—as my mother insisted—to avoid sex, and at the same time, to be polite, it was an impossible paradox. I was being incredibly impolite. But all I could think of was the book by Lombroso Mother gave me when I was twelve. It was called *Genius and Insanity* and described the grotesque syphilitic suffering of the romantic poets and musicians, and of Nietzsche, and of the homosexual officers of the Swedish army. And I was thinking about Fromm's Akt.

They were the most popular brand of condom and were sold in the men's rooms in railway stations, in vending machines which had on them cartoons of frowsy, overfed women with low-cut blouses, big breasts, and gumma here and there. The caption read: MEN, PROTECT YOURSELVES WITH FROMM'S AKT—50 PFENNIG.

When I was very young, I had a stupid fantasy. I thought the bad women Mother was always talking about were actually raping young boys, whatever that meant, and that one needed Fromm's Akt to somehow protect oneself. After I was in high school—when I was nine or so—the other boys set me straight.

It took quite some time to develop the film, and I was annoyed that I couldn't leave the room without ruining the negative. Krupinsky kept a German-English dictionary in our lab, and I wanted to get at it.

As we were leaving the darkroom, Marlene said to me, "If it is because you think I am a virgin, you are wrong."

That hadn't even occurred to me.

Outside the door, the Roumanian Biologist George Treponesco was waiting with a blond girl from Chemistry. She waved a book at us to demonstrate that they, too, needed photocopies.

His wife was a brunette from Brain Research.

Those first six weeks at the Institute, I did not even try to sleep much. I wanted to be prepared when Professor Kreutzer tested me on the journals he gave me daily. Most of the articles were on the measuring of radiation—but much to my surprise, he never even asked if I had read them. He just assumed I had. I was not treated like a student or laboratory assistant, but more like a new young scientist. And I wanted to study the assignments in biology and genetics from the Chief. I understood most of what they gave me, concentrating hard until I fell asleep over my books at night and rising early in order to arrive at the Institute in time to work with my microscope for an hour or so before anyone else came in. I hated each evening when I had to leave the Technicolor world of the Institute to descend into the gray and brown of the other Berlin—of my parents' house or my uncle's slum.

. . .

Uncle Otto and Aunt Greta's apartment was in a heavily bombed area near Alexanderplatz, across the street from the central vegetable and fruit market where the farmers brought their produce. It was a neighborhood where the poorest people lived, and it was dirty and crime-infested.

When my grandfather Josef Jacoby died, before I was born, Uncle inherited the family's furniture factory and an entire block of apartment buildings in a good residential section of Berlin. However, in 1938 the Nazis "aryanized" his assets, and now he and Aunt Greta were crowded into two wretched rooms with what remained of the Jacoby family library, silver, and china. They existed on his reduced veteran's pension and on whatever my father could send each week.

I remember his first apartment. It was large and comfortable. And since he owned the building, he had a room in the basement where, each spring, he made his own wine for Passover. Aunt Greta, for the first seder, roasted a goose, delectable, with crackling crisp skin. And the liver! Roasted goose and pâté de fois gras Strasbourg. Truffles. Mother's family had moved from Strasbourg to Berlin after the First World War and did not join a synagogue, although Uncle Otto had attended services now and then. Because they did not officially affiliate with the Jewish community, we were not on the lists the Jewish leaders in Berlin so kindly handed over to the Nazis. So it took Adolf Hitler longer to catch up with us. Grandmother and Grandfather Jacoby, "may they rest in peace," as Aunt Greta always said, both died of natural causes before Adolf Hitler came to power.

After my first day at the Institute, when I delivered that stinking salami on the way home, the shock of the difference in the ambience was so overwhelming that I splurged one mark of the food money on daffodils for my aunt. With the remaining four marks I was able to buy two kilos of old potatoes, one of wrinkled apples, one of sauerkraut, two bananas, one piece of ersatz nut torte, and two newspapers. There was more money from Father in a sealed envelope, but that was to cover their expenses for the week. I was never told the amount. In my own defense, I must say that it was the flowers that most delighted Aunt Greta and that the corn polenta and molasses from the Institute more than made up for them.

Their building was suffocating from the fetid air, an accumulation of putrid cabbage, rancid fat, and years and years of mold from the damp Berlin climate. Holding my breath as much as possible, I climbed the four flights, and before I could even knock, there they were, the door thrown open, two smiling faces. Uncle patted my back and tried to take some of the packages, but I would not let him. He wore a brace from his chin to his tailbone. Extra ribs in his neck caused him severe pain. I took the bundles into the kitchen, lifted the daffodils out of the bag, and presented them, with a little bow, to Aunt. She threw her arms around me and kissed my cheek. I had to bend way over—Aunt Greta was so short. She had tears in her eyes, but she was smiling.

"We are so happy to see you, Josef," she said. "We were a little worried. It is so late, but now you are here."

They had no way of knowing that I no longer attended high school, which was out by one and was only three S-Bahn stations from their stop. The Institute's workday ended at six and it was an hour's commute to Alexanderplatz. I did not tell them, that day, of the change, although for their peace of mind I mentioned it several weeks later. But, all along, I spoke very little to anyone about the Institute.

My coming must have been the event of the week. It wasn't just the food; that was important, of course. But they didn't have a radio—Jews were not allowed to have radios—and Uncle Otto was always anxious to hear the latest war news. So each week I would bring him two newspapers: the *Deutsche Allgemeine Zeitung—DAZ—*and a French daily, *Le Matin.*

Aunt stayed in the kitchen to put the food away, and Uncle and I settled in the *Berliner Zimmer,* a living room peculiar to that type of building, with three doors, one to the entry hallway, one to the bedroom, and the other to the kitchen. The bathroom was half a flight down the stairs and shared with the other three apartments on that floor. Uncle sat on a couch that had seen better days and I on a chair by their small dining table, which was placed in front of the only window in the apartment. Since it was dark outside, the blackout curtain was drawn.

"Ah," said Uncle, scanning the front page of *DAZ* and laughing. "I see that the 'victorious German Army' is again 'straightening out the front' in a 'victorious retreat.'" The Russians had recovered Stalingrad two and a half months before, in February, and were continuing to drive the Germans out. Even the twisted, insane news articles couldn't hide the facts. "It shouldn't be long now before the Russians are in Berlin."

"I don't know, Uncle. From what I understand, the German

Army is recovering in the spring mud on the Russian Front, and the Allies are having heavy losses to German submarines in the Atlantic."

"That's just propaganda. You can't believe anything they say."

"No, I think it's true."

"How do you know this? Josef, you haven't been listening to shortwave?" He searched my face. "You mustn't. Remember what happened to your Uncle Philip."

Uncle Otto looked so worried that I lied. "No, of course not, Uncle. You are right. If one reads between the lines the news is looking better."

"Look what our dear nephew has brought us." Aunt Greta appeared from the kitchen holding up the cone of newspaper with the cornmeal in one hand and the flask of molasses with the other. "We will have quite a feast. You must stay to dinner, Josef. I insist."

"Thankyouverymuch, Aunt, but I can't. It's late and Mother will be worried." It was absolutely taboo to eat at anyone's house and take up their rations. Aunt Greta, who had been jolly and plump, was so wasted that her skin hung in folds. She was forty and looked twenty years older.

She went back through the kitchen door and returned with the daffodils in a white vase. "I'll put these right here." She placed them on the table with the black drape as background. Then she sat down on the sofa next to my uncle, and they held hands.

"I'd really better go. I have a lot of homework." That was the truth. I wanted to read the stacks of material given to me by the Chief and Professor Kreutzer.

"Why were you so late?" Uncle asked worriedly.

"I was working on a new science project." Also the truth, more or less. I pointed to the books and journals that I couldn't fit into my rucksack. To change the subject, I said, "Aunt, I'll need that flask back."

She jumped up and went into the kitchen. I followed her to avoid further interrogation and watched her empty the molasses into a bowl, then boil a little water to swish out the residue—not a drop wasted. I wanted to return the flask to Krupinsky in the morning.

. . .

The people in my lab usually drifted in about nine, continuing the discussion they had started over tea in the cafeteria. It was always about the war. Krupinsky saw an early end in every Allied action, and his daily news analysis was hopeful, loud, and couched in a framework of sexual banter: "Hey, Josef, did you know that the condoms they issue the S.S. are perforated? And when the Americans come and get hold of them, what will that do to the Master Race?"

Amid such chatter, the daily sorting of the newly hatched flies began. Since the work was mechanical and needed no thought, the dialogue could continue throughout the morning. But one morning at the end of my first six weeks, Krupinsky was quiet. Unusual. Marlene was telling me, as we sorted the flies, about her problem in hearing BBC the night before. Most people in our wing tried to catch the news each night on England's German-language broadcast. It was, of course, highly illegal to listen to this and quite dangerous if one was caught.

"Bad reception," Marlene said.

"Why don't you try at night the normal medium waves and not rely on the shortwaves?" I said to her.

Krupinsky looked up from his silent sorting as Marlene and I talked, then asked me to join him at the far end of the lab where the Geiger counters were stored. He was most obviously depressed and spoke in a voice so low I hardly could hear him. "I don't understand how this stuff works." He waved a limp hand at the Geiger counters and other measuring equipment. "And they expect me to do it." He was supposed to measure background radiation several times each day. "I'm not a physicist or a mathematician." He slouched against the shelves. He was tall, six feet or more, and too thin. "I'm a medical doctor specializing in endocrines."

I could not think of what to say.

"Look, I heard you tell Marlene about the medium waves. You must know something about radios and electricity?"

"Yes, I do."

He waited. He touched a Geiger counter and asked me, "Would you like to learn about this measuring equipment and take it over?"

"I wouldn't be afraid of it. I would like to."

But there was more on his mind. He thrust his hands into his pockets and just stood there in front of those shelves and looked down. "Do you really know a lot about radios? I mean, how to repair them and all?"

"Pretty much."

He put his face into his hands and rocked his body. "Something horrible has happened with my radio. If I get caught it's the end of us. My wife," he moaned.

"What happened?"

"It's stuck on BBC. Last night—"

"What do you mean 'stuck'?"

"I mean stuck."

"You can't detune?"

"That's it."

"Can't you change the meter bands?"

"Yes, I can do that—I can push the button from shortwave to broadcast to long wave, but all I get on those other bands is static. And when I push back to shortwave, I either get BBC or the jamming."

"What kind of radio do you have?"

"It's a Blaupunkt, suitcase model."

"If you turn the tuning knob, does the pointer move?"

"No! That's it. The knob moves but not the pointer."

"It doesn't sound too serious. Most likely the cord from the tuning knob to the tuning condenser is broken, or a pulley has slipped, or a tension spring dislodged."

"Could you fix it?"

"Most likely."

"Then you have to come home with me right away!"

We could not leave until we had seen the Chief. He came every morning for half an hour, between eight thirty and eleven, and paced up and down our lab, often not saying a word, or sometimes asking if we'd heard the news; or there might be a few personal comments. We could ask him questions. He visited daily in each laboratory of the Genetics wing. And he knew absolutely what was going on.

While we were waiting for him, we continued sorting—Marlene, Monika, Krupinsky, and I. The new flies emerged from the pupae in the morning and had to be sorted every two hours until about one in the afternoon. They were anesthetized and put into a paper cone, which was then stuck into the polenta pudding in the bottom of a beaker. We separated the males from the females and the non-virgin from the virgin females before they were sexually mature—a matter of hours; a female only two hours old was still a virgin, and one could tell by its lack of pigmentation, by its soft, moist-looking wings. The whole thing just looked plump and still didn't have the right form.

To propagate the race, one put in three or four males with three or four females; to isolate mutations, one male and one to three females, depending on what one was looking for. The females had to be virgins, so I spent much time looking for virgins, peering at the females, at first at a distance through the microscope, and then, later, when I was more adept, with my naked eye.

In the beginning, the discovery of the variations was exciting, but soon the sorting became so monotonous that I came to prefer being assigned to monitoring the linear accelerator. Sitting in the booth of the Radiation Laboratory—even for as long as forty-eight hours—was a relief. There one could ruminate in peace with only occasional interruptions.

Krupinsky was feeling a bit more cheerful now since I told him I thought I could fix his radio, and he instructed me in a loud voice: "Look out, Josef. As soon as those females mature: *wham!* That's it, and you have to look around for another virgin."

He said *"wham!"* with such force that he blew away the little flies from the cone he held, and he had to look for more virgins himself. One had to be careful not to expel a strong current of air at them or they were gone. If one were to laugh too hard, for example, the flies would disappear.

Krupinsky delighted in pointing out the sex organ in the male—"Look, it has a built-in French tickler"—and often he asked me to notice the special comb on the legs of the male which allowed it to grip the female tight during coitus. For a boy like me, nurtured in the bosom of Victorian antisexual propaganda, the atmosphere was like that of a stag movie, and Krupinsky sustained the tension with his continual teasing and innuendo.

The Chief came into our lab before ten and sent for Sonja Press and for the Rare Earths Chemist to help complete the sorting so that Krupinsky and I could take off at once to fix Krupinsky's radio. The Chief said I needn't bother coming back until the next day, since the distances were so great, and he gave me three biology books to read. Krupinsky and I gathered together some tools and left.

On the way, Krupinsky told me about his situation. He was 100 percent Jewish, married to a Gentile, and had been working as an endocrinologist at the Charité in 1938 when Adolf Hitler banned Jews from the practice of medicine—the same law that affected my mother. The Chief took him in, but the only way they could get by the authorities was to hire him as an apprentice biologist and pay him very little. So he and his wife had an even smaller apartment than my uncle. Everything but the bath, which was shared and down half a flight of stairs, was in one room.

His wife was still in bed when we got there, and when she heard us at the door, she shouted out, "Abe, is that you?" By the time he said yes and unlocked the door, Frau Krupinsky was completely out of the bed, her arms raised in supplication like those pictures of Eve being forced out of Eden, except that Frau Krupinsky didn't have even a fig leaf. The only thing she wore was a little silver cross on a thin chain at her breasts, which were all that I noticed in my shock—not her face or her genitals but those melon-full breasts hung onto a bony rib cage, not too heavy, but full and ripe and with the rosiest nipples.

"Oh, Abe, I have been so frightened." She flew naked into Krupinsky's arms. He walked her backward toward the bed and tried to pull the blanket off to cover her while still protecting her from my view.

I could not take my eyes off his wife. I, sixteen-and-a-half-year-old idiot, just stood there gaping, with a bulge in my pants and one urgent desire: to see *them* again. Krupinsky finally got the blanket around his wife, but in doing so he uncovered the radio, which was resting on a pillow at the foot of the bed.

"For God's sake," he hissed at me. "Shut the damn door."

I closed the door.

There was some confusion. Frau Krupinsky in a blanket sat on the bed with the radio. Krupinsky, still blocking her from my eyes, tried to calm her down. "You knew I'd come back, Kirsti. I said I would. And Josef here can fix anything." He turned around and looked me down and up, his eyes stopping an instant at my crotch. "You got an eyeful, didn't you, Bernhardt?"

It was what one might call an awkward social situation, and it had not been covered by lectures in my Dancing and Social Behavior Class. Fortunately, his wife had more sense than the two of us.

"It's not the boy's fault, Abe. Leave him alone. Josef, is it?" she said to me. "Why don't you turn your back while I put something on?"

Her sweet voice restored some health to the situation. I turned around and diverted my mind by taking the various tools from my rucksack and arranging them neatly on their table, all the while translating the intimate sounds of a woman dressing: stepping into her corset, fastening the hooks, sitting on the groaning bed to pull on her stockings, sliding her slip silkily down her body.

"You can turn around now." The melody of her speech was not native German, although the accent was correct.

She wore a blue-patterned housedress that buttoned all the way down the front. And *they* were completely encaged and undistinguished beneath corset, slip, and dress. But the memory of them is vivid in my mind till this day.

I looked at her face. For those who like strong Nordic features, Frau Krupinsky would seem most attractive.

"Could we move the radio over to the table?" I said. "There's more light, and I've got my tools ready."

"I'll bet you have," muttered Krupinsky, pulling the radio to the edge of the bed.

To get to the tuning linkage, I had to pull the chassis out of the cabinet. Much work. All those knobs had to come off. At first, Krupinsky hung over me, watching, until I said, "You're making me nervous." So he went over and sat beside his wife on the bed. He couldn't keep his hands off and I heard her whisper, "Abe, not now, later." I could tell by the way she said "later" that she wanted it. Probably as soon as I left. Damn him.

My diagnosis was correct. The cord to the tuning condenser was broken and the radio was permanently tuned to BBC. The linkage in the receiver was, as in most radios, a cord kept under tension by a spring and threaded over a number of little wheels from the axis of the tuning rod to the wheel on the main triple-tuning condenser. The path of the cord was complicated. If one is lucky, he finds the remainder of the broken cord and can use it as a guide by knotting the new cord to the old one and by pulling them both through the proper pathway. And I was lucky. It had broken in the favorite spot of breakage, right where it attaches to the big wheel of the condenser. Of course, one could not buy a new cord.

I stood up and turned around. And there he was, sitting beside her on the bed, an arm around her with the hand clutching the side of her corseted breast, and the other hand Godknowswhere.

"Do you have any multistrand fishing line?"

"Nothing like it." Krupinsky disengaged and stood up.

"I've some string," said Frau Krupinsky.

"That won't do at all. Do you think you could buy some or get it from a neighbor?"

"Will that take care of it?" she asked.

"In about three minutes. I know we could get some at the Institute."

"That would take hours," said Krupinsky. "Let me see what I can do. I should be able to find some right around here."

"It has to be multistrand," I called after him as he ran out the door and left me alone with his wife.

She began to make the bed; I poked about the radio tube. Actually, I had already detuned from BBC but didn't want to give him the satisfaction of knowing. I needed the fishing line so they could continue to use the radio, and could do nothing more until I had it. So I listened to her bustle about the room, straightening, until, finally, I could hear her standing right behind me.

"I'll make some tea," she said.

I pretended to be so engrossed that I could not hear.

"Would you like some tea, Josef?" Her voice was pleasant. It had a Scandinavian melody that I could not pinpoint.

I pretended to be startled out of deep concentration. "Oh! No, thank you." What an ass I was.

"It's past lunchtime. You must be hungry. I'll cut a little sausage and bread."

"No. No. Thankyouverymuch. Not a thing." I said all this without looking at her. I knew my face was red, and I knew I was acting like a clod—but what does one do in such a situation? Should one say "I'm sorry"? Inadequate.

"I'm sorry you are so embarrassed," she said. "Please don't be."

"It is I who should apologize to you," I said, still looking down at the radio.

"I'm Finnish, you know, and we don't make a fuss about our

bodies. When I was a child in Finland, we all took sauna together: mothers, fathers, uncles, aunts, the children, and friends. Do you understand?"

Finally I looked at her. "Yes. I had a Norwegian friend—his name was Petter—and his family was just like that."

"That's right. And the Swedes, too. It's just a matter of what one becomes accustomed to."

Could one ever become accustomed to those breasts? The thought started another erection and I turned my back and fiddled with the radio until Krupinsky returned with the fishing line. He had been gone half an hour.

I was able to attach it to the old cord and just pull it over the pathway. "It's fixed," I announced. "All I have to do now is put it back in the cabinet."

They applauded and acted quite grateful, and both insisted that I have a cup of tea with them in celebration. I didn't want it. I just wanted to get out of there, but it was impossible to refuse.

I put the radio back in the cabinet, and Krupinsky and I took it off the table and put it back on the bed. I said, "You shouldn't even have the radio in this building. It's much too dangerous."

He just shrugged, but Frau Krupinsky looked at me peculiarly and said, "One must draw the line somewhere, Josef. You cannot give in completely to those swine."

Her reprimand—which I never forgot—disquieted me even more, and although she and I attempted polite conversation over tea, it just wouldn't go. For one thing, I had the feeling that Krupinsky was teasing me with his wife and trying to shock me. He couldn't keep his hands off her, even while we were drinking tea. I'd had enough, and I suggested that it was time we both return to the Institute. "It's one thirty," I said, "and we could be back there before three."

"The Chief said we didn't have to come back this afternoon."

"The Chief said I didn't have to come back. He didn't say anything about you, Krupinsky."

"Well, I'm not going. We'll no sooner get there than we'll have to turn around and come home."

I knew he wanted to stay and make love to his wife, and I didn't want him to, little bastard that I was. I began to gather together the tools.

"Leave them! I'll take them back tomorrow."

I shrugged.

I could see that Frau Krupinsky was troubled by the dissension. Her face was pale. "Thank you, Josef," she said. "I don't know how we can ever thank you." She extended her hand to me.

I fell back on the formula I'd learned in Social Behavior Class. I bowed slightly, kissed her hand, and said, "It has been my pleasure." Realizing at once what I'd said, I blushed to the roots and somehow grabbed my rucksack and got out the door.

Krupinsky followed me down the hall. "You're not really going back, Bernhardt?"

"Oh, yes, I am."

"If you do, you little pisher, the Chief will know I'm playing hooky."

"That's your problem," I snapped.

"You little schlemiel."

"You ought to go back."

"No." A malicious, lewd grin. "I have better things to do."

Ordinarily I did not talk enough. When I did, I said too much and made an absolute ass of myself. I raced down the stairs feeling as out of joint as a tin man who clanks and jangles as he moves, and so out of shape, from lack of exercise and inadequate diet, that after two blocks of jogging along, I, who had been a runner, was breathless and had a sharp pain in my side. I slowed to a shuffle, my torso bent, and squeaked and jarred along, my brain in utter confusion. Krupinsky would have her clothes off already, and the idea of him fondling them in his nauseating hands infuriated me more than the image of him actually screwing her to the bed. With her rose-tipped breasts in my fantasy, I could have done it with anyone—even Marlene—if only I had a condom. And the fact that this was so, disgusted me. There was nothing good about me; I was irretrievably rotten.

When I got back to the S-Bahn station, I headed for the vending machines in the men's room. I had fifty pfennig—half a mark—in my pocket. The machine read: FROMM'S AKT—ONE MARK. They had raised the price. I could have wept from the frustration of my own helplessness, and I was in actual pain from the continual genital tension. Alone in the lavatory, I relieved myself.

When I came out, the train for Hagen was waiting. At two in the afternoon, it was not full, and I was able to sit by a window. We would be underground for twenty minutes in dim light. I rested my head against the cool dark glass, shocked and disgusted by my violent reaction to Frau Krupinsky's breasts. With all our lack of intimacy, my family was not overly modest about the body, perhaps because Mother was a physician. But it wasn't the body. It was the sexual body, the fact that they so warmly embraced and that she enjoyed it as much as he. And it brought back the warmth and womanliness and sweetness of Sheereen, and of the way we had been together. I realized with a crunching jolt, as the train started down its dark tunnel, that at thirteen, I had been ten times the man I now was. I had deteriorated in three years into nothing but a masturbating coward.

. . .

Sheereen's father was the Ambassador from Iraq—one fifth or so of the students at the Collège Français de Berlin were children of the diplomatic corps—and at age ten, when she joined my class, she was ten times the woman the German girls would ever be, and so spectacularly beautiful that most everyone was afraid to talk to her. I couldn't believe she liked me, too. After all, there were eighteen boys in my class and only four girls.

Sheereen was absolutely the only reason I consented to Dancing and Social Behavior Class, an optional course running eight weeks each winter. Ten- and eleven-year-old boys were not supposed to have a high opinion of girls. One had to pretend to hate them, and if one showed any interest whatsoever, he was teased unmercifully by the other boys. Consequently, although I was stirred to the core by Sheereen's loveliness, I was too much of a conformist to let on. The only acceptable way I could demonstrate my feeling was by tormenting her. So in every class I tried to sit behind her—a boy never sat beside a girl—and pull her hair and poke her with my pencil. She was very understanding and would turn and smile at me every time I did this. One can imagine the effect this had on me. Secretly, I dreamed of holding her romantically in my arms, and, therefore, let Mother talk me into the class—which pleased Mother no end.

Dancing and Social Behavior Class was stupid. Imagine this group of ten- and eleven-year-old boys bowing and saying to some giggly little female, "Would you give me the honor of this dance?" And picture lectures to them on "How to Talk to a Woman in a Social Situation." The upshot always was that one must give honor to women and never indulge in street language when speaking to them.

I wasn't much of an authority on street language. When I was six, I talked my mother into letting me out on the street to play with other neighborhood children. When she called me in after an hour, I said to her, "Shut up, you stupid old wreck," and I was never permitted out on the street again. All my playmates, thereafter, were from approved families.

One would have to dress better than usual on the day of Dancing Class, and instead of my Bavarian leather shorts and favorite blue shirt, which I always wore, Mother forced me into wool Bleyle short pants that itched miserably and a white shirt, tucked in. And she would put clean white silk gloves in my pocket. One had to wear them because one sweats so when he touches a girl. And then I had to stop downtown at a flower stall and buy a small bouquet. One bows to the lady, presents her with the bouquet, and then one tries to dance.

Since I liked Sheereen so much, I dared not ask her. A private girls' school participated in the class to make the numbers even, and although those girls were cruel and laughed at the boys, the first few weeks I would ask one of them.

One of the problems was that I became quite nauseated from the waltz. It is not at all the way it appears in the movies, the couples gliding in a stately manner around the room. In a real waltz, the dancers move fast and make a turn at each step. It wasn't as difficult when the dancing masters counted and the pianist played. There were three masters, and they would walk among us shouting, "One-two-three, one-two-three." But when they put on the Viennese records, one couldn't hear the "One-two-three," and I would twirl so fast I almost threw up from dizziness. My white silk gloves would be dirty almost at once from the falls I took trying to execute the turns.

About the third week, when I thought I understood the step, I took off like the athlete I was, perhaps confusing the waltz with a track-and-field event. I got up some pretty good speed and then, somehow, lost control. I tripped on a foot—not my own—and my partner went flying backward and slammed against a wall. I spun, fell over, and, as luck would have it, landed right on the foot of Sheereen. She was gracious. She smiled and said it could happen to anyone and that I was not at all clumsy, just strong.

My partner had the wind knocked out of her and was crying. She refused to dance with me anymore, so it was all rearranged by the head dancing master when Sheereen told him she wouldn't mind.

It was accepted that she was my partner after that, and by the time I was removed from the rowing team a year or so later, we had become quite close. Of course, I was never permitted to be alone with her. She was always accompanied either by her older brother, Ahmed, who was several years ahead of us in school, or by her English governess, Miss Vinny—even her last night in Berlin, three years after we met, on her thirteenth birthday. By that time, we were deeply bound to one another.

I was thirteen and one half when her father's chauffeur delivered to my house an invitation, engraved in gold, to Sheereen's thirteenth birthday party. I should have been suspicious when both Sheereen and her brother missed school for the two days preceding her birthday. When I telephoned the embassy, Miss Vinny said they were slightly ill but would be all right by the evening of the party.

The invitation indicated dancing and a midnight supper, so I wore a suit with long pants and Mother put the white silk gloves in my pocket. She actually wanted to accompany me on the train to midtown and help me choose a very special bouquet, but I insisted that I was capable of doing this myself. She even wanted to choose the birthday present, but I had bought it weeks before at the village bookstore where my father had given me a charge account. It was a slim, leather-bound volume of Shakespeare's sonnets.

So much of our relationship had to do with books. I helped Sheereen with math and science, and she helped me with poetry, especially with the Arabic poets, whose images and metaphors were so different, and with the British Romantics and Shakespeare. Iraq had been a British Protectorate, and Sheereen and her family were fluent in English. She loved Shakespeare, especially *Romeo and Juliet* and the sonnets, which, she told me, were all about time and love.

Mother, of course, disapproved of my choice of gifts for ten different reasons. If she had seen the inscription I wrote after showing her the book, she would have denounced me to Father and both would have forbidden me from going to the party. Sheereen and I, all along, kept the depth of our feelings from our parents. Had they known, they would have used all their power to keep us apart.

And we didn't actually declare our feelings to each other, except for one little exchange: one day when we were studying together in the school library, I looked up and found Sheereen staring at me. "What are you doing?" I asked her.

"Looking at your eyes. You have very nice eyes."

"No, it is you who have the very nice eyes."

"No, you. I am lucky to have a boyfriend with such beautiful eyes."

"No, I am the lucky one."

We condensed this conversation into a little formula which we repeated every time we were together: "I am the lucky one," one of us would say. "No, I'm the lucky one," the other would answer.

This was the closest we came to words of love until her thirteenth birthday, when I inscribed the book of sonnets, *For Reenie, from her Seff, with all love for all time,* and she gave me the poem she had written herself.

The Iraqi Embassy was within walking distance of our high school in midtown Berlin, in a garden district of winding streets and huge villas where many of the embassies were located. It was decorated in white and pastels and had a very beautiful garden. I was surprised to find that there were many people there, mostly adults in evening clothes and officers in dress uniforms, and that I was the only boy from our class.

It was all quite different this year. For her eleventh and twelfth birthday parties, there had been only schoolmates, and her parents had provided entertainment for us by grown-ups who did things —a puppet show, clowns, or so—and there had been trays of brightly colored ices and cakes and a sweet red punch. But this year, as I searched through the house and garden for Sheereen, I saw that there were sweet tables with heavy pastries drenched in honey and almonds, servants circulating with trays of champagne, and in the air the delicious aroma of roasting lamb and spices, which would be served later, at a midnight supper. An orchestra was playing in the ballroom, although no one was yet dancing. There was a table piled high with beautifully wrapped gifts. I kept mine in my inner pocket, planning to give it to her privately. I carried a small bouquet of violets.

She was nowhere in sight. I joined others at the foot of the broad staircase to wait for her entrance.

I describe other women as good-looking or attractive, as pretty or as nearly beautiful, to make it clear that Sheereen was truly extraordinary. Even when she came down that staircase, stricken and ill, on the arm of her brother, she was so breathtaking that there was an audible gasp from those watching her descend. She, too, had been permitted to dress as an adult that night and had chosen a long gown of the palest blue silk, so pale that the lights from the chandeliers made it seem iridescent. And there was a net of gauzy stuff of the same blue all around her bare shoulders. The second I saw her leaning so feebly on Ahmed's arm, I knew.

At the foot of the stairs, other guests crowded around, wishing her happy birthday. I could hear her sweet voice answering, "Thank you, thank you," but I could see she was looking anxiously about for me.

I had moved to a corner, away from the stairs. When she saw me, she left her brother's arm and quickened her pace, stopping short, not touching me.

"You are leaving," I said, very softly.

"Tomorrow. I begged Father to take you with us." She began in a trembling, soft voice, but it began to rise in pitch and volume. "He said no, and I said I wouldn't go."

Ahmed was there beside us, and her governess, who looked tense and drawn. "Sheereen," Miss Vinny pleaded, "you promised me you would behave."

"I don't care," she sobbed. "I won't go."

Those near us could hear every word she said. Her brother's eyes filled with tears; I was able, by some miracle, to hold mine back. From across the room, her father glared fiercely in our direction, and I knew that if her public hysteria continued for a moment longer, he would not hesitate to send her to her room and we would not have even this last evening together.

If she had been strong, I would have crumbled. But she was not.

The news she had received two days before that they were leaving had devastated her. Strange as it may seem, her terrible suffering brought out the manliness in me, and that night—her last in Berlin—I was a rock for her, and for a time after, I was more of a man than I had ever been, until six months after her departure, when my father knocked my manhood from under me by laying the responsibility for the life—or should I say the death?—of my mother on my young shoulders, when all the time it was his failure in not taking her away and the failure of his entire generation for allowing Adolf Hitler to rise to power. It was then—without the love and support of Sheereen—that I crumbled.

Her father moved toward us.

Both her hands were touching my arm.

"Reenie," I said. "You must begin the dancing with your father, or he will send you away from me right now. I will be waiting." I folded the violet bouquet into her left hand.

Her father was there, furious, apoplectic.

"Good evening, Herr Ambassador." I bowed as I had been taught in Social Behavior Class.

He stopped short, hesitated, then turned angrily toward her.

"Oh, Father," she said in a shaky, small voice, "don't you think it is time we began the dancing?" She extended her right hand most properly, the left holding the violets crossed beneath her breast. I remember that she wore long gloves of pale blue silk, without fingers, that her nails were polished in the softest pink, and that the violets were achingly right.

Her father had used Sheereen's thirteenth birthday as a pretext for a political farewell party for himself, and had he not been sur-rounded by Nazi brass and diplomats from other embassies, I think he would have yanked her arm out of its socket, thrown her into her room, and locked the door. It was another time in my life when the black-coated S.S. officers were useful: Gestapo in the house can save one from a Caesarean section. But form is every-thing for the people of my parents' generation, and for an ambassador protocol is all. He bowed to his beautiful daughter, clicked his heels, took the little hand hanging so delicately in the balance, touched it with his lips, and said loudly, in French, "It would be my greatest pleasure, my dear." Then he whispered gruffly, in German, so I would be sure to understand, "I like to think we Arabs, unlike our cousins"—and he threw me an ugly glance—"are in control of our emotions."

She smiled at him tremulously through her tears and had the presence of mind not to turn her head even slightly to look at me.

Everyone, of course, was relieved. Nazis and other bureaucrats detest scenes. A little procession followed them into the ballroom. One could hear the orchestra begin a Viennese waltz. I was still in the corner with Ahmed and Miss Vinny, who began to prattle. "She hasn't slept. She hasn't eaten for two days. I'm half out of my mind. Talk to her, Ahmed. Tell her she must obey her father. He is very angry." The poor woman was so distraught.

Ahmed, who was a stout fellow, said to no one in particular, "If she'd eat something, it would go better for her. See if you can get her to eat."

I moved away and Ahmed followed me. We could hear Miss Vinny saying to some of the guests, "Yes, it is so sad. Of course, she hates to leave her little school friends," and "We have been very happy here in Berlin," and so on.

Ahmed said, "Let's go into the garden. I've got some good Turkish cigarettes." We were not friends. He was three years older, which is quite a difference at that age, and he never approved of my relationship with his sister, of whom he was very fond.

We passed through the ballroom. Her father, no doubt, had been to dancing class as a boy, for he was making his way quite passably around the ballroom, overweight, puffy as he was. Sheereen, whom he held at the greatest distance, was a slender blue reed.

We wandered about the garden, smoking, while Ahmed talked. "She threatened to kill herself every other minute—wouldn't eat, wouldn't drink, and read *Romeo and Juliet* about seventeen times. Miss Vinny finally talked Mother into convincing Father to let her spend most of this evening with you. You even get to sit with her at dinner. What a mess. Oh, damn, damn. All I ever wanted was to be able to go to Cambridge when I finish high school. And now it's out of the question."

"Why should it be? Iraq was a British Protectorate. You could still go there, couldn't you?"

"My dear *old chap,*" he began. We spoke French to each other most of the time, but he said *"old chap"* in English quite often when he was feeling British. "My dear *old chap,* you are most naive. Of course, Iraq was British—but the old guard like my father hate the British, and, as a matter of fact, if you had any sense at all, you'd realize from all those uniforms here tonight that my father is pro-Axis."

"You mean your father is pro-Nazi? How can he be after living here and seeing what goes on?"

"I might ask you the same thing," he said angrily.

"What do you mean? My father a Nazi? How could he be?"

"That's not what I mean. Your mother is a Jew, isn't she?"

"What does *that* mean?"

"Don't get up in arms, *old chap;* we Muslims, through the ages, have not been racial bigots."

"Oh, no? Then what did your father mean when he made that remark about his 'cousins'?"

"Don't pay any attention to that. He has good reason to be furious with you. What I meant was, your father sees what is going on here. Why the devil hasn't he taken you and your mother away? Don't you see? It isn't the separation from you that is driving my sister crazy. You know Sheereen, she's as solid as they come. But she knows that if you stay here, sooner or later . . . they will get you. She's been hysterical because she wants my father to save you. It's not a matter of money, is it? I mean, with your father?"

"You know better than that. You've been to my house."

"Then what is it?"

"I've wondered. Sometimes I think it's because my father's law degree won't do him any good in another country."

"But your mother—she's a doctor, isn't she? That'd be good anywhere. She could go to America."

I shrugged. "Her younger brother was a doctor—Uncle Philip—and he got a visa to the United States. Some people in the State of Iowa helped him get a job on a medical faculty there."

"He'll help you. If you make it to Switzerland, he could help you from Iowa."

"They caught him the day he was supposed to leave."

"*Bloody rotten,*" he said in English. "But look, *old chap,* we're going to Switzerland in the morning—Mother, Sheereen—and I'm escorting them. Father will come later. Yes, if you could make it to Switzerland, I could help you there, and then those people from Iowa could help you, couldn't they?"

"My father won't even discuss it with me, much less give me the money. I've tried. And you know that you have to have money in Switzerland or they ship you right back!"

"Maybe my father—"

"Look, Ahmed, thank you. But I won't leave my mother behind, and she won't leave my father. And then there's her other brother here, too."

He threw his cigarette on the grass and ground it out, and we both took another. "Our parents are all fools. All I want is to go to Cambridge. Ah, listen, *old chap,* my father told Sheereen that if your own father didn't care enough to save your hide, why should he? And he's right, you know. Come on. I'm starving. Let's go in the kitchen and get some lamb and rice."

It was an hour and a half, ten or so, before Sheereen was released from her social obligations. Ahmed brought her into the garden—still, she held the violets—and disappeared into the kitchen again, returning with two servants and plates of lamb and rice and a bottle of champagne for the three of us.

It was chilly outside this April evening, and I was so happy to put my wool suit jacket about Sheereen and allow myself to suffer the cold on her behalf.

We fed her—Ahmed and I—choice bits, with small sips of champagne in between, until some color returned to her face and she seemed a trifle stronger.

"Would you like to dance?" I asked her. "I promise not to throw you against the wall."

And we all three began to laugh. The tale of my waltzing accident had made the rounds at school, so Ahmed knew of it, too. It had happened so long ago, when we had been children.

But then she began to cry. "I think I could not bear to dance with you in front of all those people."

Ahmed looked despairingly at me. "We still have the *bloody* dinner to get through. And if she makes another scene, Father will kill us and fire Miss Vinny."

"All right. How should we do it? Sheereen," I said in a fake, deep voice, "you may not cry until after dinner. It is a command."

She laughed and cried, and the three of us marched up and down the garden paths. Sheereen decided that after the dinner she would defy her father and sit in the garden with me until dawn, when her train left for Switzerland.

"If he refuses," she said, "I will kill myself." And after that resolve, she was calmer. It was a matter of being in control of one's own life. It is so important.

We continued to walk about until fifteen minutes or so before the midnight supper, when Ahmed and I urged her to go upstairs and refresh herself. It was then that I gave her the little book of sonnets, wrapped with ribbon.

"What is it?" she asked.

"The sonnets."

"I knew it! Oh, Seff, I have spent the past two days trying to write a poem for you. But it is not at all good. I couldn't get it right."

"Please bring it to me. Please, Reenie."

"If you promise not to read it until I'm gone." She began to sob.
"I promise."

She turned and ran off. Ahmed and I, following at a distance, could see that she bolted up the stairs like a small child, two at a time.

After the dinner, which was the lamb and rice we had been eating all evening, her father clapped his hands and demanded attention. He wished his daughter a very happy birthday, thanked everyone for being so kind to him and his family in this foreign land, and then he announced that they would all be leaving. There were, of course, sounds of protestation and regret around the tables, but everyone knew by now because of Sheereen's scene early in the evening.

All but a few of her father's closest friends began to leave at two in the morning, and I slipped into the garden with Ahmed. Sheereen, after a battle with Miss Vinny, changed into ski pants and two sweaters and brought me a warm coat of Ahmed's, which she insisted I wear. It was chilly and damp outside—typical Berlin weather—and we sat together on a stone bench in the garden. She nestled in my arms—the tired violets crushed between us—crying quietly, drifting in and out of sleep. Ahmed walked nervously about for a time and finally stretched out on another bench and fell asleep.

It was unreal. So close to her, I could not imagine the separation. I held her in my arms for three hours, now and then interrupted by the adults. But we did not let them win this last, small battle. Miss Vinny came out and demanded that Sheereen retire to her room. "This is highly improper," she said, taking in the three of us: Ahmed wrapped in a greatcoat on his bench, and Sheereen and I, cuddled together on ours, a white mist exhaled with each of our breaths. "You will catch your death," said poor Miss Vinny.

Sheereen spoke calmly. "If you force me to my room, I will quite happily kill myself, and I mean this."

Miss Vinny stormed off, uttering threats, returned shortly, and halfheartedly ordered her to obey, but, finally, she gave in.

"Ahmed, you stay with your sister. If your father finds out, I'm finished." As she walked away, we could hear her muttering, "What is the world coming to? Everything is falling apart."

My mother telephoned. She had arranged a ride home for me, but I had refused it. I said to her, "It is not over yet. Please do not call again." And I told the servant who answered the phone not to disturb me. So I don't know if she called back or not. I knew that, in any case, I would have hell to pay when I did go home—which was not until the next afternoon, after school was over.

At five, wordless and without demonstration, Sheereen left me to prepare for her journey. I took off on foot for the railroad station from which she would leave, the Anhalter Bahnhof—a fifteen-minute walk from the Iraqi Embassy—where I waited on the platform. Her train was to leave at six thirty.

She arrived just in time, surrounded by servants, minor embassy officials, and family, and looked wildly about. When she saw me, she broke away and ran into my arms.

"I am the lucky one," she sobbed.

"No, I'm the lucky one," I said, and she was dragged weeping and falling out of my arms and into the train, and I did not ever see her again, ever.

I stayed until the train pulled out at exactly six thirty. It was too late to go home and too early to go to school, so I took the S-Bahn that circled the perimeter of Berlin and rode around for over an hour reading the poem which she must have composed in Arabic and then, painstakingly, translated into German, a difficult language for her.

For Seff from His Reenie

Tonight from the sky of your eyes,
Stars fall on my poetry,
Making lights on this virgin paper.
This is the beginning of love,
And the end of the way is foggy.

Through the windows of your eyes
I run into deserts,
Sink in the heart of waves,
Lie in the field of wild tulips,
For this is the beginning of love
In the spiritless black of this cruel world.

The chandelier of my memories of your eyes
Will light the dark temple of my mind,
For this is only the beginning,
And I cannot think of ends.
Our love, itself, is the light and is eternal.

· · ·

I closed my eyes against the light. The train had emerged from the tunnel and was aboveground.

"Is something wrong, son?"

I was startled and realized that tears were streaming down my face and that, perhaps, I had even sobbed aloud. An older woman sat opposite me.

"My father," I said, wondering, as I said it, why I had, for Papa was well.

"In the war?"

I nodded. "Wounded at the Russian Front. He was sent home, and last night . . ."

"He died? Poor dear. These are terrible times."

"Air raid," I mumbled.

"And your mother?"

"She's fine, thank God."

"Thank God." The woman crossed herself, a dangerous thing to do in public.

She looked as well-to-do as one could in these times, and I wondered if I could possibly ask her to loan me a mark. I had been giving my stipend from the Institute to Mother, keeping only what

I needed for commuting. My parents, supposedly, were well-to-do, but Mother no longer was permitted to practice medicine; Father's law practice had fallen off, and, my mother told me, the family money was "safe" in Swiss banks. If I asked her for the "extra" mark, she would want to know what I needed it for, and I preferred not to lie to her. In the future, I would hold out a bit more from my stipend, but, somehow, I would have to get my hands on one mark, fast, to buy the Fromm's Akt. Not for Marlene—I was not interested in her—but for Sonja Press, who I was naive enough to think was a virgin, and ignorant enough to assume might have carnal interest in me.

"You must be strong and be a comfort to your mother now," the woman said, and then, probably embarrassed by her kindness to a stranger, she turned her head abruptly and stared at the window.

We were pulling into Ostkreuz, the east station that connected to the trains that made the great circle aboveground around the perimeter of Berlin. The morning Sheereen left—after her train to Switzerland pulled out at six thirty—I rode the Berlin Circle until time to go to school, reading and rereading the poem she had written for me, and that night I stormed into Father's study and demanded that he take Mother and me away to Switzerland.

"You can afford it," I shouted. "You are rich!"

He, sitting in his tapestry chair reading legal papers, did not even look up when he answered, "You are too young to understand, and, furthermore, I owe you no explanation." He went right on reading.

"Of course," I said through clenched teeth in my most contemptuous manner, "I knew you would say that. But if those swine murder my mother, you will be to blame." It was the first time I had spoken to him in this way, and it was the only time in my life that he abused me physically.

He jumped from his chair, throwing his papers to the floor, slammed me back against the wall, and slapped my face. I, at thirteen and a half, was wiry and strong, but I did not raise my hand to him. Instead, I retired, without a word, to my room, and the next day began the activities with Mitzka which Father stopped six months later, after I was informed on twice in the same week—once by the Bavarian Baron next door and once by my mother.

Baron von Chiemsee informed Father that he had seen Mitzka and me rip out wires from under the hood of the Horch a Nazi official had parked down the street and throw them down the storm sewer. That same week, Mother informed my father that she caught me smuggling his Parabellum—the huge sidearm he wore as an officer during the First World War—out of the house in my rucksack.

What they didn't know was that for six months, beginning the day after Sheereen left, I joined Mitzka Avilov, at least twice a week, in riding the Berlin Circle in order to drop food to the forced laborers and prisoners of war who worked the track. Mitzka had an unending supply of cornmeal, which he wrapped in old newspapers, and, occasionally, he had a flask of molasses or vodka. In late summer, when the trees were full, we would crawl through his secret hole in the fence and collect the apples to add to our food drop.

It was doubly dangerous, for neither of us had money for the fare and we were sneaking on and off the trains. If I had been caught, it would have been as deadly for Mother as for myself. That is why I allowed Father to shock my spirit into hiding.

My conversation with him, after the denunciations, was in his study, as always, and ended in a brief exchange of non sequiturs:

"You must obey the law and avoid drawing attention to yourself. Remember what happened to your Uncle Philip!"

"Send us to Switzerland!"

"You are forbidden to see Mitzka Avilov outside of school!" And then, his final thrust: "If you continue as you are, it is you who will be the destruction of your mother."

Our nasty little game, each holding the other responsible for her life. If she were to die, whose fault would it be?

I knew that giving in to him would not save Mother in the long run, but at fourteen I was not yet ready to assume responsibility for her death. So, despising my decision, I obeyed Father. I read once in Mother's medical books that a leper's aesthetic sense revolts and he begins to loathe himself.

I detrained at Gesundbrunnen. I would not return to the Institute that afternoon. Krupinsky was a shiny ape, but he was not unkind, and I would not get him into trouble. But my God, I didn't want to go home, so I decided to ride the Berlin Circle and study the biology books the Chief had given me. The fifty pfennigs should cover the fare, and I would go home at the regular time.

. . .

I thought it augured well for me, the next morning at seven, when I found Sonja Press waiting for me in the Biology Laboratory. It was an augur, all right, but I misread the signs.

The Chief was there, too. The two of them were drinking tea and had a cup of the smoky stuff ready for me. They had somewhere an unending supply of pressed tea tablets, the size of a thumbnail, which one dropped into boiling water. It must have been some kind of a milled tea. The tablets did not dissolve completely, but there was only a little residue left in the bottom of the cup. Everyone at the Institute drank it all day and all night.

The Chief told me that later that day I would become occupied with Professor Kreutzer and the business of irradiating fruit flies and determining the physical aspects of the effects of ionizing radiation. All my education, but that of the darkroom, led to that central machine in the Radiation Laboratory—the linear accelerator.

"But first," he said, "I want to take you for a walk around the park to look at this and at that, and I wish, myself, to show you how one entices the wild ones into the small bottles which Sonja here will show you how to prepare."

It was a little graduation exercise at the end of my first six weeks.

While he paced and drank another cup of tea, Sonja and I prepared the enticing little fly traps. Twenty small bottles in a wire basket were sitting on my table; the polenta solution already was cooking in the laboratory kitchen. The two of them must have been there quite early. I carried the hot pudding into the lab, and at Sonja's direction, using a rubber tube with clamp, I transferred from the container so much of the boiling polenta into the bottom of each bottle, maybe an inch or so. We had to wait until it cooled before Sonja put in a drop or two of a yeast solution with an eyedropper. So I drank another cup of tea.

The yeast ate the polenta, and the fruit flies ate the yeast. They were wild about it, Sonja told me, and to ensure them against drowning from their own gluttony, she stuck a tight roll of thick paper, bent in a V, into each bottle. It would absorb the excess liquid and give the little fellows a place to sit after they'd eaten and laid their eggs. We stoppered the bottles with cotton, attached wires to each rim, and placed them in the carrying basket.

I carried the basket, the Chief a map of the park. He showed me that each bottle was dated, numbered, and marked on the map. We placed several immediately outside the main entrance to catch the fruit flies that escaped from the Institute—a problem often discussed at staff dinners. These fugitives limited population genetic research of *Drosophila* in the park—except, of course, for the question of how mutations spread in a given area.

"These escapees"—the Chief waved his arm at the fruit flies swarming about the double doors—"are from controlled stock, and we want as few of them as possible to breed with the wild flies. The wild ones in the park—the *Drosophila melanogaster Berlin wild*—are mixed-breeds, and, therefore, most vital and stable. Those purely bred in the Institute are, for various reasons, not fit for a free life, but will survive only under laboratory conditions."

We placed the other bottles throughout the park—on trees and hedges, on the compost heap, and in the garden. And, of course, each placement was carefully noted on the map. It took no time at all to attract the *Berlin wilds*. One hung a bottle, removed the stopper, and within twenty seconds the little creatures would be inside, eating and laying their eggs, resting on the absorbent paper.

"It's fast and easy," said the Chief, "except when the apples are ripe in the orchard next door. Then these happy little fellows disdain our cooked pudding, my curly-headed Josef, and fly through the hedges and over the fence to the sweet rotting apples, where they deposit the minute particles of yeast they always carry with them on their bodies and on their tiny legs, and they contaminate the ripe fruit, starting the process of fermentation which is such a delight to mankind.

"Happy little winemakers," he said, "the first winemakers. I wish I could fly over the fence to collect those apples when they're ripe in late summer."

I could do it. Not over the fence, but through it. I was sure that Mitzka's secret opening behind a group of willow trees was still there—the cut fence was so well hidden in the shrubbery. But I did not mention it at the time, because I was foolish enough to assume that the Chief did not know about it.

As we walked about, placing the baited bottles, he pointed out areas of special interest: the large greenhouses, the special garden, the many winding and curving drives lined with lindens, beeches, oaks, and cedars, the cultivated earth where flowers were blooming, the stone benches. And the chapel.

"Don't you think it strange, Josef, that a scientific institution should have a chapel?"

"Yes, Herr Professor." I always thought it strange that the Institute should have a chapel and a greenhouse and all those winding drives.

The Chief opened the door to the chapel, a gray sandstone structure of neoclassic design, with a dome. There were no pews inside and no altar, either. A mechanic was working at a lathe. It was a machine shop now, obviously belonging to the Physics Department, for it looked like a junk shop. But there is no doubt that the building was intended to be a little church.

In design it matched the house of the Director, which, even as a

child, when I played with Mitzka, I thought strange. Both buildings were of gray sandstone, with the false pillars which carry no
weight. The house was large, with many little parlors on the first
floor, and a small laboratory for the Chief in the basement.

I had not realized, until the Chief told me that day, why the
house was so designed: the parlors were mourning rooms, the lab
in the basement a morgue. And the chapel was for services, the
greenhouse for maintaining flowers during the winter and for beginning new plant life. The winding drives were convenient to the
gravesides. The Institute was a graveyard.

"That is, it was to have been a graveyard," the Chief told me.
"The city architects chose this location for a municipal cemetery
because the land was cheap and because it was close to the hospitals
and medical doctors who would provide the clientele. But I can't
believe the contractors were not aware of the insurmountable
problem. Do you have any idea what that might be?"

"Water," I said.

"And what tells you about this water?"

"Mitzka and I tried to dig a cave and hit water at only three
feet."

"Ah, I see you have practical knowledge of this. But tell me,
Josef, what signs are here that would tell you about the water even
before you begin to dig?"

I looked around. "Willow trees."

"Willow trees always mean water. And there are many willows.
But what did they care, these contractors and architects? They
made their fortune. They built the funeral parlor on a hill and
attached rooms for the cemetery director and his family, and they
built the chapel and put in the drives and the trees and the flowers.

"When the day came for the first burial, the poor gravedigger
must have dug down one foot, two feet, two and one half feet,
when water began to ooze into the grave. And at three feet, it
gushed forth. He must have hurried to another plot and begun
again—one foot, two, two and one half. Again the water. He tried
again and again before admitting defeat. Tell me, Josef, who

would want their loved ones floating through eternity? And aside from the aesthetic problems, if the permanent guests were floating in the local water supply, it would not be healthy for the living.

"So this place was built for the dead, and only when it became a conspicuous failure, a financial burden to maintain, did they donate it to the Kaiser Wilhelm Foundation and erect the Institute building and a few other houses and apartments for personnel who cared to live on the premises."

I was laughing. "Is it really true that they actually dug the first grave?"

"True, my curly-headed friend? If I were to tell you the real truth, I would have to lie. But look. Now the grass is clipped and the flowers tended by the gardener you see in that bed of spring flowers. It gives him work. And you and I, my son, we hang the bottles on the trees and catch the happy little winemakers, who tell us many things. And that man in the grass"—the Chief pointed—"is a scientist. He collects another kind of specimen. Like you, he is one of the special cases in our little graveyard. He is not a Jew, but a Russian prisoner of war."

The gardener and the scientist were both on their knees, and from a distance, except for their clothing, they looked like twins: two squat, bespectacled men. The Chief and I watched them. The gardener wore work clothes and was digging with a hand tool in the moist earth. The scientist, in a dark suit with vest, crawled over the grass, his face almost to the ground. The sun caught the golden watch chain hanging in an arc from his middle.

The Chief explained to me that both men were victims. "The gardener, Gunther, is feebleminded, an idiot; the Nazis, because of it, gave him a vasectomy. As a consequence, he has become the most popular man in the village. He has a happy disposition, is very kind and generous, and the women love him very much. Do you understand?"

"Yes, Herr Professor."

"The scientist, Professor Ignatov, is a genius in his field. He is the expert of the world on bubonic plague. His small plane was

shot down by the Germans when he was following the migration
of a group of gregarious rodents, some kind of ground squirrel,
which are known carriers of the plague. They thought he was a
spy, put him in prison, and almost shot him. Luckily, someone
recognized him. When I hear through the grapevine of such people, I reward a few subaltern officers and so on, and make out a
requisition form. The Institute has top-priority rating, and all I
had to do was convince certain authorities that we must have this
particular scientist to do a study on 'Population Analysis of For-
estal Rodents in the Park.'"

Ignatov was standing now and moving toward us, clutching
something in his extended fist, shouting to the Chief in Russian.
He opened his huge paw and pounded his palm with the index
finger of the other hand.

The Chief answered him in German. "Yes, yes, Boris Ivanovich,
an excellent find, excellent. One is aware that there are many *Mus
musculus,* but we've had no evidence of the *Mus sylvaticus.* An excellent find."

He had the tiny skull of a long-tailed field mouse in his hand.

"Herr Professor Ignatov, I would like you to meet our young
colleague, who, this very day, will begin research on chromosome
mutations in *Drosophila.*"

I think that Ignatov had not even noticed me until the Chief
made the introduction. Then he walked up very close to me, too
close. His teeth were bad, his breath foul, and he began to shout in
German and spit at me. A human textbook with a thick Russian
accent.

"Salivary glands," he screamed, spitting in my face, *"sal-i-vary
glands . . ."* and he jabbed me in the chest with his forefinger.
"Chromosomes at meiosis in *Drosophila* are too small to work
with, but in the salivary glands of their lar-vae"—jab, jab, into my
chest—"are giant chromosomes with distinct longitudinal differ-
entiation. In fact"—jab, jab—"they may be up to two hundred . . .
two hun-dred"—jab, jab, jab—"times the size of corresponding
chromosomes at meiosis or in the nuclei of ordinary somatic cells."

He stepped back. His large, square head drooped to one side as though he were in a trance. It would have been impolite for me to wipe his spit off my face while he stood there. I swallowed my spit, fighting nausea.

His heavy head snapped upright and he came toward me again, index finger extended. "A further advantage of the salivary gland chromosomes for cytological study is that they appear constantly to be in a *pro-phase-like state*"—jab, jab, jab, jab—"always they are in a condition appropriate for effective staining and detailed observation."

He stepped back. His head drooped. The Chief thanked him. Ignatov nodded and turned away, his right fist clutching the tiny skull. The Chief handed me a clean handkerchief. As I wiped my face, he said, "Ignatov is typical of a certain type of Soviet scientist whose entire life is his work. Extremely industrious. But only his work."

Ignatov would come to our staff dinners and parties, get drunk, and go to sleep. One never heard him speak of anything but his research, and that always in a semi-hysteria. He was humorless, illiterate in anything but science. He talked only with the Chief and Professor Kreutzer. In good weather, one could see him at almost any hour of the day, wearing a suit with vest, on his hands and knees in the park, looking for a cranium, or a tooth, or a toenail of a rodent.

The gardener had come closer, too. He and the scientist were not as much alike in appearance as they seemed to be at a greater distance. If Ignatov was a construct of thick, square blocks, the gardener was a series of balloons. His face had the round look of the simpleminded. He came up to within ten feet of us and extended his pudgy hand, which grasped three perfect red tulips.

"Come here, come closer, Gunther."

The man edged forward, smiling sweetly.

"Come, come," said the Chief.

He came to within three feet of us but would move no closer.

"Gunther, this is Josef. Josef, Gunther grows many beautiful flowers for us."

Gunther extended his hand with the tulips. "For Madame."

The Chief stepped forward and took them and bent in a brief bow. "Thank you, Gunther. She will be most pleased." Then he bowed again, and we continued our walk.

The bottles had been placed and it wasn't quite eight thirty. He suggested we had time to walk to his house at the back of the park and present the flowers to Madame Avilov. On the way, he talked more about the gardener. "He is a very happy man because the young men are all gone from home and the women left behind are lonely. He is very kind to them. It is not a bad thing to be kind to lonely women, Josef. It is almost a duty."

I wondered if Sonja Press was a lonely woman.

Madame Avilov met us in the hallway. She was tall and angular, taller than her husband, and her hair was blond turning gray. Her eyes were the same violet-blue as Mitzka's, but with no light. Today, they looked almost mauve, matching the dress she wore. Mitzka, who looked like his mother, had the vitality of his father. She had none. I knew how to act with her; she was formal, correct, and I had been trained to bow, hand the bouquet, and say the polite words.

"Madame"—I spoke to her in French—"these are from Gunther, the gardener."

"Ah, yes, dear Gunther. It has been a lovely spring, has it not? We will have some tea." She gave the tulips, with brief instructions in Russian, to the servant girl, and we moved into a small sitting room that was all blue and mauve silk and gray walls.

"And how are your mother and father during these difficult times?"

"Fine, thank you. As well as can be expected."

"And your mother, does she find her medical practice keeps her busy?"

"Not too busy, madame." Every house had its own brand of

unreality, but Madame Avilov seemed to be completely out of touch.

"I admire a woman who can keep a home and have a career."

The serving girl appeared with a tray. The tulips were in a silver vase, the tea in a silver pot with an ivory handle, and there were three glasses in silver holders. There was a sugar bowl. One rarely saw sugar in those days. Madame poured the tea. In the sugar bowl were brown pellets of rock candy. I looked at them for a moment before I took one and dropped it into my glass. I saw no spoons with which to stir, so I began to rotate the glass to dissolve the sugar. I peered at it; the sugar was still there in a brown lump. The Chief threw back his head and roared with laughter.

"One can see you are not a Russian, my curly-headed Josef. Look."

He put a pellet into his mouth and showed me that he clapped it with his tongue against the alveolar ridge, inside and above the top front teeth. And then he took a sip of the tea. Madame did not join in the tea-sipping lesson. She sat quiet, still. The Chief worked with me until I could sip the hot liquid, make it flow over the sugar I held in my mouth, taking with it enough sweetness to be satisfying. When in a few moments I'd mastered the technique, he said to his wife, "See, I told you; he is an excellent student."

"Yes, of course. Mitzka has told me many times that Josef is the brightest in the class."

Polite words without meaning. I could answer her. "Oh, no, madame, all of us knew that Mitzka could surpass any one of us at anything, if he wished to."

"If he wished to." The Chief was on his feet and pacing, his happy mood gone. "Obviously, he doesn't wish to."

Madame addressed me. "Nikolai Alexandrovich tells me that they expect great things from you. Great things."

Not true. I blushed crimson and could not answer.

The Chief was not to be restrained. "Have you heard from the boy this morning?" he asked his wife.

She answered him in Russian. I understood very little from that conversation, only the word "balalaika" and the name "Dieter Schmidt." I knew that Mitzka had a red balalaika, which he played marvelously well. He even had tried to teach me to play, but it was not for my fingers. And I knew that Mitzka left school several months before to join the Russian underground. Dieter Schmidt was my former classmate, "Commie," who disappeared from school after the Romans Thirteen episode two years before. I had not seen him or heard of him again until that moment.

Madame switched back to French and, still addressing her husband, said, "Mitzka said he would come soon to a staff dinner." She turned to me. "He so enjoys the baked rabbit." She stood.

I stood, too, and the Chief stopped pacing.

"Please do come again, soon." She extended her hand. "It is so refreshing to have young people in the house."

I had to take the extended hand and kiss it. "Thank you, madame, I will, and thank you for the tea."

The Chief bowed. I picked up the empty wire basket and he the map of the park.

. . .

Krupinsky complained that I was two hours late.

"Only an hour and a half. It's just nine thirty, and anyway I was with the Chief."

"I'm supposed to paint lurid pictures for you of the effects of radiation before Kreutzer gets you."

"Paint away."

"But first I'd like to say that my wife was right about you."

I would be a fool to take the bait; I kept my mouth shut.

"Don't you want to know what she said?"

"Not particularly."

"She said you probably weren't as big a schlemiel as you appeared to be."

"Did she now."

"No. She said you were a nice person and that you wouldn't

come back here yesterday. So I suppose I should thank you."

"You're very welcome."

"We'd better get on with this radiation business," he said.

"I have a favor to ask you first."

"What is it?"

"Can you loan me one mark?"

"Is that all? Sure. I don't have it with me, but I'll bring it tomorrow. What do you want it for?"

"It's none of your business—but for condoms."

"Where do you get them?"

"Train station. The vending machines."

"That's a stupid way to buy them. You only get four for a mark. Let me get you some from the pharmacy. When do you want them?"

"As soon as you can. Tomorrow."

"Anything else?"

"If you promise not to make fun of me, I have a question."

"Go ahead."

"Well, the girl . . . I think she may not have done it before."

"So?"

He was going to make it miserable for me. "So, can you give me any advice?"

"Sure!" He laughed demonically. "If you want to deflower a virgin, my advice is to use lots of·lubrication."

I was furious for letting myself in for this. "You know, I took quite a chance coming to your house to detune your stinking radio—"

"Who is it?" he interrupted me.

I hesitated. "I'd rather not say."

"You like her a lot?"

I nodded.

"I have an idea who it might be. And maybe I could save you some trouble if you'd tell me who it is."

"I doubt that."

"Hmm." He put his hand over his mouth and thought for a while. "Let me think about this. My wife was a virgin when we got married. It wasn't much fun for her at first. If the woman is tight, it hurts, so I wasn't kidding when I said to use lots of lubricant. And don't expect much until the soreness goes away. And she'll always be worried about getting pregnant."

"That's one of the reasons I want the condoms."

"Use two."

"Two?"

"If you really want to protect her. Those things can spring a leak. They're only eighty percent sure anyhow. Trouble is, using one diminishes your pleasure, and two is like making love through a blanket."

"It'd be worth it to protect her."

"How noble of you."

This was very embarrassing for me. I hoped he'd talk about the actual approach of the whole thing.

"Maybe you should try it with a non-virgin first and get some experience, if you know what I mean."

That man was a master at humiliation. "What makes you think I haven't?"

"Well, have you?"

Damn him. "No. And I don't want to."

"So it's like that. The love affair of the century. Why don't you marry her first, if she's a—" He stopped. "I'm sorry. That was below the belt."

Under the Nuremberg Law for the Protection of German Blood and German Honor, marriages between Jews and "Germans" was forbidden. Besides, I was not yet seventeen. I stood to leave.

"Wait!"

I sat down.

"Look, Josef, don't worry about it. If she's really that kind of girl, and she likes you, she won't be unhappy that you're inexperienced. Know what I mean?"

I nodded.

"Just be honest and don't pretend to be anything but what you are. You'll both learn together."

"Thank you." I meant it.

"And remember, it isn't as much fun at first as you think it should be. That comes later. And if you care for each other, that's what matters. And just take it slow. I'll bring those things tomorrow." He took a pencil and tablet from his pocket, made a note, then he began to try to nauseate me about the effects of radiation. But I'd read it all already.

He ended up by reminding me of the grotesque mutated *Drosophila* and by showing slides of rats which had been irradiated. "If you're not careful," he said, "you will have the same kind of crippled offspring as the flies and the same kind of degenerated bone marrow as the rats." He then threatened that radiation caused sterility and enforced this with a lecture on how the only important cells, the only thing important to life, are the sperm and the ovum. "Everything else," he said, "everything which hangs around it is just there to induce the bee to visit the flower."

"Is the sterility from radiation any different from that caused by surgical sterilization?" I asked him.

"Why do you want to know that?"

"The Chief said that the gardener, Gunther, is the most popular man in the village because of his vasectomy. Maybe a certain kind of impotency could be an asset."

Krupinsky leaned against the Geiger counters and cupped his chin in his hand. "Hmm. I'll tell you, Josef, the accidental radiation to sterilize you would be so large that you would die, and it would be impotency because of death."

But it wasn't the unseen radiation that frightened me. I felt protected from it by the lead apron, by the extra lead plates guarding the genitals. I was overwhelmed with fear of the high-voltage, high-tension equipment. One could hear it. One could see it.

The door to the Radiation Laboratory was opposite Krupinsky's lab. Signs were posted:

DANGER OF DEATH: HIGH VOLTAGE

VERY STRONG RADIATION

DO NOT ENTER

NO SMOKING

EXPERIMENT IN PROGRESS

It was locked and Professor Kreutzer had the key. Before entering, we had gone into the control booth, put on the lead aprons, and then returned to the hall to face the special entrance. The door into the Radiation Laboratory slid open pneumatically. It was of thick lead and paraffin, and when one walked in, he faced a thick wall and another door offset from the first opening. Another pneumatic mechanism slid the second thick door open, and one faced yet another wall. Then a small maze of offset passages led into that huge cement-block room—a cathedral of a room.

The pumps were gigantic, the condensers so tall they rose up two stories high. Thick electrical cables hung from the ceiling by strings. Pipes and tubes and wires everywhere. So loud! I wanted to put my hands over my ears. And there were sparks and crackles, hisses and lightning. I was terrified. And in the center was the linear accelerator, all sectioned and patched from bits and pieces of the junkyard, running diagonally twenty-eight feet or so, smaller in diameter than an oil drum—I could almost have put my arms around it.

Immediately upon entering, Professor Kreutzer went around the room with a pole, at the end of which was a chain of copper attached to a piece of pipe—another product of the scrapyard— which he used as a mobile lightning arrester by touching different points where there might be high tension. It made a terrific *bang* as it discharged, say, the condensers. Very methodically, each time he entered, Professor Kreutzer went around with that thing.

That's the way he did everything, as though he had a lightning arrester in his hand. He minimized risk to the best of his ability and went on from there. For instance, when we were in the control booth putting on the lead aprons, he took off his jacket and vest, and I noticed that he wore both a belt and suspenders.

He said I must use the lightning arrester each time I entered to make sure that all the electricity was discharged safely to the ground. And he showed me how to paste the little capsules of *Drosophila* onto the target with the dosimetry capsule, explaining that we were looking for a translocation induced by fast neutrons. The fast neutrons came from the lithium on the target of the linear accelerator. Every hour I must measure the amount of radiation, I must watch the pumps and valves and meters, I must listen for the crackling *boom* which signaled a breakdown of the high-voltage system, and I must listen for the *hsssss* which signaled a leak in the accelerator itself—which meant I must stretch a baton eight feet to the machine and seal the leak with chewing gum. And I must beware, for if it were all to stop suddenly, there would be a terrible explosion. I must immediately, if there was a failure, switch to another source of power. If the pumps had to be stopped, he must be called, for one did it by closing them down in a certain way in a certain sequence. Alone, just avoiding the mixing in the pumps of oil and mercury took expert knowledge.

In between the hourly measuring of radiation, I could sit quietly in the insulated control booth, always chewing gum, and watch through the windows of lead glass, through the aquarium of glass and water, and listen for the *hsssss* and *boom* through the intercom. And I could watch the meters and valves. If anything were to happen that I could not handle, I was to push the red emergency button, and he would come. Professor Kreutzer left me alone in the safe, warm control booth.

I had drunk too much tea. What Krupinsky once said to me was true. It was a scientific fact, he told me, that people of our background and class had a high incidence of hemorrhoids and distended bladder because they were trained from infancy to be overly fastidious about using any bathroom but their own. They developed tremendous capacity and control, and, after all, I had left home before five in the morning. It was now after two in the afternoon, and I had drunk ersatz coffee at home, tea with Sonja Press and the Avilovs and again with Krupinsky. In order to leave the control booth, I would have to push the red emergency button and summon Professor Kreutzer. I was loath to do so, probably because my mother had conditioned me to believe that calls of nature are less than civilized and that it is almost impolite to relieve oneself.

.   .   .

I was quite surprised when I discovered that other people of the same class and of even higher class had no such inhibitions. For instance, I went to the engagement party of the sister of my school friend, Petter. His sister was the first girl I ever loved—before Sheereen. Of course, she was totally out of reach, being so much older and all. The point is, I was in a similar dilemma at her engagement party.

Petter was my best friend at school, and when we were ten years old, he asked me if I thought his sister was attractive. I said, "Neither, nor," meaning that she was just a girl. He was surprised I was not interested in girls, and he told me that he couldn't wait until he was old enough to do it with a girl. Petter was absolutely astonished that it wasn't my major goal in life. He said his sister was doing it, and his whole life was aimed at the time when he could.

It gave me something to think about, and next time I went to his house to play, I looked at his sister and began to follow her about. She seemed to enjoy talking with me and was very pleasant. When she became engaged to some wretched undersecretary at the embassy, she allowed Petter to invite me to the engagement party.

Their father was the Ambassador from Norway, and they lived

in a mansion on a lake in midtown Berlin, rather than at the embassy. The engagement party was a huge event for me. They were so totally democratic. Everybody was on a first-name basis. The Ambassador and his wife were always just like any other ordinary parents—unlike the parents of Sheereen and Ahmed, who rarely dealt directly with their own children.

The party started in the afternoon and went on all day with champagne, punch for the children, and canapés, and then in the evening there was a huge meal with more champagne and punch. My bladder became overfull—and here we were, a tremendous number of people sitting at a great long table. I knew one is not supposed to get up from a table, but I thought I was going to have an accident. So I whispered to my friend.

He laughed loudly and shouted something in Norwegian. Everyone began to laugh. Someone yelled, in French, "Let's all go have a pee." So we, all the men, walked down to the lake and did it in unison. It was wonderful.

Petter was always so free. Our class took swimming at the pool of the City Police. Before we were allowed into the swimming pool, we had to strip totally and soap ourselves totally, and then the bathing master, a policeman, came with a fire hose of ice-cold water and rinsed us off.

We were always together, Petter and I, and one day, while we were soaping ourselves, he pointed to me and yelled, "Oh, I am circumcised, too." And he grabbed my penis.

The policeman came with the fire hose. "Hey, you." And an ice-cold stream of water hit us. But nothing more.

I could understand why they left Berlin the day after Germany annexed Norway, and why, that same spring of 1940, the children of the ambassadors from Holland and Belgium were gone from our school. But I could not understand why, at almost the same time, Sheereen's family left, too. After all, Iraq was friendly with Adolf Hitler.

All my friends were outsiders—like myself—and when they

went away, I was alone. By the time I was forced to leave the school, there were only six left in the class out of the original twenty-two.

. . .

Professor Kreutzer opened the door to the control booth and asked me if I would like to take a break and have a cup of tea while he was treating the Security Officer with x-ray. The Security Officer was, of course, the Gestapo in the House, and by that time I understood that his clandestine protection of the staff of the Institute was in exchange for these daily treatments of his disease.

I left for five minutes and returned quite relieved. The Security Officer had taken off his black shirt and was lying on the table with the x-ray tube aimed at his shoulder. It had to be some type of cancer. I must ask Krupinsky.

When the treatment was done, Professor Kreutzer signaled for me to switch the power from the x-ray tube back to the linear accelerator. They both left, and I settled into my chair, looking at the valves and meters before me and through the window into the deserted Radiation Laboratory. The control booth was supposed to have been shielded from the radiation by the paraffin blocks, the concrete and lead, and by the window, two sheets of lead glass separated by water. Years later, I realized that the shielding was totally inadequate, and that one was not protected. But at that time, I looked through the glass and water at the wavering image of the linear accelerator and felt more secure than I had since that moment, in 1933, when I was seven years old and I came home from the stationery store in Gartenfeld with book covers and a notebook for the new school year. All my grade school friends had bought them, too. They were covered with swastikas.

I was just beginning third grade and was quite proud that Mother allowed me to walk the three blocks to and from school alone and even to shop for school supplies myself. When I was in first and second grade, she had insisted on accompanying me, which I had found most embarrassing.

School was out by noon; by the time I finished shopping, it was half past, and I was ravenously hungry. I bounded into the house, peeked into the waiting room, one of the parlors on the first floor—only two patients left—then raced into the kitchen, slammed my book covers and notebook onto the table, and, without even sitting, began to gobble down the *Teewurst* sandwiches and hot chocolate the maid had prepared for me, all the while straining my ears, listening for Mother to come down the stairs from her second-floor office to get her next patient.

When I heard her footsteps on the stairs, I jammed the rest of my second sandwich into my mouth, ran into the hallway and into the arms of my smiling mother. She gave me a big hug. "How's my dear Butzelman?" That was her special name for me. Butzelman was a character in my favorite children's song; he was a funny, bright fellow who danced about the house. "How was your first day?"

"Neither, nor," I said.

She laughed. "One of your friends is in the waiting room. Come say good day to Herr Stenzel."

Herr Stenzel was captain of the police precinct in the village. He and his wife and children had been Mother's patients for as long as I could remember.

"Good day, Herr Stenzel," I said, shaking his hand and bowing.

"Good day, Josef. Did you go to school today?"

I nodded.

"And you are in second grade now?" he said, his eyes twinkling.

"No!" I said vehemently. "I am now in third grade, and I have my own allowance."

"How can you be so old as to be in third grade with such a young and beautiful mother?"

I looked up at Mother. She—and Father, too—had always seemed quite old to me.

Mother laughed again. "Did you buy your book covers, Josef?"

"Yes, Mutti. And a new notebook, too. Would you like to see them?" I dashed into the kitchen, returned with my purchases, and held them out for Mother to see.

All color left her face, and she exchanged an adult look with Herr Stenzel. I had done something terribly wrong.

"Excuse us, Herr Stenzel," she said. Putting an arm about me, she propelled me gently into the kitchen, where she took my book covers and notebook away from me.

It was then Mother first told me that she was a Jew, I a mixed-blood, and that I was different from the other children.

· · ·

After the engagement party of Petter's sister, I was driven home by other guests who lived in our suburb. I was so sleepy from the wine that in the car they wrapped me in a blanket, and I awakened the next morning in my own bed, beside me the bag full of cheeses and other delicacies Petter's mother had insisted I take.

When we played at his house, Petter and I were forever in the kitchen making sandwiches from all the marvelous food. I would go for the cheese and *Teewurst,* and he would stack a pile of caviar on a piece of toast.

Petter always got me in trouble in Latin class. He sat in front of me and had the fantastic ability to move both ears back and forth in rhythm to the singsong of the Latin grammar. And always, when he did this, I laughed out loud. Then the teacher stopped the lesson, reprimanded me, and wrote in the Daily Diary of the class:

Bernhardt laughed in class today.

CHAPTER FOUR

The Smells of Eden

The heart of the Institute was the Radiation Laboratory, with those condensers rising two stories in the center of both the second and third floors of the main building. It smelled of candles from the paraffin used as a radiation shield, of the oil used to lubricate the pumps, and of electricity—ozone from the high-voltage discharges. Because it was dangerous and off-limits to the janitors, it also smelled of burning dust and dusty oil.

On the first floor were the entrance lobby, auditoriums, meeting rooms, parlors, and formal dining room, all smelling of stale tobacco smoke, floor wax, and a pungent cleaning soap. Also on first was the cafeteria, which smelled of the soup of the day: cabbage or carrot or turnip.

The basement, with its storage areas, boilers, generators, and what-have-you, smelled dank and mildewed because it had been converted to double as the air-raid shelter for the Institute and, therefore, had inadequate ventilation.

Each department had its own distinctive smells. Genetics and Evolution smelled of the ether for anesthetizing the flies, of the yeast fed them, of the slightly burned polenta fed the yeast. The Chief miscalculated the quantity of polenta necessary and stored the vast oversupplies of raw cornmeal in one of the large greenhouses in the park.

He also miscalculated the quantity of alcohol necessary to pickle the Luftwaffe's brains, so our second-floor wing stank from large quantities of ethyl alcohol, which was kept in our labs, rather than up in Brain Research, because it came adulterated with other ingredients to make it taste bad and smell even worse, and the Chemistry Laboratory of the Grand Duke was dedicated to its purification, being set up, as it was, to take advantage of the various boiling points of any substance that might be mixed with alcohol, a continuous operation, running twenty-four hours, yielding approximately forty liters of vodka daily, which were then distributed to every lab at the Institute, including those of the Mantle Corporation and the Luftwaffe. There were three flasks in our laboratory of twenty liters each. Pure. According to reports filed, Herr Professor Doktor Grand Duke Trusov was deep into nuclear research, trying to separate isotopes.

Several months after I came to the Institute, the Grand Duke had a serious problem with his work and called a meeting. There were nine of us in his lab: Monika, Marlene, and two girls from Chemistry sat on high stools; Krupinsky, the Rare Earths Chemist, and I leaned against the middle table on which flasks generally bubbled and tubes usually carried liquid here and there. The Grand Duke, straight, tall, gray hair, white lab coat, addressed the Chief.

"Nikolai Alexandrovich, we are through! It is all over!"

The Chief stopped pacing and nodded for the Grand Duke to continue.

"The bastards have mixed it with petrol ether."

The Chief looked at me. "Josef, what would be the problem with separating petrol ether from ethyl alcohol?"

"They have the same boiling point," I said.

Everyone groaned.

"So! How can you separate it?" he asked me.

"You can't."

"And how do you know this 'you can't'?"

I shrugged. "I've heard it. I've read it."

"Think," he said quietly, and he paced.

I thought, shook my head, shrugged, and grew red, relieved that Sonja Press wasn't there to witness my stupidity. I'd moved no closer to her, thus far, and still had it in my mind to so impress her with my genius, that she would fall into my arms and so on.

"You think like a chemist, my curly-headed friend. Try thinking like a physicist."

I thought and became even redder. I just didn't know anything about it. But then, neither did anybody else, even the Grand Duke, who was a chemist, after all.

He asked the others—Krupinsky, the Rare Earths Chemist. "Think! Think like physicists!"

Krupinsky said, "Look, Chief, if you want to know about endocrines, ask me."

Still pacing, the Chief said, "Josef! Does ethyl alcohol mix with water?"

"Yes."

"And petrol ether?"

"Aha!" said the Grand Duke. "It's insoluble."

We all applauded. As he strode from the room, the Chief said, "Think like physicists, my friends. Think like physicists."

The rest of us stayed to watch the Grand Duke's demonstration. Here is the Recipe for Separating Petrol Ether from Ethyl Alcohol:

> Put a known quantity of the adulterated alcohol into a measured amount of water. When the petrol ether floats to the top, suck it off with a tube and burn off the residue. When the smoky yellow flame begins to burn blue, cover the vessel and preserve the rest. Before drinking, add a little more water to make it 100 proof vodka.

The next morning when the Chief came into our lab for his daily inspection, Sonja Press was with him, carrying an armload of journals. She wore a pink sweater. Her dark hair was so long that one lock rested on her breast. The Chief held a glass of tea, which he stirred with a spoon as he paced and talked.

"Josef. One can mix salt with water, and it is a solution—ionization takes place. But although it seems the same, if one were to mix sugar with water, or, say, with this tea here, as I have done, it is not the same. It is not a solution but merely a dispersement of the sugar into the water. So even if I were to put, say, twenty-five teaspoons of sugar into this cup of tea, it would not run over because it is not a solution but merely a dispersement. Correct? Or am I right?" He put the glass of tea on a table.

I more or less worshiped the Chief. Everyone did. He radiated such intelligence, such strength and power, that he would have been terrifying if it were not for a skeptical, twinkling warmth that drew all of us to him like a magnet. I took a deep breath and said to him, "I don't believe it."

"What?" he roared, trying to sound like a lion. "Speak up, speak up."

I looked at Sonja, who smiled at me encouragingly. "I think you are incorrect. Wrong." I actually smiled at him.

"We shall see," he shouted and stormed theatrically from the room. He returned, shortly, with a silver bowl filled with real sugar. White granulated sugar was a rare sight, and everyone gathered to look. I took the silver bowl from him and placed it near the cup, which was full almost to the brim. At the third spoonful of sugar, the liquid hesitated at the brim, at the fourth it spilled onto the table, at the tenth spoonful, the tea began to run from the table to the floor.

"Stop!" shrieked Krupinsky, protecting the sugar with his hands.

The Chief said to me, "I am relieved to find you think like a physicist, my curly-headed friend." He patted my shoulder before wandering off in a corner to chat with Krupinsky. All he ever was looking for was the truth.

Sonja Press said, "Here, Josef, are some articles on the theory of solutions." She smelled like roses. "I'm sure you'll have no trouble understanding them."

Sonja was warm and kind as ever, but subtly unapproachable. It was difficult to understand. I had never been particularly unattractive to girls. The others on the floor—Monika, Marlene, and the two lab assistants from Chemistry, for example—made it quite clear that they were available, but when I attempted to move in on Sonja, I would bump my nose on a Plexiglas dome encircling her.

The Fromm's Akt, along with some lubricant gel, was tucked in the back of my worktable drawer. Krupinsky had brought them as he promised. But they had yet to be used.

Our second-floor wing smelled also of the rabbits. The Luftwaffe used altered rabbits to cut the grass on their landing strips. The Chief filed a report that he needed just such stock—Albino Castrates Oldenburg Five—in order to do studies on artificial radioactive substances. Rabbits are rabbits: the Luftwaffe had an endless supply nibbling airstrips. At ten months and six pounds, they would be shipped to us. Every laboratory in the plant, including those of Mantle and the Luftwaffe, was assigned a certain number and had, in return, to supply well-documented protocols. In our laboratory, according to the files, I was doing research on "The Effects of Fast Ruthenium: A Study of Effects of Certain Radioactive Substances on the Organs of Living Rabbits." In his office, the Chief had two large stamps—TOP SECRET: ONLY TO BE OPENED BY PERSONS WITH TOP SECURITY CLEARANCE—so few officials actually looked at the reports. The second stamp read: DECISIVE FOR THE WAR EFFORT.

. . .

Neurophysiological Research, floors three, four, and five, all smelled of formaldehyde. They didn't use alcohol at all to preserve those brains. They used formalin! I had asked Krupinsky about them, repeatedly, ever since my first day at the Institute, when I visited Herr Wagenführer in Personnel and saw those jars and jars of human brains lining the corridors of the fifth floor. All I got from Krupinsky was a runaround, and I did not want to bother the Chief or Professor Kreutzer with such questions. Finally, two months after I'd first seen them, I was able to find out whose brains they were.

The opportunity came mid-June, thanks to a surprise inspection. Three or four times a month a government agency, such as the Ministry for Military Scientific Research, would make a tour of the Institute. It seemed that every office and service of the Third Reich ran its own surveillance teams, intelligence gatherers, efficiency experts, and internal security division, each group working independently and against the others, not only keeping everything a secret from the other services but also secret within their own offices. There was no central control. The Chief directed these tours. He could lecture without notes on any subject related to the Institute.

Generally, he was forewarned, either officially, or unofficially through the Security Officer, and preparations could be made. Herr Wagenführer, for example, could warn the "specials." He would search us out, wherever we were: in the labs, the cafeteria, even the bathroom. "Tomorrow morning, Josef Leopold Bernhardt"—he always addressed me by my complete name, like a surgeon who fears operating on the wrong patient—"at nine thirty A.M., it would be a good idea if you disappeared into the park. Use the Chief's stairs." The Chief had a private staircase into the park from his penthouse office. "If you are asked, which I doubt very much, you will say that you are employed by the Mantle Corporation. It will be safe to return by noon. Do you have any questions?"

Until that unexpected inspection, I was always assigned to the park, where, if the weather was halfway decent, I walked about, afraid to run for fear of drawing attention to myself. If I was tired, I stretched out in Mitzka's secret hiding place, the tunnel through the bushes leading to the apple orchard. It was still there! If it was too cold and wet, I sat in a pew in the Physics Chapel. If I was hungry, I headed straight for the large greenhouse, where they had a kitchen and endless supplies of cornmeal, molasses, and sunflower and pumpkin seeds. It was a lonely time. We, the specials, without being told to, stayed away from each other during these little exiles.

But the day of the surprise inspection was different. Instead of Herr Wagenführer, it was the Security Officer who warned us, and instead of its being well in advance, it was last-minute and hurried.

Up to that moment, the Security Officer had not spoken to me, nor I to him. I'd seen him in passing and in the Radiation Laboratory, but we did not acknowledge one another. I, of course, knew who he was and what he was, and, I rightly assumed, he knew about me.

It was he, then, who showed up in our lab that morning. Krupinsky, Marlene, Monika, and I were absorbed with the routine sorting of the *Drosophila*. None of us looked up when he entered the lab, and I was startled to find him standing behind me. At times the Security Officer wore a white lab coat—he was a chemist, after all—but this day he was in his black uniform. He was dripping sweat, breathing laboriously, as though he had been running, and there was a yellowish cast to his complexion. He looked even more ill than usual.

"You"—he exhaled the word and pointed a finger at me, then at Krupinsky—"must go to Personnel on fifth. At once!"

"Inspection?" asked Krupinsky.

The Security Officer nodded grimly.

I began to clear off my worktable.

"You schmuck!" shouted Krupinsky. "Drop it. Run! Use the central staircase."

As I sprinted from the room, I heard Krupinsky telling the girls, "Get the Roumanian and Rare Earths to help with these flies."

I ran. Once on the stairs, I easily overtook some of the other specials scrambling for safety—Bolotnikov, the dumpling who

sang off-key and worked with *Epilachna chrysomelina,* and Ignatov, the Bubonic Plague Man—but they were almost as old as my
parents. However, by the time I reached the fifth floor, I was,
much to my disgust, quite out of breath and totally terrified. Was
this, then, to be *it?* Wheezing and sweating, my heart pounding, I
leaned against the metal shelving lining the corridor, so paralyzed
by fear that, at first, I did not notice the brains. I tried to calm
down by concentrating on other people in the hallway. The specials were gathering down the corridor near the door of Personnel:
Bolotnikov and Ignatov, both of whom had passed by me without
a glance, and the pianist Rabin. All three were Russians. And there
were three others whom I'd never seen before, two men and a girl.
One of the men was thirty or so and wearing a white lab coat; the
other was just a boy, maybe a year or three older than I. The girl
was about my age and incredibly attractive—not as beautiful as
Sheereen, but certainly better-looking than even Sonja Press, who
was considered to be the best-looking girl in the Institute. She, the
new girl, had long black hair—below her waist—tied back with a
green ribbon. The men were all, more or less, huddled about her,
getting introduced, no doubt, and trying to figure out if she was a
candidate for the darkroom.

At the other end of the corridor, Luftwaffe personnel, wearing
either lab coats or uniforms, were wandering about, in and out of
what I assumed to be laboratories. Strangely enough, some of the
uniformed men seemed . . . sick . . . or not quite right. One of
them, a young man, had a noticeable limp, and two were actually
shaking—palsied.

Krupinsky was dragging himself up the stairs now, Herr
Wagenführer plodding like a solid old workhorse on one side of
him, and the Yugoslav Zoologist, who was also a ballet dancer,
bouncing on the other. Krupinsky looked ghastly gray. I wondered
if it was from the climb or from fear—most likely both. The
Yugoslav leaped onto the fifth-floor landing, jumped high into the
air, made a scissors of his legs, hit the floor on one foot, and did
three pirouettes. He didn't seem very worried.

Herr Wagenführer nodded to me and said, "This is nothing to worry about," and, kind man, trudged on down the hall toward Personnel.

"Need an elevator," said Krupinsky to no one in particular, as he stumbled up the last stair, tap-tapping at his chest with two fingers as though he had heart pain.

"You're out of shape, old man," said the Yugoslav, thrusting his arm forward in mock-fencing style, jabbing Krupinsky in the gut.

"Cut it out, you shiny ape," Krupinsky muttered, then leaned against the shelving next to me.

"What is going to happen?" I asked him.

"How should I know?"

"I'm sure the Chief and Kreutzer have everything under control," the Yugoslav said to me. "I don't think it's anything to worry about. Have you been up here before?"

I nodded. "My first day, Herr . . . Professor."

"We just call him the Yugoslav," muttered Krupinsky. "That's because he's a Russian."

"Excuse me, but I don't know your name."

"I am Russian," said the Yugoslav, "and my name is difficult for Germans to say." He smiled, in an embarrassed way. "Dmitri Varvilovovich Tsechetverikov."

"I see." Good Lord!

"Professor Yugoslav will do nicely, Bernhardt," said Krupinsky.

"Excuse me, but why do they call you the Yugoslav if you are Russian?"

"I was with the ballet in Belgrade before I came here. Other than that, my life was in Russia. I was educated there—in biology."

"And ballet," said Krupinsky.

"Krupinsky," I said, pointing to the two men in Luftwaffe uniform at the far end of the corridor, "is it my imagination, or do they both have palsy?"

Krupinsky shrugged without even looking, but the Yugoslav

gave them a glance and said, "It's not your imagination."

"How did they even get into the Luftwaffe?"

"They're always looking, in neurophysiological research, for the focus of where such problems originate in the brain," he said, nodding toward the two palsied men. "So they bring here men who have developed certain neurological symptoms such as paralysis, tremor, Jacksonian attacks—that's epileptic seizures triggered by brain damage."

"You mean they experiment on their own personnel?"

"It's routine. Don't be so shocked. In every lab the workers are experimental subjects. That's normal all over the world. They do electroencephalograms on them—record their brain waves and compare them with those of healthy people. It doesn't hurt them a bit; in fact, sometimes they can be helped. And they have the satisfaction of being useful. Obviously, they aren't fit for active service, but here they can serve as clerks."

"The healthy young ones are in the jars." Krupinsky, glumly, pointed to the brains. "You've been wanting to know about them. Here's your big chance." He pushed himself away from the shelves and slouched toward Personnel.

The Yugoslav lifted and bent one of his legs and, in one motion, lowered himself onto the floor, where he sat cross-legged, tailor fashion, beside an opened cardboard carton. He always wore those shiny black dancing pumps. "Sit down, Josef," he said in a kindly way.

I slid down the metal shelving and sat cross-legged with him, my back to the other specials down the hall.

"Reach in there and pull out a jar."

"Are you sure it's O.K.?"

He nodded. "Don't worry. I work in Neurophysiological Research—only with the primates and other animals down on first and second."

I lifted the flaps of the unsealed carton. There were three jars inside, the same kind as those containing the brains which were already on the shelves. They were packed in a shredded wood packing material and divided by corrugated cardboard.

I reached in and carefully lifted out one jar. It was about the size of a night pot, just large enough so that a human brain could rest without being crushed or damaged. Where the glass lid fit onto the jar, the glass was ground or matted so the lid would adhere securely. It was sealed with paraffin.

"What does it say?" the Yugoslav asked me.

Cradling the jar in two hands, I read the label, which was white with black stenciling and covered almost one entire side of the jar:

SEVENTH LUFTWAFFE LAZARETTO
STRELITZ
No. G. R. 041222 6700 Lt.
21 04 43
22 04 43
Compound Fracture—Sepsis
Brain Removed Intact
Preservative: Formalin
By Hans Bremer,
Medical Sgt. Major

"What do you think it means?"

"The brain was removed at the Seventh Field Hospital in Strelitz. The patient . . . the person . . . died of blood poisoning from a fracture?"

"Right. Go on."

"It . . . the brain was put in the jar by Sergeant Major Hans Bremer?"

"Bremer removed the brain and put it in the jar."

"They use formalin? I thought . . . I understood that they used alcohol."

"Nonsense. Formaldehyde. One never uses alcohol. They come here already pickled in the formaldehyde."

"But who is it . . . was it?"

"Tells you on the label. Read those first numbers."

"Number G. R. zero, four, one, two, two, two, six, seven, zero, zero, L. T.—he was a lieutenant?"

"Right."

"In the Luftwaffe? You mean these were all air force personnel?"

"Right."

"G. R. is a classification?"

"His initials followed by birth date."

"Zero four, twelve, twenty-two. December fourth, nineteen twenty-two. He is—he'd be twenty."

"Gunther Rathke, age twenty."

"Is that his name?" I looked curiously at the brain I held in my hands.

"No, I made that up. His complete history will be sent here later. Look at those other numbers. He died on April twenty-first, nineteen forty-three, and the autopsy was the next day, on April twenty-second."

"Was he, most likely, sick in some way? Epilepsy or so?"

"To the contrary, these are the brains of fallen young aviators, the cream, so to speak. Goering's superior, elite, consummate Aryan youth—second only, of course, to Himmler's beloved S.S."

"What will they do with them here?"

"Nothing."

"Nothing?"

"Nothing! There is no research. This is just a collecting place, dead storage. Sometime in the future, if they get all the papers— medical histories and all—they may try to see if any of the known physical or psychic abnormalities are reflected or can be demonstrated in the brain."

"Will they be able to tell that from dissecting his brain?" I look curiously at Gunther Rathke.

"No. Nothing. The brain itself isn't enough. They would need the spinal cord, too. And even then they'd find out nothing. In any

case, the field autopsies are too crude and insufficient, and no bio-
chemical data can be obtained."

"But that's crazy!"

"The amount of craziness in scientific research is higher than
the Chimborazo—but especially in the Third Reich." The Yugoslav stood, all in one motion. "Most especially in the Third Reich.
They want us down the hall. Put Rathke away and come along."
And before I could ask him more, he was loping down the hall
toward Personnel.

I put Gunther Rathke back in his box with the other two Aryan
creams of the crop and was about to push myself to my feet, when
I saw that Sonja Press was ascending. My God, she was lovely. She
started the last flight at quite a clip but slowed considerably as she
neared the top. When I was certain she could see me, I leaped to
my feet à la Yugoslav and bounced down a few steps to help her.

"Ohhh!" She was breathless. "Ohhhh. I ran all the way from
first." I extended my arm. She took it. "Thank you, Josef. You are
such a dear." And I, more or less, pulled her up the last few steps,
where, still, she clung to my arm. "These brains make me sick."
She closed her eyes, and I led her down the corridor toward the
others, who watched us moving toward them, realizing, no doubt,
that she would have the latest information from the Chief. As we
approached them, Ignatov and Rabin burst into rapid Russian.
Rabin, all the time he was at the Institute, never learned German.

Sonja soothed them with a few soft Russian words and slipped
into the Personnel Office. I followed her and saw that Herr
Wagenführer was pulling cards from one file and putting them
into others. Krupinsky reached in and grabbed my sleeve. "There's
someone I want you to meet."

Reluctantly, I stepped back into the corridor.

"Tatiana," he said, separating the new girl from the pack of
wolves surrounding her, "this is Josef. He's our math genius. He
knows the multiplication table backwards and forwards—even
the sevens."

Good Lord!

"Josef, Tatiana here is our new floating lab assistant." She was as good-looking up close as she had been from a distance, with strong features: large, dark eyes and a firm chin. "She's a half-Jew like you," said that stupid schmuck.

"How do you do," she said curtly, extending her hand in such a way that I knew that she, too, had attended Dance and Social Behavior Classes. Krupinsky, of course, wouldn't even know such classes existed.

"Enchanted," I said in French, just to get back at Krupinsky, and I bowed and kissed her hand. One doesn't actually touch the lips to the hand, of course.

Herr Wagenführer, carrying a long drawer of file cards, joined us at that moment, and I abruptly stepped away from Tatiana to be near Sonja. No doubt, I got off on the wrong foot with her— Tatiana—from the very beginning. Obviously, she was accustomed to having men fall all over her, so she could reject them. In any case, at that moment I was obsessed with Sonja Press.

Herr Wagenführer cleared his throat and began to speak, pausing every sentence or two so Sonja could translate into Russian for Rabin, Bolotnikov, and Ignatov. "As you must have gathered by now, we are in the process of being inspected without having received prior notice. The agency is the Ministry for the Coordination of Total War Effort, and it is interested, it turns out, *only* in the genetic aspects of the research done here and how that relates to the war effort. We foresee no problems for any of you. It is just a matter of keeping you out of the way for four hours, until two o'clock this afternoon, when you may feel free to return to your own work. These inspectors do not have security clearance to come up on the Luftwaffe or Mantle floors." He pointed to the file drawer under his arm. "Your cards are removed from these files I carry down to them."

"Herr Wagenführer," said Sonja, "at noon they will be having lunch in the dining room, and at one the Chief would like Rabin to give a concert for them in the parlor."

"Yes, all right, but I would prefer that certain others stay away from the first and second floors until all the inspectors have left the premises. Now, Fräulein Press, please inform Professor Boris Ivanovich Ignatov that he may continue with his normal activities in the park, and if he is asked, which I doubt, he may say that he is in the Department of Genetics and Evolution. Inform Stanislas Rabin that he may return to his piano and prepare a concert: no Chopin, no Russians, only German composers."

He waited until she translated, then said, "Please ask them if they have any questions?"

"They want to know if they may leave now?"

Herr Wagenführer nodded, and Ignatov and Rabin, looking relieved, walked together toward the stairs.

"Now, Professor Igor Vasilovich Bolotnikov and Professor François Marie Daniel"—Herr Wagenführer nodded to the new man, obviously French; I found out later that he was a physicist who worked with photons—"you two will go to a Mantle laboratory on fourth. Fräulein Press will show you the way. If you are asked, which I doubt, you will say you are employed by the Mantle Corporation. Once you are in the laboratory, someone will show you what your duties will be for the day. Please stay there until the inspectors have left the premises. Do you have any questions?"

They shook their heads.

"You may go now."

As Bolotnikov and François Daniel started down the hallway with Sonja, she threw me a little wave. Then that damned Frenchman, whom some might consider quite good-looking, offered her his arm, and she took it!

That left the new girl, the new boy, Krupinsky, the Yugoslav, and me. Herr Wagenführer continued his instructions. "Tatiana Rachel Backhaus and Eric van Leyden, I am sorry, but you two are so new I have not had time to make any files, so you must remain hidden in the darkroom on third until two o'clock, when the inspectors will have left the premises."

"Lucky dog," said Krupinsky, snickering. "Better send a chaperone with the lady."

"I can take care of myself," Tatiana Backhaus said firmly, tossing her chin in the air. And one had the feeling that she could.

"Where is this darkroom?" asked van Leyden, who, it turns out, was a medical student from Holland.

"I will show you as soon as I have assigned these others," said Herr Wagenführer. "Now, Josef Leopold Bernhardt, Dr. Abraham Morris Krupinsky"—he paused and took a deep breath— "and Professor Dmitri Varvilovovich Tsechetverikov will remain here on fifth in Brain Research. If you are asked, which I doubt, you will say you are in the Luftwaffe's Department of Neurophysiological Research. Could you perhaps"—he looked at the Yugoslav—"run encephalographs on each other?"

"Yes, of course," said the Yugoslav.

"Do you have any questions?"

We did not.

The Dutch Medical Student offered Tatiana Backhaus his arm, but she refused it. They went down the stairs with Herr Wagenführer; the Yugoslav, Krupinsky, and I walked into the Electroencephalograph Laboratory on fifth.

The EEG machine was housed in a Faradic cage, a copper-mesh cage that was supposed to eliminate all external electromagnetic fields, but didn't. "Not a hundred percent," said Krupinsky.

"Not even fifty percent," said the Yugoslav. "It's supersensitive to any kind of noise or vibration, so stand still while I try to adjust it."

The machine was white and quite large, the size of a kitchen table. The top had a paper drive mechanism, with paper about half a meter wide on a roll. There was a tray on each side, and the paper stretched across the machine. For recording, there were ten pens on arms, and for every pen there were three or four buttons to adjust, including one for the amount of ink flowing through. And each pen had to be calibrated so that it showed a deflection of one cm per 100 microvolts. In other words, for every pen, there was a complete push-pull amplifier—highly sensitive—with its own battery supply.

Another adjustment was that the deflection for positive or negative was the same. So the amplifier had to be balanced. Then there was an adjustment for the rejection of fifty-cycle hum. And the whole affair was run on batteries—six-volt wet cells for the heaters of the tubes, then dry batteries for the other required voltages. The Yugoslav had to check all this, including the batteries, before he could even begin to run a test.

After half an hour, he said, "I've only worked with this thing twice before, and both times the pens got to swinging and covered the paper and me with ink. O.K., Josef, sit yourself in that chair over there and Krup will hook you up."

They had a wire-mesh helmet, which Krupinsky fixed to my head with elastic adhesive. There were little wires with tiny cups which he filled with electrode jelly and then bent back so the cups would touch my scalp—twenty or so of them. It was slow work and difficult because I had so much hair.

"Won't work," said Krupinsky at one point. "We'll have to shave his head."

"Go to hell," I muttered.

When all the wires were attached, they had me stretch out on my back on a leather bench in the center of the room. It was hard and uncomfortable. Instead of a pillow, there was a neck support, the kind they use for the guillotine, except that I was face up, my helmeted head hanging over the support.

The wires were formed into cables, which, in turn, were plugged into the electroencephalograph. Then Krupinsky attached a large metal plate to one leg. I knew it wasn't going to work.

Krupinsky stood beside me. "Ready," he said.

The Yugoslav, at the controls, said, "O.K., Josef. Relax."

"Ha!" I said.

"Hush," shushed Krupinsky.

I could hear the machine whir to a start as the paper was set in motion.

"O.K., now, Josef," said the Yugoslav quietly, "open your eyes. . . . Now close your eyes and relax. . . . Now do what you usually do and think of nothing. . . . Damn . . . *damn.* There's nothing but a fifty-cycle hum in the pens. *Christ! The goddamn ink.*" I could hear him shutting off the switches, and the machine hummed to a stop.

Krupinsky was over beside the machine now, and I heard him say, "There also seems to be an EKG superimposed."

"We'll have to do the whole thing over," said the Yugoslav.

"Can you let me out of this thing?" I hollered from my guillotine.

They both ignored me and continued their idiotic conversation.

"Let me out of here."

Nothing.

"Have you tried adjusting the in-phase rejection circuit?" I called over to them.

That they heard. They walked over to me, and when I looked at the Yugoslav, I burst out laughing. His face and the front of his white lab coat were covered with black ink. Krupinsky took a good look at him and started to laugh, then the Yugoslav started to laugh, and we all laughed and laughed and laughed until we were in tears. Here I was, my cross-breed brain wired to a stupid machine, and Gunther Rathke's pure-bred Aryan brain in the hall, and those Nazis touring the fruit flies on second, trying to figure out how those happy little winemakers could help Adolf Hitler win the war. I think the absurdity of it all hit us, for, obviously, the Yugoslav must have had some Jewish blood in him, too, or he wouldn't have been hidden in the Luftwaffe's Brain Research Department.

Krupinsky finally unhooked me from the machine and removed

the helmet. "We'll have to do the whole thing over again," he said.

"What was that you said about in-phase rejection?" the Yugoslav asked me.

"I was thinking about it," I said. "As some of the interfering currents are arriving with the same phase at the electrodes, I would imagine that by balancing a circuit in the amplifier one could almost eliminate this particular type of disturbing signal. In other words, it would serve mainly to eliminate a fifty-cycle hum and the EKG."

The Yugoslav said, "How do you know so much about electro-encephalographs?"

"I don't. But I do know about amplifiers."

The Yugoslav looked dubiously at Krupinsky, who said, "I hate to admit it, but the little pisher knows what he's talking about when it come to machines. People, on the other hand, he doesn't know from borscht."

They let me at the machine, and I was able to balance the circuit in the amplifier by putting a dummy electrode into the circuit with a switch. I explained it to them. "This mimics the condition of putting real electrodes on the skull, one of the main characteristics of which is that there is a certain resistance between those two points. The higher the resistance, the more apt you are to pick up interfering signals. What you try to do is adjust these two potentiometers to eliminate all the interfering signals picked up."

"What makes the ink spray?" asked Krupinsky.

"I imagine that when all that interference comes in, the pens get to swinging wildly, and the developed centrifugal force sprays the ink." I pointed to the machine. "Look at those pens. They swung so much they got interlocked. They look like crossed fingers."

And I looked at each pen, too, not only to balance the amplification but also to check the ink flow. Just as I had thought, the ink was clotted in two of them and running too fast in two others.

When I thought it was all ready, I sat again on the chair and Krupinsky reapplied all the cups with fresh electrode jelly. Then I lay down on the couch. Krupinsky, as before, stood beside me. I could hear the machine rolling.

"Blink your eyes," said the Yugoslav. "Don't move. . . . Imagine Marlene and Monika, or how about the new girl, what's her name? Tatiana? Yes, Tatiana with the long black hair and almond-shaped eyes. . . . Now, don't move. Krupinsky will tickle you but do not move."

Krupinsky tickled my gut and under my arm, but I did not move.

Then the two of them held a conversation which was supposed to make me angry. "He's from superior stock, you know," said Krupinsky. "He's one of those high-toned Sephardic German Jews who won't have anything to do with us low-class Ashkenazis." And so on.

In two or three minutes, which seemed much longer to me, they were through. Krupinsky carefully removed the mesh helmet. Then I walked over to the machine and tried to get them to explain what the encephalogram said about my brain waves.

"It's disgusting," said Krupinsky. "If you think at all, you have nothing on your brain but evil thoughts."

"Come on," I pleaded with the Yugoslav. "What does it say?"

He looked long and carefully at the inky lines scribbled across the paper. "It demonstrates," he said thoughtfully, "that even birds have larger brains than you."

Then the Yugoslav sat in the chair while Krupinsky fitted him with the helmet and I readjusted the machine, which Krupinsky wanted to operate. I fixed it so as soon as he turned it on, he would get sprayed with black ink. Unfortunately, I stood too close; he grabbed me and I got some in the face, too.

"You little schlemiel. You did that on purpose, didn't you?"

"Tell me about my brain waves, Krupinsky."

"They are completely normal—for a schlemiel, that is."

"How do you tell?"

"We try to analyze these wiggles by shape, amplitude, and number. I've got a book in the lab."

"You mean you actually count the number of wiggles?"

"That's right."

I thought that sounded pretty clumsy. I readjusted the amplifiers, and we graphed the brain waves of the Yugoslav; we readjusted the amplifiers again and graphed Krupinsky.

By the time we were through, it was almost two, and we knew
we could return to the second floor. But it was so pleasant, we
stayed in the EEG Lab and talked for a while.

"I hate using this machine," the Yugoslav told us. "It's so primi-
tive. Down in my lab, we use light rays on photosensitive paper.
It's probably much more accurate due to lack of inertia. Those
pens are heavy."

I said, "Instead of counting a bunch of wiggles on paper, why
don't you just feed the electrical signals into counters, like the ones
we have in our lab?"

"You see how lucky you are he doesn't work for you?" Krupinsky said to the Yugoslav.

"That's a great idea," said the Yugoslav. "Could you set that up
in my lab?"

"I don't see why not."

"We can go down now," said Krupinsky. "Maybe Josef can stop
by and see your operation."

"Not looking like that, he can't." The Yugoslav pointed at me,
and we started to laugh all over again. All three of us were spat-
tered with black ink, and our hair, heavy with electrode jelly, was
greasy and standing on end.

We walked down the hallway, past the jars and jars and shelves
and shelves of the brains of fallen young aviators, then, three
abreast, down the three flights, and as one mind went first into the
kitchen off the small greenhouse in our second-floor wing to have
some polenta smothered in molasses and plenty of vodka.

After showering and shampooing to get rid of the ink and the
electrode jelly, the Yugoslav and I went over to his department,
which was in the left wing of the first and second floors, and he

showed me the animals in which he had implanted electrodes, surgically, right into the brain.

. . .

The left wings of the first and second floors had their own special smells, filled as they were with a collection of dogs, cats, and rabbits with hereditary defects mimicking some of those in man, such as harelips, shortened limbs, and club feet. They were difficult to get because the breeders destroyed the malformed, wishing to conceal the presence of deformity in their highly prized lines. Goebbels, of course, had a club foot.

There were cages and cages of primates, dogs, and cats, most with electrodes planted in their brains for recording and for stimulation. When they were not strapped down for electroencephalographs or similar tests, the male monkeys masturbated. They had nothing else to do, each kept separate, and most having had delicate brain surgery. These masturbating monkeys so fascinated the soldiers of the Red Army when they "liberated" us some two years later that they carried them off to Russia, along with the Yugoslav, as a gift to their Great Leader Josef Stalin.

After the delicate brain surgery, these animals were unstable physically and required a lot of care. But it was almost impossible to find women workers who were willing to stay on. After two or three days they would quit, complaining of the smell, or of the female monkeys who bit and scratched, but never mentioning the real reason. This particular personnel problem came up for discussion over and over during the biweekly staff dinners of the Department of Genetics and Evolution.

. . .

The biweekly staff dinners of the Department of Genetics and Evolution were private, absolutely top secret, and kept from the

Luftwaffe and from all but a few of the Mantle personnel. They began three hours after official closing time, at nine. To avoid drawing attention to these secret meetings, nothing was used from the cafeteria or dining room downstairs. Dishes and utensils were brought from the Chief's house, and all preparation was done in the Genetics wing: we men would slaughter the rabbits—pick them up by the ears and hit them with a lead pipe, bleed and skin them—but mostly the girl lab assistants would cook them in the autoclaves and also cook the polenta in the kitchen of the small greenhouse attached to our wing. Tables would be arranged in a large rectangle in one of the labs in our second-floor wing.

Between twenty and twenty-five people came: the Chief, Professor Kreutzer, and the Grand Duke always sat at the head of the table, with Madame Avilov and Frau Kreutzer, who was very good-looking and much younger than her husband. I don't think the Grand Duke had a wife. Near them sat some of the specials like Ignatov, the Bubonic Plague Man, who would eat and drink himself into a stupor and never say a word, and Stanislas Rabin, the pianist.

Some of the specials would not sit by the Chief, but way at the other end near the girl lab assistants: for instance, the Russian dumpling, Bolotnikov, and the Roumanian Biologist George Treponesco.

Or there might be, at the head of the table, visiting scientists: atomic physicists from the other Kaiser Wilhelm Institutes; or the physicist who was supposed to be reassembling the Humpty-Dumpty cyclotron the Nazis had been tricked into moving from Paris to Alsace-Lorraine—of course, it couldn't be put together again; or the one in charge of the working cyclotron belonging to the post office; or notables like Pascual Jordan. When these visitors came, the dinners were even more private, with no lab assistants invited. Because I was treated like an inexperienced young scientist rather than a laboratory assistant, I was always expected to attend. I didn't mind, because Sonja Press was always there, too.

Sitting at the middle of the long table would be the kind woman biologist Frau Doktor, Krupinsky and his wife, the Yugoslav, and the Rare Earths Chemist, who at his own discretion would bring some of the part-time Mantle Corporation people who used his lab. The Chief mistakenly trusted him. And there was that Frenchman, François Daniel, who worked with light perception, trying to measure the minimal amount of light which will evoke a response—a photon. His laboratory was over in Physics.

Some wives would come now and then, but never the wife of the Roumanian Biologist George Treponesco. This Treponesco had been sent by the Roumanian government to learn genetics, but all he was interested in were the girls. He could have sat in the middle, if he'd wanted, but he preferred to sit at the end where the young girls were, and after Tatiana came he always maneuvered to sit next to her.

The rest of us—Monika, Marlene, other laboratory assistants, the Dutch Medical Student, and Sonja Press—sat at the foot of the table. And Mitzka Avilov, when he came, would not sit with his parents at the head of the table, but below the salt with us. He was as cavalier as ever, easily maintaining the adoration of all with tales of his daring exploits in the underground. He and his confederates were stealing food and blankets from German troop trains and cleverly distributing them to Russian prisoners of war. From these Russian prisoners he received word of the atrocities—the mass murders, gas chambers, cyanide, the ovens—and Mitzka, in turn, passed this information on to us, not at the staff dinners, because even there certain subjects were not openly discussed, but in private conversation with one or, at most, two others. Krupinsky dubbed him the "Russian Robin Hood," and the new floating lab assistant, Tatiana, called him "William Tell." She would always sit beside him, and after dinner, when Mitzka amused us with his balalaika, she sang, making the Roumanian Biologist George Treponesco quite jealous. When Mitzka wasn't there, Tatiana would let the Frenchman, François Daniel, sit beside her.

The Security Officer was not invited, but would be given a tray with baked rabbit, polenta, and vodka, which he would take to his small house in the corner of the park and share with his wife and children.

There was no formal beginning to those dinners. One came in, sat down, and began to eat. There was always the rabbit, polenta, and vodka for the men and a vodka punch for the women. Sometimes there would be vegetables from the garden or greenhouses in the park and sometimes there were apples. When the apples were ripe in the orchard adjacent to the park, the Chief would say to me, "How well apples would taste with the baked rabbit tonight," and I would crawl through Mitzka's secret hole in the fence. At first, the farmer had two large dogs guarding them, so I would make only one trip. But later, I suppose he could no longer feed them, and I could make as many trips as were needed.

The discussions could begin any time, and the Chief made no opening statement unless he felt the need to impose some discipline. Then, before sitting, he would pace back and forth and talk. "Can you imagine that I just came from a laboratory in which someone had taken a liter or so of alcohol and replaced it with water?"

Everyone looked surprisingly guilty when the Chief began his tirades.

"Can you imagine that someone would think me stupid enough not to know the difference? I don't care a bit if you steal as much alcohol as you like, but to contaminate the remainder is what should not be done. Ignorance," he would shout, "is the only excuse for anyone to do anything he shouldn't. Thoughtlessness or laziness is no excuse."

"Sit down, Nikolai Alexandrovich," said Madame Avilov. "You'll ruin everyone's dinner."

He stopped pacing, picked up a glass, raised it high. "In spite of, nevertheless, why don't we have a drink?"

And we all did.

The drinking was very important, and the Chief pushed the vodka all through the dinner. It was necessary, for so deeply was it engrained in our German souls to revere authority, especially in a place like the Institute, where the difference in status between individuals was so vast, where there were so many titles and so much formality, that a younger person or a less titled person never dared contradict or interrupt, even to ask a question. As I had learned from ministers at my high school, it was more than just engrained in our souls. In Germany, the teachings of Paul in Romans 13 had actually replaced the heart, and all reverence was given to the governing authorities, no matter how evil they were, not because they were ministers of God but because they were ministers of fear. To overcome this, the Chief had to get everyone pretty well drunk, insisting that we eat vast quantities as we drank, the scientific hypothesis being that alcohol was harmless and that liver damage was caused by malnutrition and avitaminosis. Besides, we were hungry.

And although the pecking order in seating remained, he broke down the reticence, the fear of speaking, and there was much conversation and shouting up and down the tables.

"Did anyone hear Voice of America this evening?"

"Ha!" yelled Krupinsky. "If I'm going to risk my life to listen to the radio, I'm not going to turn on Voice of America to hear about Farmer Jones who milks his cows all day and tired but strong works all night in a bomber factory, or listen to Thomas Mann rattling on about what Germans in Germany should do, when he's safe in America. No, sir, Chief, if I'm going to risk my life to listen, I'll tune in to BBC and hear some news."

"He's right," said the Rare Earths Chemist. "BBC. But listen, Krup, I don't know why you're so against Mann. He'd be dead by now if he hadn't left."

"All right, all right, but he should shut up, pray hard, and stop giving advice."

Then there would be a middle-table argument about Thomas Mann, and a head-table fight, in Russian, over a ballet performance, or about how to cure tobacco, or how to keep the female flies from ovulating and the males from ejaculating under ether, or whether or not the lab windows should be closed so that the *Berlin wilds* in the park would not be contaminated by the controlled stock, or how to cover with "amplifier noise" an article on Einstein's relativity so it would pass the censors and still make sense, all this with everyone eating incredibly much and drinking and the Chief listening to everything with half an ear until something caught his interest.

"If it isn't a secret," he said to a middle group talking about forced labor, "let's talk about it together."

The Yugoslav said, "It's no secret. We can't keep any assistants in the primate wings because of the masturbating monkeys. We were wondering about forced labor. After all, we'd treat them well. They'd actually be better off here."

"No matter how well we treated them," the Chief said, "we would be in trouble. Later we would be investigated, and the authorities—the Americans or the Russians—they would say, 'How come you had here fifty forced labor?'"

"But couldn't the laborers explain how well off they were?"

The Chief shook his head. "The workers will be the first people to be repatriated and gone. If they are gone they cannot defend us. No, my friends, if you are caught with the thieves you are also hanged with the thieves." He turned to Professor Kreutzer. "Correct? Or am I right?"

Professor Kreutzer nodded agreement, pushed back his chair, stood, and began to change his glasses. He rarely spoke at the dinners, but when he did, everyone stopped eating and listened. He changed from the gold-rims to the rimless.

"I would like to take this opportunity to implore you to lower your consumption of water and fuel for the next month. Stay within the prescribed consumption. Do not draw attention to what we do here by forcing us out of budget. Also, we need more projects in order to keep supplies coming. If you have an idea, let me know." He sat down.

All resumed eating.

Krupinsky said to the middle and lower groups, "I would like to suggest a new project for the Chemistry Lab."

"What's that?" said the French Physicist François Daniel.

"Beer. They should try making beer. The stuff you buy nowadays is so bad that when I sent a sample in for analysis, the report came back, 'Your horse has diabetes.'"

We all laughed, and François Daniel said, "That's because it's made out of whey. Can't get the right ingredients, Krupinsky; there's a war on."

"I wasn't sure the French had noticed," said Krupinsky. "Say, Chief," he hollered. "We've got quite a project going in our lab. Josef here has rigged up a cigarette holder on his microscope so he can smoke and sort flies at the same time. We've got so many orders coming in for them, he hardly has time to do anything else."

That wasn't at all true. I had made a few for the microscopes in our lab. But everyone was laughing and looking at me. I could have killed Krupinsky.

Sonja pressed my arm and said, "Don't pay any attention to him. He loves to tease."

The Chief said, "I hear you've been working on other things aside from those very important cigarette holders. Eh, Josef?"

I nodded. It came quite easily for me to make little mechanical changes here and there.

"We'd all like to hear about it."

This was the moment I had looked forward to: implementing my plan to so impress Sonja with my genius that she would fall into my arms. But I was terrified of speaking publicly, and especially before this group of distinguished scientists. My major problem was that I liked to think before I spoke, so there was always a hesitation, a delay, which caused my listeners to demonstrate impatience, compounding my anxiety and making me stammer.

They were looking at me—all of them. I thought for a moment, organizing my ideas into sentences, took a deep breath, and began. "The flies were drowning," I whispered.

"Louder!" said Professor Kreutzer. "We can't hear you."

"The flies were drowning in their—"

"Speak up!" roared the Chief.

I stood up.

"Sit down!" shouted Krupinsky. "This is an informal meeting."

I sat down. Paralyzed.

The Chief raised his glass. All did and drank. I, too. They were all staring at me.

I said, "The flies when they breathe produce water vapor, and when they were put in the small airtight chambers in order to be irradiated with ultraviolet rays, they would become waterlogged by their own vapor they produced by breathing. And they would die." I held my breath.

Professor Kreutzer helped me. "The reason he assured them in airtight chambers was that they would crawl all over the target area so the radiation hit randomly. Ultraviolet radiation is too easily absorbed by other parts of the anatomy, and we want the gonads to get a full dose."

The Chief raised his glass and said, "To the gonads."

We all drank.

I said, "So we had to figure out how to hold them in such a way that only the abdomen got the radiation, and, at the same time, to keep them from drowning in their own vapor."

The Chief raised his glass. We all drank.

"So I looked at my wristwatch and got the idea to lay them on their backs in a Plexiglas capsule that has a round face like my watch and put cellophane on top, and I fastened the cellophane to the Plexiglas with the screws from my wristwatch." I showed them my bare wrist, where the watch had been. "Of course, I anesthetized them before putting them into the capsule. Just lightly squished them down so they wouldn't wiggle around. And then I had to figure out how to get air into the capsule."

The Chief raised his glass. We all drank, and, of course, the others continued to eat as I talked. But they listened.

"So I got a small motor and made it turn a screw that pushed a syringe in and out. And just that small amount of air was sufficient to keep the flies dry."

There were murmurs of approval around the room. The Chief

beamed at me and Sonja pressed my arm again. I must admit, I felt rather pleasant. Actually, I was quite drunk.

The Roumanian Biologist George Treponesco said, "That's all well and good, young man, but with all that air pushing in and out, the ether wears off and you wake up the flies. How do you intend to take them out of the capsule when they are flying all around?"

"I thought of that," I said. "I put an ether mixture into the syringe and the flies would go to sleep again."

"It's too bad," said Treponesco, "that they don't offer a Nobel prize for kindergartners."

All evening he was trying to get the floating lab assistant, Tatiana, to notice him, but she found him repulsive and totally ignored him.

The dinners always ended in a party. Some of the people would go home early—the Kreutzers, the Krupinskys, Frau Doktor, Madame Avilov, or so—but many would stay, especially the Russians—the Chief, Ignatov, who would be so drunk by the end of the dinner he couldn't move, Bolotnikov, the Yugoslav, and always, without his wife, the Roumanian Biologist George Treponesco. The Russian girls from the ballet—Die Scala—would come over after their performance, and the party would go on all night. The first six weeks or so, I went home right away; then I began to wait until Sonja Press left. She stayed only an hour or so until it began to get wild. At times she allowed me to walk her to the door of her apartment in the park, but usually the Chief would take her. In that case, I'd head right for the train station—until the time when I, too, stayed all night.

. . .

The first time I enjoyed the three hours between work and the staff dinners was at the end of June, two and a half months after I'd come to the Institute, when Sonja Press invited me, Frau Doktor, the Yugoslav, the French Physicist François Daniel, and Tatiana to her apartment for tea and cakes made from the cornmeal. Everyone was friendly, and they all just talked together. As far as I could tell, Sonja had no special boyfriend, and I decided that it was time to tell her how I felt—if only I could get her alone.

The next step was to manipulate her into inviting me, alone, to her apartment, using as a wedge her solicitude toward me when I was assigned to a forty-eight-hour stint in the Radiation Laboratory. "You poor thing," she would say, "it must be terribly lonely to sit there all those hours."

Actually, I didn't mind it at all. Although most of the time I was alone in the control booth, people did stop by to chat—the Chief, Marlene, or so. Professor Kreutzer and Krupinsky would relieve me for an hour or two at regular intervals. Someone had to be there all the time to make sure the equipment didn't break down and to measure the dose hourly. When one worked with fast neutrons from our homemade accelerator, there were too many variables: high voltage wasn't constant, ion source wasn't constant, vacuum wasn't always the same; therefore, the number of fast neutrons produced had to be measured frequently. With ultraviolet or x-ray the dose, once measured, was fairly constant. One needed to spot-check only now and then.

Mostly I liked monitoring the linear accelerator because it meant that I had an excuse not to go home for two or three days at a time. Nevertheless, I began to act sad about it when Sonja was near, and surely enough, she would press my arm and say, "You have the saddest eyes." But to get her to actually invite me to her apartment, I was forced to more or less lie.

The first week in July, the day before I was to go into the control booth for forty-eight hours, I ran an appalling, sad routine every time she walked into my lab. And at lunchtime, in the cafeteria, I sat across from her and stared down, despondently, at my cup of tea.

It was almost too easy. God, what an ass I was! I made her beg me to tell her the cause of my great sorrow. "I'll bet it's the Radiation Laboratory. You poor dear."

"No." I sighed. "It's not that. It's nothing. I'll be all right."

"Then what is it? Are you ill? Are your parents all right?"

"Oh, it's nothing like that. You'd laugh if I told you."

"Josef! You know me better than that."

"Well . . ." I wanted to appear reluctant to say it, so I had to hesitate. "It does have something to do with the Radiation Lab."

"I knew it! Why don't you let me talk to the Chief?"

"No, no." That was the last thing I wanted. "You don't understand. I really don't mind being in there at all—but I'm going in tomorrow night at seven and I have to stay for forty-eight hours." I took a big breath and did it. "And the day after tomorrow is my birthday." Actually, my birthday wasn't until six weeks later, August fifteenth.

"We'll have a birthday party for you," she said and clapped her hands.

"No! I don't want anyone else to know. Please. Just forget it." I blinked my eyes at her a few times. Girls always commented on my eyes. They were probably my only good feature.

The upshot of it all was that she invited me, alone, to her apartment for dinner on my "birthday." Krupinsky agreed to relieve me in the Radiation Lab for two hours, starting at seven in the evening.

Everything ran smoothly all night and all day, and by the time he was supposed to come, I'd had plenty of time to think about Sonja Press and how I would say it and do it. But Krupinsky didn't get there at seven. The British bombed early that night, and he was held up for two hours by the air raid. I was so upset that I blew up at him, even though it wasn't his fault. He gave me one of his expressionless looks and said, "You have three hours, you schmuck. I'll stay until midnight."

Sonja had said I could come any time after six and before nine—and here it was several minutes after nine. Fortunately, I had showered and shaved when Professor Kreutzer relieved me in late afternoon, so all I had to do was pick up two Fromm's Akt and the lubricant gel from my worktable drawer and run across the park to her building and up the stairs.

She seemed a little anxious. "I was so worried you wouldn't make it."

"Krupinsky was delayed by the British. Am I too late?"

"Well, no. We do have a little time." Then she smiled, gave me a hug, and said, "Happy seventeenth birthday. Here, I have a little vodka ready."

She handed me a glass of it, and I had to stand there while she toasted me with "Many, many happy returns of the day." Then she began to weep, probably over the contradiction of many happy returns for a cross-breed half-Jew in the Third Reich.

I was extremely ill at ease, and I already knew it wasn't going to work. When things start off so wrong—the lies and Krupinsky being late—the best thing is to drop it. But I was trained by my father, a Prussian, that once a job is started, it must be completed—right or wrong. "In the army," he said to me over and over, "if one buttons a tunic beginning with the wrong hole and discovers it halfway up, he must finish it wrong and then unbutton all the buttons and start all over again."

I stood there, rigid as a Prussian soldier, feeling totally alienated from the scene. Words wouldn't come naturally. I had to think of what to say.

Sonja gave me another hug and said, "You poor dear, sitting up all night and all day in that control booth."

I put an appropriate expression on my face and sighed. "It's not too bad. I really don't mind it." Ah, I let a little honesty creep in.

"Here! Lie down on the couch and rest."

I sank onto the couch, half reclining, a position uncomfortable for me, and she actually bent down and untied my shoes. "Take these off and stretch out a minute while I get some food on the table." I hated to take off my shoes; my socks were threadbare, darn on darn. But she left me no choice.

Stocking-footed, I stretched out and she covered me with her

shawl. She puttered about the hot plate and the table for ten minutes or so, then sat beside me on the couch and took my hand.

"Would you like some more vodka?"

"No, thank you."

"How is the irradiation going?"

"Fine, thank you. Sonja? May I tell you something?"

"Dinner is ready." She dropped my hand and tried to rise from
the couch. But I held her arm.

"Dinner is ready." She tried, again, to rise, but still I held her
arm. Gently, she pushed my hand away.

"Sonja, there's something I've been wanting to say to you."

"Josef, dear, I think it would be best if we have our dinner
now."

"Please, you must let me speak." I knew she didn't want to hear,
but I had to finish buttoning up the tunic, wrong hole and all.

She did not try to get up.

"From the very first moment I set eyes on you that very first
day, I . . . I have felt . . ." God! Her face was so anxious and pained.
"I have felt the greatest affection for you."

She leaned over, kissed my cheek, and took my hand. "You
have no idea how greatly I esteem your affection for me and how I
will always cherish your friendship." This conversation was right
out of a nineteenth-century novel. "And now, dinner is ready."

"You don't understand . . ." I began. But someone was at the
door. I heard a key turning in the lock.

Sonja jumped to her feet and I to mine. The shawl fell to the
floor.

It was the Chief. He opened her door with a key. He frowned
and said to Sonja, "What's he doing here at this hour?"

"It's his birthday today. I invited him for dinner."

He looked at me. "Happy birthday. Aren't you supposed to be
over in the Radiation Laboratory?"

I did not run. I bowed slightly. "Good evening, sir." I bowed
more deeply to Sonja and kissed her hand—"I thank you for a

most pleasant evening"—and I walked slowly toward the door.

"Your shoes," she said.

I returned, picked up my shoes, bowed again, and walked slowly from the apartment, slowly down the flight of stairs. Then I ran, in my stocking feet, through the park to the main building and up the stairs to the Radiation Lab.

Krupinsky said, "Back so soon? It's not even ten. Why didn't you get some sleep? Why are you carrying your shoes? What did you do, get caught in somebody's bed?"

"Why don't you shut up and shove it up your ass, you shiny ape."

"Good idea! He picked up his jacket and left.

A male *Drosophila* would jump on anything, even a black spot on a piece of paper. In the lab, I had made black spots on paper, watched them pounce and stagger off in confusion, return and pounce again. But I had made my sexual frustration unilateral: Sonja Press. Not like him, who had a wife, too, and who, everybody knew, fornicated with all the ballet dancers who came to the parties after our staff dinners. It had been two months since Marlene had invited me to the darkroom.

I sat all that night, checking hourly the amount of radiation given to the one hundred flies in the three gelatin capsules pasted to the target. At six in the morning, Professor Kreutzer relieved me for two hours, and I passed out on a table in our lab until eight, when I returned to the control booth. At eight thirty the Rare Earths Chemist came in with a solution he wanted irradiated. Good Lord, why him? Always him? Such a nice man. But in the first place, he forgot to use the lightning arrester, in the second place he was about to put his hand into the target area in order to paste on the small capsule of solution he wanted irradiated. I had to pull switches, causing crashing noises and many sparks. He'd been so nice to me from the beginning, directing me to the Chief's penthouse that first day, and after that always ready to explain about the Rare Earths elements, which are not really so rare, and showing me the tremendous collection of alkaloids stored in his lab, and explaining how he was always trying to isolate the trans-uranium which they knew was there from the measuring equip-ment, but which, of course, they had never seen. In the third place, his solution might give off secondary radiation. If this happened I could throw away my one hundred flies because I couldn't be sure if the effect I got was from primary or secondary radiation.

Professor Kreutzer had put me in charge of the linear acceler-ator, but without any authority. So I couldn't tell the scientists not to put their solutions on the target, or not to go into the Radiation Lab unprotected, or not to stick their hands in front of the target. I could just make the machine seem to break down.

I looked at the Rare Earths Chemist through the glass and water. And he, kind man, looked at me, waved, smiled, pointed to the machine. I said over the intercom that I was sorry things seemed to have broken down, but if he would come back at four or five in the afternoon, it should be fixed. He picked up his solution and left.

By the time the Chief stopped in to see how things were, I had rationalized my way into a fit of moral indignation over his sexual behavior. It was the only way I could handle my humiliation. He acted as though nothing had happened and began talking about statistical validity. He was forever talking about how to confirm the validity of statistical phenomena. "One must have a very large number, a very large number, and even then, Josef, one must be careful with statistics, for they are like a lady's brief bathing suit. What they reveal is interesting, but what they hide is essential. Correct? Or am I right?"

One began to notice that he repeated the same trite phrases over and over: Correct? Or am I right? And one knew also that what one does not say also hides the most essential. I was coldly polite but said little.

Krupinsky came in after lunch to relieve me. "How're you do-ing, Josef?" His tone was so kind that I became wary.

"How should I be doing?" I rose from the chair. He closed the door and blocked my exit.

"It was Sonja, wasn't it?"

I shrugged.

"I should have told you, I suppose. But you're such a damned know-it-all."

"Told me what? That the Chief's a moral pygmy?"

Krupinsky grabbed my shirtfront and pulled me toward him. "You goddam schmuck." He released me with a push; he actually had tears in his eyes. "You are so brilliant," he said, "and probably the most stupid individual I've ever met."

"It's time to measure the dose."

"A minute more won't matter. Don't you understand, you schlemiel, that the Chief is carrying you on his back—and me—and all of us, including those Luftwaffe people in Brain Research and at Mantle? Anything he has to do to keep his sanity is O.K."

"But he has a wife!" I blurted out.

"When the hell are you going to grow up? It doesn't make any difference."

I sat down again on the swivel chair in front of the control panel. "But he's so old."

"Did Sonja tell you about the Chief?"

"He walked in on us. He has his own key."

Krupinsky turned away from me, perhaps to hide a smile. I swiveled around and looked through the aquarium of glass and water into the Radiation Laboratory and saw the wavering image of the linear accelerator. "I'll measure the dose before I go to lunch," I said.

"Thanks. I can stay one hour."

After the measuring, I went into my lab. The girls were through with the daily sorting and were putting the flasks of flies into the incubators. I took Marlene aside and asked her if she would like to go with me to the darkroom.

She took a step backward, looked up at me, and nodded. A serious face. The eruptions on her skin were, most likely, not syphilis at all.

"I don't have much time," I said.

"It doesn't take much time."

So we went up to the darkroom.

It takes the flies a long time. Many minutes. The male jumps on the back of the female and holds her with all six legs. There is no struggle. Sometimes they fly around joined, but usually they just crawl or hop. But slowly—they take their time.

Marlene turned on the red light, bolted the door, and pulled the soundproof curtain. I tried to embrace and kiss her.

"Don't kiss me." She pushed me away.

There was a stack of folded blankets in the corner. She began to spread one. I helped, being careful to smooth out the corners neatly. She put a folded blanket down for a pillow, stepped out of her underdrawers, lay down, and raised her skirt above her waist. I looked.

"Don't look at me."

I closed my eyes.

"Just unbutton your pants."

It was not embarrassing to me—slightly awkward, but mainly matter-of-fact.

"Do you have a safety?"

"Two." I pulled the Fromm's Akt from my pocket.

"One will do."

I pictured the full, rose-tipped breasts of Frau Krupinsky with the small silver cross in the cleavage. Then I dropped to my knees.

Mother's medical books listed only two kinds of sexual impotency for the male: *impotentia generandi,* the inability to procreate, sterility; and *impotentia coeundi,* the inability to perform coition. To this I added a third, *impotentia Josefus,* the inability to satisfy a woman. She just lay there stiff and quiet while I did it to her.

I was able to heat up and eat three bowls of polenta with molasses in the greenhouse kitchen and return to the control booth within the hour, by two P.M.

At four thirty, Professor Kreutzer walked into the Radiation

Laboratory with his lightning arrester and the Gestapo in the House. It was time for the Security Officer's daily x-ray therapy. When I had asked Krupinsky about him, I was told that the Security Officer—who was a high-ranking officer in the S.S., an *Obersturmbannführer*—had a doctorate in chemistry, and that is why Himmler himself assigned him to keep watch over the various scientific activities at the Institute. And Krupinsky gave me a book to read about his particular disease, *Principles of Internal Medicine,* page 1317:

Hodgkin's disease is characterized by painless, progressive enlargement of the lymphoid tissue. The proliferating cells tend to encroach upon, obscure, and finally replace the architecture of the lympth node. No age is immune, and males are more frequently affected than females. The cause of these disorders is unknown.

The nodes are discrete and movable at first; only later do they become matted together and fixed. At first they are painless and the overlying skin is normal; however, when they have developed rapidly or when the nerves are infiltrated, they may be painful. The effect of irradiation may be dramatic, large masses melting away in the course of a week.

If correct diagnosis is not made early, dissemination of the disease occurs.

Correct diagnosis had not been made early in his case, and it had spread. He'd already had surgery on his underarm and groin, which accounted for his peculiar walk: a limp, a shuffle, his arms held gingerly away from his body.

He took off his black trousers and lay down on the table. Groin. Does such a disease make one impotent in any way? He had three small children. Professor Kreutzer came into the control booth and switched the power from the linear accelerator to the deep x-ray machine. The Kreutzers had no children, nor did the Krupinskys or Treponescos, only the Avilovs. They had the one, Mitzka. My parents had one, me. Uncle Otto and Aunt Greta had no children, and my mother's younger brother, Uncle Philip, was not married when he was picked up and "relocated to the East."

The flies had been irradiated forty-six and one-half hours. Enough. When Professor Kreutzer and the Security Officer were gone, I took my three capsules from the target area and stopped by Rare Earths to tell the Chemist that the Radiation Laboratory would be O.K. now, and then I went into my lab to etherize the flies and put each male in a flask with three virgins. You could figure that as soon as the virgins matured, after two hours or so, and there were male flies in the vicinity, the virgins had to be considered fertilized.

Monika was there waiting to help me. She and Marlene must have talked, for when the hundred flasks were all back in the incubators, she took my hand and led me to the darkroom. Both of them—first Marlene and then Monika—lay so silent and unmoving that I felt that although one had the ability to perform coition, one could still feel inadequate.

We were looking for the effects of radiation on unripe sperm, so those first three virgins had to be discarded into the mass grave, and the second three, and the third three. Each male went through nine or so females before he was put with those whose offspring we could check.

. . .

Our second-floor wing smelled also of the rich compost we mixed with the soil to grow the feed for the rabbits, rats, and ladybugs and to grow the tobacco. Some of it was grown in the small greenhouse on the second floor, and the remainder in one of the large greenhouses in the park.

Our wing smelled of the tobacco we grew and aged, and of the particular sauce each scientist developed to cure his own tobacco: it was air dried, hung leaf by leaf on fishing line, and then soaked in all kinds of exotic solutions including the Chief's recipe of prune juice and extract of dried figs. There was endless discussion on how long to soak, how long to dry, what sauce to use. Then it was cut, then smoked. The report filed showed extensive research on a tobacco virus called "Tabac Mosaic Virus."

And it smelled of the smoke. Everyone smoked. It was an absolute miracle there was no explosion with the building so full of alcohol and ether vapors.

I smoked a lot after coming to the Institute, and I was puffing away on a cigarette while sorting flies one day early in August when Sonja Press came to get me. She was as warm and friendly as ever. "Your mother is here," she said, touching my arm. She always smelled like roses.

I unscrewed the cigarette holder from my microscope and put it in a drawer.

"She's upstairs in the Chief's office."

There was always the problem when I stayed overnight at the Institute that my parents would not know if I was all right, and I would not know if they were. Telephone calls to check on family after air raids were against the law. So we developed a system: I would ring the house, and if everything was fine, they would pick up the phone after the fifth ring and then hang up again. It wasn't too satisfactory because often the phones were out of order, and I would end up riding through the night from Hagen, on the northeastern border of Berlin, to our southwestern suburb, Gartenfeld, only to find the house intact, my parents all right. Sometimes I would stay a few hours to help put out fires at neighboring homes and turn right around, stumble through the dark to the S-Bahn stations, and ride for two hours back to Hagen. The night before, the phones had been out of order, and I was unable to go home to check on my parents because I had to be Air Raid Warden at the Institute. We took turns being Warden.

Mother sat beside the Chief in his private office. So near to his bulk, his bursting virility, there seemed little life left in her.

Mother, a small woman and plain, wore a black wool suit. I bowed and took the frail hand she extended.

"Herr Professor informs me that your work is promising, Josef. I hope, also, you are being a good and honorable young man."

The Chief said, "I understand, Frau Doktor, he is quite good." He smiled at me.

I could not yet smile at him.

Still her hand held mine. Unusual. "Has something happened, Mutti? Uncle Otto? Aunt Greta?"

She pulled her hand away. "No. We are all fine—your father, too." A reprimand. "It concerns you." She withdrew a letter from her black purse and gave it to me. One could see from the envelope that it was from the Office of Labor.

I did not want to be taken from the Institute.

She sat erect in her chair. The Chief jumped to his feet and began to pace.

I opened the letter and read it silently. "They want me to report to the Labor Office, Section IV-B-4, within seven days, in order to be incorporated into the work force."

I did not want to be taken before my time. From 1941 on, when they were bringing in forced laborers from the conquered countries, there were rumors that the Jews were not being put into labor camps or resettlement camps but were actually being murdered. The first time I was aware that extermination was going on was in 1939. We were called into an assembly at school to hear a recent alumnus talk. He had been a soccer champion and student president of the whole school, and, of course, we all looked up to him as some sort of god. Several months earlier, he had enlisted in the Waffen S.S. and was just now returning from combat on the Polish Front. He had been asked to give a pep talk to the students so that they would go willingly into the S.S. and into the army. But instead, he stood before us and said that he could not live with what he had seen and with what he had done. He told us that in Poland they had rounded up Jews into groups and had driven their tanks and trucks into them, smashing them to death. Of course, the school officials were furious about what he was saying, and, finally, they stopped him. Later that day, he committed suicide by throwing himself off the school roof. We were called, again, into assembly and told that he had killed himself because everything he had said had been lies, and he was ashamed of the lies.

And Mitzka, every time he came to a staff dinner, corroborated all the horrible rumors about the death camps. We knew cyanide was being used—a horrible, suffocating death.

Mother said to the Chief, "Is it because he will be seventeen next week?"

The Chief stopped pacing and looked at me. "Happy birthday," he said. He took the letter from me and studied it, then said to Mother, "If you'll please excuse us, Frau Doktor, we will be back shortly. Come along, Josef."

On the way out he asked Sonja to bring my mother tea with real sugar and to have two rabbits slaughtered and packed in a basket with cornmeal and vodka for her. We ran down the steps from his penthouse and up the central stairs to Herr Wagenführer in Personnel on fifth.

"Is it that he will be seventeen soon?" the Chief asked.

Herr Wagenführer shook his head. "No. Look at this number up in the corner: fifty thousand. They have printed only fifty thousand of these form letters, so most probably it is an action against a certain group." He handed back the letter. "I'm sorry, Josef, there is nothing I can do for you, but sometimes Professor Kreutzer has ideas on these matters."

In the Physics Laboratory on second, Professor Kreutzer changed his glasses only once, and quickly, before reading the letter. Afterward, he changed slowly back to the original pair, cleaning, slowly, the gold-rims, taking off the rimless, donning again the gold, putting the rimless away in a pocket, looking at me over the gold-rims and then through the glass before he spoke. "It's some special action, in your case probably an action against mixed-bloods. If you will notice this number printed on the form, there are only fifty thousand issued, which is not many considering that they have gleaned the mailing list from files of some hundred million people or more."

"What can be done?" the Chief asked him.

"Delay."

The Chief nodded and said, "Frau Doktor Bernhardt is in my office."

"Alex," said Professor Kreutzer, "find out from our Gestapo in the House about this operation IV-B-4. I think it is not Labor Office at all but something else."

The Chief left to find the Security Officer. Professor Kreutzer packed a few things into a briefcase—some papers and journals—checked to be sure his spectacles were all in place, and he and I walked down the hall and up the staircase to the Chief's office. He bowed to my mother and said, "I am optimistic we can delay any action against your son until, we hope, there will be no further need to delay."

The Chief came, followed by Sonja Press, who carried the basket of rabbits and all for my mother. I could see the Gestapo in the House, in his black uniform, waiting in the outer office.

"No!" said Professor Kreutzer. "It would be too dangerous for Frau Doktor to carry such a basket of food on the train. We'll send it over later."

The Chief pounded his palm with his fist. "Of course, how thoughtless of me."

My mother was unable to speak. Sonja Press took her hand and held it. I, across the room from her, could not move. The Chief and Professor Kreutzer stepped to the outer office to confer with the Security Officer, returning in very few minutes.

"Frau Doktor," said the Chief, "although it comes through the Labor Office, this action is secretly under the auspices of a special department of the S.S. An appointment has been made, and Professor Kreutzer and Josef will have to pay a little call there today."

Mother stood and looked at me. I wanted to cross the room and embrace her, but I did not.

"He will be back today," said the Chief gently.

"Good-bye, Mutti," I said from my distance.

Professor Kreutzer and I walked the three kilometers to the train station without talking. Once on the train, he motioned for me to sit opposite him in the empty compartment; then he extracted two scientific journals from his briefcase and handed one to me. At the second stop, a family crowded into the small compartment with us. The father, an army sergeant, sat next to Professor Kreutzer. The mother, next to me, began to unpack sausage and bread from a basket. The four children, noisily munching, moved constantly— back and forth, forth and back.

The sergeant tapped Professor Kreutzer's arm and offered him some food.

"Look," he said, "real butter. I have just come on leave from Denmark, and we have real butter and good sausage."

Professor Kreutzer looked at the sergeant over the black-rims. "Denmark, eh? So you eat good food from Denmark?"

"Superior. I am in a hurry to return there."

Professor Kreutzer nodded and said, "Thank you very much, sergeant, but I have already eaten."

I was too worried and preoccupied to read, but Professor Kreutzer returned to his journal and was so engrossed he seemed not to notice the continuing commotion, even when the train lurched and the children fell against him with their buttered bread and sausage.

But what? I looked again at him. A spastic movement, subtle. He rubbed his back against the bench; his left shoulder twitched. Discreetly he scratched his head, his chest, his underarm; there seemed a slight convulsion of his trunk.

The mother began to look at him, too, and, I think at the same moment, she and I saw the little fleas hopping about the lap of Professor Kreutzer—hop, hop—onto the leg of her husband. At her exclamation, the sergeant, too, noticed. He jumped to his feet, brushing his chest, his legs.

"What kind of pigs are these people?" he shouted.

And he moved across and sat beside his wife, who was packing the sausage and bread back into the basket. All four children crowded near the parents on my bench, which was intended for four people. They muttered and complained. "Pigs. Fleas."

Professor Kreutzer, solitary, scratched his chest and said, "Eh? What? Fleas, madame? There are no fleas in Germany."

At the next stop the family fled from the train. I began to itch. Professor Kreutzer motioned for me to sit beside him. I hesitated, but I did it.

"Your reluctance to sit here appalls me," he said.

I shrugged.

He opened his hand. A gelatin capsule, the kind we used for irradiating flies. "Open it."

Of course. *Drosophila melanogaster vestigial*. A mutation. Withered wings. They were unable to fly but perfectly capable of hopping about like fleas and of breeding with each other to make more such useful creatures. Thereafter, I bred my own private stock and always carried a capsule of them with me on the S-Bahn.

The Central Labor Office was midtown in a massive red-brick structure built at the turn of the century without regard for taste. The windows, all boarded and bricked because of the bombing, compounded its ugliness. Professor Kreutzer unhesitatingly bypassed the main entrance and walked briskly in a side door marked *D,* I following him. To the man behind the information counter, he said, "I have an appointment with Herr Direktor Bruno." The man waved us on. Up three flights of stairs and to the right we came to a door marked 1127, Labor Department Section IV-B-4. He knocked.

"Enter," sang a woman's voice.

The anteroom was plainly furnished. A good-looking woman

sat behind the reception desk. There were three doors leading, I assumed, to other offices.

"I have an appointment with Herr Direktor Bruno. I am Professor Kreutzer."

"One moment please, Herr Professor." She picked up her telephone and pushed a button. "Professor Kreutzer is here. . . . Yes, Herr Direktor." She hung up the receiver and said to us, "Won't you have a seat, please? It will be a few minutes."

We sat on the wooden chairs. I was anxious but not afraid. If there were to be a free election for the position of God and the two candidates were the Chief and Professor Kreutzer, I would vote for Professor Kreutzer. Both were brilliant, brave, and competent, and the Chief was also warmly human and overwhelmingly charismatic. Professor Kreutzer, by comparison, was cold and impersonal. But he was infallible—and I would, ten times over, rather be ruled by a well-directed infallibility than by a well-directed charisma.

After twenty minutes or so, the receptionist's phone rang. "Yes, please? . . . Immediately, Herr Direktor." She looked toward us. "Please, you may go in now. The middle door. You needn't knock."

Behind the middle door was a short passage leading to another door, which was upholstered against sound. Professor Kreutzer opened the second door and walked in, I behind him.

The office was elegant, with oriental rugs and heavy wine draperies. There were four framed pictures on the walls: Adolf Hitler; Himmler, who was Interior Minister as well as Leader of the S.S.; and Ley, Minister of Labor. The fourth was a family group with an officer in the black uniform of the S.S., surrounded by his overfed wife and chubby children.

Bruno, in well-tailored civilian dress, sat behind an ornately carved desk and did not look up as we entered. He pretended to be engrossed in the papers before him.

Professor Kreutzer, of course, was not one to be ignored.

"Heil Hitler and greetings, Sturmbannführer Bruno." It was

barked in staccato and followed by a click of the heels and a Nazi salute.

Sturmbannführer Bruno's head jerked up. Astonished, he was momentarily impotent and could not get his hand up in a proper salute. "Heil Hitler," he muttered. "How did you get my name?"

Translated, that meant how did Professor Kreutzer find out he was an officer of the S.S. and that IV-B-4 was not Labor Department at all but a clandestine operation of Herr Himmler's. To this day, I am not sure why they bothered with such charades, and why they didn't openly concede that this department was S.S. and that IV-B-4 was a code for Jew in the Labor Force.

Professor Kreutzer answered his question. "Did you not receive a special citation in the *Schwarze Korps?*"

"Yes, I did. But that was some time ago." A half smile.

"I do not forget these things," said Professor Kreutzer and handed him my summons. The man was off-balance and would not be allowed to regain his equilibrium.

Bruno glanced at the summons, and Professor Kreutzer began his spectacle-changing routine. He removed a glasses case from one pocket and searched for the cleaning cloth in another, then removed the black-rims from the case and held them to the light from the window and began to clean them in a superior way, attacking a recalcitrant spot in the upper right lens. At this point, Bruno looked up at him. Professor Kreutzer removed the gold-rims, put them in the case and into his pocket, and donned the black-rims, then stared over them at the seated official, looking cold and controlled. He looked very important, not at all kind, very superior—and all reverence is due superiority, so deeply is it engrained in our German souls.

Bruno rubbed the side of his face with his open palm, then stood. "What can I do for you?"

But Professor Kreutzer did not answer him and began to change to the rimless, all in all the most elaborate and perfectly timed exchange I had yet seen. Bruno just stood there, gaping at the stunning performance.

I stood behind Professor Kreutzer. I was as tall as he, but I weighed one hundred and twelve pounds and had absolutely no presence.

"As you well know, Sturmbannführer Bruno, the Kaiser Wilhelm Institute for Neurophysiological Research in Hagen is involved in work of high priority and of utmost importance for the war effort of the Third Reich."

Bruno nodded. "Yes, I am aware of this, Herr Professor."

"Yes. Are you aware that I am the Chief Atomic Physicist, and that this boy has been trained to perform certain tasks? He has been trained by me to perform them well."

Bruno looked at me.

"Even so, he does not understand what it is that he does, and what the work is all about. He is a machine. I am not free to go into the details of what this work involves, and I ask that this matter be handled with top security—TOP SECURITY! If you wish, you may check into the research projects for the Luftwaffe. The numbers for this project are eight . . . six . . . seven . . . zero . . . three . . . two . . . one." Professor Kreutzer paused after each number to give Bruno time.

Bruno, meanwhile, had dropped into his chair to write the numbers. When he had them all on the pad, he nodded to Professor Kreutzer, who, nevertheless, repeated them quickly: "Eight, six, seven, zero, three, two, one. I need this boy. It would be difficult and time-consuming to replace him. I have already cleared him with the local draft board."

I cringed. An out-and-out lie. When they saw the maiden name of my mother, Jacoby, I was automatically exempted from serving in the army.

Professor Kreutzer continued. "You can be assured your cooperation in this matter will be appreciated, and you may send the approval of his working for me to the Director of Personnel, Kaiser Wilhelm Institute for Neurophysiological Research, Hagen."

Bruno tried to write all this on the tablet, but Professor Kreutzer interrupted him.

"There is no need to take more of our valuable time. Heil Hitler." Up went his arm.

He kicked my shin. "Heil Hitler," said I, arm raised.

"Heil Hitler," said Bruno, jumping to his feet again and saluting strongly.

Professor Kreutzer turned. I turned. He walked. I walked.

It was not necessary to use another capsule of *vestigials* on the train ride back. We were alone in our compartment. I sat beside Professor Kreutzer, and he explained that since my file would be marked *Top Secret,* and since few people had top security clearance, it would take months before the Labor Department would act upon it. "Do not believe for a moment," he said, "that Herr Direktor Bruno's office will ever give you clearance. All we can hope for is investigation and delay. If the Allies come soon enough, you might be lucky. Meanwhile, I will begin correspondence with the office of Reichsmarshal Goering, who is in charge of the Scientific Research Council of the entire Third Reich."

More than a year later, we received a letter of clearance from the Scientific Research Council, but it was too late for many reasons, one of which was that Goering had lost too much power by that time. Three months after our trip to the Labor Office, a letter arrived addressed to me in care of the Wilhelm Foundation, Hagen. It was probably another summons, but Professor Kreutzer told me not to open it. He sent it back marked *Wrong Address.* Five weeks later, another letter came. This time it was correctly addressed, but it was almost illegible; the type was too light. He took it back personally, saying to the secretary that the print was illegible, he had very weak eyes, and what was the Third Reich coming to that they couldn't put decent typewriter ribbons on their machines in the Labor Office?

He calculated that it took at least thirty-seven days for a letter to be received by them and dealt with, so every three or four weeks he would write a letter concerning me to the Office of Labor, saying, for example, "Why has my letter of 15 April not been answered?"—which, he said, would cause my file to be removed from the stack, reviewed, and put again at the bottom of a pile. Of course, it was all marked *Top Secret* and *Decisive to the War Effort* and one must imagine a very large red-brick building, filled with many secretaries, with many files stacked on each desk.

"Someday," said Professor Kreutzer, "there will be machines which can sort through one hundred million names in a matter of hours. Then there won't be a chance for you. But now it is all manual. You have no idea how much trouble it is for Hitler to keep track of all the Jews."

He did all this without humor, a deadly serious game, hoping to delay the action against me for at least a year, by which time the war should have been over. As it was, he was able to delay for sixteen months, until January of 1945, when General Eisenhower and his colleagues were still hesitating in France, afraid to move on to Germany.

· · ·

After I'd been at the Institute a year, Marlene got pregnant and quit. I was relieved when the Dutch Medical Student felt he had to marry her. Monika had to leave our laboratory, too, after the disaster the night I was Air Raid Warden, and there actually was an air raid in Hagen.

A staff dinner had been called at the last minute to celebrate the Russian victory in the Crimea, in the spring of 1944. But Monika and I had private plans, and I used as an excuse for missing the dinner the fact that I was Air Raid Warden.

It usually was easy to be Warden because the Allies never bombed our hospital suburb. But that night—either by accident, or maybe because the Royal Air Force had cowards like everything else—one crew dumped its bomb load on the outskirts of Berlin, in a field near the Institute.

I had just connected with Monika in the darkroom when the

building began to shake. My first impression was that I was finally getting some coital response from her, but when I realized the tremor was external and more like an earthquake, I collapsed. My God! I had left some pretty important *Drosophila* cultures on my worktable—special mutations—planning to put them back into the incubator later.

By the time I ran into the lab, it was too late. The windows had shattered, the flies on my worktable were dead from exposure to the cold, and the Chief was standing there, furious.

"Here is my Warden," he said sarcastically, and he and I set off to inspect the entire plant, including the buildings in the park. Luckily, no one was hurt, just some shattered windows here and there, and, of course, those isolated mutations on my worktable.

Everyone from Genetics had been at the staff dinner but Monika and me. Krupinsky, Frau Krupinsky, and the Dutch Medical Student were sweeping up the debris when the Chief and I returned to the lab. He began to pace furiously.

"In spite of being young," he said, "one still has to follow certain conventions, certain rules. A gentleman takes, but does not hang it on the bulletin board that he is having an affair with a certain girl, and that the affair took place during a general staff meeting, and that both were absent from that meeting, and that because of their thoughtless behavior their serious work was not properly carried on. Ignorance is the only excuse for anyone to do anything he shouldn't," he shouted. "Laziness or thoughtlessness is no excuse." He strode from the lab.

I could have killed myself.

Monika sat in the corner and cried.

"Frankly," said Krupinsky, "I can't imagine what the women see in him. Look at him. Look at all the signs of somatic degeneration. His chin is too short, his teeth are crowded, he has one nonseparated earlobe, his index finger is too short, and his shoulders—I feel sorry for his tailor, he would have an almost impossible task to hide the concave chest, the wings on his back sticking out, the narrow rib cage. And his ears—look at them: one is much larger than the other." He was sweeping up glass all the time he talked. "Really, I'm much more attractive than he and nobody ever looks at me."

Frau Krupinsky gave me a hug and helped me clean up the mess on my worktable.

Monika was still in the corner, crying. I could have killed myself.

Monika was moved to Chemistry and replaced by the floating lab assistant, Tatiana, who, as I've said, had a background similar to mine, except that her mother was a Russian Jew and a biologist, while it is mine was a German Jew and a physician. Both our fathers were one hundred percent "German" and both were lawyers. The Roumanian Biologist George Treponesco was still madly in love with her, and she still ignored him.

. . .

Our second-floor wing smelled also of the rats. We did not use the rabbits for research, and there is no such thing as fast ruthenium. But on the bone marrow and other organs of the rats we did test the effects of artificial radioactive substances produced by the particles from the linear accelerator.

PART III

OCTOBER 10, 1967
IOWA CITY

CHAPTER · FIVE

Elizabeth

Dr. Josef Bernhardt handed his resignation in a sealed envelope to Dr. Jenkins's secretary at 9:50 A.M., knowing that it would not be read until after the morning's surgery. With the vial of succinylcholine and a little bottle of Librium rattling in an otherwise empty briefcase, he walked out the tower entrance of the University Hospital feeling, somehow, lighter, and, squinting against the dazzling sunshine of the brilliant October day, hurried across the emerald lawn to Student Health for his ten o'clock appointment with Dr. Elizabeth Duncan.

Although he knew Elizabeth was always late, he arrived at her office exactly on time. "Would you mind," he asked her nurse, "if I waited in one of the examining rooms?"

"Not at all, doctor."

The nurse led him down the hallway, pushed open a door, and flicked on the fluorescent light: a tiny moss-green room, sink in the corner, small desk and chair, the window completely darkened by olive-green venetian blinds. The examining table lay beneath the window.

The nurse glanced circumspectly at his face. "Would you like to lie down, Dr. Bernhardt? It might be some time."

"Yes, thank you."

Deftly, she pulled white paper sheeting from the roll at the head and covered the table. From the cabinet beneath she took a little pillow and plumped it. "Can I get you anything?"

"No. And thank you very much."

"You're quite welcome." The nurse left, closing the door but leaving the light on.

Josef leaned the brown leather briefcase against the wall, removed his dark gray suit jacket, hung it on a hook, kicked off his black oxfords, and lay down. He felt somewhat better: his head still ached, he was nauseated, each respiration was a rasping wheeze—but he could breathe. And still he felt on the verge of tears.

To wrench his mind away from his physical symptoms, Josef willed his thoughts to the beauty of the day: the vivid colors, yellow and red against the blue sky and the green grass ... alas ... the geese rising from their noon apple-dreams.

The poem again, the little elegy. He scanned his memory for the words, feeling pressed and then panicked by his inability to remember something he had known so well. Josef sat up, inhaled deeply, pushed the breath out by tightening and releasing his diaphragm—three times—and lay down again. As with a name on the tip of the tongue, it is often best to trick it into floating to the surface. He closed his eyes and permitted his mind to free-associate: green grass ... alas ... white geese ... snow goose who cried in goose alas against the green grass.

Still it did not ring a bell.

He tried again: green grass ... goose ... alas ... beauty ... brown study ... body ... little bodies. ... His body was cushioned by the bodies of others whom he could not identify. He smashed them to bits. The trolley or the train—he couldn't remember— yes, he remembered. It was a train and it was cut open with a carpenter's ax and he was lifted out. Saved. But the unremembered others were mashed and broken, crushed and dismembered from the impact of his body—not beheaded—but their skulls smashed and their brains spilling out into pools of their own gore. Little Hans Levy and his grandmother, the button lady, were taken in July 1942, but the others, so many others, were not taken until nearly the end of the war, after the Normandy invasion in June

1944 and the liberation of Paris in August 1944. The Americans just stopped. Stopped! They could easily have marched through Germany, almost without resistance, and saved so many! But Eisenhower seemed more interested in humoring his prima donnas—Montgomery et al.—and in refereeing the little war between the Allies than in concluding the big one. His delay provoked unimaginable despair. Unimaginable! The Russians. Josef, lying on his back on the examining table, breathed deep, rasping breaths.

And yet, during a war there is hope. One can hope, always, that the war will be over and that life will be better. It is only after one is "liberated" that he realizes there is no hope at all and no reason at all. That is when the true emptiness begins.

His meditation was interrupted by Elizabeth Duncan, who, at half past ten, burst into the examining room clutching a large handbag and a grocery sack reeking so of garlic pastrami that Josef's nausea momentarily escalated into another dimension. He sat up and swung his legs over the edge of the table.

"My life is running three weeks late," she said breathlessly. "Don't get up." But Josef was already on his feet. Elizabeth dropped her purse and brown paper bag onto the table, and, as he helped her with her coat, began her inevitable apology. "I'm so sorry to have kept you waiting. I've a really sick one over at Mercy. Diabetes complicated by LSD." She shook her head. "And it's such an incredibly beautiful day that I stopped at the deli on the way back and picked up some sandwiches for us. I thought we might find a minute or two to wander down to the river and have a picnic. It's so beautiful out," she repeated, "so warm that I didn't even need my coat. Oh, no!" Elizabeth pointed to the grocery bag. "What on earth was I thinking? I bought pastrami on rye and potato chips. And with your blood pressure!"

"It's quite all right. I'm not the least hungry."

"Salt," she murmured.

They stood awkwardly, Elizabeth leaning against the examining table scrutinizing Josef dangling in the center of the little room. Although she denied it vehemently, Elizabeth was a striking woman. He had thought so since the day he met her when he was only nine and she, seventeen, had come with her father to the 1936 Olympics in Berlin. His Uncle Philip, who had just completed his residency in pediatrics that spring, was taken with her, too, and Josef would stand at the high window of his third-floor bedroom and observe the two of them as they walked together about the garden. She was to have stayed in Germany for several years, to study nursing, but the political climate was such that her father, wisely, took her home with him—back to Iowa. Who in his right mind would elect to leave his child in Germany during those dreadful years? During the visit to Germany, Josef's mother had convinced her to become a physician—not just a nurse.

"You look terrible," Elizabeth said, finally. "Seff, I know you're not going to listen to me, but please, you should go to someone a little more removed, more objective—and more qualified."

He shook his head.

"Bob Ericksen. He's a top-flight internist. Honestly, the only ills I get to work with around here are V.D.s, O.D.s, and final exams." She searched for cigarettes in her bag, offered Josef one. He refused but took the matches from her hand, lit her cigarette, and stepped back again to the center of the room. "I've got to cut down on these," she said, inhaling deeply. "Ah, doctors. We know too much. Do you want me to examine you?"

He nodded.

"I suppose we should get some tests to eliminate the nasties: pheochromocytoma, kidney problems. Do you want to arrange it, or should I?"

"Don't you bother."

"EKG, too, and a chest x-ray. Your breathing. I can hear it from here. It sounds as though you've got quite a bit of music in your chest."

"An entire orchestra."

"Here," she said, moving her handbag, grocery sack, and coat from the table and laying them on the little desk. "Take off your shirt and sit up here and tell me your symptoms."

While Josef divested himself of white shirt and tie, Elizabeth picked up the telephone, dialed one number, said, "Hold my calls," and hung up.

Josef, perched on the edge of the examining table, began his recitation: "Recurring headache, getting more severe. Blurring of vision. Tingling in fingers and lips. Runs of extrasystoles. Short spells of disorientation and panic."

"Panic?"

"Panic. Nycturia."

"Heart," she said. "I don't like it."

"Respiratory distress with and without congestion. Sudden onset of an irresistible tiredness without being able to fall asleep."

"How do you sleep generally?"

"Poorly. I wake up exhausted."

"How's your stamina?"

"I need more and more will to maintain it."

"Any disturbance in walking, in equilibrium?"

"Dizzy spells after physical exertion."

"What kind of physical exertion?"

"Running. Heavy lifting. . . ."

"How is your sex life?"

"It doesn't bother me."

"Hmpff. Take off your shoes and pants and lie back."

Elizabeth washed her hands and began a thorough, old-fashioned physical examination, saving further questions until it was over.

"You know what I've found," she said when she was through. "The blood pressure is right up there—hundred eighty over hundred and ten. You have frequent extrasystoles, pulmonary congestion, bronchospasms. I want to put you in the hospital this afternoon, call Bob Ericksen, and do a complete workup."

"No." Josef reached for his clothes and dressed while she talked to him.

Elizabeth lit another cigarette, sat behind the little desk in the only chair in the room. "How long have these acute symptoms been with you, my friend?"

"Since *Kristallnacht.*"

"Crystal Night? You were just a child. What—nineteen thirty-seven, thirty-eight?"

"Nineteen sixty-seven. Crystal Night in Montréal this spring, when the national soul of Canada erupted over the decision of a referee in a hockey game."

"Oh, yes. It made the news here. That *was* awful."

"I was on call. The injured were brought to the hospital. One had hopes that such behavior was indigenous to the Germans, that the Americans and the Canadians would not indulge in senseless, sadistic—"

"That's not fair!" Elizabeth cut him short. "You know there have always been mobs, even in America. Read *Huckleberry Finn.*"

"That's just the point, Eliza. It hit me that the Nazis are not unique. Don't you see?"

"Josef, I just can't let this pass. Crystal Night in Germany in—when was it?"

"November ninth, nineteen thirty-eight."

"That was different. It was planned by the government, by Hitler and his cohorts. It didn't just happen."

"Ah, yes. You are right. They organized, as they used to call it, 'a spontaneous demonstration of the German people.'"

"Wasn't it in reaction to something? The assassination of some official?"

"An embassy official in Paris."

"By a Jewish man?"

"He was seventeen. His father and ten thousand other Jews had been shipped off in boxcars. His name was Grynszpan."

"But, Seff—"

"They killed him, of course. Then they burned over a hundred synagogues, destroyed businesses—broken glass all over. The

Nazis called it 'The Week of the Broken Glass,' a real problem for the insurance companies."

"Seff—"

"And they arrested twenty thousand Jews. Twenty thousand. And carted them off to God-knows-where."

"That is just the point! You must admit to me that you see the difference between a drunken mob rioting after a football game—"

"Hockey."

"After a hockey game and a planned pogrom of the Nazis."

"You didn't see their faces. I did. I was walking along Côte Sainte Catherine on my way to the hospital, and I saw the faces of those people shattering the windows. Twisted. My God! Don't you realize, Eliza, that before the *planned* 'spontaneous demonstrations,' the Brownshirts in Germany had been running amuck—spontaneously—like rabid dogs? They murdered, tortured . . . broken glass. It all began with mobs."

"Of course, it's all indefensible, Seff—Montreal *or* Germany—but the Québecois were terribly ashamed by the next day. That's the difference!"

"Don't you think the German people were ashamed the day after *Kristallnacht*? And what did they do about it? Nothing! Nothing!" Josef was shouting. "I'm sorry, Elizabeth," he said quietly, his voice trembling. "I hadn't meant to give a speech. But I was sickened. And after a night at the hospital patching up the cuts and bruises, I felt ill. I took my blood pressure. It was up and hasn't come down since. Of course, it could have been up before that. I hadn't checked it for some time."

"How had you been feeling before then—say, for the past five years?"

"I was functioning. The only major problem has been with kidney stones—I'm a stone maker. If I drink enough fluids, I'm O.K. But this past summer, this fall, I've felt increasingly worse."

"When's the last bout you had with kidney stones?"

"Half a year or so ago—in the spring. I checked myself into the hospital, gave myself a shot of Demerol, and was able to pass it." He shook his head at the memory. "That pain is unbelievable."

"So I've been told. Did that happen after the hockey game episode?"

Josef thought for a moment. "Yes, I think it was after that."

"Why is it you decided to do something about your health today?"

He shrugged and looked away from her. "I don't know. I felt quite ill this morning—dizzy, headache—could hardly get out of bed. Thought perhaps I had the flu, but my temperature was normal. I shouldn't have gone to work. I am not fit."

"Did you dream last night?"

"No . . . yes. I . . . I rarely dream; that is, I don't remember my dreams."

"And last night? Do you remember?"

"I don't want to talk about it."

"Hmm. Is today anything special? An anniversary, someone's birthday?"

"Today? October tenth? Tuesday?" His breathing became more labored. He took a deep breath. "No," he said in a choked whisper. "I can't think of anything significant." Josef could not exhale. Bronchospasms again. He turned and bent over the table, back arched, mouth open wide, and tried to force the air out.

Elizabeth asked, calmly, "Does this happen often?"

He shook his head, all the while straining and pushing his neck and abdominal muscles to pull the air out of his lungs. "Once in a while," he whispered harshly. "But today—heavy."

"Do you do anything about it?"

"It goes away," he whispered, relaxing slightly as the constrictions diminished and he was able to take a shaky, quick breath and exhale. Quivering and sweating—but breathing—he turned to her. "I'm sorry," he said.

"How do you feel right now?"

"Headache." He covered his eyes with his hand, shaking his head.

"That bad?"

"Not good."

"Here." She rummaged in her purse. "Let me give you some aspirin."

"I'd better not," he said.

"Nonsense! Take these. You'll feel better." Elizabeth took a paper cone from the dispenser above the sink, filled it with water, and gave it to Josef.

He swallowed the two aspirin, crushed the empty cone, and threw it into the wastebasket.

"How's your sex life?" she asked once more.

"I'm not complaining."

"Why are you avoiding that question?"

He did not answer.

"Are you and Tanya lovers?"

"No, but it doesn't matter."

"How long has that been going on?"

"Lizzy, don't pull that psychological crap on me. I just want a physical checkup."

"Since when hasn't sex been physical? How you could marry a cold soul like Tanya, I'll never understand."

"Don't blame my failure on Tatiana. And I married her to please my mother."

"Your mother? Did she know her?"

"No. They never met."

"Then what you are saying makes no sense."

"Yes, it does, Eliza. Maybe I married her because I wanted someone just like my mother." He was dressed now—all but his suit jacket and tie.

Elizabeth was on her feet. "Your mother!" She lost all objectivity. "Your mother was the most sympathetic person I have ever known. Your wife is nothing like her. Nothing! And never will be.

Do you mistake Tatiana's coldness for strength and your mother's strength for coldness?"

Mother. Standing beside her desk, holding the black telephone receiver in one hand, beckoning to Josef, firmly, with the other, a strong motion pulling him to her. She wore a white lab coat over her black dress, and her hair was dark, almost black.

Josef felt uneasy, lightheaded, a throbbing in his ears. He could hear and feel his heart—palpitations—and his entire body was becoming one agonizing itch. "Elizabeth, I'm allergic to aspirin."

"You are flushed and developing hives. And your breathing—again."

"You'd better get me some epinephrine: one tenth of a cc of the one-to-thousand solution. No more. I'm very reactive to drugs."

Elizabeth raced from the room. Josef doubled over with abdominal cramps, unable to breathe, in an acute reaction to the aspirin. His mother lingered in the periphery but was kept at a distance by his physical symptoms. Elizabeth was back with the syringe.

"Don't give me too much," he begged.

She injected the Adrenalin subcutaneously in his arm; within seconds he could breathe freely, his cramps relaxed, and he felt the blood rushing to the upper part of his body. He sat on the edge of the examining table. Elizabeth wrapped the cuff around his arm and took his blood pressure. "Two hundred ten over one hundred and twenty," she reported. "How are you?"

"Better." He took a deep, trembling breath and was able to exhale. "But now I *really* have a headache."

"We have to consider following this up with cortisone."

"Let's wait. The emergency is over." He lay back on the table and closed his eyes. She stood beside him checking his blood pressure until, within five minutes, he opened his eyes. "I'm better," he whispered.

Tears welled up in Elizabeth's eyes, overflowed, and ran freely down her face.

Josef winced and turned away. "I'm sorry."

She wiped her eyes and blew her nose. "My dear, I am the one

who is sorry." The telephone buzzed. She answered, "Dr. Duncan
. . . yes?" She looked at her watch. "Tell him to wait—ten minutes." She hung up and turned to Josef. "It's my fault. I pushed
you too far. I had no idea the shape you were in. We've been so
busy, John and I. We should have made it a point to see you."

"Elizabeth, please. I'm better. You've got patients to see—"

"They can wait! I shouldn't have insisted you take those
aspirin."

Josef put his hand on her arm. "Listen to me. I'm better. But I'm
very tired. Would it disturb you if I rested here for a while?"

"Of course not. Are you sure you're all right?"

He nodded. "If you'd turn off the overhead light? And you
needn't stay. I'm all right."

"Are you sure?"

"I'm sure."

"It's almost eleven thirty. I've got some patients to see. But I'll
leave the door open a crack so my nurse and I can stick our heads
in to check on you."

"Not necessary," he murmured, his eyes closed.

"It'll make me feel better. Will you shout if you need
anything?"

Josef nodded. "Elizabeth, would you mind taking the pastrami
with you? I can't take the smell of garlic just now."

"Here," she said, untying his shoes, "let's take these off." She
covered him with a sheet, leaned over, and kissed his forehead.
"I'm going to leave the blood pressure cuff on your arm."

He nodded.

Elizabeth picked up the grocery bag, her purse and coat, turned
off the overhead light, and left the room.

· · ·

The itching had lessened and was tolerable, the headache bearable.
Josef was exhausted and felt he could sleep. But the moment he
allowed himself to drift off, his mother, willful as the ghost of

Hamlet's father, appeared again. As before, she was in her office, on the second floor of their house in Gartenfeld. Josef made one last attempt to rally his will, to push her away, but all he succeeded in doing was stiffening his body. He lay on his back, rigid, sweating. Consciously, he began to relax each part of his petrified frame, starting with the smallest toe on his left foot and moving up his trunk. As he did this, his mother marched through his broken defenses. But still—he could breathe. She, in her long white coat, was talking on the telephone to their next-door neighbor, the Bavarian Baron. It must have been 1932 or 1933. She was still in practice and seeing patients that day, and Josef, by the door, was quite young—six or seven. He was not at all afraid of her. He was curious. With a gesture of one hand, his mother summoned him to her. "Josef, Baron von Chiemsee reports that on many days you enter his back garden and climb his apple tree. Is that true?"

"Yes."

"What do you do there?" She put her arm, protectively, about his shoulders.

"Nothing, Mutti."

"One never does nothing. You must do something. What is it you do?"

She was not being unkind. Her manner was always brusque in those days.

"I think."

"Baron," she said into the telephone, "has my son harmed your tree or your garden in any way, or does he disturb you with noise? . . . No? . . . Then what is your complaint?" She hung up in her firm way, not a slam, but a motion with enough force to carry emphatically to the Baron's ear, then she leaned over and kissed Josef on the forehead. "I would suggest, Butzelman, that you do your thinking someplace other than the Baron's apple tree."

When her medical license was revoked, she was forty-one, just the age he was now. Her hair was still dark brown, as was his, and although she pulled it back in a bun, there were always softly curling wisps about her face. He realized now that she was almost pretty, and she looked so young! Why had he always thought of her as being old and plain—and weak? As a young woman she'd had the nerve to defy her parents and go to medical school and defy them again and marry a Gentile. When did her nerve desert her? How long did it take Adolf Hitler to break her down? *Mein Kampf.*

> *I understand the infamous spiritual terror which this move-ment exerts, particularly in the bourgeosie, which is neither morally nor mentally equal to such attacks. At a given sign it unleashes a veritable barrage of lies and slanders against what-ever adversary seems most dangerous, until the nerves of the attacked persons break down.*

. . .

Josef stirred and opened his eyes. Wearing a white lab coat now, Elizabeth, flashlight in hand, was checking his blood pressure.

"You can turn on the light," he said.

She did and returned to his side. "It's a little lower than when you came in—one eighty over ninety-five." With a shake of her head, she pulled the stethoscope from her ears and let it drop around her neck.

Josef rubbed his eyes against the light. "I must have dozed off."

"You slept an hour and a half. It's after one."

"Good Lord. I've got to get to the bank." He sat up abruptly, swinging his legs over the side of the table, and found that he had to steady himself by pressing his hands firmly on the table.

"How are you?"

"A little vertigo. But I'm all right." He shook his head. "I must have really been out." He yawned and stretched.

"We were in and out of here five or six times, and you didn't stir."

"I feel better. Almost rested." He stood. "I'll run along. I've taken up enough of your time."

"Please. Don't go."

"I've got to get to my safety box."

"You've got time." She pushed him gently backward.

Reluctantly, he leaned against the table.

"Seff, my dear, don't you know anything about yourself?"

He looked down.

"The aspirin. Didn't you know you were allergic? Why did you take it?"

The phone buzzed.

"Damn!" she said.

Josef leaned over and picked up his shoes.

"Don't go."

The phone buzzed again. "Dr. Duncan here. . . . Yes. . . . Oh, yes."

Josef, shoes on, lifted his jacket from the hook.

Elizabeth put her hand over the mouthpiece. "Please."

"Bathroom." He pointed to the door.

She pointed. "Down the hall—that-a-way."

Josef threw his suit jacket onto the examining table and left the room. As he started down the hall, he could hear her say, "Just a minute," and, very softly, "he's just leaving the room."

Carlos! Damn it. Josef stopped to listen, but Elizabeth shut the door and he could no longer hear. He hesitated, then ambled down the hallway to the men's room. He'd known the second he'd revealed that he was seeing Elizabeth that Carlos would call her. And there was nothing Josef could do to stop them from talking about him, to stop Carlos from meddling in his affairs. After the first delay of his resident's visa by the American Embassy, Josef wanted to give up his move to the U.S. But Carlos kept pushing, insisting, wouldn't give up. And Josef allowed himself to be carried along like a child, without a will of his own. He shoved open the door: MEN.

The morning surgery would be over, and the noon staff meeting of the Department of Anesthesiology, and, most likely, Carlos had heard from an irate Dr. Jenkins of Josef's resignation. As he stood at the urinal, Josef realized that he would not have to go to any more daily, interminable scheduling meetings—ever again. He breathed a deep, musical sigh of relief. It was easier.

A broad ribbon of sun shone through a south window of the lavatory, illuminating the sink. Josef rolled up his shirt sleeves and ejected three times the green liquid he needed from the soap dispenser, working it into a thick lather. The soap bubbles, like multiple lenses, refracted the sunlight in all directions; he was caught by the ever-moving, ever-changing rainbow of colors he held on his hands—multiple spectrums of all sizes and shapes. He rinsed, splashed cool water onto his face, and, as he patted it dry with a paper towel, looked at himself in the mirror above the sink. *Mein Kampf.*

> *The Germans are the highest species of humanity on the earth and will remain so if they care for the purity of their own blood and produce images of the Lord and not cross-breed monstrosities halfway between man and ape.*

Josef studied his reflection: his father's facial shape, the strong nose, the chin cleft almost in half. But his dark eyes, large and set wide apart, his curly brown hair—they were his mother's.

He blotted his hands carefully with two paper towels; his skin was sensitive, and his hands often red and sore from scrubbing up. But he would not have to scrub up again—ever. He completed the drying under the electric blower, then walked swiftly out the door and down the hallway.

Elizabeth, sitting at the little desk, smoked a cigarette and still talked on the telephone. She looked up when Josef entered and raised an index finger to indicate she was almost through. "Yes. . . . I agree. . . . I will. . . . Yes. . . . Good idea. Give me that number." She jotted a number on a prescription pad. "Yes, I've got it. . . . I'll call you at about two fifty. . . . All right, I'll make it a point, exactly ten minutes to three." She hung up.

"*En punto,*" said Josef.

Elizabeth looked up sharply. "In what?"

"Ten minutes to three *en punto*. It's Spanish, and it means 'on the dot.'"

"Did you know all along I was talking to Carlos?" She jabbed out the cigarette in the ashtray.

Josef nodded. "He's the most predictable man I've ever met. Also the most intrusive. I don't know how he does it. I had no intention of telling Charley I was coming to see you."

"If you didn't want him to know, you wouldn't have told him."

"Lizzy, please cut the psychology."

"I will if you'll stop calling me Lizzy. You know I hate that." She frowned. "Jeff, he's very worried about you."

"Good Lord, I envy him. He's the only man I've ever known who has his life absolutely under his control. That's why you must call him at exactly two fifty. His driver picks him up at the hospital at exactly two ten; they arrive at the farm at two twenty-five; he drinks a Scotch—only the best unblended malt—and nibbles hors d'oeuvres for twenty minutes while he reads *The Wall Street Journal,* and at exactly three—*en punto*—he eats a magnificent dinner prepared by his Spanish housekeeper, Camila: soup, fish, meat—"

Elizabeth took another cigarette and held out the pack to Josef.

"No, thank you. Salad, vegetables, dessert—*postre,* he calls it."

"You must really be feeling dreadful. I've never known you to refuse cigarettes before."

"Oh? Didn't Charley tell you? I've quit smoking."

"Congratulations. How long has it been?"

Josef looked at his wristwatch. "Exactly four hours and twenty minutes. I quit at nine o'clock this morning."

"Just about the time you wrote your resignation to Dr. Jenkins?"

He hesitated. "Just about."

"Dr. Jenkins wants to see you."

"I have nothing more to say to him—or to Charley."

Elizabeth closed her eyes and rested her forehead in her hand.

Josef put on his suit jacket, stuffed his necktie in a pocket, and leaned over to pick up his brown leather briefcase.

"I'll be going."

She looked him directly in the eyes. "Carlos thinks you are suicidal."

Josef shrugged.

Elizabeth scrutinized his face. "No. If you wanted to kill yourself, you wouldn't have come to see me."

"Is that what you told Charley?"

She did not answer.

"Maybe I came to say good-bye."

"No, Seff. I don't think so. I told Carlos that if you wanted to kill yourself you would not have written a letter of resignation. It's a red flag." She looked up at Josef; he stood near the examining table, poised for flight. "I understand it. You know I do. We've talked about it. The daughter of a Calvinist minister—I carry the guilt of the universe on my shoulders. I am responsible for every leaf that falls from every tree. My fault. Every morning I have to make the decision to live another day."

"That is why I knew you would understand."

"But you? *You* haven't the right. You haven't thought it through; you are in no condition to make such a decision."

"I have thought about it. For over twenty years I've been thinking about it."

She shook her head. "Looking at you, listening to you, my dearest friend, I would say that you are sliding into a serious depression."

"Most likely," he said, "I am sliding *out* of one."

"And the worst thing you can do in your mental state is to quit working."

"I *have* quit."

"They are not accepting your resignation."

"My God!" It was a wail. "Having a medical degree is the wrath of God! They have no choice! I am not well! I am not fit! Understand me and do me the favor of telling that intrusive bastard when you talk to him at exactly two fifty this afternoon that *I have quit!* I am through!"

She held her breath and waited.

"I am not a good doctor, Lizzy." He was begging now, imploring her. "I am not like you. I do not have the healing instinct. I never wanted to be a physician. I have always hated it. I do not like people."

"That is not true." She stopped him. "You are like your mother. You are a warm and loving human being."

"I am an impotent bum. I am nothing. And don't blame Tanya for my failure. I knew what she was when I married her. I never loved her."

"I don't believe for a minute that you are impotent. She's a cold fish and you know it. When is the last time you two made love?"

"Elizabeth, she didn't come down with me. Tanya is in Berlin."

"My God. You're here alone?"

He nodded.

"How long?"

"She left in the spring. May."

"You've been alone for six months?"

"More or less. Five months."

"Have you had another woman?"

He looked intently at her but said nothing. On trial for his life, he waited for her to continue.

"You are a sexual man, Seff. You need a lover. I can tell by the way you look—even at me—that you are a sensual man."

"You are a beautiful woman, Lizzy."

"I am not! I never have been. And please stop calling me Lizzy."

"No, it's true. I have always thought you beautiful. And so did my Uncle Philip."

"Philip," she whispered. "You have a gift for stopping any real conversation. But I will not let you. Those years—the war years— you never talk about them, and you hide behind a wall so thick that even those of us who love you—dearly"—Elizabeth was trembling, near tears—"even we dare not ask. It must have been terrible for you. Horrible! You have got to come to terms—"

"You miss the point completely." Josef's voice was cold and hard. "They were not horrible for me. It seems impossible for you Americans to believe that there were a few Jews and half-breed Jews surviving outside of Dachau and Bergen-Belsen. Those last years of the war were—in a way—the best years of my life."

"That cannot be true!"

"You see? You don't know what you're talking about. God!"

"How can I know? You never talk about it. After the war my father and I sent request after request for information about Philip, about your family: to the Red Cross, to the Jewish Agency, to the American Christian Committee for Refugees, to the Army, Navy, and Marines. And finally, months and months later, my father received a letter from the First Airborne Division of the United States Army. I memorized it. You want to hear?"

He nodded.

Elizabeth closed her eyes and recited in a voice trembling with emotion:

"Dear Reverend Duncan:

"In answer to your inquiry regarding the whereabouts of your friends, we have compiled the following information:

"We very much regret that as yet we have found no trace of the following: Anna Bernhardt née Jacoby, Philip Jacoby, Otto Jacoby, Greta Jacoby née Braunstein. These names will be broadcast over the widest possible network with the request that any person who has information will forward it to the Central Tracing Bureau.

"Lothar Bernhardt, attorney, and son Josef Bernhardt have been discovered at the following address: Berlin-Gartenfeld, Kastanien Strasse 95.

"They request that the following message be sent:

"'Dear Reverend Duncan. Many thanks for your inquiry. We were very glad about it. We survived all the hardships of war and we also hope to get through the winter. Our lodgings are nearly undamaged. Whether Anna, Philip, Otto, and Greta are living we do not know. We urgently hope to see you again. Kindest regards from Lothar and Josef.'

"Kindest regards!" she said tremulously, and then, again, "Kindest regards. I assumed you had been in—a camp. All I know is that somehow you survived."

"Somehow!" Josef snorted, his mouth twisted. "I was 'arrested,' you might say, toward the end of the war. But I was treated well. Before then, until the beginning of 1945, I was—quite comfortable."

"You weren't in a concentration camp?"

"Does that disappoint you? How on earth do you think I would have survived that? By skinning the bodies of my relatives for lampshades? By pulling out the gold teeth of the button lady, Frau Levy, and her grandson, Hans? That's what the American consul in Berlin assumed when I applied for a visa after the war. I had a scholarship to M.I.T., Elizabeth, to study physics and mathematics, but they would not give me a visa because I survived the war. No, Eliza, I did not lift a finger to save myself—or anybody else. I was preserved for almost three years in a lunatic asylum run by the inmates, kept pickled in vodka thanks to the brains of the Gunther Rathkes who were unlucky enough to have crashed in their Luftwaffe airplanes."

"You talk in riddles! You let no one in! I don't care if you were hidden in the Garden of Eden"—her voice was resonant, ringing—"it was *horrible* for you. *Listen* to yourself. You are *angry*. Angry and depressed. You have to come to terms with it. And *then! Then* you can kill yourself. But not now. *You have no right!*" The tears were gone, replaced by her anger. She tapped a cigarette out of the pack, struck a match so violently that it snapped in half, struck another to light her cigarette, leaned against the desk.

Josef, standing now at the foot of the examining table, dropped his briefcase on the table and turned again to the olive-green blinds. But this time he jerked the cord and rolled them up. The tiny room was ground level, and he faced—directly outside the window—a sturdy young maple, every leaf a vivid red.

"Elizabeth, do you remember a poem—I think it was some kind of an elegy about the death of childhood?"

"Can you give me more to go on?"

Still facing the window, he said, "It was in the anthology of American poetry you sent me when I first came to McGill. I can't remember the poet or the title, but it had some images of a day like this: white geese against green grass and blue sky, an apple orchard."

"'Bells for John Whiteside's Daughter,'" she said. "John Crowe Ransom."

He turned. "That's it. I've been trying to remember it all day."

"It's about a wonderfully naughty little child chasing after the geese in an apple orchard. It's about her death—a letter of condolence."

Josef, excited at remembering, recited the first four lines:

> *"There was such speed in her little body,*
> *And such lightness in her footfall,*
> *It is no wonder my brown study*
> *Astonishes us all."*

He was unaware that he had switched to the first person in the third line. "But I can't remember the rest," he said.

Elizabeth turned to him, her face and her voice tender. "You will, my dear, if you'll give yourself time. Seff, is there any way I can convince you to see an analyst?"

He shook his head vehemently. "You know I don't believe in that."

"Remember what Santayana said? 'Those who do not remember the past are condemned to relive it.'"

"Remember what Shakespeare said? Those who summon up remembrance of things past 'grieve at grievances foregone.'"

"What happened," she said, her voice tense, her words quick, "to your Uncle Philip? He wrote me that he had his visa in his hand and was on his way."

Josef, his face a storm, did not answer her.

"His things came," she said. "All his household goods, medical equipment—books."

"Elizabeth, I have to get to the bank before it closes."

"You at least owe it to me to tell me about Philip."

Josef's lips were strained taut in a sardonic grin. "He went through a red light."

"There you go again. Riddles! How can you do this to me? You are not being fair."

His mouth still twisted in a grimaced grin but now trembling, he said, "You are the one who is angry."

"Angry is not the term for it: wrath—rage." Her voice softened. "But not with you, my dear. Not with you."

"Elizabeth, he went through a red light!" Josef's contorted smile came undone, and his eyes filled with tears. "It is not a riddle." He was weeping now. "In 1938 one could take out household goods—including one car—but no money."

She nodded.

"Do you remember that my father had two cars, a Duesenberg and a Willys Overland convertible?"

"Yes, I do remember."

"Uncle Philip bought the Willys Overland from Father. All the papers came through. The day he was leaving, Uncle Philip, on the way to the ship to load the car—"

"Oh, no," she moaned.

"He was so excited," Josef sobbed, "he went through a red light."

"And that was that?"

Josef nodded, wiped his eyes, took a deep, shaking breath. "Bad luck. They caught him; he was 'taken into protective custody,' as it was euphemistically phrased. And later . . ."

"My God!" A whisper.

"Yes, my God."

Josef, leaning against the table, and she against the desk, lost in their own thoughts, were silent for some moments. Then she looked hard at him as though gauging the strength of her next assault.

"Did something happen today?" Her voice shook. "One makes mistakes . . ."

"No . . . no."

"In surgery?"

He brushed her words away. "It's nothing like that," he said. "Elizabeth, I've got to go."

"Carlos said you blew up at a resident."

Josef grimaced.

"He said you overreacted."

"Overreacted! Good Lord!" Josef exploded, pounding his fist so hard on the desk that the ashtray jumped, dumping the butts all over. "My God, Elizabeth, I couldn't have been down the hall for more than five minutes, and you two seem to have covered my entire history. What else did that shiny ape tell you?"

"He told me—" She stopped.

"Yes! Yes! Why stop now?"

"He said that he never knew you were Jewish."

"You *told* him I was a *Jew?*"

She nodded, her eyes wide. "He said he worked with you for five years at McGill—that he thought the two of you were quite close—and that he always assumed you were a German."

"A German!" Josef glared at her contemptuously.

"I would never have said anything—but I assumed, being so close to you, that he knew."

"Knew what? That I am a Jew? Am I, Elizabeth? Am I not a German? After all, my father's family are Prussians—Christians

—from way back. And my mother's lived on 'German soil' since the late fifteenth century—almost five hundred years. Doesn't that make me a German? They were Spanish Jews, my mother's family. They lived in Spain for centuries—that is, until Charley Borbon's ancestors financed the Inquisition and they had to flee to Germany—1492, just about the time Christopher Columbus was discovering America, the land of the free. So you see, Elizabeth, maybe I'm really a Spaniard like Charley, who, by the way, was born in New York City and raised on a farm in Iowa, and who is discriminated against because some people here consider him a Hispanic American, not a nice thing to be in this country of liberty.

"But I'm lucky; with my name and face, no one can tell what I am—that I'm really nothing at all, or, if anything, that I'm a crossbreed, a monstrosity halfway between man and ape." Clutching the briefcase with the succinylcholine and Librium tightly under his arm, Josef opened the door of the examining room.

"Josef."

He turned to her. "But Auguste LaRivière—that dear man—there is no hiding what he is."

"Who is Auguste LaRivière?"

"A chemist who took his doctorate at the Sorbonne."

Josef stepped into the hall and slammed the door shut.

"Josef," he could hear her call as he hurried down the corridor. He had lost track of time. It was one forty-five and the banks closed at two. He mapped out the route in his mind: the little ravine, the overpass over Riverside Drive, the Iowa Avenue bridge over the river, up the steps of Old Capitol, and a cut through the Pentacrest. Twelve minutes, he estimated—if he ran—getting him to the bank three minutes before closing. Once he was inside, they would have to let him into his safety-deposit box. Elizabeth, he was certain, would not wait until two fifty *en punto* to telephone Carlos but would track him down at once, ruining, most likely, the rest of Carlos's day.

PART IV

1944–1945
BERLIN

CHAPTER · SIX

Liberation of Paris

I, carrying the twenty baited bottles in the wire basket, and Tatiana, the map, set off through the park to capture the little *Berlin wilds* and to steal apples for the staff dinner the Chief proclaimed for that joyous night: August 26, 1944. Paris had been liberated the day before by the Americans.

After all the bottles were placed, we hid behind the large shrub which concealed Mitzka's secret passageway to the orchard, and I crawled through, ran to the trees, filled the wire basket with the green apples, made a bag of my white lab coat, tied it around my neck, stuffed it and my pockets and my shirtfront, then crawled back to her, on three paws, pushing the basket along, a most willing dog, holding the most beautiful apple, with a touch of red, in my other paw for her.

"Ah!" Tatiana sniffed the apple. "It smells just like apples."

We laughed.

The celebration started after dark, at ten, in our Biology Lab, and was restricted to personnel from Genetics and Evolution, specials, and wives. The only exceptions were the Rare Earths Chemist, who worked for Mantle, and Marlene, who came with her husband, the Dutch Medical Student. Lab assistants were excluded. Sonja Press was there, of course, and Tatiana, who was special.

Flasks of flowers from Gunther the gardener decorated the tables, and there were baskets of the polished green apples; bowls of sunflower seeds from the greenhouse in the park; and, from the garden adjoining the greenhouse, plates of radishes, carrots, and tomatoes and bowls of boiled potatoes and green beans. There were platters of baked rabbit, basins of polenta, flasks of molasses, pitchers of hot tea, and, of course, beakers and beakers of vodka.

The tables were arranged in a square, with the seating as follows:

Grand Duke	Madame Avilov	Chief	Prof. Kreutzer	Frau Kreutzer
Ignatov				Rabin
Yugoslav				Rare Earths Chemist
Krupinsky				Frau Doktor
Frau Krupinsky				François Daniel
Bolotnikov Treponesco				Dutch Medical Student
Tatiana	Reserved for Mitzka	Sonja Press	Josef Bernhardt	Marlene

I did not even try to sit next to Tatiana, because she had put a flask with autumn weeds—chrysanthemums and snapdragons—on the plate next to her, a signal that Mitzka would appear. The Roumanian Biologist George Treponesco had as usual shoved his way to her other side by putting a chair at the corner, infuriating that fat dumpling Bolotnikov, who had forgone more prestigious seating in order to be next to her. The French Physicist François Daniel, who was also quite interested in Tatiana, had some perverted Parisian idea that to win a beautiful woman one must pretend to be "disinterested," so instead of jockeying to be near her, he sat beside Frau Doktor and acted charming.

The dinner began as a jolly occasion. There were toasts to the Allies—especially to America—and many congratulations to François Daniel, who at one point gained everyone's attention by shouting out, "We French were dealing the lethal blow!"

"Tell me one thing the French did," yelled Krupinsky. "One thing!"

François Daniel stood. Head bowed, hand on heart, he said, *"N'oubliez pas nos femmes."*

"Translate, you crazy *poilu*," hollered Krupinsky.

"Don't forget our women! They demoralized the entire German occupation army."

"You're damn right!" Krupinsky jumped to his feet. "They sucked them dry. To the women of France, a toast."

All the men stood and drank and sat.

Madame Avilov, smiling, raised her glass. "I, too, will drink to the beautiful women of France and also to the men. They are wonderful, you know."

"Madame," said Krupinsky, "don't you think you are going a bit too far?"

"No, I do not go too far." There was light in her pale eyes. "The men of France are the most sensitive, the greatest diplomats in the world."

Applause and boos. Laughter.

"Nikolai Alexandrovich, tell us your wonderful story about French diplomacy." Madame turned to her husband.

"Ah, yes," said the Chief. "You must all listen to this. At a banquet celebrating the fiftieth birthday of a reigning Queen, whose name I wll not mention for the sake of tact . . ."

Laughter.

". . . every country contributed a typical dish to the meal. The *frijoles refritos* from Mexico, the *garbanzos* from Spain, and so on, very soon affected the delicate digestion of the Queen. In a moment of silence, one could hear, very definitely from the seat of honor, the sound of air escaping.

"Immediately, the French Ambassador, purple-faced, was on his feet saying, 'Madame, I beg you, *mille pardons,* but my digestive system has been very labile. I have been warned by my doctor to eat bland foods but have been unable to resist these delicacies.'

"This, of course, was a serious diplomatic defeat for the other ambassadors present, and was particularly felt by the representative of the Third Reich, one Joachim von Ribbentrop."

We all laughed.

"With a keen ear, he awaited another such happening from the royal presence, and when it occurred, he jumped to his feet, clicked his heels, and bowed, shouting, 'Madame, this one and the next three are for the Third Reich.'"

Even Professor Kreutzer removed his glasses to wipe the tears of laughter from his eyes. Grand Duke Trusov jumped to his feet and said, "I propose a toast not only to the marvelous women, not only to the liberation of the most beautiful city in the world, but also to the greatest diplomats."

Everybody stood but Krupinsky, even the women, and we waited for him, chanting, "Up. Up. Up," until he, too, stood.

"I'll drink to that," he said. "But we must drink also to the Nazis, who are so incredibly stupid, thank heavens, that even the French can outwit them."

All drank and laughed and wept and sat.

"My friends," said Professor Kreutzer, "do not underestimate them."

"You must admit, Max," said the Chief, "they haven't used their heads. Why didn't they aim the V-One rockets at the ports and embarkation points for the Normandy invasion rather than at the civilian population of Britain? Correct? Or am I right?"

"Yes, of course you are right."

"And now there stands between Paris and Germany—nothing. It is a matter of marching through. It should be very few weeks."

Applause.

Professor Kreutzer stood and began to change to the black-rims. All became quiet.

"My friends," he said, "you must remember that also there was nothing between Normandy and Paris, and it took the Allies from June to August twenty-fifth to liberate that city. I wish also to remind you that we must proceed prudently as we always have done.

"For the past year my pleading with you to cut consumption of fuel and water has been successful. Now I must plead that you use more. I do not want us to underconsume so that our budget is cut or so that attention is drawn to what we do here. I should not have to remind you that since the twentieth of July, when the officers of the army revolted, the Nazi reaction has been fierce, and times are even more difficult. You all know this. The animal is wounded. The liberation of France will cripple it more. In its pain it will strike out. Caution," he said. "Careful."

He sat.

We began to eat in earnest. There was quiet discussion around the square of tables. Will it be the Russians or the Americans? Of course, everyone wanted to be liberated by the Americans. How long will it be until they come? Shall the windows be kept closed in order not to contaminate the wild flies in the park—the *Drosophila melanogaster Berlin wild*—with the purebreds? How can one keep the females from ovulating and the male flies from ejaculating and losing their sperm load under anesthetic? What is the future of atomic power?

Abruptly, Tatiana jumped to her feet. "Shhh." She put a finger to her lips. "I hear something."

At once, all fell silent. Shouting in the park. Then machine-gun fire and rifles, a *ratatatat* and eight or ten single cracking shots. The blackout curtains were drawn, so we could not see out.

"Mitzka!" shrieked Madame. "Mitzka-aaaaa," she wailed, rising to her feet.

"Shhh!" admonished Professor Kreutzer.

Electric silence.

Madame sat down again.

I glanced at Tatiana. All color had drained from her face.

"I'm getting the hell out of here!" The Roumanian Biologist George Treponesco jumped to his feet.

"Sit down!" roared the Chief.

Treponesco sat down.

Professor Kreutzer stood. "Do not panic," he said. "That is the worst thing you can do."

"But I don't want to get caught with these people," said Treponesco, morosely.

"You will remain here," said the Chief. "You will all listen to Max."

Professor Kreutzer did not bother with a spectacle-changing routine. "Sonja," he said, "telephone the Security Officer and tell him to meet me in the lobby at once."

She ran to the phone in the corner of the lab.

Professor Kreutzer then addressed the Chief, but loud enough so that we all could hear. "Alex, I will go and see. You stay here and carry on as though it is a normal staff dinner. It would be foolish to act in haste."

Sonja called out to Professor Kreutzer from the back of the lab, "He's on his way."

"Now locate Herr Wagenführer and tell him to be prepared to come over. Do you understand? We do not want him to come now, but he is on call." Professor Kreutzer checked his pockets to be sure his spectacles were in place, then walked swiftly from the lab. It was eleven. We had celebrated for one hour.

There was no conversation now. All sat silent, listening for sounds from the park or from the corridor outside the lab. The Rare Earths Chemist excused himself. "I will be right back," he said and left the room.

I went over to Tatiana and put my hand on her arm to comfort her. She shook me away. I returned to my place at the table. Did she imagine Mitzka in love with her? He sat by her at staff dinners only because she was the prettiest girl.

Sonja, after completing her call to Herr Wagenführer, pulled up a chair next to Madame, held her hand, and talked softly.

The Chief, without rising, lifted his glass and said, "Let us drink and eat while we wait." But he did not drink.

Nor did any of us. There was occasional muted conversation around the table now but no eating and no drinking. Mostly we strained our ears to listen. No more shots. Men's voices in the park, waxing and waning, then silence. Silence in the corridors until, half an hour after Professor Kreutzer left us, he returned, followed by the Gestapo in the House in his black uniform of the S.S., carrying a red balalaika in one hand. Mitzka.

All talk stopped. I had never seen the Security Officer at a staff dinner before. The Chief jumped up. His chair fell. Professor Kreutzer rushed to his side and put a restraining hand on the Chief's arm. The Security Officer limped to where they stood at the head of the table and held out the balalaika. His mouth was open. No words. He trembled.

"Speak!" roared the Chief.

"I didn't know. I knew nothing. He was denounced by someone here, but it was not I. I swear it."

Professor Kreutzer cautioned the Chief with a raised finger and a shaking of his head.

"They got him outside. They caught him at the back of the park," said the frightened man.

"Who was it?" The Chief grabbed the black lapels and pulled the Security Officer toward him.

"Alex," said Professor Kreutzer, "I will tell you. Please sit down." He said a few quiet words to the Security Officer, took the red balalaika from him, and placed it on the table before the Avilovs.

The Security Officer left the lab.

Professor Kreutzer leaned over between the Chief and Madame

and spoke softly to them. When he was through, the Chief stood to tell us.

"My friends"—he paused and looked around the tables as though to embrace each and every one of us—"Max informs us that the Gestapo have shot him. They say he ran into the park trying to escape and that he is dead."

The Chief bent his body. His large hand encompassed his glass of vodka. He shrugged, and, body still bowed, he raised his head to see us. "I am too sad to be proud. I am too sad to be angry. Mitzka was a man. He did as he wished, knowing the consequences." He stood straight, raised the glass. "A Gestapo in the House does not always save one from a Caesarean section." And he threw the vodka down his throat, then smashed the glass on the table. He cut his hand.

The Russian pianist, Stanislas Rabin, sitting next to Frau Kreutzer, stood, drank, and threw his glass, with great force, onto the floor. Each man, in turn, did the same: Professor Kreutzer, the Grand Duke, Ignatov, the Yugoslav, Krupinsky, Bolotnikov, Treponesco, the Dutch Medical Student, François Daniel. I, too, in my turn. All but the Rare Earths Chemist, who had not returned. The Chief picked up the red balalaika from the table and carried it to where I sat. His hand was bleeding profusely.

"Play!" he said, shoving it into my hands.

"I don't know how."

Mitzka had tried to teach me, but it was not my music. Tatiana jumped up, grabbed the balalaika away from me, and began to play a rhythmic folk melody, sad and in a minor key. Russian. Bolotnikov sang along—without words—with a "Yah, dee, dah, dee dah." The Yugoslav stood and swayed in time to the music, then jumped onto the table, and, in the midst of all the plates and bowls and beakers, he danced.

Professor Kreutzer, raising his voice to be heard over the noise, said, "Krup, you'd better take a look at Alex's hand."

"Josef, come along," said Krupinsky tersely, and the Chief, Professor Kreutzer, Krupinsky, and I moved to a dark corner of the lab where most of the medical supplies were stored.

The Chief insisted on standing. I held a lamp while Krupinsky tweezed out the glass, cleansed, stitched, and bound the wound. It was a deep cut in the web between thumb and forefinger of the right hand. "It will be five or six stitches. Would you like a local?"

"Sew it up," growled the Chief, "and hurry. Are you certain," he said to Professor Kreutzer, "that he has not gone to lead them up here?"

"I checked in Rare Earths. He made it quite obvious that he took a supply of strophanthin with him."

"Then he plans to kill himself."

"Latte is positive that the denunciation was *only* against Mitzka and his companion—and done only to save himself. It seems the Gestapo had been pressuring him for information." Latte was the name of the Security Officer.

"I hope he waits to take the strophanthin. If he dies too soon, it will draw attention to us. Damn it, Krup, aren't you through fiddling with my hand yet?"

"Hold still, damn it. Two more stitches."

"Obviously, they need to be fed more denunciations," said Professor Kreutzer. "We have become careless."

"Ah, yes, the gods must have sacrificed to them so many virgins, so many youths. We could try the alcohol again."

"We've done that too many times. Let me think about it."

"Hold still, Chief, please. I've just got to bandage it. Josef, hand me the gauze—and hold that lamp still!"

"Do you know the name of the other lad?" the Chief asked.

"Schmidt. Dieter Schmidt."

"What will they do with him?"

Professor Kreutzer shrugged.

"Are you sure they will not search for others?"

"No. Latte told me that they knew there would be two only—Mitzka and the Schmidt boy. They are propitiated. And Alex, they were told by our friend, most clearly, that the denunciation of your son and his 'comrade' came from you because of your hatred of Communists and your devotion to Adolf Hitler. I corroborated this tonight. You will be called upon to do the same."

"Corroborate," muttered the Chief.

"You must do it."

"I will. I will. Is there anything we can do for young Schmidt?"

"Nothing. He's as good as dead."

"He'd be better off dead. Ask our Gestapo in the House if there is anything we can do."

"There's no use, Alex. We must not endanger the rest by contradictory actions.

"At least ask Latte. That can do no harm."

"It's done, Chief," said Krupinsky. "You might want your arm in a sling to keep from banging it."

"No, thank you, Krup. Thank you very much. Max, what of Mitzka?"

"They would not leave the body. I made a small plea for the sake of Madame. I'm sorry. I could not push them."

"Of course not. Krup, I want you to give Madame a sedative—a strong one."

"O.K. Will you be taking her home?"

"What do you think, Max, is it safe to walk her across the park?"

"They are gone, I tell you. They have what they came for."

Sonja Press and Frau Doktor escorted Madame Avilov home and stayed the night with her. Krupinsky went along to administer a sedative, then returned to the lab. Professor Kreutzer, who also had a house in the park, took his young wife home and returned at once. He never allowed her to stay for the parties. I don't blame him. She was much younger than he and very pretty. The Dutch Medical Student and Marlene went home.

The Chief and everyone else stayed on. The girls from Die Scala showed up near midnight. By that time an accordion and another balalaika had appeared, the tables were pushed against the wall, the glass was swept under the tables, and the party had begun in earnest. At first, Professor Kreutzer preached caution. "Careful," he said, removing his spectacles and looking severe. The Chief, beyond reason, would not listen, and ordered me to fetch more jugs of vodka from labs on other floors. They drank and danced, wild Russian dances, all but Professor Kreutzer, the Krupinskys, Tatiana, and me. Tatiana was perched on a worktable, her feet on the chair, playing Mitzka's balalaika; I stood near her. Mitzka was, of course, running to escape through the apples when they shot him.

The wake became so wild, that Tatiana—Tanya—still playing the balalaika, sidled over to the edge of the table, nearer to me. The clowns had begun to line up to pay her drunken court, and I think it made her feel uneasy. One of the first was the Frenchman, François Daniel: he muttered a few quiet words to her, then stopped in front of me.

"You will never win her," he said. "Never," he repeated. "You will never learn to keep the distance until she is ready."

When the greatest buffoon of them all, the Roumanian Biologist George Treponesco, staggering drunk, paid his call, squatting at her feet, embracing her legs, she completely recoiled in disgust. I disentangled his arms from her legs and pushed him backward onto his *derrière,* and she, holding the balalaika above her head to keep it from harm, jumped to her feet and took my arm. That ass Treponesco rolled over and actually crawled away on all fours.

We joined Professor Kreutzer and the Krupinskys, who stood near the door, stonily staring at the bedlam. The lab was a disaster. Drinking was encouraged at staff dinners, and, usually, there was a strenuous party afterward with the ballet girls and all, but it was always within some sort of limits. Everyone would help clean up from the dinner, put everything away, and push the tables back in place, so that next day the routine work of the lab could be carried out. That was most important to the Chief, the research. But oh, my good Lord, the tables had been shoved back helter-skelter with all the food and dishes still on them, there was broken glass everywhere, and the Chief was as I'd never seen him. He always drank a lot, but I had never seen him drunk before, and there he was, squatting on the floor, trying to do the *tcherzatskaya,* but so looped he had to be held up by two Die Scala girls, one on each side. His great head was thrown back, his mouth opened wide while Bolotnikov poured vodka down his throat. The others were drinking and jumping and shouting and clapping, encouraging him. He always danced the *tcherzatskaya* for us—we all loved it when he did this—but he'd never needed anyone to hold him up. He was panting like some great beast; his face was beet red, and he was sweating copiously.

"He'll have a heart attack," said Krupinsky, tapping his own chest, as though he were in pain.

Professor Kreutzer pointed to the door. The Krupinskys, Tanya, and I followed him down the hallway until it was quiet enough for us to converse in low voices. Tanya had taken Mitzka's balalaika with her for fear it would be broken in the frenzy.

"How long," Professor Kreutzer asked Krupinsky, "can they keep this up?"

"Hours—it's after one thirty now—there's no way of knowing." He tapped his chest, again, as though he were in pain.

Professor Kreutzer took a glasses case from his breast pocket, removed from it the black-rims, which he held to the light, squinting at them through the gold-rims he was wearing; then, instead of cleaning the black-rims—which was the next step in the routine—he shoved them back into the case and into his pocket. "The best thing we can do is get some rest. I will stretch out in Physics. I suggest that all of you find a quiet place. It's too late, in any case, to get the train."

"I will go to my room," Tanya said. It was in a building in the park.

The door to our Biology Laboratory opened, and Rabin stepped timidly into the hall, looking this way and that before walking over to us and making a brief statement in Russian.

"He says," Krupinsky translated, "that he is not very drunk."

"Ask him how much longer it will go on."

"He doesn't know," translated Krupinsky. "Two hours, three."

Rabin shrugged apologetically and spoke again. This time Tanya translated. "He will play for us," she said.

"Fine," said Professor Kreutzer. "I will be in my lab if you need me, and I will meet you, in any case, at seven, in the cafeteria kitchen downstairs."

The Krupinskys, Tanya, and I followed Rabin down the stairs and into the parlor. Krupinsky and his wife nestled close together on one couch; Rabin settled at the piano, eyes closed, head bent, as though asleep; Tanya and I sat apart on the same couch. She held Mitzka's balalaika on her knees. Rabin hit the keys and the hair on the back of my neck stood up: an orgy of Rachmaninoff and Tchaikovsky—magnificent, technically perfect, passionate, some pieces over and over without stopping.

Berlin is cold at two o'clock in the morning, even in August. I left the parlor long enough to fetch two woolen blankets from the bomb shelter in the basement. I tucked one around the Krupinskys, huddled lovingly together. Frau Krupinsky kissed my cheek. The other I took to where Tanya sat, tight against the end of the couch. She put Mitzka's balalaika down beside her, where I had assumed I would sit, took the blanket from me, and covered herself. I could have fetched another for myself, but I did not. And I did not sit again on her couch, but chose, rather, to listen until dawn from a hard chair as far from her as possible.

At seven, Professor Kreutzer joined us in the cafeteria kitchen and, over a hurried cup of tea, gave us instructions: Krupinsky was to check to see how Madame Avilov was doing, then see if Sonja and/or Frau Doktor could be spared to help with the cleanup, which Tanya and I were to begin at once.

The Krupinskys left to cross the park to the Chief's house. Professor Kreutzer, Tanya, and I walked through the lobby just as Grand Duke Trusov came down the front stairs—a Die Scala dancer on each arm—looking for a cup of tea. He glanced out the windows, dropped his dancers, and came tearing toward us.

"Max!" he shouted. "An inspection team!"

We all ran to the windows. Three black cars—two Mercedeses and a Thule—were coming around the circular drive.

Professor Kreutzer snapped orders: "Tatiana, run after Krupinsky and tell him to come back. You, Duke, find Alex—he's probably asleep in his office—and tell the dancers to vanish." To me, he said, "Telephone the Security Officer and tell him to hurry over. Quickly."

I raced up the stairs to the phone in my lab, then decided it would be safer to use the private telephone in the Chief's penthouse office. Grand Duke Trusov was already there bending over the Chief, who was collapsed on the floor, clad only in a shirt, a Die Scala girl naked in his arms. The Grand Duke couldn't waken either of them. He was slapping their faces and dousing them with cold water.

"Bernhardt," he ordered, "run down to my lab and get some vodka. That will wake him up."

Through the window, I saw the Krupinskys running cross the lawn. I telephoned the Security Officer. Krupinsky came dashing up the outside steps to the penthouse and into the office.

"Good Christ, Duke!" he shouted. "What are you trying to do, drown him?" Krupinsky turned to his wife. "Run to the lab and get my stethoscope and sphygmomanometer." He knelt beside the Chief to take his pulse. "Listen, Duke, you go down to Chemistry and get me two ampules of Polybion, one Bexatin Fortissimum, and one Cebion Forte."

"Vitamins?" shouted the Duke. "Vitamins? Why don't you give him a shot of Adrenalin?"

"I want to wake him up, not kill him, damn you. His only son got murdered last night, he is dead drunk—what the hell do you think his blood pressure might be?" He turned to me.

"Josef, run along to the lab and get a new sterile syringe, needles, cotton, and alcohol."

My good Lord, the lab was in chaos: rabbit bones, broken glass, dirty dishes, congealed polenta, apple cores, Bolotnikov asleep under one table, and the Roumanian Biologist George Treponesco and a girl under another. Tanya had begun to clear away the mess on the worktables. The morning sorting of *Drosophila* would have to be done no matter what else was going on.

I hurried back to the penthouse.

"One hundred sixty over one hundred and ten," said Krupinsky. "Lift the girl off and help me turn him over."

The Chief muttered and shook his head at the needles but did not wake up.

"I want to get his head down. Don't want him aspirating vomitus."

We wrapped the Chief in a blanket, dragged and carried him through the outer office, and laid him on his stomach down the stairs. Grand Duke Trusov and I, at the top of the stairwell, held his feet, and Krupinsky sat by his head, talking quietly.

"Hi, Chief. Time to get up. Good morning. The sky is blue, and we have visitors."

The leonine head shook away the sound.

"Good morning, Chief. Another day, another dollar, your pulse is steadier, time to get up."

Eyes opened. *Blink.*

"Good morning, Chief. How's the head?"

Blink. "Krupinsky, is it true that I am hanging down the staircase?"

"True."

"I cannot understand what this fuss is all about. I was extremely tired and was only resting." He tried to jump to his feet, but, of course, it was impossible. Head down again, eyes closed. "Tell them to let go of my feet."

"Just a minute, Chief. We have a logistics problem. Listen, Duke, you and Josef swing his legs around, and for Christ's sake, both of you move in the same direction—I've got his shoulders: Christ, Chief, you are heavy—and let's get him all on one stair."

The Chief sat up. "Take this damn blood pressure cuff off me," he growled. "Why didn't you let me sleep?"

"Chief, there's an inspection team downstairs," said Krupinsky. "What is it they want?"

"I don't know," said the Grand Duke. "Max is with them."

"All right." The Chief jumped to his feet, wrapping the blanket around himself. "Josef, be a good boy and brew me a pitcher of tea. Strong. And bring it to me in my shower. And Krup, will you stop fiddling with that damned stethoscope. There's nothing wrong with me."

The dancer was still asleep on the floor of the Chief's office. Krupinsky took her blood pressure, and then he and the Duke wrapped her up in a blanket and carried her to the darkroom on the third floor, leaving Frau Krupinsky to watch her.

The Chief drank the first four cups of tea under water. When Professor Kreutzer stepped into the bathroom, the Chief emerged from the shower holding the fifth cup. He beckoned to me to hand him the huge bath towel hanging on a hook, and gave me, in exchange, the cup and saucer. "What is it they want, Max?" He began to dry himself.

"It is, again, the Ministry for the Coordination of Total War Effort—eleven 'inspectors.' They want, and I quote them, 'to see the linear accelerator and know its place in the atomic potential of the Third Reich.'"

"Are they scientists?"

"Only one. He's not a physicist, but a biologist, and not quite as stupid as the rest. The others are the average Party officials—

grocers and schoolteachers. I told them, of course, that the work here is Top Secret and that they must undergo strict security clearance—which would take some time, several hours or so. Latte is interviewing each one separately, then checking their clearance. He will let six or seven through, but for sure not the scientist."

"Our Gestapo in the House is not too useful, is he?" The Chief enveloped himself in the great white towel.

"He's as surprised as we."

"This inspection has nothing to do with what happened last night?" the Chief asked quietly.

"No. I am almost certain it is coincidental, although both are reactions to the twentieth of July and to the liberation of France. It will get worse."

The Chief nodded, grimly. "I see. What time is it?"

"Eight fifteen. The security check will keep them busy for at least another hour."

"How much time do we need to get the Biology Lab cleaned up, the flies sorted, and a demonstration made ready in the Radiation Lab?"

"As much time as you can give me."

"Then I will lecture to them in a meeting room on the first floor for three hours." His hair still dripping wet and plastered onto his forehead, the huge white towel wrapped about him like a toga, the Chief raised his right arm and began an oration in his penthouse shower room. "I will begin with Empedocles and Democritus, from the Greek *atomos,* 'indivisible,' hence, 'that which cannot be split,' and on through Dalton and Thomson and to our good friend, Niels Bohr, with his simplistic image of a miniature solar system, with its planetary electrons in circular orbit about the nucleus, but one must not mention Einstein to the officials from the Ministry for the Coordination of Total War Effort of the Third Reich. No! But I will say that now, with all we know since Democritus, we are unable to measure or conjecture, for it is wave yet particle, empty yet full, forward yet backward. It trembles, sputters, radiates, expands, collapses, splits, absorbs, discharges, and reappears. And though we cannot define it, we can release, in theory, its power. And then I will give them an equation, a formula for population casualties—I'll need a blackboard for that—and I'll tell them about fallout, *retombées radioactives, radio actionye ossadkye.* Then I'll show slides, myself." He looked at me.

"Hide this boy," he said, "and the others. Tell our Alsatian friend to switch the records of all our specials and keep them out of here.

"I will show them slides of radiation burns, of destroyed bone marrow, of grotesque mutations in rats. I will talk for exactly three hours. And then, Max, you can put on a show in the Radiation Laboratory, after which we will serve them dinner in the dining room downstairs and answer any questions they might have."

"I'll need the boy," said Professor Kreutzer.

"No. Let him hide upstairs with Krup. We have lost enough boys."

"I need him in the Radiation Laboratory. He will be all right."

I was to remove the shielding from the ultraviolet lamp, a mercury-vapor arc enclosed in quartz, so that it would fill the room and do two things: make the air smell of ozone and make certain things glow—teeth, buttons, fingernails, and the collection of minerals I took from the Rare Earths Laboratory. The Rare Earths Chemist was not there, so I had to take them myself.

When I was finished with that, Professor Kreutzer and I rigged up an old spark rectifier which had a point as an anode and a flat plate as a cathode, and when it reached approximately 250,000 volts, a spark jumped almost twenty inches every ten or fifteen seconds. And then we reconnected an old x-ray tube whose anticathode was radiation-cooled, so after a while it emitted very bright lights.

After that, we tidied up the Radiation Laboratory: picked up the tools, oil rags, glass tubing, and all the other junk lying around on the floor.

Finally, we tested our equipment and had a dress rehearsal of our light show, beginning with Professor Kreutzer and his terrifying lightning arrester. Even without our theatrical tricks, the Radiation Laboratory was a frightening place, with its high-tension, high-voltage equipment. It is ironic, though, that the greatest danger—the radiation—is not picked up at all by the senses.

These preparations and the rehearsal took until noon—well over three hours—and when Professor Kreutzer had no more use for me, I went into my lab. They seemed to have everything under control. Sonja, the Krupinskys, and the Yugoslav were carrying the last of the dishes, all washed and dried, down the hall to Physics, where, most likely, they wouldn't be noticed among the junk. Tanya and Frau Doktor were sorting the flies.

I walked over to them and said, "Good afternoon."

Tanya ignored my salutation.

Frau Doktor turned to me. "Good afternoon, Josef. How are you?"

"Fine, thank you, Frau Doktor."

"He was a close friend of yours, wasn't he?"

"We were schoolmates since I was nine—and friends since I was twelve."

"He is . . . was your age then?"

"Older. Mitzka was almost twenty."

Tanya twisted in her chair and looked up at me. "And you are eighteen!" she said unpleasantly.

"He was a brave young man," said Frau Doktor. "A great loss."

"*He* was a hero!" snapped Tanya, accenting the *he*.

"And *I* am a coward!" I answered, accenting the *I*.

"I didn't mean it that way," she said.

"Oh? What did you mean?"

"Please," said Frau Doktor. "This is no time for dissension."

Tanya jumped to her feet and walked quickly to the far corner of the lab. I followed.

She had deep shadows under her eyes, making them look bigger, and her thick long hair was working loose from the green ribbon that always held it back. I wanted to put my arm about her to comfort her.

"Do you really want to know what I've been thinking?" she said.

I nodded.

"May I be frank?"

"By all means."

"I think that you waste your time and talent."

"What has that to do with my cowardice?"

"Nothing. I don't know why I said that. And Mitzka . . . he was brave, but also very foolish." She began to cry. She was so very tired. "His activities with the underground are one thing, but coming back here—to show off—was another. It was dangerous for him and put all of us in jeopardy—his own father and mother! He put *my life* in danger. *My life!* He was a fool!" Tanya sobbed.

"I didn't know you felt that way about him. I thought—"

"You thought I was in love with him. Well, you don't know the first thing about me, Josef Bernhardt. Everybody loved Mitzka. He was dazzling. But there is a difference between loving someone and being 'in love' with someone." Tears were streaming down her face. "And besides, I don't think he was capable of loving anybody—but himself."

Ah, so she knew he didn't love her. I put my hand on her arm to comfort her, but she jerked violently away from me.

"And you," she sobbed. "Josef, I don't think of you as a coward."

"And how else can you think of me, hiding here under the umbrella of his father, while Mitzka loses his life to help others?"

"How do I think of you?" she said in a quiet, quavering voice. "I think of you as brilliant. I have been told that you have a genius for mathematics—that you could be a great mathematician. But you are already eighteen years old and would have to begin to work for it now." She took a deep, shaking breath. "But instead, what do you do? You waste your time. You go to the darkroom with every girl at the Institute."

So that was it. "Every girl?"

Her tears had stopped. "You know what I mean."

What could I say? "Every girl" was a gross exaggeration. As a matter of fact, since Marlene got pregnant, Monika was almost the only one who actually had sex with me in the darkroom. The others whom I had been seeing regularly—two girls from Chemistry—had an apartment in the village of Hagen and insisted I come there. It was awkward: I had to climb up the drainpipe in the dark, after their landlady was asleep, and sneak out again before she woke up. I would have preferred the darkroom, but every girl had her own form of discretion.

"If you wonder why I have not been sitting by you at the staff dinners, it is because I can't stand men who cannot control their animal appetites."

"Yes?" I said sarcastically. "And yet you sit by that Roumanian, Treponesco?"

"I don't care about him!" It was a wail.

There was a commotion at the door to the lab. Professor Kreutzer had just come in with Herr Wagenführer, who was clapping his hands to gain everyone's attention: "Attention, everyone. The following people will report to the Luftwaffe, Squadron Clerk, Sixth Floor, for work assignments for the remainder of the day: Professor François Marie Daniel, Tatiana Rachel Backhaus, Eric van Leyden, Professor Igor Vasilovich Bolotnikov"—he paused and took a deep breath—"and Professor Dmitri Varvilovovich Tsechetverikov. At this time, I cannot tell you how long before you can go back to your regular work. You will be informed. Hurry, there is no time for questions. Josef Leopold Bernhardt?" He looked about for me.

"Here!"

"You will be employed by the Mantle Corporation today and are assigned to Professor Kreutzer here. Make haste, all of you. There is no time." He clapped his hands again.

"What about my wife?" shouted Krupinsky, as the specials hurried from the room. "She's here, too."

"Darkroom," said Herr Wagenführer, as he hurried from the lab.

The Chief, finished with his three-hour lecture, escorted the inspectors to the hallway outside the Radiation Laboratory, where Professor Kreutzer dressed them elaborately: extra lead plates over their genitals; lead aprons around their shoulders like a cape, covering their entire bodies; safety glasses. In through the pneumatic doors they walked, smelling the ozone, seeing the purple phosphorescent glow, and Professor Kreutzer with the lightning arrester making sparks, crackles, *bangs,* hisses, and lightning, and the sparks flying, the bright lights emitting from the x-ray tube, and the corona glowing about the high-voltage condensers, cold colors of the spectrum—blue, white, violet. And I, hidden in the dark control booth, pulled the levers. Through the thick windows of glass and water, I could see the purple phosphorescent glow of the teeth of the inspectors from the Ministry for the Coordination of Total War Effort.

Fingernails and buttons glowing, and teeth in the grimaced faces, the seven inspectors who passed our Gestapo's strict security check huddled, terrified, in a corner of the Radiation Laboratory, as far from the linear accelerator as they could get. The biologist was not among them. Did they think we had enough energy to make a bomb, when in reality all we could do with the little atom smasher Professor Kreutzer made, himself, out of bits and scraps, was irradiate a few flies—if they were left long enough on the target?

The Chief often said that Adolf Hitler must have astute advisers who told him, all along, that Germany did not have the capacity to develop these weapons. On the offchance, however, heavy water was made available from Norway, and a small amount of experimentation was allowed, as if someone was hoping for a miracle, some breakthrough, afraid to let go altogether, for, after all, it was all there in theory. But the technical aspects—anyone with any kind of a brain and some basic knowledge knew that technically it could not be achieved without untold space and untold wealth. But these people were desperate, looking for some miracle to help them, hoping they were seeing it in the purple phosphorescent glow.

We hadn't even turned on the linear accelerator. Why take the chance, Professor Kreutzer said, that one of the inspectors would be harmed by the radiation or why take the chance that the linear accelerator, itself, would be harmed by the high voltage I was throwing through? After all, it was the center of the Institute. The Chief said it often enough after a vodka or three: "This place is a cow with three hundred teats," he would bellow, "and the linear accelerator is the bull, and with the coupling of the two, Max and I have pressure over some government officials who have interests in certain businesses which produce things—counting amplifiers or pumps, for example. But to produce these counting amplifiers and pumps, these businesses need raw materials and labor, and for this they need authorization permits, which must be issued by other government officials who, in turn, are made silent partners in the businesses which produce the counting amplifiers and pumps, and who, therefore, are interested in finding research projects which need the products that happen to have the exact specifications of those manufactured by the businesses."

I thought it like the *Contes de ma mère l'oie*—the *Mother Goose* Mother had read to me when I was quite young. It wasn't "The House That Jack Built," but, rather, "The House That Fission Built": This was the house the scientists built, that enriched the government officials and the manufacturers, who protected one another and the Institute, that protected its scientists and workers, who used the Radiation Laboratory to retard the cancer of the Gestapo in the House, who, in return, kept the Chief and Professor Kreutzer informed, and who cleverly denounced the Institute in small, intelligent, harmless ways, regularly enough to keep the pressure off. For example, it was the Security Officer who re-quested—at the suggestion of Professor Kreutzer—that the ethyl alcohol be delivered adulterated with petrol ether. But it was not he who offered Mitzka as the scapegoat. It was, of course, the Rare Earths Chemist. He had been harassed for information. Denouncing Mitzka, he must have felt, would take pressure off him without jeopardizing the good, secure life he enjoyed at the Institute.

. . .

One month after Mitzka's murder, the police telephoned the Institute to report that an employee had died of a heart attack the night before in a public air raid shelter during an air raid. The Rare Earths Chemist had waited one month to take the strophanthin in order not to draw attention to the Institute.

By that time, the Roumanian Biologist George Treponesco had already been transferred into the Rare Earths Laboratory, Tanya to that of Frau Doktor to assist with the larval transplants, and Marlene was recalled to work in our laboratory. Her mother took care of the baby.

Professor Kreutzer's prophecy at the celebration dinner that times would be even worse, that the Nazi reaction to the liberation of Paris would be fierce, was correct. They did strike out in every direction, increasing their efforts to round up and exterminate what remained of the Jews, during those last nine months of the war, from August 1944 until April 1945, when the Americans stopped—*just stopped*—when they could have marched through with so little resistance and saved so many. Uncle Otto and Aunt Greta, for example.

. . .

Uncle, bent over from the pain in his neck and back and extremely agitated, was waiting for me outside his apartment building. Face red, arms waving wildly, he blurted out in a loud, quavering voice, "You must be a good boy and bring us tomorrow two wool blankets and some soap—for the trip. Is it too much trouble?"

"Uncle. Please! Calm down and tell me. What trip?"

"If it's too much trouble, I understand. Two blankets and some soap. We have the rest."

Because his building was across from the Farmers' Market, there were many people on the street, and his excitement was drawing their attention. "I will bring whatever you want, but it would be better to talk about it upstairs."

"No! No! I don't want you to upset your aunt." He shoved an envelope into my hand. "This came yesterday." Uncle Otto was so weak, and in such pain, that his legs trembled and he hardly could stand.

I put a hand on his shoulder and gently propelled him through the door of the apartment house. Although it was a cool evening, it had been a rare warm day for September, and the heat had amplified the putrid air in the building. "Sit here on the steps, Uncle." I helped him to lower himself onto a stair, then opened the envelope.

While I read, he chattered nervously. "I served the Kaiser loyally. I was decorated for bravery in the First World War. I am sure I will not be harmed. The Jacoby family have been good German citizens since the beginning of the fifteenth century. That's almost five hundred years."

GERMAN INTERIOR MINISTRY
DEPARTMENT OF THE DELEGATE FOR SPECIAL
DEPLOYMENT

18 September 1944

Herrn Otto Israel Jacoby, and
Frau Margaret Sara Jacoby née Braunstein
Berlin Alexanderplatz
Grosse Frankfurter Strasse 47 Fourth

You are herewith advised that you have been selected for special employment for the general war effort of the German Reich.

You have been assigned the following numbers:

Otto Israel Jacoby   236
Margaret Sara Jacoby née Braunstein   752

and are expected to be ready for transportation on 21st
September at 2 A.M. to a location that will be announced to
you at an appropriate time.

Your baggage is limited to 10 kilograms each and
should include heavy work clothes and provisions for three
days.

Noncompliance will be severely punished according to
special provisions by the Law.

With German Greetings!

[illegible signature]

"Uncle, do you know what this means?"

"Yes. Yes. I must do as they say."

"You can't let them take you. You must hide. And Aunt Greta."

"No, no, Josef. Look." He reached up and took the summons
from my hand. "See, they say we are to be employed. And it is so
polite—they send greetings."

"Uncle, they are always polite." There he sat, a brace from his
chin to his tailbone, weak and in constant pain. *Heavy work clothes!*
"Let me go up and get Aunt Greta, and I will take you to our
house, to Father. He will help you."

With great effort, he pushed himself to his feet. "No, we could
not do that. We must obey the law. Remember your Uncle Philip.
We must do as they say. I was decorated by the Kaiser for bravery.
They will send us to Theresienstadt."

Theresienstadt. I could not believe I was hearing this. I shoved
my rucksack with their weekly supply of food, money, and ration
stamps into his arms, dropped the bag of groceries I had just
bought, and, before he could say another word, fled out the door
and back to the Farmers' Market, where I walked back and forth
among the stalls. It was inconceivable that he didn't know. Wasn't
everyone aware that the Nazis put up façades—Potemkin villages,

Theresienstadt—advertised as places for certain people who were "acceptable" despite being Jews, people who would be "reabsorbed" when the rage against the Jews subsided? It was all fantasy. There was no one place big enough for every Jew and other undesirable who thought he was special. And besides, going to Theresienstadt was no guarantee—conditions there were horrible and getting worse. Shortly before his death, Mitzka had told me about it and about the jammed boxcars with unhygienic conditions beyond all imagination. Surely, Uncle knew what this really meant.

At a flower stall I bought six yellow gladiolas for Aunt Greta and raced back to their building. Uncle had started the long climb, and I found him on the third-floor landing, leaning against a wall and panting. I took back my rucksack and the bag of groceries and put an arm about him. He leaned heavily against me as we climbed slowly up the last flight to his fourth-floor apartment.

"Don't upset your aunt," he pleaded.

"Does she know?"

"Yes. But don't upset her more."

She was waiting for us outside their apartment. "Aunt Greta, please, talk some sense into Uncle."

"I am sure we will not be harmed, Josef. Don't worry. Your uncle served the Kaiser loyally and was decorated for bravery—"

"I know, Aunt, but that means nothing to these swine."

"Hush!" said Uncle Otto, who seemed more in control of himself now that he had his beloved wife to protect. He opened the door to the apartment, and we all went inside. "I have some things for you." He hobbled over to the dining table in front of the window, where there were two packages neatly wrapped in old newspaper.

"Uncle, listen to me." I put the grocery bag on the table. "Every day when I walk from the village of Hagen to the Institute, I pass a labor camp—barracks, really—where they have workers from France. They work for the hospital, and they are free to come and go. You speak French like a native. Come with me. Now. Come on the train, you and Aunt, and just walk into the place. They wouldn't even notice you."

"Josef," he said in a patronizing way, "in the first place, you know your aunt doesn't speak one word of French—"

"She could keep quiet. Really, they wouldn't even know."

He held up his hand to silence me. "I have something for you." He patted the newswrapped packages on the table.

"Uncle—"

"Shhh." He picked up the larger bundle, "Händel," he said, "the *Concerti Grossi*. These are my favorite. I want you to have them."

"Uncle—"

"And this"—he picked up the smaller packet—"this is a prayer book. It belonged to your grandfather Josef Jacoby, after whom you are named."

"Please, Uncle."

He shoved them at me. "Take them."

I was still holding the yellow gladiolas. "Uncle, listen to me— just for a minute."

"No, Josef. You listen to me," he said firmly. "Sit down, please." He lowered himself onto a chair, but I refused to sit with him. "In the book is a paper with the dates of the deaths of your grand-mother and grandfather Jacoby. On the anniversaries of their deaths, I ask, as a special favor to me, that you remember them by lighting a candle that will burn for a day and a night and by saying the prayer for the dead—Kaddish. It is in the book."

"You know I can't read Hebrew."

"When the time comes, open the book. You will be able to read it."

"Uncle, please. Come with me. Aunt Greta . . ."

And then Uncle Otto gave me the ultimate family answer: "When you are more than three cheeses high, perhaps you will understand." I was too young. I was too young to understand.

It was hopeless. "If you won't run and hide, then at least turn on the gas for a while, light a match, and blow yourselves up." I dumped the contents of the rucksack on their table and ran to the door.

"You will bring the blankets and the soap?"

"Yes. Tomorrow." And without even saying good-bye to them, I was out the door and down the stairs, still clutching the flowers in my fist, Händel and the prayer book under my arm. I will never forgive myself for this, for not saying good-bye, for not staying to plead with them, for not telling them about the gas chambers and the ovens and the trains.

I had no stomach for facing Mother with the news, so although it was already eight o'clock and quite dark and cold, I, stupidly, took the train back to Hagen, hoping to get some advice and comfort from Tanya. Since our "talk" by the Geiger counters, we had been going together, more or less; that is, Tanya was not the kind of girl one took to the darkroom. I had virtually stopped seeing Monika —one cannot be totally impolite—my visits to the two girls in the village, about which Tanya never knew, were less frequent, and I would leave them, now, after the British had finished bombing, around midnight or so, and take the train back to Gartenfeld, which meant that I was not getting much sleep and was very tired.

I ran the three kilometers from the station to the Institute and through the park to Tanya's building. It was dark, and the weather was unyieldingly Berlin—damp and cold. I raced up the stairs and knocked on her door. She had not yet let me come in her apartment, and there was to be no exception this night.

"Oh, Josef. I thought you'd gone home." She opened the door a crack.

I bowed, slightly, and handed her Aunt Greta's gladiolas. "Please, I need to talk to you."

"Is something wrong?"

I nodded.

"Just a minute, I'll get a sweater, and we can walk around the park and talk."

"It's getting quite chilly outside."

"Then I'll get a coat."

As we walked, I told her exactly what had been said at my uncle's. At one point, we sat on one of the stone benches along the winding drive. She, bundled in her warm coat, a wool scarf over her head, did not sit close to me. The bench was cold and hard. I was not dressed warmly enough. I am not certain what I expected from her.

"Your uncle is a fool!" she said. "One must fight! One must see the danger and use one's strength and will."

And then, as I sat there turning to stone, she told me a long story of how, when her mother received word she was to be taken, Tanya's father put her on a train and had her ride around for days and days; then he sent her to a farm they knew in the country. At the same time, he sent Tanya to his friend—the Chief—at the Institute. The narration was filled with irrelevant detail—every train, every stop, the mechanics of contact—and full of sermons and vehemence. By the time she was through, I was frozen to the core.

"And that is why I am here at the Institute. I have no patience with people who will not fight! It is cold. I am going to my room."

I walked her to her door. She unlocked it and stepped across the threshold.

"May I come inside?"

"You know I don't permit that."

Before she could shut the door in my face, I turned and ran down the stairs. I was a fool for looking for any comfort from her. She was a selfish, coldhearted bitch, as unlike Sheereen or Sonja Press as one could be, and any budding affection I might have had for her was killed that night.

I walked the three kilometers back to Hagen, took the train through Berlin, was held up for three hours because of the

British—God bless them and help them smash the place to hell—arrived in Gartenfeld at three in the morning, and tiptoed into my parents' bedroom. Dritt, who always slept on their bed at my father's feet, raised his sleepy head and smiled at me. Good old Dritt. Mother slipped out of bed without waking Father.

In the kitchen, I told Mother about the summons and about Uncle and Aunt's request for two blankets and some soap.

She, of course, was horribly upset by this, and began to wring her hands. "The blankets, yes, and soap. I will waken your father. He will give them money. They'll need money if they are to make a journey."

"Mutti, I think they should not go. They need to hide."

"No, no," she began.

"Listen to me. I have a friend at the Institute whose mother was sent such a letter, and her father put her mother on a train and had her ride around for days and days and then arranged to have her hidden at the farm of a friend. She is still alive! Surely Papa has family who will hide them."

"I don't know . . ." But she was hesitating!

"Mutti, they are shipping the Jews out in cattle cars, packed like sardines in a can, and they are—"

"Hush, Josef. Where do you hear such things?"

"Mutti, listen to me. I have not told you these things because I cannot bear to upset you. But it's true. Mitzka Avilov told me. He saw these things and he heard about them from the Russian prisoners of war. Mutti, there are gas chambers. They use cyanide. They—"

Mother was on her feet. "I'll talk with your father. He will want to give them some money. If they are to take a trip, they will need money. Are you hungry? There is a potato soup with good garden vegetables in the icebox."

"Yes. I'll eat something." I was hopeful for the fifteen minutes Mother was gone that my parents might, this one time, come to their senses and face reality. While waiting for the water to boil and the soup to warm, I celebrated by helping myself to two liberal slices of bread and wurst. My disappointment, when Mother and Father remained true to form, was tenfold.

Mother returned with a small leather suitcase. "Here are the blankets, soap, some aspirin, money, and ration stamps. Can you think of anything else they might need? You said provisions for three days? There is bread and wurst. I'll send that."

"Mutti."

She raised a hand to silence me. "Your father feels that they must obey the law. Your uncle was decorated for bravery during the First World War and will be treated fairly. Your father assumes they will be sent to Theresienstadt."

"Mutti, Theresienstadt is not what you think."

"Josef, you are too young to concern yourself with these things. I know how very tired you must be, but your father feels you must get back to your uncle's with the suitcase as quickly as you can just in case they are asked to leave earlier. You must catch the first train—but by no means are you to draw attention to yourself by running. Do you understand?"

"Mutti. They will be transported in cattle cars and murdered—"

"Look what you have done! You have eaten the bread and wurst. Now I have no food to send them."

The 4:09 arrived on the lowest-level track at Friedrichstrasse at 4:31; a five-minute climb to the upper level to catch the 4:38 for Ostkreuz, which arrived at Alexanderplatz at 4:44; a ten-minute walk—I could have made it in six minutes running—to Grosse Frankfurter Strasse 47. At 4:54, I ran up the stairs. I was too late. They were gone. All that was left in their two rooms were the dining table covered with a soiled white linen cloth with Grandmother's initials monogrammed in white on the corner and, under the table, a small silver napkin ring with the initial O for Otto, and a Schiller, with the cover gone, stinking of mildew.

I folded the cloth neatly and placed it in the suitcase with the two blankets, the soap, and all, and put the silver napkin ring in my pocket. Then I leafed through the Schiller. It was an anthology of his plays. Uncle Otto had marked up the *William Tell,* and from what he underlined I realized that he had known, all along, and that I would never be able to forgive myself for not pleading with him, for not insisting, for not telling him what I knew.

> *Cast off, Ruodi! You will save me from death! Put me across.*
>
> *Hurry, hurry, they are close on my heels already!*
>
> *I am a dead man if they seize me.*
>
> *What! I have a life to lose, too. Look there, how the water swells, how it seethes and whirls and stirs up all the depths. I would gladly like to rescue you, Baumgarten, but it is clearly impossible.*
>
> *(Baumgarten still on his knees): Then I must fall into the hands of the enemy with the nearby shore of safety in sight! There it lies! I can reach it with my eyes. The sound of the voice can reach across. There is the boat which might carry me across and I must lie here, helpless, and despair.*
>
> *Save him! Save him! Save him!*
>
> *Righteous heaven! When will the savior come to this land?*

I should have refused to leave their apartment, should have forced them to listen, should have threatened to be there when the Gestapo came after them. I would never forgive myself.

The line the Chief parodied, "A Gestapo in the House saves one from a Caesarean section," was from the first scene of the third act: Tell is in the courtyard in front of his house. Having just repaired the gate with his carpenter's ax, he lays his tools aside and says to his wife, Hedwig:

244 · BERLIN WILD

> *Now I think the gate will hold a good*
> *long time. The ax at home often saves*
> *one from the carpenter.*

William Tell had been my childhood hero. I pictured him
striding about, saving the innocent, the crossbow on his back fastened across his breast by a colorful band. He saved Baumgarten,
of course, by rowing him across the seething water, and then he
saved the entire country with his crossbow and one apple.

When I returned to the Institute that same morning, I spread one
of Uncle's blankets on the floor under my worktable, covered myself with the other, and slept. Krupinsky and the others began the
morning sorting and let me sleep. I awakened at noon, ate four
bowls of polenta, and drank hot tea laced with vodka.

I did not even bother discussing the matter with Tatiana, nor
did I tell her that I no longer cared for her, even though I knew
that she felt we were officially going together. I began the retreat
into a dead place within myself, and without comment I would
listen to her daydream about our future: I was to be a famous
mathematician and she a biologist; we would have two children, a
boy named Josef and a girl named Tatiana. It was too late for me
to become a mathematician, and I would never, never bring children into this hideous world. The more removed I felt and acted
toward her, the more interested she became in me. François Daniel
was right. The only way to win a woman like Tatiana was to seem
to be disinterested. It is even more effective if the disinterest is
genuine. *Seems, Madam. Nay, it is; I know not "seems."* I did my
work at the Institute efficiently, increased my visits to the darkroom with a grateful Monika, and visited more often the two girls
from Chemistry who lived in the village of Hagen, staying until
dawn, then returning to the Institute in the morning. I returned to

the house in Gartenfeld only five times between September twenty-first, when Uncle Otto and Aunt Greta were taken, and October tenth, when they took my mother. So I saw her— Mother—only five times those nineteen days between, and I was so non-communicative that we hardly exchanged a word.

. . .

On Tuesday, Ocober 10, 1944, at five in the afternoon, nearly two months after the liberation of Paris, we were finishing up in the lab when the Chief came to tell me that my parents had called. "Your parents called. Don't go home tonight. Stay away. They are expecting visitors."

I telephoned, but there was no answer. I left at once. The walk through the fields and forest and the little village of Hagen. The train to Potsdamer Platz. I watched passing trains for the face of my mother. The Americans had the habit of sending a few fighter bombers over, now and then, in the early evening, to stop the railways from running, and the trains held at the Potsdamer, which was underground, for almost three hours. It was dark when I arrived in Gartenfeld. I ran fast. I could not see and bumped myself on a corner mailbox, tearing my leg. Very painful. Bloody. A Jew dare not use a flashlight during a blackout and draw attention to himself. Remember Uncle Philip.

Father sat in his great chair before the fireplace in the small parlor on the first floor. There was no fire. He was wrapped in his overcoat. Dritt sat quietly on his lap.

"Where is my mother?"

"She is gone."

"Did she receive a letter?"

"No. A neighbor called. Her husband was taken and she saw your mother's name on the list."

"Why didn't you take her away?" I was shouting now. "How

could you let them take my mother? Why didn't you just shoot her and be done with it?"

"You are much too young to understand, and, furthermore, I owe you no explanation. But I will say this to you, Josef. Heretofore, the actions have been against households which are one hundred percent of your mother's background; they have been predawn and secret. The S.S. has no desire to draw attention to what it is doing. But this present action, as I understand it, involves too many German households, is being carried out in daylight, and, therefore, it will draw attention to itself. Because of the outcry from the German involved, it will be abortive. If she were to try to evade arrest, they would get her on a criminal charge and there would be no recourse. Remember what happened to your Uncle Philip."

"I despise you for bringing me into life."

I went upstairs to Mother's office to cleanse and bind my leg. The bleeding had stopped, but it would need several stitches. On her desk was her potato peeler. I put it in my pocket, then went up to my room and packed a suitcase.

He met me at the front door. "Your mother left a letter for you."

I stuffed the letter in my pocket. On the way back to the train, I avoided the corner mailbox. The British were bombing again; the Wannsee Bahn waited at Potsdamer for many hours.

10 October 1944

My dear son Josef,

I have two wishes: that you study medicine and become the gifted surgeon you could be, and that you, as always, be honorable in your life and in your relationships with other human beings. There is no time to say more, but you know of my love for you.

Perhaps a moment more. Socrates has been no small comfort: "Those of us who think death is an evil are in error. For either death is a dreamless sleep—which is plainly good—or the soul migrates to another world. And what would not a man give if he might converse with Orpheus, Musaeus, and Hesiod and Homer."

Ever,

Mutti

The second train arrived in Hagen shortly before dawn. I went to the apartment of Sonja Press and awakened her. She was alone. I thought she might comfort me in her bed, but she offered me only words—"Oh, my dear, I am so sorry!"—tea, vodka, and some of the Chief's tobacco, which she rolled for me into a cigarette. I stood in the middle of her living room.

"Horrible," I said.

"It should be good, Josef. It's his new recipe, you know. He soaks the tobacco in prune juice and citric acid."

"One might as well smoke stinking weeds. They are all crazy and they are all stupid. They think this stinking tobacco is good. It is not, I tell you. It is no damn good, and you know it." I threw the burning cigarette to the floor.

She picked it up. "Sit." Gently, she pushed me toward the couch. "Sit." And she bent to untie my shoes. "Lie back, Josef. It's almost morning."

"Lie with me."

"I can't."

"He does it with everybody."

"You don't understand."

"Of course not. I am much too young to concern myself with such matters."

"You don't understand our Russian men. To them it is like drinking a glass of water. As important but also as unimportant. With the women it is different. For me there is no one else. Lie back. No one is too young now."

I lay back. She removed my shoes, covered me with her shawl, pulled a chair beside the couch, and put her hand on my arm. It was dawn. *And oh my good Lord said I knew you before I created you in the womb of your mother and I separated you before you were born by your mother. But I said, Oh, my good Lord, I am not fit because I am too young. But my good Lord said to me, Do not say I am too young, but you should go where I send you. And the Lord stretched his hand out and touched my mouth. . . .*

"Josef, Josef, wake up." The Chief was bending over me. He shook my arm. "Come now, Sonja has tea and cakes for us. We've half an hour to breakfast and go over to the lab."

Ah, the wound in my leg was throbbing. And my head.

"Come! Sonja has prepared tea and cakes."

But I was not hungry. I left without eating and hobbled across the park. As I entered the Institute, I heard Stanislas Rabin practicing on the Bechstein in the parlor on the first floor. I sat and listened. Over and over and over the same scales of the Chromatic Fantasia of Bach, expanding, intertwining, unfettered. He would reach the trill and return over and over and over to the beginning. One could run statistics on how many people would be using the train system in Berlin on a Tuesday morning at, say, six thirty, but if one wanted to choose one person only from the population of the city and determine whether or not this one person would be on the train at six thirty Tuesday morning, how could it be known? Or one knows that half the atoms of radioactive substances will have disintegrated in a certain length of time, but how can it be known which atom will go first? And how can it be said which follicle of the thousands in the ovary—for after all only one, rarely two or more—is destined to complete its development? Why that one? In my high school, the Calvinist ministers preached that those who reach grace are set apart before birth. Did they believe that Paul's follicle was set aside in the ovary? *But when he who had set me apart before I was born, and had called me through his grace. . . .* And Jeremiah: *And the word of the Lord happened to me and said, "I knew you before I created you in the womb of your mother." . . . But I said,*

"Oh, Lord, Lord, I am not fit because I am too young." But he said to me, "Do not say, 'I am too young.'" Rabin began again. I had visitors. The Chief came in twice for five minutes, paced, walked out. Not a word. Then Tatiana stood before me.

"I am sorry about your mother."

I shrugged and remained sitting.

"Why did you go to Sonja rather than to me?"

I shrugged again. She left. She helped now in the lab of Frau Doktor, the kind woman biologist, and still there was the problem of the clumsy mechanical handling of the larvae which I had noted my first day at the Institute. Each pair was taken from the slimy solution, put on a slide, and then operated upon. It came to me that it could be remedied by a turning disk, with space for several pairs, like that on a phonograph, going around endlessly, listening to Rabin over and over and over, I pictured the disk to myself, planning so that I could explain it to the mechanic in the Physics Chapel in the park.

The Chief came again, this time with Professor Kreutzer, who stood before me and began to change his glasses. One feels most uncomfortable when he begins this. I stood.

He put on the black-rims, put away the rimless, and stared at me.

"Yes, Herr Professor?" I said finally.

"We are not getting any reproduceable effects from the ultraviolet radiation of the flies. The variations are wild. See what you can come up with on this."

"Yes, Herr Professor."

He stood there looking at me. The Chief, of course, was pacing. Stanislas Rabin began again.

"Well!" barked Professor Kreutzer. "What are you waiting for?"

So I left the parlor and went up to the lab. Marlene and Krupinsky were there. He said, "Sorry to hear about your mother."

"Will you take a look at my leg? I think it needs stitches."

I lay down on a worktable, and he collected his paraphernalia.

"Listen, Josef, you need about five stitches, which means ten pricks with the needle. I can give you a local anesthetic, which means about four or six pricks, and, of course, means more chance of infection."

"What kind of anesthetic?"

"Novocain."

"Do you have any books on anesthesiology? I was wondering, if we changed from ether to something else, would the flies still ejaculate and lose their sperm when we anesthetize them?"

"Good Christ, Bernhardt, you won't ejaculate if I give you Novocain, unless you have some strange perversion."

"Do you have a book on anesthetics or not?"

"Not. Now don't move!"

The Chief came to watch. Krupinsky washed the wound, sprinkled it with sulfa powder.

"We'll try it without Novocain. If it hurts too much, give a yell, and I'll deaden it. O.K.?"

He told the Chief I'd probably lost a bit of blood and that I should take it easy for the rest of the day. And he gave me a handful of vitamins and aspirin.

"I'm allergic to aspirin."

He took the aspirin out of my hand. "Go home and rest."

"Can you possibly find one for me?"

"What the hell are you talking about?"

"A book on anesthetic gases?"

"Christ, you never give up, do you?" He took two steps to the shelf where he kept his medical texts and grabbed a large volume. "Here!" He shoved it at me. "*Pharmacology*. That's the best I can do. In Great Britain anesthesiology is an important specialty, but in Germany it is not. Here the gas is given by a subassistant or a nurse, and they mostly use ether because it is safest in the hands of the inexperienced."

"Could you get a British text for me?"

"Now where in the hell am I supposed to lay my hands on

something like that? Look, if it's gases you are interested in, the *Pharmacology* should do it."

I thumbed through the book:

ETHER: $(C_2H_5)_2O$ *One of the safest and probably the most widely used of all the inhalation anesthetic agents. It is irritating to the respiratory tract. Its administration may be followed by increased secretions in the pharynx, trachea, and bronchi, by swallowing of ether-laden mucus, and by nausea and vomiting in the postoperative period.*

I crossed the park to the Physics Chapel to find the mechanic. Together we dug through the junk looking for an old turntable to make the revolving-disk operating table for Frau Doktor. I was pleased to find an old record-cutting machine with a turntable ten times as heavy as an ordinary one. I had the mechanic cut it to a diameter of eighteen centimeters. It sat on an axle in which there was a friction bearing. I had him screw the whole thing onto a chunk of iron. Then we cut a Plexiglas disk, which fit with three prongs into the three slots we made in the turntable. We made twelve divided hollows in the disk—and twelve tiny removable cups to put over each hollow—in the same position as numbers on a clock, so the two larvae—donor and donee—could be placed side by side in the hollows. We cut grooves running to a reservoir in the center to be kept filled with saline solution so the larvae wouldn't dry.

The day was gone. I hadn't hooked up the motor yet, but I was dizzy from not eating, so I walked back to our building just as they were closing up.

Krupinsky said, "What are you doing here? I thought I told you to go home."

"I don't have a home."

"Oh, come on, Josef. Why be self-destructive? Besides, your father—"

"Krupinsky, has it ever occurred to you to mind your own business?"

"No, I don't think that it has. Did you take your vitamins?"

I nodded.

"What are you going to do? Where are you going to sleep? There are no empty apartments in the park or in Hagen."

I shrugged. "I'm hungry." My hands were shaking.

We made some tea and Krupinsky slaughtered a rabbit and asked Tatiana to put it in the autoclave. Then he and I drank tea with vodka and he left.

I stretched out on a worktable and let her watch the baking rabbit and warm some polenta. My throat was raw, my nose beginning to run. She brought a blanket and covered me.

"Thank you."

"You're welcome. Josef," she said, "I want to know why you went to her instead of to me."

The upper part of the spindle will be surrounded by a coil, an electromagnet. Parallel will be a large capacitor, and the battery can be switched on or off by a foot switch.

"Why don't you answer me?"

She had tears on her face.

"I know you're upset," she said.

"I'm not upset. You're upset."

"I am sorry about your mother."

I closed my eyes, on the verge of sleep.

"Why won't you talk to me?" Her voice was shrill.

I opened my eyes. "I did not come to you, because it was too cold at four in the morning to sit with you on a cement bench in the park."

"Where will you sleep tonight?"

I closed my eyes and drifted at once into sleep. . . . **The train, racing toward the end of a long, dark tunnel, collided with a brick wall. My body was cushioned by the bodies of others—Mitzka Avilov and Dieter Schmidt—and others whom I knew but could not recognize. The train was cut open with a carpenter's ax, and I** was lifted out and saved. I looked back down into it and saw the others, mashed, broken, and dismembered from the impact of my body, their skulls smashed and their brains spilling out into pools of their own gore.

Tatiana was shaking me. "Josef, Josef, wake up. You are having a nightmare."

I sat up, confused and frightened. "Where am I?"

"You are in the Biology Lab. You were having a bad dream. Come, the rabbit is done. We can eat."

We ate in silence, and I, instead of trying to sleep again, returned to the Physics Chapel and worked all night. By morning it was finished, and after the sorting of the flies, I took it in to Frau Doktor.

"The brake is very smooth-acting because of the capacitor, Frau Doktor, so because of the smoothness, the braking action doesn't start immediately upon activating the foot switch, nor does it close, suddenly, upon disconnecting the battery with the foot switch. You must work with it until you have a sense of the rhythm of the time lag."

We loaded the first twelve pairs of larvae onto the disk, and Tatiana and I watched while Frau Doktor lifted the cups and performed the transplants. It was efficient, and she was most pleased.

"You are talented in many ways." She touched my hand. "What will you study when this war is over?"

Tatiana said, "Mathematics!"

"I'm not sure," I said.

"What do you mean? We've always said you'd be a mathematician."

Frau Doktor said to me, "Are you considering other things?"

"I haven't really advanced at all in math for three or four years. It may be too late by the time this is over."

Tatiana said, "Don't be a fool. Newton quit school when he was fourteen and didn't even go back to begin the study of mathematics until he was your age."

"There is no one here who knows more about mathematics than I do, Tanya. There is no one here to teach me. There are no books. It is finished!" I turned to Frau Doktor. "I think it would be better to have two disks so that Tanya could prepare the second group of twelve while you worked on the first."

Tatiana was angry. She left the room.

Frau Doktor embraced me and kissed my cheek. "My dear, if there is anything I can do for you, all you have to do is ask." She looked something like my mother, but was quite a bit younger, thirty or so.

I returned to the Physics Chapel to make the second disk. Tatiana came at closing time, bringing me some bread, sausage, and tea.

"Thank you very much."

"Where will you sleep tonight?"

I had a full-blown cold and my chest felt heavy. I was having trouble breathing.

"You've got to sleep somewhere."

"There's always the cement bench in the park."

She began to weep.

"Why do you cry, for Lord's sake?"

"You can't sleep outside in this weather. What would people say? And you already have a cold."

"Oh, my good Lord, Tanya, since when do you give a damn what happens to me? I'll sleep under a table in the lab, or there are cots in the basement."

And I was thinking of the problem with the ultraviolet radiation. One exposes the flies to it and tries to measure the effect. These results have to be quantitatively or qualitatively reproduceable. For example, take a blue dye. You have to check the sensitivity of the blue dye to light, so you expose a solution of dye to a certain amount of light and then measure the change.

"It wouldn't be right for you to sleep in the lab or in the basement."

"My good Lord, Tanya, don't you have anything else on your mind?"

She left.

It might turn out to have less blue or green in it, or maybe it becomes dirty-looking. So let us see, if one exposes this blue dye to the equivalent of one month of sunlight and one finds a reduction of blueness of ten percent or nine and three quarters percent or eleven and one tenth percent—finally, adding up to nine and four fifths percent—one can make a statistically valid statement of nine and four fifths percent. If, however, each time it is totally different, then something must be wrong. Too much variation in a controlled experiment means the experiment is not controlled. I was finished with the second disk and walked back to the main building. It was ten at night.

Tatiana was waiting for me in the Biology Lab. "Would you like a cup of tea?"

"Yes, thank you."

The water was already boiling on the Bunsen burner. She handed me the hot tea and asked me where I was going to sleep that night.

"I could always go over to Monika's."

"Monika's? Did she invite you?"

"Should she have?"

"No!"

"Then why ask such silly questions?"

"Do you want to go to Monika's?"

"Should I want to?"

She left. I could hear the air-raid sirens in Berlin. I lay down under a table, covered myself with a blanket, and fell, at once, to sleep. **The train raced toward the end of a long, dark tunnel and collided with a brick wall. My body was cushioned by the bodies of others—Mitzka Avilov, and Dieter Schmidt—and others whom I knew but could not recognize. The train was cut open with a carpenter's ax, and I was lifted out and saved. I looked down and** saw the others, mashed, broken, and dismembered from the impact of my body, their skulls smashed and their brains spilling out into pools of their own red gore.

I heard screaming. I sat up. It was I. I had been screaming.

Krupinsky's *Pharmacology* was on my worktable. Was there such a thing as an anesthetic gas that allowed one a dreamless sleep?

> CYCLOPROPANE $(CH_2)_3$ *A colorless gas with a not unpleasant characteristic odor resembling that of petroleum ether and having a mildly pungent taste. In anesthetic concentrations it is odorless. Induction with cyclopropane requires only two to three minutes. It is pleasant, more rapid than with ether, but less so than with nitrous oxide or ethylene. Unconsciousness occurs in 20 seconds to three minutes. Cyclopropane does not cause dreams, as does, say, nitrous oxide.*

Other gases are not so pleasant:

> HYDROCYANIC ACID (HCN) *A colorless, volatile, extremely toxic, flammable, aqueous solution of hydrogen cyanide, used in the manufacture of dyes, fumigants, and plastics. Also called "Prussic Acid" and "Hydrogen Cyanide." Hydrocyanic acid is one of the most rapidly acting poisons. The symptoms appear within a few seconds after the ingestion of compounds or the breathing of vapors containing the ion, and consist of giddiness, apnea, headache, palpitations, cyanosis, and unconsciousness. Asphyxial convulsions may precede death. As long as the heart continues to beat there is a chance of saving the patient since effective antidotes are available. Diagnosis can be made by the characteristic odor on the breath of the poisoned individual (oil of bitter almonds).*

A punishing, suffocating death.

*

By morning my chest was congested, my eyes and nose running.

Krupinsky said, "If you want to commit suicide, let me give you a gun."

I coughed. He looked at my leg, listened to my chest.

"Your leg is coming along. And you don't have pneumonia yet, but you will. There's a lot of music in your chest. I suggest you go to bed for a few days."

"No." Coughing and sneezing, I limped—my leg more sore than ever—into the lab of Frau Doktor with the second disk.

"My dear boy," she said, "you should be in bed." She put her hand on my forehead. "I have a couch in the living room of my apartment. Why don't you take the bus over there and lie down?" She had an apartment in Hagen. "Here." She began to dig through her purse. "I'll give you the key."

Tatiana sat at her side of the microscope, pale, lips tight.

"No, thank you. I'm all right, Frau Doktor. Just a little cold." And I limped, coughing, from her lab.

Tatiana came running after me. "I have just one small room," she said, "with a bed, a table, and two chairs. Where would you sleep?"

"There's always the cement bench in the park." I coughed, sneezed, blew my nose. "Or Frau Doktor's."

At that moment the Chief and Krupinsky came talking down the hall.

"Do you think it is a good idea for you to contaminate all the personnel with your disease?" said the Chief.

"Go home and go to bed," said Krupinsky. "And take your vitamins."

"You must promise to sleep with your clothes on," Tatiana said quietly. She had a strong face but pretty, a pointed chin, large dark eyes set wide apart, but most beautiful was the thick dark hair that fell below her waist, tied always with that green ribbon. I would like to see it free, cascading, like the hair of Sheereen.

She took a key from the pocket of her white lab coat. "Here. I will come at noon to give you lunch. You are not to move from that bed until you are well."

I took her key and limped off to the lab to pick up my suitcase, the charts on ultraviolet radiation, and those on the search for an alternate anesthetic which would keep the females from ovulation when gassed and the males from losing their sperm. I took, also, several of Krupinsky's medical texts, including the *Pharmacology*. I found only two references even slightly related in the *Pharmacology* text. The first was in relation to gas: *Occasionally priapism may develop under cyclopropane anesthetic.* And the other was in relation to ethyl alcohol:

> *Much of little worth has been written on the subject of the relation of alcohol to sexual activity. It is a popular notion that alcohol is an aphrodisiac. Shakespeare, however, realized that inebriation interferes with coitus. In* Macbeth, *for example, the following conversation occurs (Act 2, Scene 2, translated by Tieck and Schlegel):*
>
> MACDUFF: *What three things especially does drink provoke?*
>
> PORTER: *Marry, sir, nose-painting, sleep, and urine. Lechery, sir, it provokes, and unprovokes; it provokes the desire, but it takes away the performance.*
>
> *The experiments on the effects of alcohol on the sexual reflexes of normal dogs support the observations of Shakespeare: in neurotic dogs, alcohol has some therapeutic value.*

The dream returned every time I fell asleep. I began to drink myself senseless each night before we got into bed, I, in the patched remnants of my pajamas, Tatiana fully clothed, her long dark hair brushed and plaited into one braid and tied with a string. Nothing I could say or do would induce her to let it lie free.

My cold abated after one week, although the bronchitis never really left me, and I developed a wound infection in my leg. It was localized; I didn't die of blood poisoning like Gunther Rathke, the fallen aviator whose brain lay in a jar on the fifth floor. In spite of the stitching, one part opened, providing drainage. I carry the scar to this day.

I stayed at Tatiana's a nightmarish three months—until early January, when my summons came. After three weeks of my heavy drinking, during which I completely ignored her, she, misunderstanding my motives for drinking, gave in. The French do understand women.

"I see no reason to torture you any further, since of necessity you must stay with me at night. But you must promise to marry me when the war is over."

I had not so much as jumped on a black spot since I had been sleeping beside her.

"You must promise," she repeated.

I promised to marry her!

I used two Fromm's Akt to protect her and lots of lubricating gel to make it easier, but she was tense and tight—rigid—and nothing could induce her to relax. I was not permitted to touch her breast or to kiss her, but was allowed, only, to lift my leg to a tree once each night to relieve myself. She would not untie the ribbon on the thick braid, plaited behind the ear and falling, like the string of the bow or the band on the balalaika, across her breast to her waist. She lay still, unmoving, silent. *Impotencia Josefus,* the inability to satisfy a woman. When I tried to talk to Tatiana about it, she said, "I will not allow myself to enjoy it until we are married."

When one knows the answer to a riddle, it all seems so simple that one wonders why it was such a revelation: when the flies are mature, they become fully pigmented in the abdomen; therefore, the ultraviolet was not penetrating to their gonads or was penetrating in random amounts. We were careful, thereafter, to use flies only so many hours old. Young enough not to be fully colored but old enough to be sexually mature.

CHAPTER · SEVEN

Berlin

I did not want to be taken from the Institute.

"You must leave," Professor Kreutzer said. "Come to see me after you've talked." And he left me standing with my father in the Chief's office.

How old Father looked—but then to me my parents always were old—and his face was distorted, the right eyelid sagging, and the left side of his mouth. How perfectly dressed: his wardrobe of shoes, alone, would have lasted another ten years, and his spats, various lengths in gray, black, and white. Did he suffer not being able to wear the uniform of a German officer? He'd been ambitious as a young man, but marrying my mother, of course, ruined everything.

"Professor Kreutzer advises that you should report to I. G. Farben as ordered and you will be all right."

I was smiling. My teeth felt like fangs, my lips curled back. "Little chance of that, is there! Why didn't you take us away? It wasn't a matter of money!"

"Your mother and I discussed it many times, and we talked it over with friends who were in situations similar to ours. We all agreed." He lowered his eyes. "It did not work in her case, but nevertheless I will explain to you our thinking." He took a deep, shaking breath, then looked again at me. "We felt that the two of you were not in such immediate danger as fully Jewish families. This was reflected in the semiofficial designation as 'privileged' and also in the Nuremberg Laws, in which mixed marriages and the offspring from such marriages were set apart. Within mixed marriages, there are also two categories: one where the father is Aryan, the other where the father is a Jew. The families with Jewish fathers were treated much more severely by the law. Your mother and I felt that you both were in a relatively safe and protected category.

"For reasons as much out of our control as the Nazis themselves, the measures by other countries to control emigration from Germany were so strict and limiting that the few visas which were available, we felt, should go to the most endangered part of the German population. The immigration quotas were insufficient and filled up much too fast, and, for the unprivileged, totally inflexible.

"Those are the reasons why we did not apply for immigration visas for the two of you."

It was the longest speech he had ever made to me.

"I see," I said. "Then it was for the sake of—others—that you did not save my mother or me."

"Others without privilege."

"I see. How noble of you. You are as great as Abraham, who was willing to sacrifice Isaac for the glory of God, or as William Tell, who used his son's head from which to shoot an apple. I have not gone through a red light and neither had my mother." I shouted and waved my summons. "Will this, too, be abortive?" And I ran from the room. On the stairs from the penthouse to the second floor, I had to slow down—vertigo—and I was having difficulty breathing. My lungs were never the same after that terrible cold. I walked slowly to Professor Kreutzer's lab in Physics.

He sat on a stool at a worktable, fitting together two pieces of junk, the same posture as the first time I had seen him. I thought he didn't see me until he said, without looking up, "You will be all right." Then he turned to me, changed his glasses, routinely, looked at me through the lenses of the second pair. "We fight them like the devil, but we are not suicidal. If you stay here any longer, they will come after you. I have made some telephone calls and advise that you go to I. G. Farben as ordered rather than trying to hide. You are all right. You will be all right. Keep your eyes open. Do not talk to any of the other workers. You will find that at this particular factory they are, for the most part, free workers, refugees from the Baltic states. They out-nazi the German Nazis. Therefore, I repeat: Do not talk. Listen. Do not join any groups. Be alone. You've got more brains than all the rest of them put together. As for surviving the war, unless a brick falls on your head, you have a much better chance than the men your age who are in the army. They will die, or be maimed, or be prisoners for years. Furthermore, you have nothing to fear from what comes after. In that sense you are privileged."

He stood and shook my hand—for the first time—at the moment of my abandonment.

"It is a matter of months. Come back here when it is all over."

I returned to my lab and found the Chief talking to Krupinsky. When I began to pack away my microscope, the Chief stopped me. "Leave it!" he shouted. "You will be back." And he embraced me, crushed me in his arms against his massive chest. A bear. Then he walked quickly from the lab.

Krupinsky said, "Chief says there's a good chance you'll be O.K. They need workers. Your girlfriend was here. She said to tell you to hurry back to her room."

"She knows?"

"I told her. She thinks you should run off and hide, both of you. She has a point, you know."

I nodded.

"What did Max tell you?"

"He said I would be all right at Farben." I shrugged. "He made some telephone calls."

"He probably has friends over there."

I nodded. "He said I'd be all right—if I kept my mouth shut."

"That ends your chances right there." Krupinsky put his arms around me and gave me a hug. "Put your money on Max," he said, and he turned away, blew his nose, and wiped his eyes.

Tatiana was in the room packing our things.

"Why are you packing?"

"We will run away and hide together."

"Oh, my good Lord, Tanya. Don't be ridiculous. They're not after you."

"You will walk into their hands? Are you as big a fool as your mother and your uncle?"

I reached for her hand. She jerked it away.

"Tanya, listen to me. Professor Kreutzer said I will be best off to follow the orders. He has checked it out—made phone calls. I'll be all right."

"My God, that's what they all say. No! You must run! We will go to my parents."

"What do you think would happen to me if I got caught? What do you think they'd do to the Chief and the others here if I should disappear? No! I trust Professor Kreutzer's judgment. As far as I am concerned, he has never been wrong."

"And me? Don't you trust me? What of me? What have I done? What have I done?" She threw herself face down on the bed, sobbing.

I sat beside her and put my hand on her back.

"I am nothing to you," she sobbed, shaking my head away. "You are self-centered, selfish, and not honorable."

"Listen, Tanya. It's early, two o'clock or so. Maybe we can find someone to marry us this afternoon. We can get married if you want."

Mottled red face, snuffling nose, she sat up. "There isn't time, and you know it. Besides, it would draw attention to us. We can't do that."

The offer mollified her enough that she let me put my arm

around her, but there was no molding into the curve. We sat rigidly. Her ear was near my mouth. I dared not even kiss it. My hand was near the green ribbon, tied in a simple bow. I pulled it; the hair released itself, slowly, to its fullness.

Ah, there it was. She sprang from the bed, shaking her mane, and it flew free and cascaded wildly. Her eyes narrowed as though against the sun, her nostrils were dilated, teeth bared, hands on hips, skirt swirling. Fire! But just for an instant.

"Is that all you think of?" she screamed, throwing her head forward to collect her hair in one hand, then braiding, furiously, tying it with a plain white string and winding it tight around her head, not even allowing it to fall acrosss her breast like a crossbow. I stood to leave.

"Good-bye, Tanya. Maybe while I'm gone the Chief would again permit you to use Mitzka's balalaika to keep you company."

. . .

The little atom looks around him and knows one day he'll emit a quant or two and be altered, but he doesn't know when, and does it make any difference why? Until that time, he can wander here or there, no matter how many statistical studies are run on the number of atoms apt to take the 6:30 A.M. train from Hagen to Friedrichstrasse on a Tuesday morning in early January. It cannot be known if our little atom will or will not be on the aforementioned train; however, if he has in his pocket a form letter such as I had in mine, it is easier to assume he will.

Labor Office Berlin.
Berlin, 7, I, 45.
Dept. II, 4. Operation: Mixed-Blood.

NOTICE OF OBLIGATION

according to the order of the deputy of the four years plan
in order to secure forces for tasks of special political signifi-

cance to the State, from February 13, 1939, Reich Publications Law I, p. 206, and the Obligation Execution Order of March 2, 1939, same issue, p. 403.

Occupation according to labor book: lab technician	Herrn: Josef Leopold Bernhardt
	Born: 15, VIII, 26 in Berlin.
Citizenship: German Reich	Address: Gartenfeld, Kastanien Strasse 95

You must report at 8:00 A.M. on the 9th day of January 1945, to I. G. Farben Co., in Lichtenberg, as a Manual Auxiliary Laborer.

LABOR DEPARTMENT, BERLIN

[signature]

DISTRIBUTION:
1. To the obliged one.
2. To the receiving company.
3. To the contribution company, Kaiser Wilhelm Institute, Berlin-Hagen.

WHAT IS SAID ON THE BACK OF THIS FORM IS TO BE NOTICED!

FOR NOTICE! You have to report as specified. You are obliged to follow this order in every case even if you protest it. The service begins with the stated time. The time of employment is as specified. The employing company has already made the contract and cannot refuse you employment. Employment can only be changed with the consent of the Office of Labor. You are on leave of holiday from your previous employment. You cannot be discharged or fired from your previous employment without consent of the Office of Labor. You may be entitled, if separated from dependent family, to separation payment to aid said family. Put in application. You are entitled to compensation given you. If you previously were insured, then insurance should continue. Take with you your papers and this notice of obligation so as not to delay employment. The original of this notice is only for the obliged one and no one is entitled to use it but the obliged one. NON-FOLLOWING OF THIS NOTICE OF OBLIGATION OR INFRACTION AGAINST THE OBLIGATION TO WORK IS PUNISHABLE BY JAIL AND FINES! THE LATTER WITH LIMIT, OR WITH ONE OF THESE PUNISHMENTS (Second Order for Four Years Plan, N4, I, p. 936).

I was on the 6:30 train the next morning, Tuesday, from Hagen to Friedrichstrasse, where I transferred to another train for the suburb of Lichtenberg, which is on the eastern periphery of the city. I had with me a small satchel with changes of clothing and, in my pocket, a tube of Veronal tablets.

When I left Tatiana in her rage the day before, I'd gone directly to the Rare Earths Laboratory, where certain poisonous substances were kept along with the rare earth elements, alkaloids, and radioactive material. Theoretically, it was all under lock and key, but actually the cupboard I wanted was not locked; there was the symbol of a skull and crossbones pasted to the door. On the jar of Veronal was a warning: *Use of Veronal should be discouraged in favor of a barbiturate less potent, shorter-acting, with noncumulative effects.*

The Roumanian Biologist George Treponesco—who was in charge of Rare Earths now—said nothing as I shook twenty tablets into my hand and put them in a small tube, which I stoppered at both ends with cotton. He was still infatuated with Tatiana. In any case, he shook my hand and wished me good luck. Maybe he wasn't such a bad person after all, or maybe he was hoping I would take the Veronal.

I should have taken a later train than the 6:30, for I arrived at 7:29 and stood outside the gate of I. G. Farben for half an hour looking through the barbed-wire fence at the huge complex: two large factories, several smaller buildings, and an acre of temporary structures—*Nissen Hütten*—of one floor each.

At exactly 7:59, one hand in my pocket clutching the tube of Veronal, the other holding the satchel and my papers, I approached the entrance. There were guards at this gate, but they waved me on without even looking at my papers. I, however, stopped and asked one of them where I was to go. He read the summons and directed me to Building 7, a temporary hut not far from the gate. Outside the door of Building 7 stood a man in a white lab coat.

"Bernhardt?" he said.

I nodded.

He walked away as I entered the building.

The official at the desk was polite. I presented him with my summons, and he gave me forms to fill out for employment, taxes, and insurance. While I was writing, the man in the white lab coat came into the room and began to complain to the official.

"My laboratory assistant was taken away two months ago—two months! And you promised you would find me some help. How do you expect me, alone, to keep up with all the lab work for the entire factory?" He left without so much as glancing at me.

When I returned the completed forms, the official said, "You are to sleep in Building Twenty-seven; you are to eat in Building Ten; you will be working for Dr. Schmidt in the laboratory in the Administration Building. You will have off every other Wednesday"—he consulted a calendar, looked up at me, and smiled—"starting tomorrow." He handed me back my papers!

"Tomorrow?"

"Tomorrow." He smiled at me again.

"Do I have to take the day off tomorrow?"

"Yes, but you can stay in the barracks, or there are day rooms with libraries, radios, and you are most welcome to use them."

I stood and bowed to him. "Thank you very much."

My good Lord, how on earth could I go back to the Institute the next day after the tears and farewells the day before? After I'd picked up the Veronal, I'd gone to the greenhouse to see if there were any flowers. There were not, but Gunther the gardener gave me some leafy sunflower plants, not blooming yet, which were grown to feed Bolotnikov's ladybugs, and I borrowed from Gunther a pair of white gardening gloves. Then I returned to Tatiana. The Chief had sent over a bottle of real wine, Sonja had baked a cake with real sugar and eggs, and they'd given us a rabbit and all.

During the meal, we listened to the news and music on the new Allied Station—Soldiers Transmitter West. Tatiana would not touch even a drop of the wine, but she did eat some. And after our dinner, when a mellow Glenn Miller began on the Allied Station, I put on the white gloves, stood, bowed as I had been taught in Dancing and Social Behavior Class, and presented her with the green bouquet.

She took the sunflower plants but would not dance with me. Her hair still was braided tight around her head, and she still was weeping. So I finished off the rest of the wine, plus vodka, drank myself senseless, fell into the bed, and awakened in a sweat from the dream.

No, in my fantasy, I could picture a return to Tatiana the very next day. Besides, I did not want to talk anyone. I was very tired, and I did not want to talk.

The man in the white lab coat whom I'd seen at the entrance to Building 7, and again when he came in to argue about a lab assistant, was waiting outside the building for me. "I am Dr. Wilhelm Friedrich Schmidt. I am a physicist. You will be working with me. Do you know anything at all of polymerization?"

"Nothing." I walked beside him across the compound.

"I hear you know a lot about electricity. You can tell me about it."

My dear Lord, Professor Kreutzer's umbrella still covered me.

The Administration Building was red brick and looked like my high school. The lab was old-fashioned: high ceilings, gothic windows, square wooden worktables. There was a very clean bathroom with a shower. The factory produced perlon fibers, and the job of this lab was to measure the viscosity of the polymers and the tear resistance of monofilaments. It took less than an hour a day to do this, and after Schmidt showed me how, he didn't do anything at all but smoke and talk and, more or less, continue my education for the brief time I was there.

That first day he gave me books to read, and because he hadn't anything else to do, he made up a formal written examination to quiz me on what I had read. Stupid.

EXAMINATION

I. G. Farben Corp., Lichtenberg   By: Dr. W. F. Schmidt
II, I, 45.   For: J. Bernhardt
Subject: Polymerization

1. Why do we measure the viscosity of resins? (Discuss the relationship between degree of polymerization, length of chain, and viscosity.)

2. Why do we measure tear resistance and stretchability of monofilaments?

3. Describe the influence of temperature upon the viscosity of liquids. Consult the article by Andradi in *Nature*, V. 125, p. 582, 1920.

4. Describe the difference (temp.) of the Du Pont Nylon and our product.

5. Discuss the electrical properties of thermoplastics in great detail.

Ha! The last question was because he really didn't know and was too lazy to read up on it himself. Professor Kreutzer never questioned me on what I'd read. Nor did the Chief. But since I had nothing else to do, I wrote out elaborate answers for three days— he said it was all right if I studied in the lab on my day off—until I was so bored I asked Schmidt if he would like me to make the entire operation of measuring the viscosity completely automatic.

"That's a wonderful idea," he said.

The viscosimeter was a long tube filled with the hot, syrupy stuff. One dropped a steel ball and timed its trip through the tube; in short, one measured how long it took to sink to the bottom. I began to figure out how to measure the drop of the steel ball electrically, so we wouldn't have to watch it and time it, which would give us both absolutely nothing to do. The tear-resistant test took no time at all—one merely tied weights to a thread of determined length and weight to ascertain how much it stretched and when it tore.

I had just begun to assemble the equipment to make an automatic viscosimeter when someone must have denounced me—perhaps a loyal Nazi in the personnel office took a good look at my forms, or maybe one of the other workers resented my privileged position. I received another summons less than a week after coming to Farben. I was to appear the very next morning, Tuesday, at eight, at another factory closer to the center of Berlin, near Ostkreuz. So I had no opportunity for a second day off to see Tatiana. I could have telephoned her, I suppose, but I didn't want to. It occurred to me, also, that I should let Professor Kreutzer know what was happening to me, but I did not wish to burden him with my existence any longer. I was very tired. I did not want to talk.

. . .

Berlin is dark at 6:30 A.M. in mid-January. There no longer was snow removal and after the sunrise one would be able to see the dirty, gray snow. I had all my papers with me, my small suitcase, and the tube of Veronal tablets. There was nothing to keep me from taking the train anywhere—to the Institute, to the house of my father—but they would look for me there. I spoke French like a native and could have gone into a free French labor camp, or I could have sought out some of my father's family—Gentiles. Surely, they would hide me? I understand now that I was ill and depressed, and I did as all the others—I followed the orders of the governing authorities. One cannot pass judgment unless he has been in a similar circumstance.

The I. G. Farben plant was a city compared to Wolff Printing and Dyeing Company, which was on a side street, ten minutes by S-Bahn from Lichtenberg. It was one U-shaped building, behind a dirty red-brick wall with barbed wire on top. There were guards at the gate. They took all my papers, and one of them "escorted" me to the personnel office, where, once again, I was asked to fill out forms for employment, insurance, and taxes.

When I had finished, the personnel official said, "You are assigned to the dye kitchen. Do you prefer day or night shift?"

"Night."

He made a notation, then recited: "It is forbidden to leave the premises without orders. This is an industry which is directly under the Interior Ministry for Total War. Any infraction against the rules, which include rules of safety, loitering, and tardiness, will be mercilessly punished under martial law. Your work begins promptly at six o'clock in the evening. You will report to the foreman of the dye kitchen, Herr Freulisch, at five fifty-five!" He handed me a card. "His name is on this card. His orders to you will be the law! A foreman in the dormitory will assign you quarters." He handed me a canteen book. "You have here coupons for three meals each day."

He did not return my papers.

My "quarters" were a cot in a room with twenty-four others. The barracks were not in separate *Nissen Hütten* but in an older section of the factory building along with the canteen. Although they were not as clean as those at Farben and not as warm, and the bathrooms were filthy, I felt more secure, for at this second factory, the workers mostly were free Germans, some of whom lived in the barracks, and the forced laborers were either Russians or people with a mixed background similar to mine. There were no Balts, as far as I could tell. The German free workers did not bother the others, displaying no feeling one way or the other. But at the first place, Farben, the "Folk Germans," as they were called, who had migrated east to Lithuania, Latvia, and Estonia, had maintained their ties to Germany with exaggerated patriotism. Professor Kreutzer was right about them—they out-nazied the Nazis. I was afraid of them, although they hadn't time to actually bother me at Farben. Following Professor Kreutzer's advice, I stayed to myself in both places and kept my mouth shut.

I was hungry. The food at Farben had been inadequate. I put my suitcase under my cot and went to the canteen to eat lunch: one meal ticket for a plate of stew, bread, and ersatz coffee which was undrinkable. The food was all right, except that the three meals amounted to only 800 calories. Then I returned to the dormitory, where I crawled into my cot with my clothes on—a sweater, too—covering myself with the two warm blankets they provided. I could not get warm, and I was very tired. I dreamed my dream and awakened after five in the afternoon, went to the canteen for the supper of stew, bread, and ersatz coffee, and, after asking directions from the dormitory foreman, began to look for the dye kitchen.

It was in the basement of the boiler house, a section of building at the tip of the U nearest the front gate, behind two huge, closed iron doors. I was ten minutes early—it was a quarter to six—and worried that someone might assume I was loitering. At five minutes to six, I tried the great doors, but they would not budge, and I worried that the foreman would turn me in for tardiness. Remember Uncle Philip. At one minute to six, nine other night workers gathered. At six, on the dot, the great doors opened and the day workers moved out, silent and hurried; the night workers filed in, silent and slow. I entered last, following them through the heavy iron doors, which clanged shut behind me.

I was in a stinking, smoky den, warm and moist. Sooty beads of water slid down blackened concrete walls. Shaded lamps hanging by a single cord from the ceiling illuminated the work areas like the lamp over the billiard table at my father's club. Four giant vats steamed on a gas fire, vats so tall the workers climbed a three-rung ladder to a catwalk circling them to stir or add or take away. In the center was a large platform scale; in the shadows were hills of bags—starch, sugar, and dye—and buckets and buckets of milk.

The workers all were old, as old as my father. They stood together beneath a lamp, immobile, eyes cast down. I stood out of the light.

A low voice, monotone, most likely the foreman, said, "You! Bring me the fuckin' bucket."

A worker left the group, plodded fifteen paces or so, holding his lower back, groaning as he bent to pick up a galvanized iron pail. He carried it to within three paces of the foreman and released the handle. The bucket fell, clattered to the floor, and rolled over, bending the rim. The foreman let it lie and gave assignments in a language I could not understand—Berlin dialect—a ten-word vocabulary covering the spectrum, totally metaphorical and esoteric, each word with a hundred meanings covering a hundred circumstances.

In response to the orders, four of the men moved slowly, muttering softly to themselves, to the vats, to the scale, to the piles of starch and dye. The other four lay down on the stacks of bags. No one communicated with another. The foreman picked up the galvanized bucket lying on its side near his feet, moved to the scaffolding surrounding the vats, climbed the three rungs with heavy legs, walked along the planks, stirred the contents of the vats with a wooden shovel, tasted, and called out, "more blue shit," or "more fuckin' shit," or "more shit"—random amounts, random temperatures. At the Institute I had to measure a speck with a Geiger counter or determine if there was a little vein missing from the wing of a fruit fly. The foreman filled the iron pail from one of the vats and climbed down from the catwalk, swearing quietly to himself. When he was again on the floor, several of the men resting on the bags rose, came to him, scooped up pudding from the bucket he held, drank it, scooped up more, and returned to their sacks. The foreman put the bucket down, threw himself, sighing, upon the bags, and closed his eyes.

"Pardon me," I said from my shadow, "are you Herr Freulisch?"

"Eh?" He opened one eye.

"Pardon me." I moved closer, bowing slightly. "Are you Herr Freulisch? I was assigned to work duty here."

I did not understand his reply to me, so I said, "I beg your pardon?"

He was on his feet in an instant, mimicking me. "I beg yer pardon, I beg yer pardon? Get his. Hey, get his." He made a mock bow to me. "Lah-dee-dah. I beg yer pardon."

Two apparitions arose from their starch bags and floated into the light, bowing and bending in curtsies. One picked up an empty bag and hung it from his shoulders, like a cape or a royal train, and the other lifted its edges. They pranced and bowed, clicking their heels and I-beg-yer-pardoning.

Freulisch said, "Well, they done it. They sent us a rich pisher. How d'ye like the way the real people live, rich pisher, little pisher? Here now, little pisher, pick up that fuckin' bag of shit." He motioned toward a bag of starch.

It was over a hundred pounds. I lifted it an inch from the stack. The room was hot and humid; I was dizzy and weak; my legs folded, and I was on the floor.

"All you can do, you limp prick, is fuck a juicy broad, but you can't lift this fuckin' shit," said the one with the cape. And with that assessment of my character and strength, all but the foreman returned to their bags.

I jumped to my feet, lost my balance, and sat down hard on the floor.

The foreman gave me a metal cup and motioned toward the bucket of pudding. I stood up, slowly, walked to the bucket, dipped in, and drank. Sweet, rich, it was made of potato starch, sugar and milk. He motioned for me to take more. I did. I drank a liter or so and then sat on the bags and waited for someone to tell me what to do. It was warm and dark and wet—a womb. One became used to the stink. I was tired and my stomach full. I lay back on the soft bags, slept, and dreamed my dream.

Clanging and pounding on the closed iron doors awakened me abruptly. Two workers grabbed my arms and jerked me to my feet; a third put a shovel in my hand. "Shovel that shit, little pisher."

The iron doors burst open. I shoveled blue dye from a mound on the floor into a bucket. All the men worked furiously now— shoveling, carrying, weighing, stirring. Through the opened iron doors clattered a warehouse truck carrying two empty vats, pushed by two shouting men: "Two blue shit. Two blue shit. Two blue shit."

The empties were exchanged for two full, steaming vats lifted with an overhead crane on a trolley, and, grunting and swearing, out through the doors went the two men, pushing the full vats on the platform truck.

Freulisch slammed and locked the doors—the only ventilation—and the moist heat and the smell settled again. The workers opened their hands and dropped their shovels, buckets, bags of starch and dye. Four returned to sleep. Freulisch and the other four began to fill the empty vats according to a formula called out:

"Piss to fuckin' blue line.

"One fuckin' shit.

"BL blue shit."

I drank another cup of pudding, curled up on my sacks, and was asleep.

They awakened me again for the air raid. It was ten at night, which meant it was the British. We hurried down to a subcellar beneath the basement kitchen, ten men and two buckets—one filled with fresh, hot pudding, the other for us to fill. There were several cots and more piles of bags in the subcellar. I drank another half a liter of the pudding and slept until they awakened me for the all-clear: "Up, little pisher." Then I slept in the dye kitchen until shortly before six in the morning, when the night shift hurried out and the day people shuffled in.

I went directly to the canteen for a breakfast of stew, bread, and ersatz coffee, then to the dormitory, where I showered, shaved, dressed in clean clothes and a sweater, and climbed into my cot, covering myself with two blankets. The moment I fell asleep, I was on the racing train. I awakened, exhausted, at noon to eat lunch; slept again until shortly after five; ate my supper of stew and so before going to work, where I was given an assignment: to weigh the dry ingredients for the first batch. I stood in the circle of light beside the scale.

"Number three fuckin' shit," the vat man yelled at me.

Two other workers began to shovel potato starch onto the platform of the scale. I just stood there.

"Number three, little pisher," yelled the vat man.

The two workers stopped working and leaned on their shovels. "Number three, little pisher," said one.

A row of weights sat on a shelf behind me. Each had a number or a letter or two on it, but no weight. I found one that read 3, hung it on the balance, and asked the shovelers, "How many pounds is that?"

They did not answer. They shoveled until the No. 3 balanced out. Only then did one of the shovelers answer me: "Do you think it puts more fuckin' shit in yer belly if yer know what the shit weighs, little pisher?"

"BL, BL blue shit."

I found the weight marked "BL" and hung it on the balance. While they carried the blue color to the vats, I read the recipes pasted to the scale. Here is the recipe for blue dye:

> *Water to blue line.*
> *Milk to red line.*
> *No. AS wt. sugar.*
> *No. 3 wt. potato starch.*
> *No. BL wt. blue dye.*

We then prepared a batch of green and a brown. After two hours, my work for the night was done. I drank some pudding and slept—on the train—until morning, interrupted now and then by the warehousemen, exchanging empty vats for full, and by the British.

I was forgotten by the authorities. No more orders. Unlike some others—unlike Mitzka Avilov—all my actions were self-protective. Stay quiet. Stay safe. I drank at least three liters of pudding each night, and I slept my unrefreshing sleep on bags of starch. I was very tired. I dreamed one dream. If there were others, I did not remember.

During the day, too, I slept, waking to eat the three meals in the canteen, to shower and shave, to wash my clothes in the laundry room every other day, and then to sleep again. I could not read; there were magazines in the dayroom—propaganda—and the classics—Goethe, Schiller, or so—but I could not concentrate on even the simplest ideas. I did not know when February came or March or April. I moved only where I had to move, said only what I had to say. Mostly one was able to be silent. But not always.

Respecting Professor Kreutzer's admonitions, I always ate alone. But one day, at lunch, a man approached me. He was of early middle age and dressed in work clothing.

"Josef Bernhardt?"

I looked up at him.

"Mind if I sit down?" He spoke in High German.

I extended my hand toward the empty chair across the room.

Still standing, he said, "Name's Schneider. Professor Schneider, University of Heidelberg, Department of Sociology."

"How do you do, Herr Professor," I said, rising slightly from my chair.

"Sit down. Sit down, son." He sat. "We've had our eye on you."

I said nothing.

His eyes appeared larger than normal through the thick lenses of his spectacles. "You must wonder how I knew your name?"

I nodded.

"We have our resources." He smiled broadly. "We know that you are one of us." He indicated with a nod a group of ten or so sitting at a table in the corner. "You are welcome to join us at any time."

"Thank you, Herr Professor," I said. Do not talk. Be alone. Do not join any groups.

"And I bring to you the collective sympathy." He laughed. "We understand they put you with those subhumans in the dye kitchen."

"I beg your pardon?"

"Did you know that the difference between the higher and lower human beings is greater than the difference between the higher primates and man? Ah, well, I see you think me unkind, Bernhardt. And perhaps you are right. They are not to be blamed; it is due to environmental retardation rather than heredity. I've had a field day collecting data during my . . . 'holiday' here."

One must answer something. "My aunt is a sociologist in America," I lied, for no reason I could understand.

"Oh, is that true? A fascinating science, a new science. And even while on . . . 'holiday,' I try to keep up. Do you know, has she published?"

"We haven't been in touch recently, Herr Professor. She's in Iowa."

"Iowa? I know my colleagues at Harvard, Chicago—people of that ilk." He smiled down at me. "But I don't think I know of any sociologists from Iowa."

So deeply is it engrained in our German souls to revere superiors and teachers, I rose and extended my hand across the table to him. "Well, thankyouverymuch, Herr Professor, for your kind invitation."

He stood and shook my hand. "That's quite all right. Courage, Bernhardt. This will all be over very soon, and people like us will be the future leaders. The privileged status will belong to us." He rejoined his privileged colleagues, several of whom waved at me from across the room.

For the next meal, I brought along a volume of Goethe from the dayroom and pretended to be deeply engrossed as I sat alone and ate. Thereafter, I always carried a book, even to work.

My new habit did not escape my colleagues in the dye kitchen, one of whom summarized the situation. "Sure," he said, "you can read a fuckin' book, you limp prick, but you can't fuck a juicy broad."

But they would do me no harm. I had the same right to eat the starch pudding and to sleep on the bags. I was absolutely part of the gang. And although they thought I "talked funny," mostly they asked no questions. Once only, when I was at the scale, a shoveler resting on his shovel said, "How come you aren't a soldier?"

"My mother was a Jew."

Several nights later when I was again at the scale, he said, "I think my daughter was livin' with one of them. They got taken away to a concentcamp early on, and he wasn't no commie."

Which gave me the courage to approach him after a week or so. "Don't you like the commies?"

"Crooks. They cheat us."

"Do you think the workers are treated well now?"

He snorted and walked away. Almost a week later, he shook me awake, gently, as I lay on my bags of starch.

"They all cheat us, little pisher," he said. "The commies and the rich fuckers. We like to choose our own crooks from amongst ourselves."

It was he, along with Freulisch, who warned me, the two of them motioning me aside just as we were filing down into the subcellar for a nightly air raid. I actually knew it already—my "privileged" co-workers had not shown up for either lunch or dinner that day—but I refused to let myself recognize the implications.

"They took some o' them others," said Freulisch, handing me a card. "This is sent for you."

"The ones like you," said the shoveler.

The note was handwritten, unsigned, and not dated: *Josef Leopold Bernhardt is to report to the Personnel Office with all his belongings at promptly 6:55 tomorrow morning.*

We hurried to join the others, for the bombing seemed particularly close and heavy.

In a thunderstorm one sees the lightning and then hears the thunder. With a bomb, the order is reversed. One hears the howling even underground, then feels the shaking, and then there is dust. One cannot see anything, and can hardly breathe. Then one hears booms and crashings and feels a jolt. All is very silent until people begin to cry and one hears glass breaking. The lights were gone. We were in total darkness. Even from the subcellar we could tell that the factory had been hit.

"Let's see if we can get out of here."

Someone lit a candle.

"Put out that fuckin' candle. You'll use up the air."

Darkness.

Freulisch: "There might be gas leaking. No fuckin' matches." He sent someone up the stairs to see if we were trapped.

Very shortly, a voice shouted down to us, "We can get out easy, Freulisch."

Freulisch: "D'ye think we can wait till the fuckin' planes are gone?"

Voice: "I don't think so. Gas leakin'."

I did not want to leave. And yet I knew that I must, for I was certain that in the morning I would be "relocated to the East." I had not been out-of-doors since I came to Wolff in January. I had not heard a news report or read a paper. Obviously, the war was not over. Maybe it never would be over. When it was, if I survived, I was obligated to marry Tatiana and be a mathematician and have two children, a boy named Josef and a girl named Tatiana. I always carried the Veronal with me. It was against the law to be on the streets during air raids. I had no papers. Our basement kitchen was probably the only warm place left in Berlin. It was a crime to bring children into this fucking world. I did not want to leave the dye kitchen.

We filed out of the cellar and, because of the smell of leaking gas, ran through the dye kitchen, up the stairs, and into the open air. Most of the building was standing, although one section was badly damaged. There was no big fire, only small ones here and there, giving enough light to see. The brick wall surrounding the compound was intact. The snow was gone. We huddled together inside the gate. The bombers had moved on, but the all-clear had not yet sounded.

I said to Freulisch, "My papers are in the office. I don't have any papers."

He didn't answer me.

"My papers are there. I don't have papers."

"They're hangin' them without papers. Especially the young ones."

"Who?"

"The young ones without papers. Deserters."

"Who's hanging them?"

"You can see them hangin' from the light posts on every fuckin' corner."

I was cold. The all-clear sounded and they began to move slowly toward the factory, leaving me standing alone by the gate. The streets beyond were jammed with people swarming from bomb shelters. There were fires everywhere. I slipped through the gate and, in an instant, was in the middle of a moving mass of bodies, pressing and crushing toward the trams and trains. I shoved and pushed to stay in the center. Two corpses, both young men, dangled from a dark lamppost on the corner. The fires illuminated large white placards attached to the ropes on their throats; there was not enough light to read the inscriptions.

Berlin had gone wild. Jammed in the midst of the living throng, I let myself be carried into the Ostkreuz S-Bahn station. The train toward Friedrichstrasse would take me deeper into the heart of Berlin. I had no ticket. Most likely, they would not be checking for tickets; if they did, I was lost. I had no papers. Remember Uncle Philip. Staying in a crush of other bodies, I jumped onto a train which would take the Berlin Circle north—toward the Institute. At Gesundbrunnen, a busy transfer point, I moved in a jam to a train heading northeast. Three stops before Hagen, the crowd became dangerously thin, and I detrained in the center of a group and cut off across the fields, stumbling and falling in the darkness. I came across no one at all; it was quiet and very peaceful, and yet I knew to be found wandering at night was suicidal, so I stopped and hid in dense shrubbery until, at the first light of the eastern horizon, I ran through the fields and woods to the tiny village of Hagen, past more fields, the little forest, the hospitals to the Institute, through the guardless gate, around the circular drive, past the flagpole that still flew no flag, and into the park, where I sat on a stone bench along the winding drive. It was chilly. I could smell the apple blossoms from the orchard beyond—and lilac. It must be late in April.

. . .

Everything looked the same—deserted, of course, because of the early hour—but well-kept. I knew I must hide; the Institute was the first place they would look for me. And I knew that if I went to anyone but Tatiana, the wrath of God would descend upon me, and it would come from her. I pictured her, the braid falling across her breast, one fist clutching shut the pink quilted robe—worn and mended—eyes narrowed, lips tight. If the proper wife were to be chosen for me, I supposed it would be someone like Tatiana. But sitting on a stone bench in a garden in April, I could not help but think of Sheereen, that lovely face engraved permanently in my memory, and I thought of the breasts of Kirsti Krupinsky. I stretched out on the cold slab and closed my eyes to dwell on my fantasy, holding, in my pocket, the glass tube with the twenty Veronal tablets.

The sun was up. There no longer was an excuse to avoid Tatiana. I arose from my slab and walked slowly toward her apartment building, feeling hopelessly trapped and guilty. I did not love her, and perhaps that is the only characteristic I had in common with Mitzka Avilov.

She wasn't there.

I knocked lightly. "Tanya? Tanya. Psst, Tanya. It's Josef." My first assumption was that she did not want to open the door to me. It was terribly early, and I didn't want to awaken the other tenants, so I avoided loud banging. I wasn't alarmed yet, although it did occur to me that she might be gone, that they might have tried to "relocate" her, too. If so, Tatiana most certainly would have fled to safety. This, of course, would not release me from my obligation.

I ran into the next building, where Sonja lived, and knocked on her door. When she didn't answer, I pounded, then began to yell and shout. She wasn't there, either, and nobody came out of the other doors to complain of the noise I was making. That is when I realized that something terrible must have happened.

I tore down the stairs and across the park to the main building. To my relief, I was greeted by a swarm of little escapees who wanted to rejoin their pure-bred colleagues inside. Research on the *Drosophila,* then, was still going on. I shooed the little fellows in with me, then ran, my heart pounding from anxiety and from the unaccustomed exercise, through the deserted lobby and up the stairs of the right wing to the Biology Laboratory.

In any case, no one would be there this early. I checked the mass grave: fresh bodies. The flies had been sorted and dated the day before and marked *April 18.* This, then, had to be April 19. I looked at a calendar to discover the day—Thursday—and at the clock on the wall—6:50. It was Thursday, April 19, 1945, at 6:50 in the morning. I had been gone for three and a half months.

My Greenough binocular sat on my worktable, just as I'd left it. I opened the top drawer of the table and found the terrible cigarettes I'd left, lit up, and inhaled deeply. If I were found, it would be dangerous for the Chief and everyone else—if they were still at the Institute. But if not, who was doing the sorting? Bach? Very faintly, I could hear the fugue, delicate, passionate, and joyful, wafting up the stairwell from the first floor. My good Lord, Rabin.

I disposed of the cigarette, then slowly, cautiously, walked down the stairs and across the empty lobby toward the music, stopping at the parlor door. Rabin did not take kindly to being disturbed when he was practicing. I entered quietly, but he heard me.

"Yosup!" He jumped up from the piano, ran to me, embraced me, kissing me three times on each cheek, then pound-pound-pounding me on the back. "Yosup! Yosup!"

I was overwhelmed by his joy at seeing me. "Rabin! Where is everybody?" I hugged him and pounded him on the back.

Unfortunately, I spoke no Russian, and Rabin, although he had been at the Institute longer than I, had learned hardly a word of German.

"Tatiana," I said. "Tanya? Where is Tatiana?"

He nodded, beaming, made a circle with the thumb and first finger of his right hand, and said, "Goot. Pfery goot."

"Tanya's good? Very good?"

He nodded again, smiling broadly. "Tatiana—*Mommá, Poppá.*"

"Tanya's with her parents, her mama and papa?"

"*Da, da. Mommá and Poppá.* Pfery goot."

"The Chief? Professor Kreutzer? Krupinsky?"

Still nodding. "Pfery goot. Chief, Professor, Krupinsky. Pfery goot." Rabin then pointed to the ceiling and made flying motions with his arms.

I looked puzzled. "Birds?"

He shook his head, pointed again to the ceiling, made an airplane of his right hand and arm, and flew about the room. "*Bzzzzzzzzzzzzzzz.*"

"Ah, the Luftwaffe."

"Da, Luftwaffe." He saluted briskly. *"Bzzzzzzz. Pffft."* And he blew them all away.

"Gone? The Luftwaffe is gone?"

He nodded vigorously. *"Pffffffftt."*

"All of them? All?" I indicated many numbers with my fingers.

He nodded, then held up five fingers and then ten.

All gone but ten or fifteen. My God, the air force people comprised two thirds of the entire staff of the Institute—some 130 or so people out of the 200. That would explain why the apartment buildings were empty. Most of the space had been taken up by Luftwaffe personnel.

"Why?" I pointed to the ceiling, extended my palms up, with a look of amazement on my face.

Rabin marched ten paces forward and ten back. "Russkies," he said gleefully. "Red Army."

"Here?" I pointed to the floor, to the walls.

He laughed and held up one finger, then two, and marched again.

"One day? Two days. They'll be here?"

"Da! Khoroshaw! One day. Two day."

My good Lord, talk about relativity—seven kilometers by train, seven more on foot, the war was over, winter was gone, and it was spring.

"Trusov!" said Rabin. *"Pffft."*

"Grand Duke Trusov? He's gone, too?"

He nodded.

"Where's Sonja? Sonja Press?"

His expression changed to one of great seriousness, and my heart jumped into my throat.

"Madame Avilov," he said sadly.

"Yes, Madame Avilov. I understand. *Ponimayu.*"

Rabin pretended to slit his throat from ear to ear, slash both wrists, and swallow two fistfuls of pills with water. "Mitzka," he said.

I nodded that I understood. Madame was dead. Sonja had, most likely, moved in with the Chief.

He played an arpeggio on an imaginary piano, then embraced me again before returning to the Bechstein.

It had not occurred to me that anyone would be overjoyed at my return.

With the Russians so close, the S.S. would not come as far east as Hagen to hunt me down. I knew I would endanger no one by being there, so I returned to the Genetics wing—to the kitchen in the greenhouse. There was no polenta on the stove, no cornmeal or molasses, but bowls and bowls of sunflower seeds, vats of vodka, and canisters of the milled tea. I made myself a cup of tea laced with vodka, cracked a mound of sunflower seeds—tedious work —before I began to eat.

I must admit, I was looking forward to the welcome from Krupinsky and the others. I decided that I would be hard at work when they walked in and that I would act as though nothing had happened.

At nine, Krupinsky wandered in with his wife, Kirsti. Both of them ignored me completely—not even a nod or a "good morning." I wouldn't give him the satisfaction of reacting, so I just sat at my microscope sorting flies. Finally, Kirsti could stand it no longer. "Abe," she said, "this is too cruel," and she threw her arms about me and wept. "My dear, my dear, how wonderful to have you safe!"

Krupinsky rolled back on his heels and grinned.

"Rabin told us," Kirsti said. "He came running out into the lobby. And Abe insisted we tease you."

"Where have you been? Nobody knew where the hell you disappeared to after you left Farben." Krupinsky looked even thinner and not at all well.

I shrugged. "Rabin tells me the war is over here."

"Who knows? The German troops came through in a big hurry

a couple of days ago—said the Russians were only ten, fifteen miles to the east."

"That close?"

"That's what they said. Nobody knows where the Americans are. Anyway, did Rabin tell you that most of our people left? Almost all the Luftwaffe."

"He mentioned the Luftwaffe—and Tanya."

"Just a few civilian doctors left up in Brain Research, and a few Mantle chemists, and all the specials: Rabin, Bolotnikov, Ignatov, François Daniel, the Yugoslav. Who else is here, Kirsti?"

"The Chief and Professor Kreutzer."

"Tell him something he doesn't know."

"George Treponesco and Latte—that Gestapo."

"Tell him something he wants to hear," said Krupinsky. "Frau Doktor and Sonja."

"Gunther the gardener?" I asked.

"Yes, he's here, and the janitors and kitchen help—although there's nothing much to eat. I'd say there are fifty or so people in the whole place, plus some wives. Monika's gone, and Marlene and her husband. Did Rabin tell you that Trusov left?"

I nodded.

"The Duke thought we should all leave. He said he's more afraid of the Soviets than he was of the Nazis. They killed all his family, you know, during the revolution."

"What did Professor Kreutzer think of that idea—of leaving?"

"He said that Berlin was in chaos."

"It is."

"We heard that there are barricades and fighting in the streets, and that the S.S. are hanging people on lampposts. I haven't seen it myself—we moved out here right after you left."

"Our building was bombed," said Kirsti.

"I can't believe how peaceful it is," I said.

"The food's mostly gone," said Krupinsky. "All the rabbits, and no fresh fruit or vegetables yet—it's too early. All we have is the dried corn and sunflower seeds—no molasses. But we have water and electricity still, and lots of vodka."

"And tea," said Kirsti. "Enough tea. Most of the apartments are empty, so you can just take one."

"Tanya is with her parents?"

Krupinsky and Kirsti exchanged meaningful looks, and Kirsti said, "That's right. Her father came out and got her."

"Did she get a summons, too?"

"No. They just thought she'd be safer with them. She was upset. Professor Kreutzer said you could have kept in touch—at least at first. She was quite angry with you."

"So what else is new," said Krupinsky. "She was always mad at him."

I shrugged. Krupinsky was right. "She never approved of anything I did."

"That's not fair, Josef. How would you have felt if she'd been taken?"

"That's just the point. Tanya would not have let herself be taken."

"I think you've grown taller," Krupinsky said, "three inches or so."

"One and a half!"

"And fat. You are positively gross." He slapped my back.

We all three laughed. I now weighed one hundred and twenty-seven pounds, and I was almost five feet ten inches tall.

"Come on, where the hell have you been?"

"I'll tell you Krup, it's like this. The first week at Farben I got into trouble."

He nodded, his lips pursed. "Yes, go on."

"I noticed that the bread rolls were getting smaller each day, and I began to complain to the baker, 'The bread is getting smaller.' Well, to make a long story short, they had a meeting of the bakers' association and got a petition to have me thrown in jail for saying 'The bread is getting smaller.'"

Krupinsky nodded again. "Uh-huh," he said, cupping his chin in his hand.

"So I was thrown in jail. As you can imagine, the food was so terrible, I almost starved, but for one of the bakers, whose conscience began to bother him."

"I'm with you," said Krupinsky.

"So he smuggled in bread to me, every day, through the key-hole."

"I see."

"And all that bread—that's why I'm so fat."

"Bernhardt, your brain has atrophied. I told you that joke the first week you were here."

"And my grandfather told it to your grandfather."

We continued the routine sorting of the fruit flies and waited for the Red Army, which came the next morning.

CHAPTER EIGHT

Last Day

I was to hoist a white flag on the pole out in front that had never known a flag.

"Timing is essential," said Professor Kreutzer. "There is a possibility that German military still might be retreating through here. If they spot a flag of surrender, they will open fire on us. On the other hand, if the Red Army doesn't find one, we will all be killed."

"Scylla and Charybdis," said the Chief. "If one isn't smashed on the rock, he will drown in the whirlpool."

"We will tell you when to raise it," said Professor Kreutzer. "Have the flag ready and test the pulley mechanism on the pole." And he and the Chief, that day of my return, having toured all the labs in the Institute to give the final orders for the moment of liberation, returned to their telescope on the roof.

All that day, occasional refugees fleeing the invasion sought brief shelter, reporting that the Red Army was on their heels. From our lab, I could hear tanks and trucks, an occasional cannon firing. The Chief and Professor Kreutzer, on the roof, could see them. They actually arrived at the Institute the next morning, Friday, April 20, 1945, at ten.

"This is it! This is it!" The Chief ran down the hallway, shouting into each lab. "Josef, put up the flag. Now! Put up the flag."

Krupinsky and I raced down the stairs, out the front doors, tied a white lab coat by the sleeves, pulled it up the virgin pole, and beat a hasty retreat just as a truck with armed Soviets drove through the gate and around the circular drive.

Confusion. Krupinsky and I slammed into the lobby. The Chief, Professor Kreutzer, and Krupinsky were there, and some of the others. The Chief had a liter of vodka in one hand and a broom handle with a white rag attached in the other. "We will greet them on the front steps," he said breathlessly.

"No," said Professor Kreutzer calmly. "We will wait here in the lobby. Krup, you take the flag and stand in front, near the door. I'll open it so they can see you. Talk to them in Russian."

Reluctantly, Krupinsky relieved the Chief of the broom handle and moved, trembling, to the double doors. Professor Kreutzer opened them wide, then stepped back beside the Chief.

The rest of us huddled directly behind them: Rabin, Ignatov, Bolotnikov, the Yugoslav, the French Physicist François Daniel, the Roumanian Biologist George Treponesco, and I. The other men—the civilian doctors remaining in Brain Research, the two chemists left from Mantle, the custodians and kitchen workers— were told to stay in their work areas and pretend to be busy. The women—Frau Doktor, Sonja, Kirsti, the female lab assistants, and the wives—were hiding in the darkroom or in the various labs. Word had come from the refugees that the troops following the first, elite attack troops were raping all the women. The Security Officer, in civilian dress, was also "working" in one of the labs.

Through the open double doors, we could see twenty soldiers jump from the truck, holding submachine guns and rifles; some running into the park, the others advancing, slowly, toward the building.

"Wave the white flag," said the Chief. "Go to the door and let them see it. And speak Russian!"

The broom handle advanced, quaking, to the threshold.

We could not see the soldiers. They had flattened themselves against the building. A voice shouted, in German, "Let all German soldiers step outside with their hands up."

Krupinsky stepped outside.

One could hear the same voice. "Are there more?"

"We are not soldiers," said Krupinsky in German. My good Lord. He forgot to speak Russian.

"Krupinsky, speak Russian," hissed Professor Kreutzer through the door.

"You! Tell everyone to come out, slowly, with their hands up."

Professor Kreutzer nodded for us to obey; in a tight pack, we followed him and the Chief.

"One at a time!" Shouted in German.

We exited onto the stairs, one at a time, with our hands up, and, immediately, were surrounded by ten tense Soviet soldiers, pointing submachine guns and rifles at us. A young officer, followed by an aide, broke through the armed soldiers and addressed himself in German to Krupinsky, who still stood at the head of our little group.

"All soldiers and fascists must surrender. If any resistance is offered, this entire place will be destroyed and everyone become a prisoner. They can be assured of humane treatment by the great Red Army. We have no animosity against the German people. The Hitlers come and go, but the German people remain."

Krupinsky's voice was a squeak. "We speak Russian here," he said in Russian and pointed to the Chief. The broom handle was shaking violently.

The young officer looked toward us: the Chief and Professor Kreutzer standing in front, and the rest of us clustered behind them. Then Rabin shouted something in Russian and came forward very slowly.

When the young commissar saw the pianist, his face registered disbelief and then expressed such joy and amazement. Apparently, the Soviets did not know that Stalin's favorite pianist—famous all over Russia—was still alive.

"Rabin!"

They embraced.

The Chief came forward, raised the liter beaker of vodka, and said, "To the success of the great Red Army toward victory and peace," drank deeply, and handed it to the young officer, who said, "To the great Stalin, liberator of all people." He did not drink but, instead, pushed the beaker into the hand of Professor Kreutzer, ordering, "Drink!"

Professor Kreutzer bowed slightly and drank deeply. Only then did the young officer drink. He scanned the rest of us huddled together. "This young man," he said in German and pointed to me. "Is he not a soldier?"

"He is a Jew," said Professor Kreutzer.

"His papers!"

"He has none," said Professor Kreutzer, stepping forward as he spoke. "He escaped from a labor camp."

The officer cocked his head to one side and looked at me for an instant, then thrust the beaker toward me. "Drink!"

I did.

"You are lucky," he said. And at a sharp command from him in Russian, the soldiers pointed their weapons to the floor.

The entire plant had to be searched. Those of us in the lobby were ordered to remain where we were. An armed team took Professor Kreutzer along as hostage and looked into every building, every room, every corner of the park.

The young commissar stayed in the lobby and talked, in Russian, with Rabin, Bolotnikov, and Ignatov. The soldiers relaxed, some sitting on the floor, others standing easy or leaning against the walls, almost all smoking; and when they offered us cigarettes—*papirossi* with a long mouthpiece and small bit of tobacco, or *mahorca* tobacco in *Pravda* newspaper, rolled with one hand in their pockets—we relaxed, too. Krupinsky, the Yugoslav, and I sat on the stairs and were joined by François Daniel and that schlemiel Treponesco. The Chief paced back and forth between the two groups and listened.

"What we need to think about at this very moment," said Treponesco, "is how we are going to eat for the next year."

"For Christ's sake, you shiny ape," said Krupinsky. "What we have to think about is the welfare of our wives. You heard what's going on. The Russians are raping and killing."

"Not these," said the Yugoslav. "These first troops are elite and disciplined."

"And the mark will have no value whatsoever," continued Treponesco. "We need to think about how to get some occupation money."

The Chief, pacing in our direction, overheard Treponesco. "What we need to be thinking about," he said, "is how to continue our research."

"I think," said that schmuck Treponesco, "that we should take advantage of the tremendous sexual appetite of the Red Army. How if we get half a dozen ladies from the tenderloin district in Berlin, put them in the empty apartments, and say to the Russian soldiers, 'Be my guest'—for a slight fee, of course."

We laughed at this—all but the Chief and Krupinsky, who was too worried about his wife to think anything funny. Our mood was lifting. We were not afraid, at that moment, of the Soviets, and slowly it began to dawn that we may have been liberated.

"There must be another way," said François Daniel, "short of turning the Institute into a brothel."

"How if we use the fertilizing concept?" said the Yugoslav.

"What the hell does that mean, Mitya?" asked Krupinsky.

"Use your imagination. The doctors up in Brain Research are sitting on a huge supply of sulfonamides and condoms, and Treponesco has been collecting watches, jewelry—"

"That stuff's mine," Treponesco said, petulantly.

"Like hell it is," said the Yugoslav. "You got it on Institute requisitions!"

"Not all of it. I bought and traded."

"That's enough!" said the Chief, infuriated. "I am one hundred percent against the idea of selling anything here."

"But Chief, how will we eat?"

"I will find a way. Max and I. No doubt we will be supplied with what we need for survival. There will be no funds for new experimentation for a while, but we must continue with what we can. There will be no time for commerce. This is a place of serious research!" And he stalked off to listen to the other group.

The search team returned with Professor Kreutzer, and, after a brief conference, the commissar addressed us again in German: "So far all is clear here. But my men have found some interesting things." He laughed. "The most interesting might be those monkeys on the second floor.

"This place," he continued, in good humor, "is so full of women and inebriating substances, some of which may be poisonous, that if the soldiers following us get into it, we might as well stop the Berlin offensive."

We laughed.

"So I must declare this place off limits to our soldiers, or we would lose the war in Berlin. The attack groups are well disciplined, but those that follow us are disorderly. For *your* protection I leave an armed guard to keep the Red soldiers out." He turned to the Chief. "The colonel who will be in charge of the hospitals needs help from any physicians you have here who can speak both Russian and German."

"Of course," the Chief said. "Dr. Krupinsky here speaks Russian and is a fine medical doctor."

Krupinsky, at the mention of his name, stepped forward smiling, blushing like a bride.

"Would you mind coming with us now, Dr. Krupinsky, to the hospitals?"

"I would be overjoyed to be in a hospital again." He actually had tears in his eyes. "Can I get my things? My medical equipment—and my wife?"

"Yes, of course. But perhaps your wife would be safer here for a day or two."

Krupinsky hesitated.

"But you may take her, if you wish." He turned to the rest of us and said, "One more announcement. This Institute is hereby placed under the jurisdiction of the Commander of the Hospital Section, Berlin-Hagen. Starting tomorrow afternoon or, at the latest, the day after, your personnel will be placed on hospital officers' rations. Three good meals a day will be brought over."

We all looked at each other and smiled very much.

"We go now," said the commissar. "Sergeant Lazar and his guards are here. He will be in shortly to introduce himself."

It was noon. The young commissar and his troops left. We, still standing in the lobby, "liberated," were not certain what to do next.

Professor Kreutzer took command and captured our attention by changing from the rimless to the black-rims. We mustered about him to await orders. "My friends," he said, so softly that one had to strain to hear, "do not forget that there are guards at the gate."

"But Max," said the Yugoslav, "it is for our protection."

"Guards have two functions. One is to keep people out; the other is to keep people in. Do not forget that even under Nazi rule there were no guards at our gate."

"It is true," said the Chief. "'Protection' is a term common to both Nazis and Bolshevists. The first and foremost purpose of this 'protection' is to prevent any of us from leaving. We are under house arrest. Being under the protection of the Red Army is the same as being a prisoner. Correct, Max? Or am I right?"

"You are correct," said Professor Kreutzer. "Quiet! We have company."

A Soviet soldier had entered the lobby and was looking, hesitantly, in our direction. An older man, late fifties or so, he approached us, removed his cap, and bowed deferentially. "Hello, will you please excuse me," he said in what sounded like Middle High German. "I am Sergeant Lazar. My guards have surrounded this place, and you will be safe." No, it was Yiddish. He was speaking a patois of German and Yiddish.

"How many are you?" growled the Chief.

"We are only fourteen, but with automatic weapons that is sufficient, believe me."

"Sufficient to keep us locked in as prisoners, you mean."

"Oh, no, Herr Professor! Not at all! We are not NKVD. You are free to go and come. Believe me. I am not even a real soldier, even though I have been in one army or the other all my adult life; I am a farmer and I never once volunteered. Oh, no, to the contrary, we are here to protect you from the troops that follow. They are . . . let me put it this way: Are you aware of what the Nazis have done to the land and to the people?"

"We have heard of the concentration camps—the atrocities," said the Chief.

"Whatever you have heard," said Sergeant Lazar, "it is wrong. It is not enough. No words can describe what I have seen." He had tears in his eyes and took a great red handkerchief from his pocket, wiped his eyes, blew his nose before he could go on. "You see, it has made the Red Army very angry." He sighed. "But this place? This place is heaven, and I am very happy to be assigned here to help you, and so are my men."

"You're not Russian, are you?" asked the Chief.

Sergeant Lazar smiled. "No, I am not. I am from Galicia."

"Yet you have been in the Russian army all your life?"

"Did I say that? Oh, no, I said I have been in the army all my life—but not the Russian army. You see, I was in university—agriculture—when the First World War began, and I was conscripted into the Austrian army. After the war, I went back to university and was promptly drafted by the Polish army for several little wars. In 1939, I was taken prisoner by the Reds and was given the option to go to Siberia or to join the Red Army. So here I am. All the time I have distinguished myself by never rising above the rank of sergeant."

The Chief began to laugh. "Josef," he said, "give our friend here some vodka."

"Oh, no, thank you. I don't drink."

The Chief turned to Professor Kreutzer. "Max, what do you think? Can we trust this commissar? Is it safe to dig into the supply of cornmeal we've been saving and eat all we want?"

Professor Kreutzer shook his head, "Let's wait! There's enough for all personnel to have a bowl for each meal for several weeks. We'd better wait and see."

"Excuse me, Herr Professor," said Sergeant Lazar, "don't you worry. If the commissar said there will be food tomorrow, then there will be food tomorrow and plenty of it. This place is heaven," he said again, rolling his eyes.

And, indeed, the food came the next evening. Stew so rich and thick with meat, mostly meat, with peas and carrots and potatoes; good bread—moist, dark, heavy sourdough—and sausages, as good as before the war; real coffee, cream, and white sugar; Russian cigarettes; and American chocolate bars; all in generous amounts. But the day of our "liberation," we continued with the rationing, and life went on much as usual. As soon as Sergeant Lazar left us, Professor Kreutzer said, "Josef, it's time for Latte's x-ray treatment. Would you give me a hand?"

This, then, was what it was like to be liberated.

There were guards at the gate, a Soviet flag on the pole, and I sat in the small control booth of the Radiation Laboratory, watching the valves and meters, looking through the aquarium of glass and water at the wavering image of the Security Officer, who removed his white lab coat and lay down on the table, and at Professor Kreutzer, who fussed with the equipment. Today the neck. One wondered how long he would go on? It was the same as always, except that now our Gestapo in the House no longer wore the black uniform of the S.S.; Krupinsky and Kirsti were gone; it was more convenient to be advertised as a Jew than as a German; and I was beginning to worry about Tatiana. She should have stayed at the Institute.

When the x-ray treatment was over, Professor Kreutzer told me to shut down the high-voltage generators. The pumps for the linear accelerator had been turned off permanently in January, when the Russians had crossed the Oder. Professor Kreutzer said he could not take the risk of a sudden power failure; besides, there was no money to run anything. So when I shut down the generators, the Radiation Laboratory was silent and dark.

· · ·

Sergeant Lazar allowed selected Soviet soldiers into the building to shop. The Roumanian Biologist George Treponesco opened his store in Rare Earths and sold the watches and jewelry he had been collecting. The physicians up in Brain Research opened a drugstore in a lab on third and sold sulfonamides and condoms. The French Physicist François Daniel had a couturier shop in Physics: bathing suits, silk stockings—whatever he had been able to get his hands on. The most popular concession of all, though, was the Yugoslav's. He charged admission to see the masturbating monkeys.

Having been away, I was unable to make such preparations, but the good sergeant from Galicia, Lazar, gave me a brilliant idea when he wandered into my lab and mentioned that he had sent a picture of himself to his wife when he was in the Austrian army in 1914, again when he was in the Polish army in 1920 and 1938, but that in all his years in the Russian army, he had not had a portrait taken.

"Poor woman doesn't know what I look like anymore."

"How would you like it if I took your picture so you could send it to her?"

"Like it? I love it."

"Give me an hour to set it up, and I'll take your photograph."

"You come find me. I be out in front—by the door."

As soon as he left the lab, I ran up the stairs to the darkroom on the third floor, picked up the old box camera, film, and lights, took them back to my lab, arranged the camera and lights, hung a dark blackdrop, pulled up a chair, just so, and then ran down the stairs and out the front door to invite Sergeant Lazar to be the first to have his picture taken, free of charge.

I had a slight problem with the paper. All we had at the Institute was electrocardiogram and electroencephalograph paper made for optical writing. So the pictures not only had too much contrast—stark light, stark dark, and no grays—but also faded rather quickly. By the time the pictures arrived in Russia, they would mostly be faded. My studio was popular, almost fifteen to twenty customers every afternoon—after the sorting of the flies— thanks to Sergeant Lazar, who did an especially good job of soliciting for me.

Still, the Yugoslav's concession was the star attraction. The Russian soldiers were entranced by the masturbating monkeys and crowded in to see them. They were so popular, in fact, that the young commissar who had "liberated" us in April stopped by on his way back to Moscow, in June, to pick them up.

The Chief summoned us all to the lobby to have a final vodka with our "liberator." By the time I got down the stairs, there was an intense discussion going on between Professor Kreutzer and the commissar.

"They will not travel," said Professor Kreutzer. "They have all had delicate brain operations. What he tells you is true. They will not survive the journey. They will all die."

"Then he is responsible that they live," said the commissar, nodding toward the Yugoslav. "He will come with us."

"Let me talk with him," said the Chief. "I will convince him of the folly," and he argued with the commissar, heatedly, in Russian, the Yugoslav and Ignatov joining in.

Professor Kreutzer stepped back to where I stood with François Daniel, and began to change his glasses, absentmindedly: that is, he took off the gold-rims he was wearing, wiped them clean, and put them back on.

The Yugoslav, in utter despair, left the discussion and joined us. "It seems they want to give them as a gift to Stalin from the 484th Platoon. If it weren't for the rest of you, I would kill myself right now and save them the trouble. They will never survive the trip, the primates, and when they die, I will be killed."

Within an hour, the trucks were loaded—the primates in their cages, the Yugoslav under armed guard.

Ignatov and Rabin went with them of their own free will. There would be no more music.

When they were gone, François Daniel said, "I'm getting out of here."

"Where will you go?" Bolotnikov asked.

"To the Americans, wherever they are."

"I go, too," said Bolotnikov.

Back in my lab, I had time to take one photo before the Chief stormed in, in such a rage that my clients, waiting patiently in line to have their pictures taken, fled in fright.

"Because of this"—he waved his arm at my photography shop—"because of these markets, they have taken Mitya." He paced furiously.

I turned to my worktable. Because there was no money, no new experimentation was going on, and although I, alone, was left in our laboratory, I continued the routine sorting of the *Drosophila* for three or four hours a day, putting up cultures, examining them after ten or twelve days, making statistics and analysis. But the Chief was not pleased with this, either. "And you!" He was standing behind me now. "How dare you make only one hundred or one hundred and fifty cultures. Your statistics mean nothing. Statistical analysis requires a large number, a very large number."

I was silent.

"No one is listening to me," he said. "Things fall apart." And he stalked from the lab.

At least I was keeping the flies going by not allowing them to breed themselves to death in the small flasks, clearing out those which were not useful, putting them into the alcohol bottle, the mass grave.

It needed emptying. The *Drosophila* were heaped well above the level of the alcohol in the wide-mouth jar, the new flies falling onto the heap, dying slowly from the fumes rather than instantly from the liquid itself. But they were gassed, sleeping, and felt no pain.

The last few to be discarded were asleep on a white index card. I uncorked the alcohol jar, tapped the anesthetized flies onto the heap, recorked the jar, and then immediately uncorked. One little fellow on top was moving. I inserted my pencil; he climbed onto it, and I lifted him out onto the white index card. He was wet from the moisture in the jar and quite drunk from the alcohol vapor and the ether. He looked wingless, the wings pasted to his body by the moisture. But he could walk, barely. Stagger, stop, weave. Quite drunk, but living. He stood in one place now, rubbing together his two front legs, rubbing them against his face and head, freeing one wing and then the other. The staggering became less severe; he could walk a straighter line. Hop. He lifted himself off the ground. Hop. Then took a small flight. I made black spots on the white card, then put a small splash of polenta pudding with yeast on the card. And there he was, landing, ignoring the yeast and hopping the spots.

I corked the bottle. Other flies had attempted to escape, but the fumes were too much. They would have had to have been helped.

I walked down to Chemistry to see if one of the girls would like to go to the darkroom. They had given up their apartment in Hagen and were living in the complex in the park, which at that time was mostly empty.

I still had no word from Tanya.

. . .

Twice in June and once in July, I walked into Berlin—the trains were not yet running—to Tanya's western suburb, Dahlem, which was not far from my father's house. On the first two trips, I found their house occupied by Russian officers; on the third, by Americans, none of whom could—or would—give me any information about the family. I began to imagine that I was in love with her, and I blamed myself for every failure in our relationship—until mid-July, when the Americans restored phone service city-wide and I was able to talk to her.

I was alone in the lab, sorting the flies, when the Chief came in. "We have telephones again," he said. "See if you can reach Tatiana."

I thought, at first, it was she who answered.

"Hello? Hello?"

"Tanya?"

"Hello? No, this is not Tanya."

"I beg your pardon." My heart was pounding. The Chief stopped pacing and stood beside me. "Is Tatiana Backhaus there?"

"Who is calling?"

I looked at the Chief, who was pacing again, and took a deep, shaky breath. "Josef Bernhardt. Is she there? Is Tanya there?"

"Josef! I told her you would call."

"Is she all right?"

The Chief, again, stopped pacing and growled, "Well, is she there?"

"Tanya, Tanya," I heard her mother's voice call. "It's Josef. I told you he would call."

I shoved the phone at the Chief. "She's there."

"Hello?" He waited. "Tanya, my dear child, are you all right? . . . Thank God! Your mother and father? . . . That is wonderful. . . . I am fine. . . . He is fine. We are all fine. Good . . . good. Here is Josef. He will tell you all the news." The Chief handed me the phone.

I could hear Tanya's voice calling, "Josef? Josef?"

The Chief, tears in his eyes, smiled at me. "Two children saved," he said. "That is something, is it not? Two children saved?" And he strode from the lab.

"Tanya, how are you? Are you all right? I've been to your house three times."

"Mother said you would call. I'm fine. How are you? It was terrible, but we are all right, all of us. Josef, I am so sorry I did not dance with you."

"Where were you? We were really getting worried."

"Oh, Josef, it was terrible. The Russians."

"Did they hurt you?"

"No. I was hidden near Königswusterhausen, but there was no food, and it was cold, and when we got back to Berlin there were American officers living in our house, and we had to stay with friends until they moved out. They were very nice, the Americans, when they found out we were not Nazis. They gave us food. We have food. And you? What happened to you? We knew you were taken from Farben, but that's all."

"I was forced labor at Wolff's—a factory near Ostkreuz—and I escaped."

"*You* escaped?"

Ah, the old chill was back. "Yes, *I* escaped."

"How did you do that?"

I did not answer her.

"Josef?"

"Yes? I'm here."

"Did you call your father yet?"

"No, and I don't intend to."

"He is very ill, Josef, and worried about you."

"And how would you know this?"

"I have visited him. Almost every day, since we got back. Our fathers know each other."

"How nice."

"He is not well."

"I can't come just now, Tanya. The Chief needs me. I'm the only one left to sort the flies."

"Oh, no. Did something happen to the Krupinskys?"

"They're all right. He's working in a hospital nearby. And almost everyone else has left."

"Professor Kreutzer?"

"He's still here, and Frau Doktor and Sonja."

"Is that all?"

"Treponesco."

"Monika? Is she still there?"

I was silent. Monika had been gone for quite some time, but, at that moment, I did not want to give Tatiana the satisfaction of knowing.

"So! She's there. You should know that your next-door neighbor has moved into *your* house to take care of *your* father."

"My next-door neighbor? You don't mean that idiot Baron is living in my house?"

"His was bombed and burned down. You should be grateful. Your father is really helpless, and it is your duty to care for him."

I sighed. "Does Father have food?"

"Yes. Some American friends sent cartons and cartons of cigarettes—through some colonel they knew—and you can buy anything with American cigarettes. He bought you a motorcycle, a BMW, with four cartons and a sailboat for two cartons. Josef? Did you hear me?"

"Yes, I heard you."

"So he has food now. But for a while he didn't. He was more upset about not having food for his dog than for himself."

"Dritt? How is Dritt?"

"Dead. Your father couldn't feed him."

Poor old Dritt. I couldn't even save him.

"I told your father about us."

"Everything?"

"No, not everything. I told my mother everything, and she understood. She said you would call me. He has given me a ring."

"A what?"

"Your father gave me a ring—your mother's diamond."

"That's quite nice, Tatiana. I think the two of you will be quite happy together."

. . .

There developed a little inner circle, which was in the habit of having all three meals together at the same table in the cafeteria—the Chief and Sonja Press, Professor Kreutzer and his wife, Frau Doktor, the Roumanian Biologist George Treponesco, and I. Breakfast was at seven thirty, lunch at noon, and dinner at six thirty in the evening. We regrouped again at nine to do some serious drinking and to talk about what lay in store.

Each of us was concerned with his own small life and future. The Chief and Professor Kreutzer dreamed of starting a university in a Kaiser Wilhelm Institute in the American Sector of Berlin and had actually made several trips to Potsdam to promote their idea. All the others—except for Treponesco—wanted to be on the Chief's faculty to continue research and to teach. I, of course, had visions of being their student in this imaginary university.

Our self-interested preoccupations continued throughout the summer, until August sixth, when the atomic bomb was dropped on Hiroshima.

That night, at shortly after nine, the inner circle was gathered at our table in the cafeteria, settling down with glasses of vodka, American cigarettes, Russian caviar, and Swiss chocolate bars—all but Professor Kreutzer, who generally listened to the BBC at nine and then reported the latest news to us.

He arrived breathless and ashen, and without changing his glasses even once, he said, "BBC reports that the Allies have dropped an atomic bomb on Japan."

Stunned silence. Then shock and disbelief and everybody talking at once.

Finally, one could hear Frau Doktor say, "Are you certain you heard it correctly?"

And we ceased talking and listened for Professor Kreutzer's answer.

"I am sure!"

"It's just a bluff to scare the Soviets," said Treponesco.

"I don't think so," said Professor Kreutzer. His voice was shaking. I had never seen him so profoundly disturbed.

"Did they say anything about uranium in connection with it?" asked the Chief.

"No. They spoke of the bomb as being equivalent to tens of thousands of tons of TNT."

The Chief began to pace, hands locked behind his back. "My God," he said. "If they really did it, what kind of an airplane must they have developed to drop that thing."

"You are assuming that they had to drop a whole reactor," said Professor Kreutzer.

"What else could it be?" said Treponesco.

"There are many possibilities," said Professor Kreutzer. "But, fortunately, none that we know of here in Germany."

"It's all a bluff," said Treponesco again, "to scare the Soviets."

"Then how do you account for the reference to tens of thousands of tons of TNT," I said sarcastically.

"The Soviets," said the Chief, thoughtfully. "If it is, indeed, a uranium bomb, I don't think the Russians are in on it. Max!" He stopped pacing and looked at Professor Kreutzer. "That would explain the disappearance of Heisenberg and Hahn and all the other nuclear scientists in the American and British sectors. The Americans and the British have had a deep interest in the subject, but obviously the Russians have not been thinking about it at all."

Professor Kreutzer removed from his pocket the black-rims and began a cleaning and changing routine. We waited, silently, for him to continue.

Finally, he donned the rimless and spoke. "The next newscast is at nine o'clock Greenwich Mean Time, which is midnight here— Moscow time. They promise to have more information by then. Let us all listen together and after carefully evaluating this development, let us make our decisions."

Shortly before midnight, we gathered around the radio in the Chief's private office: Professor Kreutzer, Treponesco, Frau Doktor, the Physicist of the cyclotron at the post office—who, because of the news, had hurried out to the Institute—the Chief, of course, Sonja, and I.

At exactly twelve, the volume was turned up:

> *This is London. . . . Twenty-one hours Greenwich Mean Time . . . BBC World Service. The news tonight is dominated by a tremendous achievement of Allied scientists—the production of the atomic bomb. One has already been dropped on a Japanese army base.*

"I don't believe it," said Treponesco. "I just—"

"Shhhh."

"Quiet, damn you."

> *. . . and reconnaissance aircraft couldn't see anything hours later because of the tremendous pall of smoke and dust that was still obscuring the city of once over three hundred thousand inhabitants. The Allies report that they have spent over five hundred million pounds on the project; up to one hundred twenty-five thousand people helped to build the factories in America and sixty-five thousand are running them now. Few of the workers, it is reported, knew what they were producing.*

They could see huge quantities of materials going in, and nothing coming out—for the size of the explosive charge is very small.

At this, all in the room exchanged significant looks.
Then came the final confirmation:

The American Secretary for War has announced that uranium was used in making the bomb.

"My God, three hundred thousand dead?"

"They didn't say that."

"Madness!"

"There must have been tremendous cooperation among the Americans and the British to do this thing."

"Thank God Hitler threw all the great physicists out of Germany—Lise Meitner—all of them," said the Physicist from the post office.

"When Hahn first made his discovery," said the Chief, "and realized the implications of uranium fission, he wanted to throw all the uranium into the sea just to avoid such a catastrophe."

"Why didn't he?" said Frau Doktor.

"Poor Heisenberg." Treponesco snorted. "It makes him out a failure."

"Nonsense!" said the Chief. "Don't you believe for a moment that Heisenberg or Hahn wanted the atomic bomb for Adolf Hitler."

"What I cannot understand," said Professor Kreutzer, "is why they waited so long to drop it on the Japanese."

"Maybe the Allies thought they would surrender right after Germany," said Treponesco.

"No," said the Chief. "They didn't have it any sooner. If they had, they would have dropped it on Berlin."

My God. We were all silent for quite some time.

Sonja served tea.

"It was political," said the Physicist from the post office. "It is a warning to the Soviets."

"That's what I've been saying," said Treponesco.

"You said it was a bluff," I corrected him.

More silence. We drank our tea. The Chief jumped to his feet and tried to pace, but the room was too crowded. Professor Kreutzer took a spectacle case from his pocket, took out the gold-rims, began to clean them, removed the black-rims he was wearing, and put on the gold. We watched him and waited.

"It is obvious," he said, finally, "that with the dropping of this bomb by the Americans and the British, interest in anything nuclear will be intense."

All nodded in agreement.

He continued. "The Soviets have the habit of packing up everything and shipping it off to Russia."

The Physicist from the post office jumped to his feet. "They wouldn't do that to me," he said. "Why, the magnet alone, of my cyclotron, weighs some two hundred twenty tons. Even the Russians couldn't be that stupid."

"One must not forget," said Professor Kreutzer, "that the Germans found a working cyclotron in Paris in 1941, took it apart, and shipped it to Alsace-Lorraine, where our colleague is still trying to put it together."

"Yes, but that was different."

"In what way different?"

"The post office cyclotron was built only because our transmitter wasn't in use and there sat idle a huge power plant. It would be sheer folly to try to move it. The Paris move was sabotage."

"I think I could persuade them," said the Chief, "that our small atom smasher would not survive the trip, that they would be better off to let us continue our research here."

"Were you able to convince them that the primates would not survive the trip?" asked Professor Kreutzer.

"You're right, Max. You're right. But Max, if I serve them the pure wine, and they know what I've done here, surely then—"

"The pure wine, Alex? What is the pure wine?"

"It is the real truth of my loyalty."

"What loyalty?"

"To Russia rather than to Germany."

"And tell me, my good friend, as you would tell it to them, of the real truth of your loyalty to Stalin, liberator of all people."

The Chief threw back his head and rumbled a desperate deep laugh. "If I were to tell them the real truth, dear Max, I would have to lie."

"I see!" said Professor Kreutzer. "My friends, we must proceed carefully, as before. These Russians—they are no different from the Nazis. Perhaps the sheer magnitude will keep them from moving the cyclotron at the post office. I don't know. But you, Alex, should take Sonja and leave at dawn. Go to the Americans!"

"No! I will stay. My work is here. But I will hide our small bit of uranium."

"I wouldn't do that. That's the first thing they'll come looking for. That would be a mistake. A fatal mistake."

"But you, Max, you should leave."

Professor Kreutzer sighed. "You are making mistakes. To hide the uranium is a mistake. To stay is a mistake."

"I will stay," said Treponesco.

Then the Chief polled each person in the room, one at a time, starting with Frau Doktor.

"Ruth," he said, "there is no need for you to stay. You can carry on your work in other places. As much as I would miss you, I beg of you to leave."

"Oh, Alex, you know I have been in contact with our colleagues in Great Britain. But I can't go. Not quite yet."

"I think you should leave immediately," said Professor Kreutzer. "In the morning."

She shook her head. "I am in the process of gathering my research notes. Even if I hurry, it would take me at least another week before I could put it all together. But then I will leave—in a week or so."

"Max?" said the Chief.

"I will send my wife away at once. But I will stay," said Professor Kreutzer.

"Josef," said the Chief. "You must leave."

"You must," echoed some of the others.

I, also, did not want to leave that garden of a graveyard. I did not want to leave them. They were all the family I had.

"I will stay."

Knowing the consequences, we all made the same choice as Uncle Otto, Aunt Greta, and my mother, the same choice, we were discovering, as millions of others.

One lives one's present naïvely.

. . .

Using metal mine detectors, the day after the second atomic bomb was dropped, on Nagasaki, they easily found the kilo of uranium in the bulky lead cases which the Chief had buried in the earth in the large greenhouse in the park. The buildings and grounds swarmed with green-capped, armed Russians. Sergeant Lazar from Galicia and his friendly guards were replaced with NKVD. Everyone at the Institute was interviewed. We were ordered to continue our scientific work. And we were all placed under arrest—forbidden to leave the grounds.

The next morning, shortly after dawn, as I lay sleeping in my apartment in the complex at the back of the park, I was awakened by a large convoy of trucks pulling into the circular drive at the entrance to the Institute. It was Saturday, August 11, 1945. I dressed and hurried across the park to see what was happening.

They were taking it apart—the Institute—loading everything into the empty trucks: chairs, tables, drapes, dishes. The Bechstein piano, my good Lord, was being carried down the front steps.

The soldiers ignored me as I walked through the lobby and up the steps of the right wing to the lab. Sonja was there, pacing and wringing her hands. "Oh, Josef. Alex wants to see you right away. Hurry."

I ran up the circular staircase to the penthouse. There were two armed guards at the door to his private office. They allowed me to knock.

I could hear the Chief say, "Enter."

They allowed me to pass and to close the door behind me.

The Chief was stuffing papers into a small suitcase on his desk. He took my face into his great hands. "Josef, the Soviets take not only equipment but also people."

I tried to pull my head away. His hands were so large for a man of his height. He looked into my eyes. I knew what he was going to say, and I didn't want to hear it.

"It would not be good for you in Siberia." He dropped his hands and turned his back on me.

"I do not want to leave you, Herr Professor."

He sighed, his back still to me. "During the night, Max and I talked at great length about your future. Also, I have been, for some time, in contact with your father."

I had not been consulted.

"You must hide yourself and escape through the apples. Go to your father. When you leave me now, you must go immediately to Max. He has certain papers for you and will tell you of our wishes for your future." He turned again to face me.

I shook my head.

"Your father is ill. He needs you." Again, he turned his back on me and began to sort papers and put them in the suitcase.

"Herr Professor," I said.

But he would not look at me. He continued to sort the papers as though I no longer existed.

I left him, walked past the guards, past Sonja Press, who sat weeping at her desk in the reception office, and down the circular staircase to Physics. There were two armed guards by the open door of the lab. They let me pass. Professor Kreutzer was sitting on a high stool at a worktable. I stood, silent, as he changed to the black-rims.

"You are nineteen years old," he said. "You know that you have missed the boat on mathematics."

I nodded. Tears filled my eyes, and I wept. He turned from me until I was in control; then, facing me again, he gestured, both hands open, palms up. Then he, too, began to weep and turned away, again, until he was in control. Then, looking at me, he said, "Do you understand why I say this, Josef?"

"Yes, Herr Professor, I do."

"I offer you a bouquet of dead flowers when I tell you that we, Alex and I, feel that the kind of creativity you were capable of in mathematics reaches its peak by the time one is in his mid-twenties. Newton, by the time he was twenty-four, had made the two fundamental discoveries which have transformed mathe-matical science, that of the differential, which he shared with his teacher, Barrow, and that of expansion into infinite spheres.

"Pascal published his study of mathematics at twenty-one and then went on to other things—philosophy. Einstein published his theory of relativity when he was twenty-five, but he actually thought it through when he was an adolescent.

"Your teacher in high school taught you all he knew by the time you were fourteen and was unable to arrange for you to move on. And when you came here, not one of us was capable of carrying you on in mathematics. Crucial years wasted. I regret this. I regret this waste more than anything else. The flower of western civiliza-tion was slowly wilting, but Hitler and his cohorts ground it to dust beneath their boots." He removed his glasses, put them on the table, rubbed his eyes. "Sit down, sit down, Josef." He peered at me. He hardly could see without his glasses.

I sat on a chair and looked up at him.

"It might be years yet before you could be with the right people. We tried. I, myself, went to Potsdam to see if we could convince the Americans to let us open a university in the Kaiser Wilhelm Foundation buildings in their zone in Berlin. But they were using it as a hotel and playground for their officers." He sighed. "They are entitled. Furthermore, the best people are gone."

He wiped his eyes with a handkerchief, cleaned the black-rims, and put them on.

"Alex and I also agree that, aside from mathematics, your creativity lies in practical things. You have a talent for mechanical invention. It is our opinion, and, I might add, our strong wish, that you try to emigrate to the United States as soon as you are able, matriculate at the Massachusetts Institute of Technology, and study nuclear physics."

I looked away.

"With the breakthrough in atomic energy, I foresee a good future for you. I see that in twenty-five or thirty years, the world will be powered by nuclear energy, which force, at the same time, might be the one thing to keep mankind from war.

"But again, most physicists have done their best work by the time they are thirty or thirty-five. Max Planck published his quantum theory when he was thirty-two. It is imperative that you get to the United States as soon as possible to begin your training."

He took an envelope from the inside pocket of his suit jacket. "Here are two recommendations: one from me, the other from Alex. We are not unknown in scientific circles. With these you should be able, not only to gain acceptance in Massachusetts, but also to be awarded a full scholarship."

"Professor Kreutzer, I would like to go with you and the Chief."

"No. It is all over for us. Our hope is in you."

I sat there, the envelope in my hand, and wept.

"Josef, you must understand that the Soviets will try to put me to work to build weapons. I have decided that under no circumstances will I cooperate in the creating of atomic bombs. You know what that will mean for me?"

"Yes, but I—"

He interrupted me. "Are you aware that the Soviet government has denounced the Darwinian theory of evolution and has gone back to Lamarck, and that the Mendelian theory of genetics is in disfavor also?"

"No, Herr Professor. I didn't know that." That meant, of course, that there wasn't a chance the Chief could continue his work in genetics, and that he, too, would be in disfavor.

"You are aware that the Avilovs fled Russia when Stalin came to power?"

"Yes, Herr Professor, I knew that."

"No, Josef. It is all over for us."

"But Herr Professor, I could be of help to you. Excuse me, but I... and I am younger, perhaps I could make some things easier for you."

He turned from me. We sat in silence. I held the envelope in my hand. It was sealed. Finally, I rose from my chair.

"Herr Professor, I . . . I thank you."

He nodded, his back to me.

I left Physics and walked down the dark hallway. There were two guards at the open door to the Rare Earths Laboratory. I waved to Treponesco. He waved back.

Frau Doktor's Biology Laboratory was next. Although there were no guards at the door, two Russian soldiers inside her small lab were "packing"; that is, they were tearing her lab apart and throwing everything, indiscriminately, into a large crate: books, papers, test tubes, the two binocular microscopes, and even the incubators with the *Drosophila*. She, crumpled on a chair in the corner, was in a state of such absolute shock that she was unable to respond to my greeting. Usually immaculate and in control, she was now disheveled, her lab jacket open, her blouse half-buttoned, locks of her abundant dark hair—always pulled back severely into a bun—hanging loose.

I continued my walk down the hallway. There were two guards at the open door to my lab, and inside at the worktables sat Krupinsky and Kirsti with their suitcases.

"It seems," said Krupinsky, "I am no longer needed as an interpreter and order clerk at the hospitals, but now I am needed for my great nuclear knowledge. They won't believe me that I know nothing about it."

I could think of nothing to say.

"I am not a physicist or a great mathematician like you, Bern-hardt, but I was doing some good work in my specialty when they let me. It would be hard for a person like you to understand that all I ever wanted to be was a mere medical doctor."

"Abe, please." Kirsti took my hand. "Josef, he doesn't mean what he says."

"Do you have any idea what they have had me doing? I am an endocrinologist; I keep telling them that. But all I've been is a goddam purchasing agent, ordering rubber gloves and gauze in Russian, German, and English. I wasn't even allowed near a patient."

I had no words. I left the lab and walked across the hall to take a last look at the Radiation Laboratory—at the linear accelerator.

NKVD were dismantling our patched, homemade machine, created by Professor Kreutzer from bits and pieces of the junk-yard. The Security Officer stood watching, more stooped than ever, ghastly thin, his face gray. There was much swearing in Rus-sian and much ill humor. I watched. When the soldiers tried to disconnect the huge pumps, oil began to pour out all over the floor. The officer screamed, "Sabotage! Sabotage!"

I ran from the cement-block room, slipping and sliding on the flood of oil, back into my lab. Krupinsky sat with his head in his arms at a worktable. I opened the drawer of my table, and, after a quick survey of the three-year accumulation of junk I'd collected, stuffed my mother's potato peeler, four chocolate bars, and the Fromm's Akt into my pants pockets, then picked up a wire basket and the map of the park.

"Take my wife." Krupinsky's voice was muffled, his face still buried in his arms.

Kirsti said, "No."

Krupinsky swung around in his chair. "Here, send this telegram as soon as you are able."

I looked at the words he had scrawled on the paper:

Dear Herr Stalin:

Fuck you. Strong letter to follow.

Abraham Morris Krupinsky, M.D.
Kaiser Wilhelm Institute
Berlin-Hagen
11 August 1945

I carried the basket and the map of the park into the little greenhouse kitchen off our lab, burned the "telegram" over the gas flame, filled four bottles with water and put them in the carrier; and then I went down the hall to the laboratory of Frau Doktor. She sat as before, only now, with a dazed look on her face, she watched the two Russian soldiers actually removing the panes of glass from her windows.

"Frau Doktor. It is time to collect the *Drosophila melanogaster Berlin wilds* in the park."

She looked at me.

"Come!" I said. "It is time to collect." I took her arms, pulled her to her feet, and picked up her handbag, which was on the floor beside her. The soldiers were intent only on their panes.

My hand on her arm, we walked from the lab and down the hall to the bathrooms. "Frau Doktor, go in there and relieve yourself. Take your time. Then comb your hair and arrange your clothes."

She seemed loath to let go of my arm. Gently, I detached and gave her the handbag. "I will be waiting right here. Now go."

She obeyed me as one in a dream. As promised, I waited at the door for her, and when she emerged ten minutes later, her hair was combed neatly, her face powdered, and her lab jacket buttoned. She followed submissively, allowing me to take the lead, enough in control to cooperate fully, but trembling and terrified.

Somehow her helplessness brought out the strength in me and gave me courage.

We walked down the hallway together, I carrying the wire basket and she the map of the park. On the staircase of our right wing, we were stopped by a Russian guard, who jabbed me in the side with his rifle butt.

"What do you do, you Nazi?" he said in German.

I pointed to the wire basket. "We pick up bottles of fruit flies from the trees and bushes in the park." I nodded toward the map in Frau Doktor's hand.

She opened it and showed the guard. "There, there, there, there." She pointed.

He shoved me again with his rifle butt. "Do it!" And he followed us down the stairs to the main entrance in the lobby and pushed me out the double doors with his rifle and a boot on my ass.

Under the scrutiny of the guard, who watched us from the entrance, we consulted the map and picked up two bottles which were on bushes near the front door, then began working our way into the park, picking bottles off trees and bushes, until, toward the back of the park, we came near the willows guarding Mitzka's tunnel to the apple orchard.

We stayed in that area until there was absolutely no one in sight. Frau Doktor first, then I, slipped behind the trees and into the shrubbery, crawling on our hands and knees partway through the hole to the little area Mitzka and I had cleared, where we used to lie, side by side, our bodies touching, plotting the destruction of Adolf Hitler and his Thousand Year Reich. There was very little room, and Frau Doktor and I had to sit very close, touching. As soon as she felt we were out of immediate danger, her entire body began to shake and she was racked with sobs. I put my finger to my lips, cautioning silence, and took her in my arms, letting her bury her face in my chest, my lab coat and shirt becoming soaked from her tears. I had a genuine affection for this woman who had been so kind to me from the very beginning. We were quite good friends, despite the difference in our ages.

Even this far back in the park, we could hear the racket those Russians were making with their "packing," and we knew, without saying it, that we could not make any noise whatsoever. All the while, I felt certain that they would not find us. Mitzka had chosen well, and as far as I could tell, these units had no dogs with them. Tracking dogs would be the only way they could find us; that is, by smell. Furthermore, we would not be missed. I wasn't considered important enough, and Frau Doktor's research had nothing to do with munitions.

After an hour, I suggested we stretch out and try to get some rest. It was unusual weather for Berlin, sunny and warm. I cleared away twigs and stones, then lay on my back, making it possible for her to rest partly on my body, with her head on my shoulder. I admired her that she did not pretend to be compromised, as Tatiana would have done. It was an obligatory intimacy. There simply was no room. We rested and slept quietly, with careful changes in position, until when darkness came she was calm, all was quiet, and we felt safe enough to converse in whispers.

"What will happen to them?" she asked, a rhetorical question requiring no answer. "I am so angry with myself," she continued. "I am so greedy. I should have left at once as Max suggested."

"You had a good reason. Your work. Years and years of work— gone."

"What does it matter now?"

"It will matter. You know that."

A tremulous sigh and she began again to weep—quietly.

"I have some chocolate bars and a little water, and I'll crawl through the fence and get us some apples."

"Are you sure it's safe?"

"Oh, yes. I'll be right back."

I retrieved a lab coat full of apples, and we sat unavoidably close, our bodies, of necessity, in sustained contact. As we munched on chocolate bars and sucked the sour apples, we discussed our escape, deciding it would be safer to wait until morning. To be found wandering at night was far more dangerous than walking, openly, in the fields in daylight. And our discussion inevitably led to our plans—when and if we made the escape. She would make her way to friends in Great Britain. I had no idea where I would go the next day.

I pulled the sealed envelope Professor Kreutzer had given me from my pocket and put it in her hand.

"What is this?"

"Letters of recommendation from the Chief and Professor Kreutzer to M.I.T. They want me to go to the United States and study nuclear physics."

"Do it. With their recommendations you will be accepted. You will have to begin at once to get a visa. Your father will be able to help you."

"I do not want to go to my father's house!"

"Where else could you go?"

"I don't know. Things happened so fast today, I haven't had time to think where I'll go or what I'll do. What would you say if I told you I've been considering medicine?"

So close, her body resting against mine, her mouth so near my ear, I could feel her negative reaction. "My dear," she said, "with your aptitudes, your intelligence, that would be a tragic mistake which you would regret forever. Do as the Chief and Max advised. Use all your power to get to America. Max is always right."

"If he is always right, why did he let himself be caught by the Russians? Why didn't they leave when there was still a chance?"

"I think perhaps he has had enough. He is tired. Both of them—Alex, too. But you are young, you have a life before you. Don't waste it."

"My mother wants—wanted—me to be a physician. I was thinking about anesthesiology."

"Anesthesia! That isn't even a specialty in Germany."

"Krupinsky said that it is in England and Canada. I could go to Canada or to the United States."

"And Tanya?"

"I promised to marry her."

"Are you going to do that?"

"I don't know."

"Josef, listen to me. I care for you too much not to say this to you, at least once. Medicine is not for you. Tanya is not for you."

I was silent.

"I know. She worked with me, in my lab, for six months—from the time George Treponesco had to move into Rare Earths until she left. We spent ten hours a day together for six months, and never once did she share anything with me."

"What should she have shared?"

"Oh, how can I say this. There are some people who are unable to make a bridge to another person. No, let me try it this way. Friends share personal thoughts. Tell things about themselves, trusting." She was silent, for a moment, thoughtful. "All the while she worked with me, Tanya was polite and correct, but this politeness and correctness was never broken by one instant of sharing, of warmth. I think that Tanya may be incapable of intimacy. Intimacy and sex are not the same thing. Surely," she said, "you know what I mean."

"Yes, I know what you mean."

"Ah, well. Enough! You do not need all this motherly advice. You will work it out for yourself, when the time comes. Tell me, Josef, how do you happen to know about this hiding place?"

I thought for a moment before answering. Frau Doktor sat quietly, comfortably molded into my body.

"I know about this place because I was dropped from my high school rowing team when I was twelve years old."

"You must admit, that is a curious answer."

"Yes. But it's true. Because I was dropped for no good reason from the rowing team, Mitzka befriended me. That was quite wonderful for me. Mitzka Avilov was the school god."

"I see. It was his secret place, and he showed it to you to cheer you up."

"Yes, more or less. My school activities were curtailed then—it was 1939—and I began to divert myself by building a secret cave in my own back yard, which gave Mitzka the idea to make this one."

"Tell me about your secret cave."

There flashed into my mind the image of my father's feet—his shoes and gray spats—at the edge of the hole Petter and I dug in my back yard. I pushed it away and changed the subject. "Excuse me, Frau Doktor, I think it would be safe for you to crawl through the fence into the orchard to relieve yourself. There are bushes on the other side, too. And then, perhaps, we should settle for the night."

She agreed, and I held the cut wires of the fence as best I could. She was only slightly scratched crawling through. When she returned, I made my trip; then we settled for the rest of the night. It was cool now, and I had her nestle spoon-fashion into my arms, covering her with both our lab jackets, holding her very tight, my arm under her breast. I could feel her heart beating rapidly, and she could not help but feel my erection pushing against her.

She reached around and held it in her hand. The only problem was her corset, an armed guard around her vital parts. She detached the garters from her hose and we tried bending it upward, but the metal stays stabbed her so, she gasped in pain. "I'll have to take it off," she whispered. But there was so little room, she couldn't maneuver in our little space, and, finally, I had to crawl halfway through the hole in the fence to give her room to stretch flat and wiggle out of that thing.

"I have a condom," I said.

"No," she whispered. "I want to feel *you*."

I was so ready, I shot off like a gun—would *ejaculatio praecox* be *impotencia coeundi* or merely *impotencia Josefus,* the inability to satisfy a real woman?

"Never mind," she said. "It just means that you find me desirable. Stay where you are."

I did, and she kissed me, warmly, and moved in such a way that within five or so minutes everything was all right—more than all right. Her response was so deeply passionate that I actually had to put my hand on her mouth to keep her from crying out. And she moved in waves and convulsions. I mean she actually enjoyed it, tremendously.

She lay panting and warm and sweating in my arms for twenty minutes, and we did it again and again . . . and again.

Toward dawn, we fell into a deep sleep, and I dreamed a new dream—of my father's feet, with shoes and spats, standing beside my secret cave in our back yard. I awakened, thinking I was in the hole in my own yard, but when I opened my eyes, I realized that I was lying on my back, with Frau Doktor in my arms, her nose shoved into my neck, in Mitzka's secret place, thinking, again, about the feet of my father.

Our actual escape through the apples was anticlimactic. Leaving behind the wire basket, the map of the park, and our white lab coats, we crawled through the fence and walked, as we'd planned—slowly, hand-in-hand through the orchard and the fields—hoping to look like lovers. She wore her long hair free to complete the picture.

"We *are* lovers," I said.

"Even though I'm old enough to be your mother." She said it ruefully.

"Only if you were married at ten."

"Fifteen. I am thirty-four years old," she offered.

"I hope you're not sorry."

"That I am thirty-four?"

"You know that isn't what I meant."

"Not at all, my dear. I feel so lucky to have known you in this way before we parted."

"I am the lucky one, Frau Doktor."

"Ruth."

"Ruth."

By design, we bypassed the S-Bahn station in Hagen, walking the five kilometers to the next stop. The train was jammed beyond capacity and went only as far as Gesundbrunnen. The undergound tunnels had been flooded during those last days of the war and were not yet in use, and the rail lines circling the city aboveground —the Berlin Circle—were, in parts, still hopelessly torn up. So we walked through the dust and rubble that was once Berlin—at its best it was an ugly city—ten or so kilometers, from the Russian Sector, through the French, stopping, finally, in the vicinity of the zoo—Zoologischer Garten—which was well within the safety of the British Sector. We then stopped to make love one more time, before parting, in a basement under a house which had collapsed.

PART V

OCTOBER 10, 1967
IOWA CITY

CHAPTER NINE

Kaddish

Dr. Josef Bernhardt—the brown leather briefcase with the succinylcholine and Librium under his left arm, his elbow crooked to
secure it—raced across the campus of the University of Iowa
toward his safety box in the vault of the First National Bank:
across the green lawn of the hospital complex, down twenty-eight
steps to the little landscaped ravine—a blur of October greens and
browns, reds and yellows—and up and around the corkscrew pass
over Riverside Drive; he, who in his youth had been a runner,
squeaking and creaking like the ungreased wheels of a railway
carriage. On the bridge over the Iowa River he slowed to a jog,
then, feeling that his heart would burst and his lungs collapse, to a
walking limp the last short block to the wide cement stairs leading
up to Old Capitol—the heart of the Pentacrest. Wheezing and
gasping, right fist pounding his chest to ease the substernal pain,
Josef threw himself onto the lawn at the foot of the steps and
dropped his briefcase beside him.

He was so obviously in distress that he attracted the attention of
some of the students hurrying by and of others sprawled on the
green grass enjoying the beautiful autumn day. Almost all, Josef
noticed through the wavy distortion of his tears, were wearing the
student uniform—faded and patched blue jeans, blue work shirts
or colorful T-shirts—and carrying khaki knapsacks.

"Hey, mister. You O.K.?" A flat midwestern twang. The students formed a friendly ring about him, some on the sidewalk, others on the lawn.

"What is he? Having a heart attack or something?"

"Maybe he's stoned."

"People dressed like that don't get stoned."

"Maybe he's drunk."

"You O.K.?"

Prostrate on the green lawn, charcoal suit soaked through with sweat, mouth open to maximize air intake, eyes wide with the strain, lungs emitting rasping and gasping asthmatic counterpoint, Josef realized he must have looked like a lunatic and, hit by the irony of his maniacal race toward death, he twisted his yawning mouth into a crazy grimace and tried to laugh. But it came out as a convulsive, shuddering sound. Mitzka had been racing toward the apples when they got him.

The circle of concerned eyes watched Josef until, within a minute or so, the music in his lungs quieted, the chest pain waned to discomfort, and he tried to stand. Hands reached out and lifted him to his feet; a long-haired student picked up the brown leather briefcase from the grass and gave it to him. Josef doffed an imaginary hat and bowed as he had been taught in Dancing and Social Behavior Class. Then, to aid his respiration, he hunched over and straightened—as though rowing a skiff—and sailed up the incline and around Old Capitol. Imminent death gave one the freedom of a madman. Correct? Or was he right? And what did it matter if he dropped dead on the spot from an infarct?

The First National Bank was two blocks farther, and he had five minutes before closing. He had gained two in the run and lost them again in the grass. . . . Alas. . . . There had been such speed in his little body and such lightness in his footfall, he could hardly believe he was so out of shape. He walked quickly across the Pentacrest toward Clinton Street and cut through a line of war protesters in patched denim uniforms passively picketing on the sidewalk, phlegmatically waving banners and posters, watched by two equally passive city police in dark blue uniforms with shiny buttons, sitting in a black-and-white parked at the curb right where Josef intended to jaywalk across Clinton.

"Dr. Bernhardt!" A female voice.

Josef turned and looked at the line of war protesters.

GET THE TROOPS OUT OF VIETNAM

MAKE LOVE NOT WAR

FUCK THE DRAFT

FUCK ME

"Dr. Bernhardt," she cried, again, stepping out of the picket line.

It took him a moment to realize it was the nurse from Four North, Susan Ingram. She looked so different: instead of the stiff nurse's cap and the white uniform, buttoned to the throat, she wore a blue work shirt, unbuttoned and tied at midriff, and jeans, hugging her hips well below the navel, revealing a firm, flat gut— an altogether attractive upper and lower quadrant. Her brown hair hung in two long braids.

Josef bowed slightly to her, pointed to his watch, turned again toward Clinton, and stepped off the curb right in front of the parked black-and-white.

"Look out for the police," she yelled.

Josef looked up and down Clinton. No cars coming. He started to walk.

"Hey, fella!" shouted the officer out the squad car window.

Josef kept on walking. A capital crime? The officer jumped out. Josef heard the car door slam but did not stop.

"Hey, you there!"

"Pig. Pig. Pig. Pig. Pig," chanted the war protesters.

The policeman grabbed Josef by his suit sleeve. "Hey! You can't jaywalk here."

Josef looked up at the tall young officer and then down at the huge pistol in holster low on one hip. *"Vot yay-vok?"* he asked, smiling idiotically.

"Let me see your driver's license," said the officer as he pulled Josef by the sleeve toward the curb.

"Pig. Pig. Pig. Pig."

There were cars now, and two bicycles and a motorcycle stopped by the obstruction, and their drivers honked and some joined the cantors: "Pig. Pig. Pig. Pig."

Although he came along willingly, Josef's suit jacket was pulled clean off one shoulder by the time they reached the curb in front of the squad car.

"Your driver's license," the officer repeated.

"Pig. Pig. Pig. Pig."

Josef shrugged, smiled, and threw out a hand to indicate that he did not understand. With the other hand, he clutched the briefcase. The cantors cheered.

The other policeman, still in the car, stuck his head out the window. "Hey, you, where you from?"

"Ich bin ein Berliner," said Josef in harsh *Schweizerdeutsch.*

"Oh, great," said the arresting officer, "he don't even talk English."

"Let him go," said the one in the squad car. "He's just a dumb foreigner." And he pulled his head in and shut the window.

Josef noticed Susan Ingram walking toward him, a look of concern on her face.

The officer tugged at Josef's sleeve to get his attention. "Cross at the corners," he said very loud and very slow. He pointed first to one intersection and then to the other while Josef, nodding vigorously, mimicked the action, pointing with index finger to one intersection, then to the other, then to himself.

"That's right," the officer articulated carefully. "Cross at the corners." And, satisfied, he opened the car door, bent his long frame double, and slipped into the driver's seat.

The cantors applauded, booed, and hissed. *"ssssssssSSSSSSS pig!"*

Josef, on the curb again in front of the black-and-white, looked at his watch. He had lost three minutes, leaving only two to cover the block and a half to the bank.

Susan Ingram was beside him.

"I'm late," he said, looking down her cleavage. Kirsti Krupinsky. She wore no bra, and the peace symbol on the delicate gold chain rested between her full breasts. He glanced, then, to his left—no cars; to his right—a double-take. Carlos Borbon.

Still in hospital greens, mask dangling and flopping about his neck, Carlos was galloping across the intersection, without fear of Uncle Philip, against a red light, toward the First National Bank.

Josef made a diagonal dash to the left across Clinton. He could hear the policeman hollering, "Hey. You. Fella," and the students' monotone, monosyllabic song, "Pig. Pig. Pig. Pig." At the corner, he stepped onto the curb and found himself in a scene that looked like the day after *Kristallnacht,* a bookstore, the huge display windows boarded over, and also the doors where the glass had been. There was a placard on the door:

VARSITY BOOK

IS

OPEN

Without looking back to see if he was being followed, Josef slipped inside, panting and gasping, and leaned against the doorframe, his head thrown back, his eyes closed.

"You'll have to park your bag," said a flat male voice.

Josef, bewildered, opened his eyes and was startled to see a uniformed police officer—city police—with sidearm in holster.

"I beg your pardon?"

"You'll have to park your bag," repeated the guard, pointing to the brown leather briefcase under Josef's left arm.

Josef straightened up and looked around. There were lockers lining the walls in front of the boarded windows. Tightening his grip on the briefcase, he moved forward to the checkout counters, the guard following. There were no customers on this spacious first floor—and no books—only supplies: papers, pencils, greeting cards, calendars, mugs, cups, and other paraphernalia, T-shirts, sweatshirts, and other clothing, all in yellow with black lettering, all printed either with *University of Iowa* or with the university logo, an ugly beaked hawk. The Hawkeye State.

"Who broke the windows?" Josef turned to the guard standing at his elbow.

"Students."

"When?"

"Every time they put them back in."

"Why?"

The guard shrugged. "You can put it in one of the lockers and take the key."

"Thankyouverymuch, officer. I prefer to carry it with me."

"You can't. It's the rule," the man said peevishly, tugging at the briefcase.

"What do you mean, I can't?" Josef snapped at him, pulling the briefcase and nudging the guard with his elbow.

"Can I help you?" A pleasant-faced man, young middle-age, in his uniform—a pale blue smock coat—monogrammed over the breast pocket, *Varsity Book,* underneath which was pinned an identification card, with the man's name, his title, *Mgr,* and, so there could not possibly be a mistake, his picture. Apparently one needed more security clearance to enter a bookstore in Iowa in 1967 than to enter the Kaiser Wilhelm Institute in Berlin-Hagen during the Second World War.

"I want to buy a book."

"Books are downstairs," said the manager obligingly. "Anything special I can help you with ... uh ... er ... Professor?"

"Doctor. M.D." Josef watched the manager's eyes light up with dollar signs. Medical texts are expensive.

The guard, a sullen expression on his face, moved back to the lockers lining the front wall.

"We have a large selection of medical texts, doctor." The manager was affable. "I'll take you down myself and show you around. If you'll just park your briefcase with the security man over there?"

"I'll take it with me," said Josef, agreeably, moving toward the stairs to the lower level. He was stopped by a restraining hand on his arm.

"We can't make exceptions. You understand." The voice was still congenial.

"No, as a matter of fact, I don't understand."

"Oh, come on now, doctor." The manager slipped from affability to condescension, then slid halfway back to conciliation. "If we let *them* in here with *their* bags and sacks, they would steal us blind."

"Do you mean the students?"

"Yes. And if you make an exception, even in the case of a fine citizen like yourself . . ."

"*They* would break your windows."

"You've got it."

"I see." Josef nodded his head as though in agreement, reached in his back pocket for his wallet, from which he extracted his card, still with his Montreal address, and handed it to the manager. "Here's my card. Give me a call when you put fresh crystal in those windows," and he turned and strode to the entrance.

"Dr. Bernhardt!" The manager's voice was all sarcasm. "This is the only store in the state with any selection of medical books. There are no other medical schools in Iowa."

"You're breaking my heart," said Josef.

"Of course, you could drive to Chicago, or, same distance, to Omaha, Nebraska. They have two medical schools in Omaha— only six hours each way."

Josef enunciated each syllable clearly and distinctly. "I wanted to buy a po-et-ry book," he said and opened the door.

"Try Epstein's," he heard the manager call after him. "It's right up Clinton."

. . .

He was a wanted man. Josef flattened himself against the boarded-up windows outside Varsity Book and stealthily scanned Clinton, his eyes coming to rest on Susan Ingram and the other war protesters mid-block across the street. The black-and-white was nowhere in sight, nor was that green prick Borbon. As he suspected, Elizabeth had not waited until two fifty *en punto* to telephone but had obviously reached Carlos at once and sent him stalking the streets of Iowa City. Josef curbed his impulse to run, for he did not want to draw attention to himself. Instead, he walked quickly three storefronts up Clinton to a bar-café which had large plate-glass windows—crystal still intact.

He stepped inside and surveyed: two empty tables in front of the windows; a long bar against the wall opposite the entrance extending halfway into the long, narrow room, also empty; the inevitable booths toward the back, one filled with four students. The predominant smell was of freshly popped corn.

Despite the brightness of the day and the large windows, the interior was dim, and Josef felt he would be safe at the far end of the bar with his back to the light. But the moment he settled himself on the barstool and laid his briefcase on the bar, he realized that he hadn't the vaguest idea what to do next. The banks were closed now, and Carlos was, no doubt, still cruising the streets. He couldn't get into his safety box until the next day: his mother's jewelry; his father's rings and studs, tie pins and cuff links and gold cigarette case—Josef patted his breast, then side pockets, for cigarettes; image of Carlos reaching across the desk for the pack of Camels—three pocket watches in gold cases, Swiss, one from each grandfather and one from his father, and underneath all the artifacts, in the back of the largest safety-deposit box he could rent, under the Swiss bank account books and stocks, under the wills, under the insurance policies and passport was the package he wanted. He would destroy it, make a fire and burn it. All the rest could be sent to Tatiana in Berlin. Josef felt blood rushing to his face. Trembling, flushed, he inhaled deeply and was able to push the air noisily from his lungs and breathe again. What is it one has to show for a lifetime? One potato peeler, first-rate; a schoolgirl's love poem, in her own hand, on a tattered sheet of blue linen stationery; one tarnished silver napkin ring, engraved with an *O* for Otto or for O Lord, when will the Savior come to this land; one short, final letter from one's mother, apropos of nothing that had to do with any reality he had ever wished to live; and one old Hebrew prayer book handed down from Grandfather Josef Jacoby to Uncle Otto Jacoby to him. Gold watches and prayer books. He found it on his desk, the prayer book, the day he returned to his father's house after leaving Frau Doktor—Ruth—at noon, after loving her one more time in the basement of a collapsed house, in the safety of the British Sector, near the zoo. From Zoologischer Garten, he had taken a trolley, the main trolley of his childhood, No. 177, which was the most direct route from Gartenfeld to the pet shop in Steglitz, where he bought the semi-rotten meat for Dritt and Mies; to Uncle Otto's original apartment buildings and furniture-manufacturing plant in Schöneberg; to his father's office in Tiergarten; or to the zoo, which, when he was quite young, he and his mother often visited, a ride of half an hour in the late 1920s and early 1930s, but which in August 1945, with sections of rail still missing so that the passengers had, several times, to leave the tram car and walk a block or two, took twice as long—an hour. So after making love to Ruth one more time, after the hugs and kisses, the tears and lamentations, finally, he left her, and, an hour later, arrived at his father's house, shortly after one in the afternoon, planning to pack a few things in a suitcase and leave immediately, without speaking to his father, this resolve reinforced when the next-door neighbor, that idiot Baron von Chiemsee, opened Josef's front door.

Josef brushed past the chattering old man, up the stairs to the third floor, where he found his room intact, the prayer book on his desk where he'd left it, wrapped in newspaper, tied with twine, just as it was the day Uncle Otto had given it to him, the day he and Aunt Greta were taken. Josef unwrapped it—an old, black book, leather-bound, all in Hebrew, but Uncle had inserted a page in his own hand, a transliteration of the Kaddish so Josef could sound it out himself, and on the same sheet, the Jewish dates of the deaths of Grandfather and Grandmother Jacoby. Intermittently, outside the bedroom door, Baron von Chiemsee's quavering voice, "You must see your father. He's in his room. He calls for you."

The Baron remained outside the door until Josef, suitcase in hand, emerged from his bedroom and headed down the stairs. Von Chiemsee ran after him and as Josef, without pausing on the second floor, where his parents'—his father's—bedroom and study were located, took one step down toward the first floor, Von Chiemsee shouted, "He is a good man, your father. He saved my life."

That stopped Josef dead in his tracks. He turned to face the Baron. *"He* saved *your* life?"

"Josef, Josef, is that you?" From behind the closed bedroom door, Father's voice, but thin, without timbre.

Josef stepped up to the second-floor landing and moved menacingly toward Von Chiemsee, who shrank against the wall. He was an old man now, thin and small. Josef dropped his suitcase and knocked on the door.

"It is not locked."

Father was in the bed, propped up against pillows, his green corduroy dressing gown over pajamas, covered, on that warm August day, with a down quilt. The glass was gone, the windows boarded over, and the only light was from a reading lamp over the bed. His slippers were beside the bed, which meant, most likely, that he was able to walk about. There were legal papers and newspapers stacked neatly on the bedside table. Their cat, Mies, slept at Father's feet.

Josef stepped to the foot of the bed. Father was emaciated; his right eyelid sagged and the left side of his mouth drooped.

"I came only to pick up some things."

Father looked down.

"I will not stay."

"I ask you to hear me out before you leave." He looked up at Josef. "You are well aware that the events of the recent past have proven me wrong."

Josef did not answer, but, a jury of one, listened to the obviously rehearsed defense delivered in a voice without emotion but trembling from weakness.

"You must take into consideration, Josef, that you did not have the burden of my generation, which made the past epoch inconceivable. I say inconceivable because it was inconceivable that in a civilized country the government that had remained in power for twelve years was totally composed of criminal elements. I believed . . . I truly believed that the juridical system in Germany would have been strong enough to survive with integrity. But I was wrong.

"In my own defense, I must say that I stayed, hoping to do some good. But the elected leaders and spokesmen opposed to the Nazis just packed their suitcases and saved their own skins first, leaving behind the people who elected them—leaving them defenseless and without representation. The only ones who tried to stay were the Communists—and those who did not go underground were put in concentration camps.

"At the very beginning, when a resurrection of law and order and human decency within the German Reich still would have been possible from within, the surrounding countries—indeed, the entire world—turned a deaf ear—yes, even supported the Nazi government by flocking to the Olympics in Berlin in nineteen thirty-six. The treatment of the . . . the people of your mother's background in Germany was considered by the rest of the world an internal German affair that had nothing to do with the world at large. That was the beginning of the end.

"I made the decision to stay and to do what I could. I was wrong. I made the wrong decision. I know that now. But before you go, I have something for you. There is an envelope on the desk in my study."

"Von Chiemsee tells me you were most effective in saving *his* life."

"His life? He said I saved his life?"

"That's what he told me. He said that you are a good man because you saved his life."

"The Baron is a fool. Shortly after the Russians liberated Berlin, he decided it would be a good idea to turn himself in. 'I will tell them of my nominal Party affiliation,' he said to me, 'and they will treat me kindly if I volunteer.'"

"And you defended him?"

"Nothing of the kind. I merely advised against it and quoted a proverb to the old fool that made him change his mind: 'Go not to your lord, if you're not called.' So he did not turn himself in—and the Americans came shortly thereafter. They are much easier on Nazis than the Russians."

"I will be going," said Josef. "I came only to pick up some things."

"There is a motorcycle for you in the garage, a BMW."

Josef was silent.

"It is not from me. It is from Reverend Duncan and his daughter, Elizabeth. Do you remember them?"

"They came here in nineteen thirty-six for the Olympics."

"They sent twenty cartons of American cigarettes. One can buy anything with cigarettes. The motorcycle cost four cartons, the sailboat two. There are fourteen cartons left. Take them. I have for you, also, some papers which I have prepared. There are stocks and money in Zurich, in the Handelsbank and in Bank Leu."

"I don't need them."

"Don't be a fool. They are—were—your mother's as well as mine."

"How long is that Nazi going to stay in this house?"

"He's leaving soon to go to his estate near Munich. As you no doubt saw when you came today, his house was destroyed."

"You have been feeding him?"

"He has been helpful to me. I . . . I was unable to . . . to walk after the stroke."

"You can walk now?"

"Yes. I can make it to the bathroom by myself. And your friend Fräulein Backhaus comes each day, in the morning, to make order in this room."

"And you have food?"

"Now I do. At first there was no food. But the Americans have been very kind to us. The kitchen is full of K rations. In the winter, however, we will have no fuel."

Mies stood, stretched his long gray body, yawned, and looked at Josef, who gathered the cat in his arms. "Mies, Miesian," he said. "How are you, old fellow?"

"Mies has enough to eat, too," said Father. "He survived on mice and rats and birds. But Dritt. I didn't have enough for Dritt." His mouth twitched; his eyes filled with tears.

Josef looked curiously at his father. He had never seen him cry.

"I couldn't even save little Dritt." Father put his face in his hands and began to weep. "I had a little stone made for him, with his name. It is in the garden. Would you like to see it? I will show it to you." Tears streaming, Father threw aside the quilt and stood. "Please, will you hand me that shawl?"

"It is quite warm outside."

"I cannot get enough warmth."

Father walked so unsteadily that at the top of the stairs Josef had to put an arm around his waist to support him and, halfway down, when Father's knees buckled, Josef swept him into his arms—he was fragile as a bird, feather and light bone—and carried him down the rest of the stairs, through the house, and out into the garden. "There is an old motor or so in the basement, Papa. I will make you a little chair to take you up and down the stairs."

Papa lived seven more years, spending most of his time writing useless letters and receiving useless answers in return:

AMERICAN JOINT DISTRIBUTION COMMITTEE
KRONPRINZENALLEE 247
BERLIN-ZEHLENDORF

21 October 1946

Herrn Lothar Bernhardt
Kastanian Strasse 95
Berlin-Gartenfeld

Dear Herr Bernhardt:

Re: Otto Jacoby and Frau Margaret, née Braunschweig.

In possession of your writings of September 23, 1946, we have established communications with our official offices. We have now received the report that the above-mentioned were deported to the East with the East Transport on September 22, 1944.

They have not returned and are not on our lists.

We regret that we cannot give you more favorable news and remain

Yours truly,

Larry Lubetski
Tracing Office
American Joint Distribution
Committee

AMERICAN JOINT DISTRIBUTION COMMITTEE
KRONPRINZENALLEE 247
BERLIN-ZEHLENDORF

21 October 1946

Herrn Lothar Bernhardt
Kastanian Strasse 95
Berlin-Gartenfeld

Dear Herr Bernhardt:

Re: Frau Dr. Anna Bernhardt, née Jacoby.

In possession of your writings of September 23, 1946, we have established communications with our official offices. We have now received the report that the above-mentioned were deported to the East with the East Transport on October 13, 1944.

They have not returned and are not on our lists.

We regret that we cannot give you more favorable news and remain

Yours truly,

Larry Lubetski
Tracing Office
American Joint Distribution
Committee

Josef had a file drawer filled with such answers, his favorite from the Bubonic Plague Man, Boris Ivanovich Ignatov, answered, in German, three years—*three years*—after Father's inquiry.

15 May 1951

Comrade Lothar Bernhardt
Kastanian Strasse 95
Berlin-Gartenfeld

My dear Comrade Bernhardt:

I received your enthusiastic letter shortly after you sent it to me. As you know, I am happily engaged in very important work to benefit all mankind, and you will, therefore, excuse my delayed answer.

Let me assure you that our dear friends and comrades are in the best of health and spirit and are working happily and productively and undisturbed for the betterment and improvement of the human community.

Some of them have finished their important work and are taking their well-deserved rest. Others are well provided with all necessities of life and can dedicate themselves to nothing but their work. So they even get a visit from their barber once a week.

Contrary to what the Western Imperialist Propaganda claims, you can see that justice is fair and equal within the great Soviet Union.

As I am getting older, I experience more difficulty keeping my mind on the scientific problems which confront me, and I, therefore, ask you not to interrupt me again.

Boris Ivanovich

There was no return address.

Josef's dark eyes brimmed with tears. He lifted his head from his hands, patted his pockets for cigarettes—Carlos—and scanned the entrance area for a cigarette machine: up front, in the corner. He took a deep breath—still musical, but better. He was better. There was just a remnant of the headache; his blood pressure must be slightly lower. The substernal discomfort was gone; probably it was just a muscle spasm from the unaccustomed running. He was slightly nauseated, and he was thirsty, terribly thirsty, dehydrated from the running and sweating. If he failed to keep up on fluids, he would form stones. Ordinarily, he was conscientious about drinking two or three liters a day.

He looked at the bartender, mid-bar, who was engrossed in counting the change in the cash register, then at the signs posted randomly on the mirror behind the bar:

BEER: PITCHER OR FROSTED MUG

NO CHECKS CASHED

NO CREDIT

TRY OUR REFRESHING LEMONADE

KITCHEN CLOSES AT 2:30

Bottles of hard liquor were arranged neatly on a counter behind the bar, and a mimeographed menu with plastic cover was stuck into a metal holder next to an ashtray on the bar.

"I'll have a lemonade," Josef called to the bartender. He was a young man, most likely a student, but out of uniform. Although he had long sideburns and a handlebar mustache, his moderately short hair was neatly combed, and he wore a black plastic bow tie, black slacks, and a white shirt with his name, *Murphy,* in spidery red thread over the pocket. Murphy was now writing on a form attached to a clipboard.

"Are you open for business?" Josef raised his voice.

Murphy dropped the clipboard with a clatter and, reluctantly, looked up.

"A lemonade."

"Large or small?"

"Large."

Murphy scooped a tall glass full of ice, slammed it on the bar, and before Josef could stop him, filled it from a pitcher with a pale yellow liquid.

"No ice, please."

"You asked for a large lemonade?"

"I did."

Murphy pointed to the glass. "That's a large lemonade."

"I want a large lemonade without ice."

With one smooth movement, Murphy swooped up the glass and threw the contents into the sink. He then placed a smaller glass— half the size—onto the bar and filled it from the pitcher.

"This is a large lemonade?" asked Josef.

"Without ice."

"I see." Josef drank it in one gulp. "Another, please."

Murphy, face devoid of all expression, refilled the glass. Josef, again, drank it in a swallow and ordered another.

"Where you from?" Murphy placed the small glass of lemonade on the bar.

"Iowa City."

Murphy mopped the clean bar in front of Josef with a dry rag. "How long you been here?"

"Two weeks."

"Where were you before you came here?"

"Montréal."

Murphy stopped polishing for a moment. "You at McGill?"

Josef nodded.

"Great school. I've got a friend goes up there."

Josef drank the lemonade. He needed more fluid.

"Your accent doesn't sound Canadian."

"Most likely not."

"How do you like it?"

"Like what?"

"Here. America."

Josef leaned back on the backless barstool and fixed Murphy with his eyes. "There seems to be a war going on—at least in Iowa City. Why did the students break the windows in the bookstore?"

"You mean the Screw?"

"I beg your pardon?"

"Varsity Book and Screw. That's what we call it."

"Why?"

"Well, you know, because they screw the students—you know, rip 'em off."

"I beg your pardon?"

"Rip off. You know, steal. They've got a monopoly, so the professors order textbooks there, and we have no choice. They way overcharge. It's a rip-off."

"There are other bookstores. Why don't the professors order from Epstein's?"

"A few do. But most of 'em are just motherfuckers."

"Motherfuckers," Josef repeated. "Tell me, why don't the students break the windows here?"

"Here? Are you kidding?" Murphy was astounded. "They know we don't rip 'em off!"

"What do you call this?" asked Josef, pointing to the small lemonade glass.

"I call that a large lemonade without ice. At least it was before you drank it."

"I see. What do you think is the liquid capacity of this glass?"

"Five ounces."

"Are you sure?"

"Sure I'm sure." Murphy reached under the counter and came up with a Pyrex measuring cup; he filled it to the five-ounce mark with water and then poured into the juice glass. "See? Five ounces, exactly."

"And the large glass?"

"Ten ounces. Double."

"May I have it, please? The large glass?"

Murphy slammed the large glass onto the bar, and Josef poured the contents of the juice glass into the taller one, motioned for Murphy to fill up the small one again, then poured the additional five ounces of water, filling the taller glass to the brim.

"Ten ounces, just like I said."

"Now," said Josef, picking up the ten-ounce glass, "pour out this water and fill it up to the top with ice and put exactly five ounces of water into the measuring cup."

The young man did so, grinning slyly at Josef.

"And now pour five ounces of water over the ice."

Murphy poured slowly. At one and one half ounces, the tall glass was half full. At three and one half ounces it began to over-flow onto the bar and he stopped pouring and mopped up the water.

"Do you fill all soft drink glasses with ice?"

Murphy nodded affirmatively.

"If I were the students," said Josef, "I would break the glass here, too."

"They wouldn't!" Murphy was upset now.

"And why not?"

"Because they know I'm one of them."

"How do they know that?"

To Josef's amazement, Murphy reached to the top of his head and pulled off his hair. "It's a wig," he explained, turning around so that Josef could see that his own long brown hair was pulled tightly back in a ponytail, fastened with a rubber band, and then looped about the top of his head and held in place with bobby pins.

Josef could not help but smile as he watched Murphy's reflection in the mirror manipulating the wig back into place. "The management lets us have mustaches but no beards." He tugged it this way and that, tucking up strands of his own hair which had escaped the rubber band and bobby pins, then grimaced at Josef's smiling image in the mirror. "Go ahead! Laugh! I need this job to get through school."

"Please excuse me," said Josef. "You caught me off guard. I had no idea it was a wig."

"Hey, Murphy," called a voice from a booth in the back. "How about drawing us another pitcher?"

While Murphy filled a large glass pitcher with draft beer and delivered it to the booth, Josef studied the mimeographed menu. Despite the mild nausea, he was hungry. Forgetting again that he had stopped smoking, he patted his pockets for cigarettes. Damn. Carlos.

"Murphy? I'll have a cheese sandwich on rye and French fries."

"Kitchen's closed."

Josef looked at his watch. "It's only two twenty. Sign says it closes at two thirty."

"Can't help it. Cook leaves early on Tuesday. Has a class." He sighed. "How about some popcorn? Just made it fresh right before you came in."

"O.K. Please—butter but no salt."

Murphy filled a large glass bowl with the yellow popped corn and put it on the bar. "It's already salted, and we use margarine," he said, soberly. "But it's free of charge. On the house."

"Why?"

Murphy threw up his hands. "It's so salty that it makes you thirsty so you'll buy more to drink."

"I see." Josef tried the corn, three or four kernels, then pushed the bowl away. "Too salty."

"All bars do it. Standard practice."

Josef snorted and looked at the array of bottles on the counter behind the bar. "Is that vodka?" He pointed to a bottle of clear liquid half hidden behind the bourbon.

"That's gin. But we've got vodka."

"I'll take some."

"How do you want it?"

"In a glass, without ice."

Murphy put a tiny shot glass on the counter and filled it to the brim with vodka.

"Good Lord. How much is *that* supposed to be?"

"Ounce and a half."

Josef picked up the shot glass and dumped the contents into the empty five-ounce glass. "Another." And then, "Another." Murphy looked on, aghast, as he realized that the five-ounce glass was only slightly more than half full. "Your shot glass," said Josef, "is only one ounce, not one and a half."

"That does it!" shouted Murphy, reaching up to pull off his hair again.

"No! Stop! Don't do that!"

Murphy dropped his hand. "Tell me one reason why I shouldn't quit right now."

"Because you need the job and quitting would just be giving in to those swine."

Murphy nervously mopped the clean bar with the dry cloth. "You think we oughta break all the windows in town, don't you?"

Josef shuddered. "No. Believe me, Murphy, that does no good." He swiveled on his barstool and gazed absentmindedly at the large plate-glass windows of the bar front. Carlos.

Borbon was across the street talking to Susan Ingram, gesticulating wildly with his arms. Josef swiveled quickly and faced the back, his heart pounding.

"So what should we do?" asked Murphy.

Most likely there was an exit through the kitchen—into an alley, perhaps. Or he could hide in the men's room.

"What do you think we oughta do about it?" Murphy repeated.

"I don't have any answers," said Josef.

"What are you, a nihilist or something? You come in here and tear the place apart and then you don't do anything about putting it back together."

"Murphy, do you see a man—right across the street—wearing hospital greens?"

Murphy turned and stared out the window for some time, but did not answer. Josef heard the entrance door open, and the hair stood up on the back of his neck. "Did he come in here?"

"No."

"Is he coming over here?"

"No."

"What's he doing?"

"Talking to a little lady with boobs. No, wait, he's leaving."

Josef was afraid to turn his head. He contemplated a bolt into the kitchen. "Where is he going?" Josef inhaled a deep, musical breath and held it.

"He's getting on the Cambus." Pause. "He's gone."

"Good!" He exhaled in a loud wheeze. The Cambus would take Carlos back to the hospital. Josef turned toward the window. Customers—two women students—were settling at a table in front.

"Was he looking for you?"

"Yes. One thing you could do is pressure your professors to order books elsewhere—at Epstein's—and get the university to open its own bookstore. Another thing—you could put less ice in the glasses."

"But—"

"You've got customers." Josef nodded toward the front.

Murphy sighed, dropped his cleaning cloth, and moved heavily to the end of the bar nearest the front. Josef swung his barstool about and stared through the windows at Susan Ingram across the street. What had Murphy called her? Josef patted his breast pocket, feeling for cigarettes, stood, searched through his pockets for change, and headed for the cigarette machine near the front entrance. Little lady with boobs. They reminded him of Kirsti Krupinsky. He dropped forty cents into the vending machine and pushed *Camels*. Little lady with boobs. Little lady with rod that made them rise from their noon apple-dreams and scuttle goose-fashion under the skies—that damned poem. Rise and skies . . . scuttle and . . . little . . .

> *. . . little*
> *Lady with rod that made them rise*
> *From their noon apple-dreams and scuttle*
> *Goose-fashion under the skies!*

While walking back to his end of the bar, he opened the pack, stuck a cigarette in his mouth, and cupping his hands, lit it, inhaled, and exhaled with a racking cough. Still he could close his eyes and bring forth the image of those breasts—and still that image aroused him. Kirsti. She, most likely, had made it—survived—but Krupinsky had not. Josef took another drag from the cigarette, drawing the smoke deep into his lungs, and began retching coughs so profound he almost vomited. He was dead. It was no good. He snuffed out the cigarette in the ashtray. Josef picked up the glass of vodka. "Lieber Herr Schtalin," he whispered harshly, "fuck you," and threw the three ounces of vodka down his throat, gasped, choked, coughed again, then shuddered all over. It was raw stuff. He took out his handkerchief, wiped his eyes, blew his nose, and then brought forth from the depths a belch that relieved the nausea. He found out about the Krupinskys and the others from the Roumanian Biologist George Treponesco, returned from the USSR to teach at the university. That was five months after the escape through the apples. The University of Berlin reopened in January of 1946, and in his first class after lunch, he sat high in the back row of the tiered benches, waiting, along with sixty-five other students, for the zoology professor to appear. The university was in the Russian Sector, and Josef was wondering what kind of an idiot they had found who would be willing to teach the biological sciences under the control of the Soviets, who denied Darwin and Mendel in favor of Lamarck, when in swaggered Treponesco, slammed his books onto the table, then tried to push it aside—the way the Chief used to do—but it was bolted to the floor. He tried to lift off the lectern, but it was screwed to the table. He began to pace, hands locked behind his back, looking at the students—just the way the Chief had done it. He hadn't yet seen Josef.

"Ladies and gentlemen." Treponesco paced as he talked. "This is a course in zoology, simplified for medical students. No credit will be given for majors in the sciences. Since you are medical students, you will probably have difficulty with it. Correct? Or am I right?"

Josef, his head pounding, hardly able to breathe, pushed his books and notebooks onto the floor, and then his pencils, sending them flying. Treponesco could not help but notice. He stopped pacing.

"Bernhardt, I want to talk to you. Come down."

Josef stood and began to walk toward the front.

"Bring your books!"

Josef began to pick up his books, notebooks, and pencils. The two women seated on either side of him dropped down to help. Since there were very few men left in Berlin, his class was mostly women. Treponesco waited silently below until Josef was face-to-face, then, remembering the sixty-four other students, he turned to the class and, after two brief bows, said, "Excuse me, please. A long-lost friend. Excuse me a moment."

Josef followed him into the hall.

"I do not want to see your goddam curly face in my classroom again!"

Josef stood, silent, and looked Treponesco in the eye.

"Oh, come on, Bernhardt. Read the book. You'll pass the exam with flying colors. This stuff is so elementary you know it already. And anyway, what are you doing here? I thought you were sup-

posed to be at M.I.T.? What's the matter, weren't you accepted?"
He snickered.

"I was awarded a full scholarship, but I couldn't get a visa."

"The Americans wouldn't give *you* a visa? Why not?"

"Because I'm a German. Weren't you taken with the others?"

"We were all taken. They let me come back to teach."

"Did any of the others make it back?"

"My wife. She's divorcing me."

"I don't blame her."

"Neither do I. What about Tatiana?"

"She's enrolled here, unfortunately in biology."

"Good!" He rubbed his hands together. "She'll have to take my class. You two still going together?"

"We're engaged."

"Congratulations."

"Thank you. What about the others?"

"I ran into Rabin in Moscow; that is, I went to his concert and caught him afterward, backstage. He was really glad to see me." Treponesco shrugged. "Told me that the Yugoslav was dead."

"Mitya? What happened?"

"Seems that the monkeys started dying—during the trip. So he just injected the rest of them . . . and then himself. He did himself in."

"My God!"

"Ignatov's O.K. Rabin says he got his old position back—you know, doing research on the plague—in Kiev. Soviet Academy of Science and Medicine."

"What about the Chief and Sonja and Professor Kreutzer and the Krupinskys?"

"Look, Josef, I've got students in there. Meet me after class in that café on the corner. We'll have a beer, and I'll tell you what little I know."

After the beer, Josef had gotten on his BMW and raced out to the Institute for the first time since his escape through the apples.

*

His body swayed, a momentary vertigo; he held on to the bar. He had small tolerance for alcohol and had done little drinking since the Institute. Dizzy, he turned slowly on his barstool and looked out the plate-glass window. There she was, the little lady with boobs, Susan Ingram, picketing against war:

MAKE LOVE NOT WAR

Josef reached for the little calendar note pad and pen he kept in the inside pocket of his suit jacket and wrote: *Her wars were bruited in our high windows,* and under that, in his illegible physician's **hand,** he wrote the first four lines of the poem that had been plaguing him all day:

> *There was such speed in her little body,*
> *And such lightness in her footfall,*
> *It is no wonder her brown study*
> *Astonishes us all.*

He paused, then sketched in other words and phrases as they came to him. It was rhymed, or near rhymed, so he should be able to reconstruct it all once he found the words: Her wars were bruited in our high windows . . . apple orchards and beyond . . . Lazy geese who cried in goose alas! for the little lady with rod, that . . . harried onto the pond the lazy geese . . . dropping their snow on the green grass . . . Alas! To the little lady with rod . . . noon-apple dreams.

He had the first verse and much of the middle, but was having trouble with the end. He wrote *"Bells for John Whiteside's Daughter" by John Crowe Ransom* and put the note pad and pen back into his pocket. He needed a little help with the ending and decided that he would wander up Clinton to Epstein's and look up the poem in an anthology. It had been years since he had allowed himself the joy of browsing through the stacks—not since his youth, when his father gave him a charge account at the bookstore in Gartenfeld. Both Mutti and Papa encouraged him to buy as many books as he wished, and his third-floor bedroom was filled with them.

"Can I get you anything else?" Murphy's voice seemed far away.

"No, thank you." Josef stood. His lips were numb, fingers and toes tingling, and his legs lead. He was quite drunk.

"You leaving?"

"How much do I owe you?" Josef reached for his wallet.

"I have no idea what to charge you."

Josef dropped a ten-dollar bill on the counter.

"That's too much."

"Keep your hair on," said Josef and walked toward the entrance.

"Hey," shouted Murphy. "You forgot your briefcase."

. . .

Unsteady enough from the three ounces of vodka to be conscious of each careful step, Josef wandered up Clinton, his briefcase, held by the grip, swinging by his side. The city noises came from a great distance; the center of a quiet, glowing circle, he crossed the intersection with the light, aware that others, without fear of Uncle Philip, were ignoring the traffic signals, and that he, Josef, actually was enjoying the warmth of the beautiful October day. As he strolled along, studying the storefronts on both sides of the street—crystal intact—looking for the other bookstore, Epstein's, his attention was captured by the colors in the window of a men's clothing store, and he stopped to stare through the glass, mesmerized by the rich hues of a carefully arranged display of autumn leaves and matching wool sweaters—russet, gold, burgundy, brown.

"Buy it." Susan Ingram had slipped up beside him. He could see her reflection in the glass.

He turned slowly, so that he would not lose his balance, and looked down at her—the open work shirt, no bra, her full breasts. "Miss Susan Ingram, R.N." He slurred the words.

"I am surprised you remember my name."

"You are quite memorable, Miss Ingram." He pointed to the sweaters behind glass. "Which one? The brown?"

"The red! Your suits are too dark. You always look as though you're going to a funeral."

Josef cocked his head to one side and contemplated the wine-red sweater. Tanya would have said that he was too old to wear red.

"Look, Dr. Bernhardt, what have you got to lose?" She slipped her arm into his and propelled him through the door of a store that, obviously, catered to the more conservative element of Iowa City. There were standard dark suits and quiet sport coats and slacks along one wall; shirts in proper boxy cubicles along the other; sweaters and other accessories neatly stacked on tables in the center. No blue jeans or work shirts here.

An odd couple: Susan Ingram, looking like a hippie, and Josef in prudent charcoal-gray, carrying a fine leather briefcase, with the only hint of improvidence the unbuttoned collar, the missing necktie which he had stuffed into his jacket pocket after Elizabeth's examination; of course, he was drunk, but that, he assumed, would not be noticed by anyone.

The two salesclerks, men in quiet suits, surveyed them with lowered lids but did not rush to wait on them.

Susan pulled Josef along to the stacks of wool sweaters and picked up a burgundy long-sleeved V-neck. "Dr. Borbon was looking for you," she said. "He stopped to talk to me in front of the Pentacrest. It was after you left the bookstore and went into the bar."

"Why didn't you tell him where I was?"

"It was obvious you were trying to avoid him."

"But you knew where I was all along?"

She nodded. "Have you been drinking?"

"Is it noticeable?"

"Yes. Do you drink a lot?"

"Not recently. Tell me, Miss Ingram, how long have you been following me?"

"About a month. Will you please call me Susan?"

"Susan. I've been in Iowa City slightly more than two weeks."

"I know. But I was interested in you even before you came. Dr. Borbon talked about you a lot. Especially after you finally got your visa and were coming down soon."

"Are you a friend of Dr. Borbon's?"

"Not exactly. I am . . . was a friend of a friend of his for a while. One of the writers over at the Workshop."

"I see. Do you specialize in friends of Borbon?"

"I could do worse. He likes to collect brilliant people around him—like Dr. Matsumoto, the biochemist, and some of the writers over at the Workshop." She looked up at him, her face serious, her dark eyes wide. "He said you have an I.Q. of two hundred and five and that you're separated from your wife, which is good because she was bad for you."

"Good Lord," said Josef.

"Is it true? About your marriage?"

Josef thought for a moment. "True," he said.

"Do you want to try this on?" She waved the burgundy sweater at him.

"I'm too sweaty to put on clean clothes."

"My apartment's right across the street—above Burger Qwik. You could shower there . . ."

Josef looked down her cleavage. "Are you sure?"

"Yes."

"Can I help you?" A thin-nosed, balding clerk, finally, approached them.

Josef bought the burgundy sweater.

. . .

He awakened in some confusion, dreaming of the cave in his back yard, of Papa standing there beside the hole looking down at him and at Petter, and he realized that he was a collection of symptoms: intermittent epigastric pain, distended abdomen, mild nausea, and urinary urgency—but his headache was gone, and he could breathe. Petter! He had not thought of his high school friend for years. To relieve the pain in his gut, he needed to flex his knees, to pull his legs up a bit, but he did not want to disturb Susan, who lay sweetly sleeping on his shoulder, her tousled hair hiding her face. He had asked her to unbraid her long dark hair, brush it, and let it lie free.

Another pain, sharper this time, lower, and the muscles in his legs involuntarily spasmed. Susan's hand, resting on his belly, began to stroke lightly, moving down to his sex.

He stopped her, gently lifting her hand. "I don't think I can," he said.

She pulled her hand away abruptly and tried to sit up, but Josef restrained her.

"Don't be angry."

With one hand securing the towel he had tucked between her legs, Susan sat and pushed her back against the wall, the flowered sheet settling around her waist.

He sat, too, and looked at her—her face, her breasts. "Look," he said, taking her hand and placing it only briefly on his stiffening sex before releasing it.

"Then what's wrong?"

Josef shoved back against the wall. "Most likely, I'm working on a kidney stone."

"Oh, no. Are you in a lot of pain?"

"Not yet, but if it's true to form, I will be before long."

She took his hand. "I'm so sorry."

"I'm the one who's sorry. I so wanted to take you to dinner this evening."

"Another time."

"Of course." He sighed. "I'm a stone maker," he said. "Whenever I fail to drink enough fluid—become dehydrated—I can count on it."

"Maybe we shouldn't have made love."

"No, don't say that. You have no idea. . . ." His voice trailed off.

He had not so much as jumped on a black spot since *Kristallnacht* in Montréal in the spring—not with Tanya, who had left shortly thereafter, and not with anyone else.

"Can I get you anything?"

"Perhaps something to drink, if you don't mind."

"I've got some wine. Do you drink a lot?"

"You asked me that in the sweater store. Would it concern you if I did?"

"Yes. You said you hadn't been drinking lately."

"I said 'not recently.'"

"What do you mean by that?"

"Not since the war."

"Which war?"

Josef, startled, looked at her to see if she was serious.

She was not smiling.

"The Second World War, twenty-two years ago."

"I don't remember much about it. I was only six when it was over."

"It would be fair to say that I was at least mildly drunk, at least once a day, each and every working day for the last two years of that war."

"Not at work! You weren't drunk at work?"

"That's the only place I was drunk. My parents would not have permitted it at home."

She laughed. "Where on earth was it? A winery?"

"Not quite," he said. "It would take a long time to tell you. But except for those years, I have rarely been intoxicated."

"Except for today."

"Except for today," he echoed. "Today, I drank vodka, which I did not tolerate very well. But to tell you the truth, I did have one bout with drunkenness slightly earlier in my life. Would you like to hear about that?"

Susan nodded.

"I was only six or seven, and for some reason I don't understand, my father had taken me with him to a café in the village where he and a client celebrated winning some case or other. My father was a lawyer. They ordered a bottle of champagne and gave me a glass. I thought it quite delicious. They were involved in talking with each other and didn't pay attention to me, so I helped myself to more champagne and then more—maybe three glasses in all."

"Was your father mad at you?"

"At first. Then, I remember, they both began to laugh—my father and his client—and they half dragged, half carried me to my father's car and shoved me into the back seat. It was the Duesenberg."

"Duesenberg?"

"Yes. Duesenberg. A year or so later we had, also, a Willys Overland." Josef stopped and gasped. A sharp pain shot from his kidney, down the ureter track into his groin and testicles.

"You O.K.?"

He nodded. "Sorry. I dozed off during the short ride home— our house was only twelve minutes' walking from the village of Gartenfeld, so the car ride couldn't have been more than two or three minutes—and I woke up to find myself being carried up the stairs in Papa's arms. He thought I was asleep, but I was not." Josef's voice broke. He was, again, on the verge of tears. He took a deep breath, still musical, but he exhaled without difficulty. "Would you excuse me?" He swung his legs over the side of the bed.

"Should I get you some wine?"

"Water would be fine," he said, his voice shaking. "I would like to try to float out this stone."

"Are you in a lot of pain?"

He nodded, stood, and moved quickly toward the bathroom.

"I'll make you some herbal tea."

His mother's and father's voices had seemed to come from a great distance. "What happened to him?" Mutti said from the top of the stairs; she sounded so worried. Papa's wool suit was rough against his face, and it smelled of the aromatic pipe tobacco he smoked before the war.

"He's drunk," Papa said.

"Drunk?"

"Champagne." Papa laughed. "Hans Georg and I were talking, and Josef must have helped himself to several glasses before I noticed."

Mutti laughed, too. "Better take him in the bathroom, or he'll wet the bed."

They pulled down his pants and Papa stood him at the bowl. "He's heavier than he looks."

"He's wiry and much stronger than one would think."

Josef let go a strong stream. His urine smelled pungently aromatic, fruity. He flushed the toilet and put down the seat and lid.

"We've got a doubles date with Kahns in the morning, eight o'clock," Mutti said. "Our little tennis ball fetcher will, most likely, not be awake. That will make him very unhappy." She laughed again. "Can he walk?"

Josef looked at the door. He could have walked, but he let his knees buckle—on purpose—so that Papa, once again, swooped him up. "He is so thin, one would think he would weigh like a feather."

Chilled and nauseated, experiencing excruciating intermittent pain originating in the kidney area but radiating across his abdomen and down into his genitals and the inner side of his thigh, wearing, now, his new red sweater, Josef sat at the table in Susan's tiny living room, before him a pot of herbal tea, a mug, a legal-size lined yellow tablet, his pen, the telephone, and the Iowa City telephone directory. Susan was in the shower; he could hear the water pinging hollow against the metal shower stall.

He turned to the Yellow Pages—*C,* Churches—and shivered. *Churches-African Methodist Episcopal; Churches-Assemblies of God;*

Churches-Baptist—two and a half pages. He flipped back to the second page and ran his finger down the *C's, E's,* to the *J's:* Churches-Jehovah's Witnesses; *Churches-Jewish, See Synagogues.*

> *Synagogues*
> Agudas Achim Congregation
>   602 E. Washington   555-8818
> B'Nai B'Rith Hillel Foundation
>   120 E. Market   555-8816
> Rabbi David Brockman

"Hello?" A child answered the phone. Josef couldn't tell if it was a boy or a girl. He could hear other children shrieking and laughing in the background.

"Is this Agudas Achim?"

"What?" shouted the child. "Hey, you guys, shut up, I'm on the phone. Hello?"

"Is this the synagogue?" asked Josef.

"Yeah."

"Is Rabbi there?"

Josef winced from auricular pain when the synagogue phone was dropped with a reverberating crash onto a tile counter. He could hear the youngster shout, "Hey, you guys, tell Rabbi Brockman telephone." Then once again into the phone, "Hello? Just a minute, please. I'm in the kitchen and Rabbi's upstairs."

Josef held the phone away from his ear just in time to avoid the resounding of another crash. He listened to the riotous sounds of children playing for several minutes before the Rabbi picked up another phone.

"Hello?"

"Rabbi Brockman?" he shouted. "My name is Josef Bernhardt."

The noise from the kitchen was so intrusive that Josef could barely hear the Rabbi's voice. "Just a minute, please." Rabbi Brockman apparently put his hand over the mouthpiece before shouting, "Robin, will you run down and hang up the phone in the kitchen? I can't hear a thing."

Finally, "Sorry." A chuckle. "The children. I didn't catch your name?"

"Bernhardt. Josef Bernhardt."

"What can I do for you, Mr. Bernhardt?"

"I . . . I was wondering if you were having a . . . a prayer service this evening."

"We usually don't have a minyan during the week, but I can get one together in a hurry. Do you have yahrzeit?"

"I beg your pardon?"

"A yahrzeit," repeated the Rabbi, "the anniversary of a death?"

"Yes," said Josef. "That's it. I . . . I would like you to find someone to say Kaddish for my mother. It is . . ." He stopped.

"Is it the anniversary of her death?" asked the Rabbi, gently.

"Rabbi, I don't know." Josef's mouth twisted, his eyes burned with tears, and he had difficulty speaking. "She was taken on this date. I know she's dead. But I'm not sure how or when that death occurred."

"When was she taken?"

"Nineteen forty-four. In Berlin. We lived in Berlin."

"Are you new here, Mr. Bernhardt? In Iowa City?"

"Yes. I . . . I joined the medical faculty just two weeks ago."

"Dr. Bernhardt, excuse me, but why is it that you want me to find someone else to say Kaddish? Why don't you say it yourself?"

"I'm not sure I may. I am just half-Jewish. My father was not. And Rabbi, there were others: my uncle—that is, my uncles and aunt—and . . . others, my friends, many of them. Mostly, I know only when they were taken. I have few death dates."

"Dr. Bernhardt, it's five o'clock. I'll be teaching Hebrew school until six. Could you come over then? I'll get a minyan together, no problem. Do you know where we are?"

"I'll find it."

"Wait! Before you hang up." The Rabbi paused for a moment. "Dr. Bernhardt, the old Rabbis were very wise. They tell us that there are only two ways to become a Jew: one is by conversion and the other is if one's mother is a Jew. There is no other way, and there is no such thing as half a Jew. You are a Jew, Dr. Bernhardt, and there is no reason why you cannot say Kaddish for your family and your friends."

"Rabbi, some of them were not Jewish."

"Why don't you write down the names—all of them—and give them to me before the service. I'll read a special prayer. Just a minute, please."

Josef could hear papers rustling.

"Here it is. I'll read it to you.

"'In this solemn hour, we reverently recall the martyrs whose ranks have been tragically augmented by untold numbers of our fellow men and women in our generation. Never shall we forget those who sacrificed their lives for the sanctification of thy name. We remember also the heroes and righteous men and women of all nations who lived and died for justice, truth, and peace.

"'Though our departed are no longer with us, their memories are forever enshrined in our hearts and their influence abides with us, directing our thoughts and deeds toward the lofty purposes they cherished and for which they strived.'

"And then we say the traditional Kaddish. The whole service— Minha, Ma'ariv, and the memorial prayers—takes about twenty minutes. Does that sound all right?"

"Yes," Josef whispered. "Thank you, Rabbi. I'll be there at six, and I will bring a list."

He had one hour until six. The synagogue was not far, only six blocks up Washington from Susan's apartment.

Josef turned again to the Yellow Pages: Taxicabs.

SUPER CAB INC
   404 E. College   555-0300
YELLOW CHECKER CAB CO INC
   404 E. College   555-1313

"Super Cab."

"Yes, please, could you please have a taxi pick me up on the corner of Clinton and Washington, in front of the Burger Qwik, at five forty-five?"

"Burger-Qwik on Clinton, quarter to six."

"Can I count on it being on time?"

"Why not?"

Josef dialed again. Carlos would just be waking from his siesta and would be planning to take a twenty-minute swim in his indoor pool before shaving, showering, and dressing elegantly in a three-piece suit to head over to the hospital, arriving at exactly seven so that he could read for an hour in the anesthesiology library before making rounds.

His Spanish housekeeper answered. "Dr. Borbon's residence."

"Doña Camila, this is Josef Bernhardt. May I speak to Carlos?"

"Don José," she exploded. "Where you been? Don Carlos, he is half crazy looking for you. Don't hang up. You stay." She put down the phone, and Josef could hear her calling. "Don Carlos! Don Carlos!"

"Hello? Dr. Borbon here."

"Charley?"

"Seff? You goddamned sonofabitch, where the hell are you? Jenkins is ready to kill me, goddammit. He won't accept your resignation. Jesus Christ!"

Josef held the phone away from his ear until the tirade subsided.

"Seff, you there?"

"I'm here."

"Where the hell are you? Goddammit, Elizabeth says your blood pressure is astronomical. You've got her absolutely in pieces. Jenkins said he'll give you a leave of absence—three months—but no more. Maybe six months. Why the hell—"

"Carlos, listen to me."

"We've been so worried, we have the police looking for you. I even called your wife."

"Tatiana? You called Berlin? Why in hell did you do that?"

"What else could I do? I've looked everywhere. The police even broke into your house to see if you were hanging in the basement."

"Now that's a novel idea."

"What the hell is the matter with you? This is completely out of character."

"Charley, I'm in terrible pain."

"What's wrong?"

"Kidney stone."

"Again? How bad is it?"

"Bad. But it's still intermittent, and I can feel it moving down. It should localize soon."

"Where are you? Do you want me to come get you?"

"Yes. Charley, I am sorry to have been such a pain to you to-day—and to Elizabeth. It's been an insane day. I . . . I blanked out in surgery this morning."

"You blacked out?"

"No. I was not unconscious, but I lost track of what I was doing during the operation."

"You're just exhausted, Seff. You need a rest. I'll take you to my house in the Canary Islands. It's so peaceful there. You need time to think."

"We'll talk about it."

"Look, it'll take me five minutes to dress and about twenty to drive into town—if that's where you are."

"Yes. Please pick me up at Sixth and Washington. That's the Agudas Achim Synagogue. I'll be done there by six twenty or so."

"I know where that is. Seff, why the hell didn't you ever tell me that you were a Jew?"

Josef's mouth curled in a paroxysm of pain.

With his black ink pen, on the legal pad, he built it carefully, printing in large block letters so that Rabbi Brockman would be able to read the list without difficulty. The names came easily, and the dates after only a minute or so of reflection. By the time he was done, Susan was out of the shower and in the bedroom drying her hair; he could hear the whirring of the small motor of her electric dryer.

Anna Jacoby Bernhardt, taken October 10, 1944, death date unknown
Otto Jacoby, taken September 21, 1944, death date unknown
Greta Braunstein Jacoby, taken September 21, 1944, d/d/u
Philip Jacoby, taken June 21, 1938, d/d/u
Maximilian Kreutzer, taken August 11, 1945, d/d/u
Nikolai Alexandrovich Avilov, taken August 11, 1945, d/d/u
his wife, Madame Avilov, died in January 1945
his son, Mitzka Avilov, died August 25, 1944
Dieter Schmidt, taken August 25, 1944, d/d/u
Sonja Press, taken August 11, 1945, d/d/u
Abraham Morris Krupinsky, died August 16, 1945
Dmitri Varvilovovich Tsechetverikov, died in June 1945
Lothar Leopold Bernhardt, died November 2, 1952

Pen poised, Josef hesitated, then added another name.

Gunther Rathke, died April 21, 1943

"No," he said aloud, crossing out Gunther Rathke.

But there were so many others, he could not begin to list them all. Josef added two more names, thinking for almost a minute before writing their date.

Frau Levy, taken July 1942, d/d/u
her grandson, Hans, taken July 1942, d/d/u

. . .

By the time the prayer service was over, there was no longer intermittency. The pain, constant, was the most exquisite Josef had ever suffered. Carlos and the Rabbi helped him out the door of the synagogue, down the steps, and into the back seat of Carlos's BMW. Carlos slid in beside him, and his driver made a smooth fast acceleration. Down Washington, across Clinton, flying now, over the river, past the train station, the tiny village of Hagen, the little farms, the fields and small forest, through the guardless gate, and around the circular drive. There was no flagpole at all! They had taken even the flagpole. And the Y-shaped building was a shell. The Roumanian Biologist George Treponesco told him, over the beer in the café, that the NKVD loaded everything and everybody into the trucks, even the shelves and shelves and jars and jars of the brains of the fallen minions, and the racks with the incubators containing the pure-bred *Drosophila*, and that en route all the happy little winemakers died; that Abraham Krupinsky had a fatal heart attack after four brutal days on the road and that his corpse and his wife were dropped in some small village in the Ukraine; that he was separated from the others in Moscow and had no idea what became of them; that the Security Officer, because he was obviously so ill, was the only one given the option to remain behind, in Hagen, with his wife and children, but that he elected to follow the linear accelerator into Russia, even though the Chief and Professor Kreutzer insisted that it never would be put together again.